Voice in the Wilderness

Book 1
Against all Enemies Series

H.L. WEGLEY

Political Thriller with Romance

Publisher's Note: This is a work of fiction, set in a real location. Any reference to historical figures, places, or events, whether fictional or actual, is a fictional representation. Names, characters, and incidents are the product of the author's imagination or are used fictitiously, and any resemblance to actual persons, living or dead, or to events is entirely coincidental.

Cover Design: Samantha Fury
http://www.furycoverdesign.com/

Interior Formatting: Trinity Press International
http://trinitywebworks.com/

Copyright © 2015 H.L. Wegley

All rights reserved.

ISBN-13: 978-0996493703
ISBN-10: 0996493700

Also available in eBook publication

DEDICATION

This book is dedicated to all the men and women in uniform, as well as those elected to public office, who truly mean their solemn oaths to defend—not reinterpret—the Constitution of the United States. May God help you to stand firm against all political and cultural pressures to violate your word.

The Presidential Oath

I do solemnly swear (or affirm) that I will faithfully execute the Office of President of the United States, and will to the best of my Ability, preserve, protect and defend the Constitution of the United States.

Officer's Oath of Commissioning

I ... do solemnly swear (or affirm) that I will support and defend the Constitution of the United States against all enemies, foreign and domestic, that I will bear true faith and allegiance to the same; that I take this obligation freely, without any mental reservation or purpose of evasion; and that I will well and faithfully discharge the duties of the office upon which I am about to enter; So help me God.

ENDORSEMENTS

A terrifyingly real political thriller!

How much power does one voice have? H.L. Wegley has
written an action-packed, politically terrifying, hair-raising
thriller about the need to guard our freedoms--lest they be
snatched away. An edge-of-your seat race to keep one man
from taking over the United States--don't miss it!
--- RITA and Christy Award-Winning Author, Best-Selling
Novelist, Susan May Warren

If you're looking for a rich and creative adventure through
a dystopian future in the heart of America's powerbase,
then Voice in the Wilderness will be a wild ride that you
won't forget anytime soon. Watching this duo tackle this
massive mission, which stretched across the US in
mesmerizing detail, from DC to Oregon, was such an
enjoyable read....I would recommend it to anyone. KC and
Brock, an insider who knows where the bodies are buried
and her longtime protector and friend, must rise to this
dangerous occasion to prevent the unthinkable from
happening. Every scene seems essential, and there weren't
any sections that I found myself just "getting through". I
enjoyed it all - thoroughly, and I can't wait to see where
this series goes from here. Wegley has a sizable talent, to
be sure.
--- Author, John J. Staughton

Voice in the Wilderness brings to mind the concept of
"Romancing the Thriller." This is an action-packed
romantic suspense story that doesn't slow down for a
moment.

The novel opens with tension. The main character, a
freckle-faced, red haired beauty named K.C. Banning
receives a text message from inside the White House that
she's being set up. She's a techno-genius who works for
the government. There's one thing for certain, the author
knows his technology.

As K.C. sets off across the country to get as far away from the beltway as she can, the author's skill shines in painting a clear picture of the beauty of rural America.

K.C.'s childhood, Christian political-blogger friend, Brock Daniels, sees her image on a television news program and knows exactly where she will go to hide. Brock draws upon his deep faith and this sustains him. K.C. struggles with God, but as things get darker she begins to rely upon Him. Her fledgling faith is presented in a natural way. The author shapes a story sending both characters into what looks like will be their doom, but somehow there is hope. There is also a wonderful use of humor which lightened some of the more terrorizing moments.
--- Author, Nike Chillemi

There are several avenues authors take in writing about the disintegration of the political systems, especially the government as it functions in the US. Each has an audience but few other authors are as successful as Wegley in finding that fine line of terror and intrigue and eventual hopelessness, then leading the story into an inspirational realm. That is talent and Wegley has it.

Tension and very realistic factual descriptions of all aspects of this story make this a film waiting to be produced. A very fine, entertaining read.
--- Hall of Fame Amazon Reviewer, Grady Harp

What a powerful and compelling book! And to think it is "only" a fictitious portrait of modern America and things that may actually come to pass unless "We the people" do something to prevent them from happening. Multiple kudos to Mr. Wegley for having the courage to use his talents to "tell it like it is.

"Mr. Wegley is a talented writer, and he keeps the story moving right along while allowing us to cheer for the good guys and boo the villains. A definite page turner...not necessarily recommended for bedtime reading.
--- Author, Roger Bruner

CONTENTS

ACKNOWLEDGMENTS

Many thanks to Susan May Warren, award winning author and writing coach, who helped me brainstorm part of the plot for *Voice in the Wilderness* and coached me on character development and the romantic thread. Thanks to my wife, Babe, for listening to me read to her all fourteen drafts and for helping me fill the plot holes and fix the logic as the story iterated to completion. Thanks to my beta readers, Duke Gibson, Don and Carol Ruska, David Lewis, and to my critique group, Dawn Lily and Gayla Hiss for their suggestions.

Thank you, Samantha Fury, for developing a cover that captures the feel of the story, and for figuring out how to get Photoshop to capture all of KC Banning's beautiful red hair.

Thanks to the team at Trinity Web Works/Trinity Press International for their work in preparing this manuscript for publication, including editor, Dr. Caroline Savage, as well as Shawn Savage for web site work and book formatting. Thanks to their fearless leader, Tony Marino, and his assistant, Tom Blubaugh, for planning the publishing and marketing of this novel and to Lynn Marino for managing book promotion.

Thanks to our Lord for allowing me to be born in the USA and for leaving me enough wits and words to write another novel. May He bless and challenge us all through the lessons learned and the courage displayed by the young man and young woman featured in *Voice in the Wilderness*.

PROLOGUE

Hannan's Rules for Radical Reform

Abandon all morals and ethics. They are impediments to establishing the world as it should be.

Absolutely nothing is sacred, so never behave as if anything is.

Make pragmatic concerns my only concerns. The end I envision justifies any means.

Reject all knowledge and wisdom from the past, because people cannot distinguish myth from history.

Build political apathy, by fostering consumerism, using entertainment, technology, pornography, addictions—anything that will reduce political interest and participation.

Destroy all sense of community, isolating individuals by motivating them to focus on private concerns, with the exception of communities of special-interest voting blocs that support me.

Remove religion from public discourse, confining it to private worship.

Attack and ridicule opponents, criticizing them harshly and personally.

Agitate the population, making chaos and crisis the norm so extreme measures also seem normal.

Never let the media, or my enemies, focus on one "scandal" too long. Give them something even more egregious to discuss, an endless cascade of "scandals" so they can never catch up.

Chapter 1

Washington, DC, 10:00 p.m. the National Mall

UR being set up. Watch your back, PL. More later. B.

The text message sent a shiver through KC Banning despite the warm, late June evening. Secret Service Agent Belino had probably risked his career to warn her, but what kind of set up was the young marine in the West Wing implying? Set up to be fired or—no one would kill her for what she had done ... would they?

PL, pretty lady. Despite her angst, his flirtatious acronym almost made her smile.

KC closed her cell, dropped it into her shorts pocket, and glanced behind to see if anyone was following her. No one.

She hurried down the path between two rows of dim walkway lights, lining the wall of the Vietnam War Memorial.

Soon, the lights ended and the overhanging trees turned her surroundings nearly black.

The crunch of footsteps came through the trees on her right.

KC whirled toward the sound.

Two shadowy figures popped out from behind a large bush and walked away toward the east end of the mall.

She released her breath in a sharp blast.

Only a young couple, with arms intertwined. She had

interrupted their romantic interlude.

KC continued down the walkway but stopped when she reached the paved circle drive. To her left, the Lincoln Memorial glowed like a lantern as its light reached out into the surrounding darkness.

The senator said to meet him inside the Lincoln Memorial at 10:00 p.m. in the Second Inaugural Address chamber. And he'd emphasized that they shouldn't be seen together. For his sake or hers? After reading the text message, maybe for both.

Most of the tourists out tonight had headed toward the African jazz concert near the east end of the mall, leaving the memorial nearly deserted. When KC strode ahead, the lights in front of the temple-like structure seemed to expose her like a spotlight hitting a performer on a stage. The sense of vulnerability sent her trotting up the steps to the protection of the memorial's walls.

Inside the large chamber, two women stood in soft conversation beneath Lincoln's left knee.

Time to play the role of a tourist, pretending to be transfixed by the magnificent sculpture. That wasn't difficult. Even with her apprehension, how could she not be awestruck by this statue of the great man?

KC looked up and studied Lincoln's face. His eyes held a sad, pensive look, an expression that would be sadder still if he had suspected a man like Abe Hannan would someday hold the highest office in the land.

Would KC's life end like Lincoln's, with a bullet through the back of her head?

Something moved on her right. KC spun toward it.

A bald head ringed with silver hair stuck out from behind one of the large pillars. Senator Richards.

She released the breath she'd been holding. Maybe the senator's answers would end her role in this drama that had intensified from mysterious to threatening over the past several hours.

He motioned toward the back wall of the chamber where spot lighting illumined the inaugural address engraved on the wall.

KC walked into the chamber and headed toward the figure of an eagle, where the senator had stopped beside the stone bench lining the wall. She read the six words directly above Senator Richards's head, "... for the widow and his orphan ..."

Orphan ... that would be KC.

When she stopped near him, the smile that normally appeared when she visited the senator's office had been replaced by pursed, pale lips.

"KC, you called my office several times and left four messages. You shouldn't do that. It's a dead giveaway that you're raising sensitive issues." His steel-blue eyes pierced her with an icy stare.

What was that about? She was the one with the upsetting news. "Senator, I didn't reveal anything about—"

"Just don't do it again." He sighed and shook his head. "I'm sorry. But, I think my phones are being monitored. And there are other suspicious things happening."

Suspicious? That was putting it mildly. "Senator Richards ... you've helped me so much since my parents died but, tonight, I really need your help."

"What's the Defense Information Systems Agency up to now?"

"It's not DISA. It's Hannan. He may be targeting me."

"The president targeting you? He wouldn't have *you* fired, unless the man's an idiot. Sometimes I wonder about—what does your supervisor, Major Grieve, say?"

"Sir, I think POTUS might have more than firing in mind. Maybe ... eliminating."

"That's absurd. What could you have possibly done to— no. Even Hannan, scoundrel that he is, doesn't go around murdering people."

"But he *does* tap into the classified networks in the DUCC ... from his private study."

"And how would a DISA recruit, fresh out of school, know that? Besides, you work *under* the West Wing, not *in* it."

How would she know? The back of her neck grew hot, the precursor to an eruption. "I'm twenty-one. And, if you'll recall, I graduated top of my class with a masters from MIT, and hired in well above starting grade. You ought to know, senator. You helped me get the job." KC's red hair and temper were getting the better of her. She needed to keep it down. Senator Richards had always seemed like a kind, friendly man. She'd never seen him so agitated and hostile.

He stepped close to KC. The blue bags under his eyes, and deeper wrinkles at their corners, made him look like he'd aged several years since she saw him last month. The senator lowered his voice. "You need to tell me what led to your suspicions."

"That's what I was trying to do." She took a calming breath and tried to speak more softly. "Last night, while I was monitoring networks, we had an apparent cyberattack."

"On the classified defense networks?" His eyebrows rose. "That's darned near impossible."

"That's what I've always thought. Well, it turned out to be an exercise, or so I was told by Major Grieve. I trapped the malicious data packets and checked out the network configuration of the impacted subnet to see if we were okay. That's when I saw a new machine connected to the router."

"So you stopped the attack. But a new machine on the classified networks ... wouldn't you have known about that? Shouldn't it be part of standard procedures to notify your group?"

"Yes. That's why I made the effort to identify the machine. It matched the fingerprint of the laptop in the president's private study."

"But that's outside your area of responsibility. The WHCA should—"

"The White House Communications Agency is where I got the fingerprint database. A certain young man who works for them gave it to me. And don't look at me like that. It's not classified information."

"You take too many risks, KC. I've warned you before about—"

"I know you have, sir. But I needed to know if the defense networks had been compromised. So, I went up to ground level and—"

"Don't tell me you examined POTUS's laptop. Young lady, you—"

"You need to listen for a moment. Hannan has a newly installed network jack hidden under the desk in his study. Plug into it and you're on the defense networks. I tested it. But someone working below had to configure that machine into the authorized address tables or it wouldn't have had access. That means Hannan has at least one accomplice in my group. He has classified network access, and he has the military communications software to make use of it loaded on his laptop."

The senator frowned. "Which means?"

"It means he can communicate directly with any military organization at any level, anywhere in the world. Are you getting the picture, senator?"

His squinting eyes said he wasn't. If he wasn't such a good friend, she'd be screaming at him. "You're the head of the Senate Intelligence Committee, for goodness sake."

He recoiled from her insult. But, the wide-eyed expression on his face said the lights had come on. "POTUS must want direct control. He wants—"

"He wants to use his authority to intimidate the troops. In principle, isn't that what Hitler did? Used authority to coerce people into doing what they might not otherwise do?"

"Does Hannan know that you—"

A tune played on KC's cell, an incoming message. "Just a second."

She pulled the cell from her shorts pocket, opened the message, and nearly choked.

Hannan just declared U a domestic terrorist based on the laptop incident. Says UR dangerous. He's not talking catch. U need to disappear, ASAP. Take care, PL. B.

"He knows what I did and ..." She croaked out the words through her constricted throat. "I think he means to kill me."

"Kill you? Not even this president ..." The senator's eyes pinched hard until his bushy eyebrows touched. "Hannan ..." He shook his head. "How do you know he wants to kill you?"

"That message just told me I'm now a domestic terrorist, and someone in a position to know says Hannan isn't planning to catch me, just ... eliminate me."

"How credible is this person?"

She peered into the senator's eyes. "He probably heard it straight from Hannan's mouth. Look, he risked his job and probably his life to warn me. I believe him."

The senator's eyes softened. "I never thought this would involve you, but now it does. Don't repeat what I'm about to tell you, KC. Do you understand?"

She nodded, but she felt like running. She didn't want to hear any more threatening news. KC only wanted to leave this place where truth had become only what powerful people wanted it to be, while everyone else had to pay the consequences.

Richards placed his foot on the low stone bench and leaned on his knee. "My committee has launched an investigation of President Hannan's abuses of authority and blatant violations of the constitution, an investigation that could end with his impeachment and, hopefully, removal from office."

Ordinarily, this news would have called for a celebration. But everything ordinary had vanished with the arrival of a text message. "I love this country. That's why I took my job with DISA. I'll testify at the hearings, if you need me."

The senator studied her face for a moment, as if trying to read her reaction. "Because of the investigation, I've received some threats. Normally, I ignore such things. But with Hannan and what you've just encountered ..." He shook his head. "Your testimony, as part of my investigation, increases the odds of Hannan's removal from office. Depending on what he's done, maybe it will send him to prison. But you have to be alive to testify. If he's caught wind of—I don't know how to say this any other way." The senator pulled his foot from the bench, stepped closer to her, and placed a hand on her shoulder. "KC, whoever warned you is right. I think you need to take this threat seriously, very seriously."

KC's heart pounded out the realization of her danger. Hannan was like a venomous snake, the ones in her nightmares. That thought sent her mind back seven years to another viper, the rattlesnake coiled inches from her bare leg, the one her dearest childhood friend, Brock Daniels, had killed when he saved her life.

At this moment, she would give nearly anything to have Brock standing beside her with his arm draped over her shoulders. Thoughts of him didn't come as often now, but when they came, they completely consumed her.

"... hide, understand, KC?"

She needed to focus. She'd missed part of what Richards had said. "You think I need to run and hide, don't you?"

"Do you know a place to hide where no one can find you?"

"I ... I think so. But it's 2,300 miles away."

"The farther away the better. Now, here's what you need to do."

Over the next ten minutes, Senator Richards told her how to escape the Beltway and gave KC instructions for traveling so that detection was unlikely. His directions about getting new identification and avoiding video were detailed. What all did they discuss in intelligence committee meetings ... covert operators?

When he finished, KC's mind was a slurry of pureed thoughts. His advice went in but, with panic now pounding in her chest, could she pull anything meaningful from the mixture?

"Don't go back to your apartment, not for any reason. They'll be watching it. Is there someplace you can spend the night?"

"Yes. I can go to—"

"Don't tell me where. Just get there like I told you. Withdraw as much cash as you can and leave on the heels of the commute tomorrow. Got it?"

"I think so."

"Buy a cheap, disposable cell phone and call me when you see the message about the hearing on my senate web page. I'll be praying for you, KC."

"Thanks." Maybe his prayers would accomplish more than hers. Sometimes, she wasn't sure why she even bothered.

He squeezed her shoulder. "You need to go now. I'll wait here a few minutes so no one sees us together. Take care, young lady."

She hugged the senator. "You take care, too. And nail that rattlesnake, Hannan."

KC turned and strode into the main chamber of the memorial. It was empty.

Music from the concert played in the distance.

She looked down the steps, surveying the lighted area in front of the memorial. The tourists had all left. KC scurried down the steps and ran into the darkness to her left, toward the Rock Creek Trail.

A loud crack sounded behind her. It resonated in the Lincoln Memorial's chambers, jolting KC with its sound and significance. Someone had fired a gun inside the memorial.

She leapt to her left and hid behind a bush. KC looked back at the entrance, trying to slow her panting to normal breathing.

A dark-clad figure exited the main chamber and ran to the south, away from KC, jumped down to the grass, and then leaped the remaining ten or fifteen feet down into the bushes and trees on the far side of the memorial.

Had that person seen her while she was inside the memorial? If so, the shooter could have killed them both. Did that mean she *wasn't* a target? No. Only that she wasn't *this* killer's target at *this* time.

Tears trickled down her cheek. The man who had mentored her, watched out for her for the past three years, was probably dead. It had been Senator Richards, not her, that met Lincoln's fate tonight. But if Hannan had already sent someone after her, there was still time for KC to die before morning.

Regardless, this was not a time for tears. She wiped them away and focused on reaching a Metro station to get to her friend's apartment.

Boarding Metro here in DC wasn't a good idea. She might be spotted. Boarding on the Virginia side would be safer. Maybe in Rosslyn.

The Arlington Bridge was her best route to get to Rosslyn Metro Station on foot, but the shooter had disappeared near the north end of that bridge. She would take the Roosevelt Bridge, instead. Regardless, she needed to get away from the Lincoln Memorial before it became an official crime scene.

A siren sounded somewhere to the north. It grew louder, revving her heart near its red line.

Her adrenaline rush turned to explosive energy. She ran

down the Rock Creek Trail and up onto the Roosevelt Bridge. As she ran the bridge, between KC's heavy breaths and the occasional noise of a passing car, from somewhere behind her, sounds reached her ears ... the cadence of running feet.

The sounds grew louder.

If the running feet caught her, KC's evidence would die with her.

Then Hannan wins and America dies.

It couldn't end like that. She wouldn't let it.

KC broke into an all-out sprint.

Only 2,300 miles to go.

Chapter 2

A small village near Chisec, 290 klicks north of Guatemala City.

The moment Brock stepped from his tent into the humid Guatemalan morning air, Jeff and Allie cornered him.

Trapped.

For the past week, Brock had managed to avoid this conversation with his fellow team leaders as they rode herd on an energetic bunch of high schoolers on a short-term mission trip.

Brock scanned the metal-roofed, wooden, village huts to his left and the young people's tents to his right. The fourth adult member of the team, Julia Weiss, was conspicuously absent. He had politely avoided the cute, petite brunette who had an obvious interest in him. That would be the subject of this war of words and wits. Brock resigned himself to the inevitable and waited.

"Mi Amor, I've got this." Jeff waved Allie off. "Why don't you and Julia get the kids up for breakfast?"

"You sure, Jeff?" Allie's large brown eyes questioned him as her fingers played with strands of her long, dark hair. With her Hispanic heritage, Allie looked like a Spanish rancheros daughter, the one the cowboys fought over in old western movies. Jeff was a lucky man.

"Yeah. This is guy talk. I've got it covered." The tall former Olympic decathlete, with brains and brawn, made a formidable opponent.

"You blow this and you're in big trouble." Allie's smile lacked much of its usual warmth as she turned and sauntered toward the young people's tents.

Jeff plopped a hand on Brock's shoulder. "What's wrong with Julia?"

Right to the issue. That was Jeff. "I didn't know anything was wrong with her. Enlighten me."

"That's precisely what I intend to do. Why don't you and I take a morning walk?"

Brock would stall, stonewall, and play stupid, anything to cause Jeff to give up or cut short this inquisition. "A morning walk? Will that fix whatever's wrong with Julia?"

"Could be." Jeff gave him a smirky smile.

He was a good friend, but Brock had never told Jeff about the summers at Crooked River Ranch, about KC, or the devastating letter. Maybe it was time. Maybe Jeff could help Brock with his dilemma. Maybe he could even—no, too many maybes.

Jeff nudged Brock and the two started up the dirt trail following the small stream toward its source, a mountain shrouded in mist, the remnant of last evening's showers. The mountain would soon be uncovered, exposed to the hot Guatemalan sun, just as Jeff's questions would expose events from Brock's shrouded past.

"Brock, she's done everything but throw herself at you. I think you two would—"

Brock cut him off. "There's someone else." There. For better or worse, he had finally admitted it.

"Bro ..." Jeff's eyebrows rose as he cocked his head. "You been holding out on me?"

"Not exactly. This story starts before I met you ... about thirteen years—"

A scream stopped Brock. It came from the village. "Allie must have seen another big spider."

"That wasn't Allie." Jeff whirled and sprinted back down the trail.

Brock was fast, but Jeff, a world-class athlete, pulled away from Brock until they rounded a turn, bringing the village into view. Jeff slowed and Brock caught him.

Julia ran out the door of a rusty-roofed hut and pressed a hand over her heart.

Allie and a group of teens ran toward Julia, but she shoved her palm at them. "Stay back," she warned, then turned toward Jeff and Brock. "Brock, hurry. It's little Itzy."

Jeff was in the lead. He was the leader of this team. But Julia's eyes had focused on Brock.

Like it or not, Julia was placing her trust in him. It wasn't a good thing for anybody to do, to depend on someone who let people down, someone who always came up short. But Brock couldn't ignore the plea to help a seven-year-old orphan who had quickly attached herself to Julia.

"I'll help her, Jeff." Brock trotted up to the small hut that housed five people. "What's wrong with Itzy?"

Julia's wide eyes and body language said she was on the verge of panic. "She got sick yesterday. Said she had a splitting headache and went to bed. But now she has a high fever. When I walked in, she spewed vomit clear across the hut."

Brock stepped through the doorway.

"Brock, whatever this is it scares me. Don't expose yourself."

"I'm just going to take a look. If it's some airborne virus, we're probably all exposed already. If not ... well, I'll be careful."

Brock waited a moment for his eyes to adjust to the semidarkness inside.

The tiny girl lay on a mat on the floor, moaning, holding

her stomach with one hand, her head with the other. The contents of her stomach lay splattered in a line three feet across the floor.

The girl knew a bit of English, probably from visiting missionaries. He needed to see her eyes. "Itzy, can you open your eyes and look at me."

In a couple of seconds, her eyes opened, blinked, then focused on him. They looked like blood might drip from them any second.

Brock's gut tightened as he recognized the extent to which the disease had ravaged Itzy's body. "Show me where you hurt."

Her tiny hands patted her head and stomach. On her head, above her hairline, several sutures created a jagged line in the girl's beautiful hair. Who had treated her?

"We're going to get some help for you. Julia's praying for you, Itzy."

He backed out of the hut and turned to face Julia. "Have you touched her?"

Julia stared at him, her eyes full of worry, searching his for answers. "This is more than just stomach flu isn't it?"

Instead of replying, Brock waved at Jeff. "Jeff, come here. You need to hear this. We've got some decisions to make." He waited until Jeff stopped beside them. "I've never heard of it being in Central America, but this looks like some kind of hemorrhagic fever."

"You sure, bro?" Jeff spoke in the low monotone he reserved for moments of crisis.

"Remember that short-term trip to Africa I almost went on?"

Jeff nodded.

"Before my trip was cancelled, I spent some time with a missionary home on furlough from Africa. He saw an Ebola outbreak and described it in gruesome detail. I know they've never had an outbreak in Central America, but Itzy's symptoms, the projectile vomiting—it all fits the pattern. And it's spread by contact with body fluids."

Brock turned toward Julia. "I need to ask you again. Have you touched Itzy?"

"I ..." Julia stared at the doorway for a moment, then at Brock. "I may have touched things she touched, but not her."

"When she vomited, did—"

"No. I was on the other side of her bed."

"How did you know she had a fever?"

"Itzy's foster mother said she was hot. The family left the hut this morning when they saw how sick she was. It frightened them and then they came and told me."

"I need to talk to Itzy's foster mom."

A short woman with long, straight black hair stepped from behind Allie and peered at Brock. "You need talk me?"

At least she knew some English. "Yes. Itzy's forehead." Brock traced a line on his own head. "How did she hurt her head?"

"Fall." The woman pointed toward a large rock at the corner of the hut. "Rock."

Brock made a sewing motion with his hand. "Who sewed it up?"

"Doctor. Clinic." She pointed down the stream, below the village.

The cut was healing well. But how long ago had it been? "When?" Brock lifted a finger at a time. "Four days? Five? Six?"

The woman raised all of her fingers.

Brock did the same. "Ten days."

The woman smiled. "Yes. Ten."

About right for the incubation period. They had only one choice for seeking immediate medical care to save the little girl's life. It was a risky choice for more reasons than the risk of exposure to the disease.

17

"Brock ..." Julia touched his arm. "You said when you took a walk yesterday an armed guard stopped you at that clinic and asked you to leave. But they must treat sick or injured villagers if they sewed up Itzy's cut."

"Yeah. But they also run people off with their assault rifles."

"We've got to help her." Tears welled in Julia's eyes.

Jeff emptied his lungs with a loud blast and shook his head. "We're responsible for our kids' safety. If there's even a remote possibility of an outbreak of something like hemorrhagic fever, I've got to get them out of here."

The tears flowed freely down Julia's cheeks now.

Brock's resistance crumbled. "I'll take Itzy to the clinic."

Hemorrhagic fever, projectile vomiting and all. He couldn't believe he'd said that. Brock looked at Julia's face again and saw the relief his words had brought. He'd made the right decision. Now he needed to figure out how to take Itzy without risking exposure or hurting her in the process. The clinic was a mile down the trail.

"Bro, you sure about this?"

Brock met Jeff's intense gaze and nodded.

"Okay. I've got the satellite phone that Allie's dad donated. I'm calling for transportation to the airport. Our emergency plan was to use the guy here in Chisec. That's better than waiting six hours for someone from Guatemala City." Jeff waved Allie toward the young people's tents. "Allie, tell our kids to get packed and be ready to leave in an hour. Hope the guy with the vehicles has the day open on his schedule."

"Brock, I'm going with you to the clinic. You'll need help with Itzy." The look in Julia's eyes said he'd lose if he argued with her.

He nodded to Julia. "Jeff, what about Julia and me? No telling how long this will take."

"Don't worry. We'll arrange a ride for you and leave a

note here with the details."

"You'll need to take care of something else, too, Jeff. Though you have to be symptomatic to be contagious, which takes at least five or six days, you should tell our airline in Guatemala City about Julia and me. I think the airline is supposed to call the WHO."

"Will do. But that means the U.S. will know about us before we hit LAX. Customs in LA will probably give us all the third degree."

"Yeah." Brock shook his head. "We may not get home any quicker than if we'd stayed another week. But we've got to protect the villagers, too. I'll talk to Chac in a few minutes. He knows English better than anyone else in the village. I'll tell him how to clean up the hut after Julia and I take Itzy."

Jeff laid a hand on Brock's shoulder. "But who's going to protect you and Julia?"

"I've got a plan for that, too."

Thirty minutes later, with Julia beside Brock and Itzy trailing a safe distance behind them on an improvised travois, they rounded a sharp bend in the trail and came face-to-face with the same armed guard who had stopped Brock yesterday. Like yesterday, he wore no rank insignia or emblem of any kind.

The guard gave them the universal stop gesture, then stared at Brock for a moment. "You again. I could hear you coming for the last fifteen minutes."

"It's not like we were sneaking up on you. We've got a sick child from the Mayan village. She's really sick. Maybe hemorrhagic fever." Brock studied the man's face. His reference to hemorrhagic fever didn't get a rise out of the guy. Nothing. That was strange.

"Stay where you are. Do not come closer. I'll see what I can do." The soldier pulled out a two-way radio and walked a short distance away, turning his back on them.

Brock studied the soldier, then shot Julia a glance. "Sure wish I could hear what he's saying."

"You mean you can't hear him at all?"

"Do you mean you can?"

"I've got a hearing disorder. Can't hear the high notes, but human voices ..."

Brock moved closer to Julia. "What's the guy saying?"

"Something about Carter, about leaving, and making us wait." Julia shrugged and looked down at Itzy who seemed to be sleeping fitfully at the moment.

"Then, I guess we wait."

"You know, Brock, what we're doing isn't without risks. It isn't safe."

"Neither is life. It seems to kill everybody."

Julia gave him a strange look. "More of Brock Daniels's philosophy or—never mind. What I meant to say was thank you for helping Itzy. Most guys wouldn't have."

Itzy coughed and moaned.

Brock looked down at the small girl. "Kids like Itzy, born in one of the most isolated people groups in the Western Hemisphere, in one of the poorest countries, have the deck of life stacked against them from day one. That's why our team came down to help. Right now, this is what that help requires."

"You're a good man, Brock Daniels.'

That was debatable and it depended upon who made the assessment. But it wasn't a conversation he wanted to have with Julia, someone he barely knew.

A movement caught Brock's attention.

Two men came out of the cinder-block building, one in military clothing, the other a civilian with dark sunglasses and a hat pulled low on his face. Brock nodded toward the civilian. "Incognito? What's that guy thinking? This ain't Hollywood. And there are no paparazzi running around in Central Guatemala."

The man stumbled when he stepped off the concrete porch near the clinic door. His sunglasses slid off the bridge of his nose and fell. The man snatched them before they fell to the ground and shoved them back into place.

That face. He'd seen it ... somewhere. Julia's words, Carter ... leaving. Brock drew a sharp breath.

Julia clamped a hand on his arm. "What's wrong, Brock?"

"Let's pretend nothing's wrong. And keep your voice down."

She leaned closer to him. "But something *is* wrong isn't it?"

"Yeah. Something's sure not right."

The two men climbed into a four-wheel-drive vehicle and drove away, heading toward Chisec.

Brock let out the breath he'd been holding. "That was Secretary of Defense, Gerald Carter, and he didn't want anyone to know it."

"*Our* Secretary of Defense?" Julia cocked her head. "What would he be doing at a place like this?"

"That's the salient question."

"Salient? Oh, yes. You're a writer."

"I'd like to think so. But think about it for a minute. The place is guarded by soldiers wearing no insignia of rank or national identity. The defense secretary makes a secret visit, a cabinet member who happens to be in Abe Hannan's inner circle. Now, add to all that the fact that Itzy contracts hemorrhagic fever one incubation period after being sewn up at this clinic. And, did you notice, the guard didn't even flinch when I tossed out the words hemorrhagic fever. This smells like a black operation linked to Hannan. At least that's how I read it."

"Is this the kind of stuff you post on your blog? Conspiracy theories?"

"And what makes you ask that?"

Julia smiled at him and cute turned to beautiful. "I've visited a few times."

"Did I get a new follower from those visits?"

"Yes, you did, though I don't spend much time on the Internet."

"I'm not a conspiracy guy. Mostly, I blog about truth and reality—truth in religion, politics, and morality, using concepts from Christian Apologetics. Once a month, I make a prediction about where the nation is going in the next few years. That's when the posts go viral."

"Viral? You must have a lot of followers." She shot him a glance.

"Over a million last time I checked."

"Wow. I'm standing beside a celebrity." Julia was attempting to flirt with him, as much as that was possible in the current situation.

Brock wasn't sure how he felt about that. She was a good, selfless woman and way more than just attractive. "Celebrity? I don't know about that, but I do know here comes trouble."

The guard had left his position by the clinic door and walked toward them, radio in one hand, assault rifle in the other. "The child can come in now."

Brock grabbed a corner of the blanket they'd laid Itzy on and stood.

"I said the *child* can come in. You two stay outside."

"But doesn't the doctor want to hear how long she's had symptoms?"

A tall man stuck his head out of the clinic and looked at them. He looked about sixty, cranky, but most of all, arrogant. "You can bring the kid in now."

Julia stood. "Her name is Itzy and she has symptoms of—"

"I know. Hemorrhagic fever. She'll be fine in a few days and we'll return her to the village."

Brock stood up beside Julia and raised his voice more than the distance required. "She'll be fine? The kill rate on these diseases can be over 90%, so how do you know—"

"As I said, she'll be fine. You can count on it. Now, you two need to leave." The doctor motioned to the guard. "Sergeant, see that they do."

As the guard approached, Julia knelt down by Itzy's tiny body. "Itzy, honey ... can you hear me?"

Two brown eyes opened part way. They were red and bleeding. Itzy gave a weak nod.

"I have to go now, but there's a doctor here that's going to make you well."

Another weak nod.

"Finish your goodbyes and then you need to leave." The soldier stood as if ready to raise his weapon.

This guy liked to intimidate people. Brock usually confronted bullies. He had ever since he stood up for KC. He'd learned that planting his six-foot-five, 235 pound frame in front of them was usually enough to make bullies back off. But not when they held an automatic rifle in their hands.

Julia reached out toward Itzy's face.

"Julia, no!" Brock reached down and gripped her arm.

She pulled her hand back.

"Bantiox, Miss Julia." After her thank you, Itzy closed her eyes.

"Hulaj chik, Itzy." Julia stood, after saying goodbye, turned, and strode toward the trail leading back to the village.

Brock hurried until he caught up with her. "You okay?"

She shook her head and swiped at the tears on her cheeks. "Was the doctor lying to us? Will they even take her inside? Or will they just ..."

"We're going to find out." After they rounded a sharp bend in the trail, Brock hooked her arm and pulled Julia into the bushy trees on their left.

They crept through the vegetation, toward the clinic, until it came into view.

Two men wearing something like hazmat suits loaded Itzy on a stretcher.

Brock continued watching until they entered the building, then he backed out of the bushes and stepped onto the trail. "We'd best get out of here before the guy with the gun catches us."

Julia looked up at him with a questioning frown. "So, that's it? We just leave?"

"That's all we can do. She's under the doctor's care at the clinic. That's better than we can offer. Julia, Itzy would die in our care."

She nodded and a tear trickled down one cheek. "I guess all we can do is pray for her."

"And for our team and the other villagers and ..."

"And us." Julia said in a hoarse whisper.

"Yeah. And us. We've been careful, but you and I are still deep in the woods with this nasty little bug."

Chapter 3

Under the streetlights with no place to hide, KC sprinted hard across the Roosevelt Bridge until her breathing turned raspy, then to choking. Despite her exertion, she had hyperventilated.

Stop or pass out? She had to do one or the other, but neither seemed like a good choice.

She glanced back. No one. But the concrete walkway seemed to rock back and forth. Or was *she* rocking back and forth?

KC stopped and leaned against the railing to steady herself. She cupped her tingling hands around her mouth and nose, trying to rebreathe her air.

A runner appeared in the distance, coming toward her.

If she tried to run now, she would fall.

Get yourself under control, KC. Now.

She willed her breathing to slow and tried to focus on the runner.

A man. He wore running shorts and a T-shirt. The runner cut across the empty lanes of traffic to the west side of the bridge. Just a guy out for his evening run. But had someone been chasing her? Or had she imagined it?

Soon the world stopped rocking. KC jogged along the walkway, following the off ramp on the south side of the river until the walkway became a trail. Seeing no one behind her, she jumped off the trail into bushes lining it and hid. If someone was following her, they couldn't have seen her leave the trail, but she would soon see them.

She waited two or three minutes. Nobody.

Traffic was light as KC worked her way across the maze of roads at the south end of the bridge until she reached Wilson Boulevard. She followed it toward Rosslyn Station.

With Senator Richards presumed dead, KC had no one to turn to but a handful of college friends. Her former roommate from Georgetown U, where KC did her undergraduate work, lived in Alexandria.

KC hadn't seen Amanda Willis in a few months, but Mandie had always been a person KC could trust. A short ride on Metro would take her within a few blocks of Mandie's apartment.

Catching Metro was risky, if people were looking for her. At Rosslyn Station, KC lingered in the shadows for ten minutes before the train arrived. When she stepped onto it, there were only two people in the car, both elderly and harmless, except for their eyes. And her long, wavy, red hair was a neon sign, advertising KC Banning, domestic terrorist, latest addition to the FBI's most wanted list.

On the ride to Braddock Road Station, only one more passenger had entered the car, but it only took one to identify her and send the police to the right neighborhood. As she walked up Braddock, no one seemed to be following her.

When KC approached Mandie's ground-level apartment, she pulled out her cell to check the time. Half past eleven. Mandie was a night owl and the glow from her living room window said that hadn't changed.

Rather than alarm her, KC selected Mandie's entry on her cell's contact list and held a finger above the call icon. Were the police tracking KC's cell? So many things to consider when trying to stay invisible, especially when one moment of visibility could end her life.

She turned off her cell, opened it, and removed the batteries, dropping them into her shorts pocket. That would prevent anyone from tracking her by GPS.

KC knocked, softly.

Footsteps approached the door. The light coming through the peephole darkened. Mandie was looking out.

"Mandie, it's KC. I need to talk to you."

The door opened and the pretty, petite young woman dressed in a tank top and shorts with skin two shades darker than the sun could produce reached for KC with open arms.

"No, don't touch me yet."

Mandie pulled her brown arms and pink-palmed hands back. Her dark brown eyes widened.

"Not until we talk." Leaving DNA evidence could implicate Mandie. What else should KC worry about? She stepped inside and closed the door behind her.

Mandie scanned KC's face. "KC, you're scaring me. And that look on your face—after rooming together for three and a half years, I know what it means. So, what kind of trouble are you in this time?"

"I'll tell you enough so you can decide if you want me to leave, but not enough to get you into trouble."

"You're just *trying* to scare me now. Girl, you are staying, no matter what." Mandie pointed at her couch. "Sit down and spill it ... all of it."

That was Mandie. Never the manipulative approach many women used. Though she stood only five-foot-two, Mandie gave orders like she was a giant.

KC looked at the logo on the TV screen. "Is that the eleven o'clock news?"

"Yes. It's just going off."

"Did you watch it?"

"Yes." Mandie frowned. "Why? Don't tell me you're on the news."

"It's possible. Did you hear anything about Senator Richards?"

Mandie gasped. "It … it was the breaking news story they closed with. They said the senator had been shot in the head but didn't provide any other details."

KC's eyes overflowed. She wiped them, but the tears wouldn't stop. "That's what I—I hoped I was wrong." She choked out the words between sobs and then brutally stuffed her emotions. "Senator Richards was my mentor. He helped me a lot after Mom and Dad were killed in the crash. Now he's dead and it might be my fault."

"Your fault?" Mandie shook her head. "That's crazy. Girl, you're no killer."

"No, but he arranged for us to meet secretly inside the Lincoln Memorial, because I wanted to talk to him. He didn't want us to be seen together, so I left first. Shortly after I walked out, I heard a gunshot and saw a man running away. I ran too, then someone chased me across the Roosevelt Bridge and—"

Mandie placed her hand on KC's shoulder. "Could someone still be following you?"

"No. I made sure of that. I need to tell you enough of the story so you understand what's happening. But that could endanger you, Mandie. I don't want you ending up like the senator. I can leave right now if you want me to. Or, I can sleep here on the couch and leave in the morning. You know, hide among the commuters."

"You're staying. I don't have to work tomorrow. So we have all night for you to tell me your story."

KC told enough of the story to Mandie to keep her safe, but left out details that might cast suspicion on her if she revealed them to the police. "So, you see, Hannan's not who he pretends to be, Senator Richards is dead, and I'm a terrorist."

"And you had to run. Couldn't even go back to your

apartment. Is there anything you need?"

KC gave Mandie a half-hearted smile. "Plastic surgery."

"Girl, nobody that looks like you needs plastic surgery. But you do need a disguise and I can help with that. Let's see. How about dying your hair dark brown and getting you some sunglasses? I've got some makeup that will cover your ..." Mandie raised her eyebrows, and scanned KC's face.

"Go ahead and say it." KC pointed a finger at her cheek. "My freckles."

"But I know you hate them."

"No, it was actually my father who hated them. But ..."

"But your father's dead. Now the senator is dead. Do you have anyone to—"

"Anyone to run to? I'm not sure. But I do have a place to hide where no one can find me ... except for one person. Someone who saved my life, saved me from ..." KC wiped her cheeks.

"You're crying again. Is it because of this guy?"

"I didn't say it was a guy."

"You didn't have to. That look in your eyes said plenty."

Mandie had always read her well. Maybe KC should tell her part of the story. With her parents dead, no one but KC knew about her and Brock. "He's someone I met as a child. His name is Brock Daniels."

"Daniels? You mean the blogger?"

"I don't know. Do you know something about him?"

"Well, yeah. Just about anybody who's concerned about the direction our country's going knows about him." Mandie stood and put her hands on her hips. "Are you still avoiding the Internet like the plague?"

"It's not as bad as the plague, but I don't surf much, and I try to keep only a tiny footprint in cyberspace."

"Let's get you out of the Dark Ages." Mandie walked to her desk, wiggled her laptop's mouse, and clicked on something. "Come here and take a look at this."

KC followed Mandie to her laptop.

She pulled out her computer chair. "Here. You check out his blog while I run to the store."

"Please, don't buy just sunglasses and hair coloring. Somebody might notice and—"

"Don't worry. There are a few things I need too. The store's not far away. Be back in a half hour, after you reacquaint yourself with Mr. Daniels. He's certainly got a way with words." Mandie grabbed her purse and left.

Got a way with words. That was an understatement. Brock always could dazzle KC with his words. He could steal her heart if he wanted to. But, evidently, that was something Brock hadn't wanted to do.

KC pulled up Brock's most recent post, one that had apparently gone viral. It contained Brock Daniels's forecast for the USA. He talked about the direction President Hannan's progressives were moving the nation, toward a secular society where freedom of religion would be curtailed. He predicted over the next fifteen years, many Christians would lose their businesses, and some would go to prison for practicing their faith. Brock also forecasted that the demographics of the country would change sufficiently that no patriotic, constitution-loving American could possibly be elected to the presidency again, ever.

In so many words, Brock had predicted Uncle Sam's funeral, a funeral where, in twenty more years, there would be few mourners left.

How many people read Brock's posts? The comment count read over twenty thousand. If that many people felt compelled to leave their thoughts, probably several million people had read this post.

Brock had one tiny headshot of himself on his blog and the "About" section didn't mention anyone else. There was a link to Brock's Facebook author page. She clicked on it and checked the "About" section there. No mention of any relationships. Maybe Brock had left the door open for her. Maybe ...

The front door clicked and opened. Mandie entered, carrying a shopping bag.

Had KC been engrossed in Brock's blog and social media for a half hour? Evidently.

Mandie dropped the bag on the desk beside KC's arm and grabbed KC's wrist. "Girl, it's time for you to tell me how you know this guy and how much of your heart he owns." She pulled KC back to the couch.

KC settled onto the couch, slipped off her shoes, and pulled her feet under her. How much of her heart Brock owned—could she answer that? She chose to ignore the question, but she needed to be careful about the details she revealed to Mandie.

"I've known Brock since I was 8 and he was 12. There's a ranch, one of the most beautiful places in the US. My parents spent a month there every summer to play in the golf tournaments. The summer Brock and I met, I couldn't find anybody my age to play with, and so I hung out around the ranch basketball court. Some of the older boys there were bullies. They started calling me names. When the names turned from carrot top to gutter language, and the biggest boy shoved me, Brock told the big kid to stop. He didn't."

The scene replayed in her mind and rekindled old emotions. The events of thirteen years ago seemed like yesterday.

"Don't leave me in suspense like that, KC." Mandie poked her shoulder. "Come on, girl, finish the story. What did Brock do?"

"He's really strong, Mandie, and he knows how to box. He beat the crud out of that big bully. Sent him running home with a bloody nose and what turned into the ugliest black eye I've ever seen."

Mandie laughed. "Served him right, but that must have cost Brock some friends."

"Yeah. No one would play with either of us after the fight. But he had just become my hero. So, I kept following him and suggesting things Brock and I could do together, things like hiding by the golf course and moving grumpy old duffer's golf balls when they couldn't see us. If I heard them swearing, I gave their ball a really bad lie. I could hardly believe it when Brock said he'd like to do that with me. What twelve-year-old boy would play with a girl more than three years younger than him? Well, Brock and I played together, we dreamed together, we explored the ranch—spent every summer together for the next five years, until ..."

The summer she turned fourteen brought back both wonderful and painful memories. KC wiped her eye before it overflowed.

Mandie poked her again. "Until what?"

"The summer I turned 14 was right after ... well, I had matured, very noticeably."

"Did Brock notice? He must have been what ... about 17?"

"Oh, he noticed. And I noticed that he noticed. That's why neither of us noticed that I'd walked up on a rattlesnake, coiled under a bush about two feet from my leg."

"Is that why you're terrified of snakes?"

"Yeah. But only the poisonous ones terrify me." KC paused as she pictured Brock's hand reaching to the ground and his fingers curling around a rock. "Brock is tall, strong, and he can throw really hard, harder than most major league pitchers. He threw a rock that nearly tore that snake's head off. Saved my life. Then I told him about Dad moving us to DC and that we'd be leaving in three days. And I asked him to throw another rock, one with our initials on it. That rock sailed what seemed like a mile out into the canyon, then splashed in the river. Somewhere in the river, at the bottom of that canyon, Brock and I are still together."

"Mmmhmmm, sounds like more than just friends, you were—"

"We were soulmates. I don't know how to say it any other way than ... we completed each other. I've never experienced anything like our relationship and if I don't stop talking about it right now, I'm going to start blubbering like a fool."

Mandie's face grew serious, her eyes questioning. "Only one more question then ... why aren't you two together now?"

"I don't know. But our initials are together at the bottom of the river running through the canyon."

"You are a romantic, girl. How come I never noticed that before?"

"I'm not a romantic, Mandie, I was just a girl with a broken heart. When I left on that last day, I was crying, my nose running. I kissed Brock anyway. We both promised to write, to stay in touch, and that we'd never forget each other. We didn't stay in touch, neither of us. But I've never forgotten him."

"We were roommates for like three and a half years and you kept all this bottled up inside?" Mandie shook her head. "Girl, I'm surprised you didn't explode."

"Well, now you know." She'd told Mandie more than KC had intended and they'd been distracted from important issues for too long. KC glanced across the room at Mandie's wall clock. 12:30 a.m. "Isn't there a news program coming on now?"

Mandie nodded. "But they only cover a few of the big stories for the day."

"Can we watch it? I need to know if KC Banning is a big story."

Mandie picked up a remote control from the end table and pointed it at the flat-screen TV on the wall in front of them. "Here we go."

The fanfare for the nightly news program ended. A woman appeared. The camera quickly zoomed in until she became a talking head. Instead of an overview of the night's news stories to be covered, the anchor went directly to a breaking news story.

A picture of Senator Richards filled the screen. "Senator Daniel Richards, head of the powerful Senate Intelligence Committee, was murdered this evening inside one of the chambers of the Lincoln Memorial. The DC Metro Police Department has issued a Be on the Lookout alert and the FBI have started an intense hunt for the suspect, domestic terrorist, Katheryn Banning, daughter of the late Senator Justin Banning."

KC jumped up from the couch. "Those filthy lying s—" She stomped her foot to release the rage and bit her tongue to cut off words she tried to keep from her vocabulary.

A sketch of KC appeared. No photo. It was understandable. Since her father's election, KC had successfully evaded the media, and she avoided cameras. They wouldn't have a picture of twenty-one-year-old KC Banning. Even her driver's license photo was nearly four years old. Eventually, they would get her DISA photo, a color shot that showed every freckle on her face. But, hopefully, she would be outside the Beltway before that picture hit the news.

The news anchor continued. "Ms. Banning allegedly called the senator, lured him to the Lincoln Memorial, and shot him in the back of the head, which is almost too ironic to be believable ..."

KC glanced at Mandie. She hadn't said a word. Hadn't moved. "Mandie ... say something. Anything. Do you want me to leave? What are you thinking?"

Mandie blew out a blast of air. "Girl, I'm thinking we need to get you disguised before they get a real picture of you to show."

"So you don't believe them?"

"If President Hannan's behind this, how could I believe it? He's a lying—you know, what you almost said."

"I don't want to endanger you. Maybe I should leave now."

"The only place you're going right now is to my bathroom. Get that bottle of dye on the desk and let's get rid of that auburn hair. Plus I'm giving you some makeup to cover up those freckles."

"Thanks, Mandie. You're the best friend I've—"

"Don't you lie to me, girl. I'm the second best friend, after Brock Daniels."

Despite her situation, Mandie's words drew a smile from KC. "Okay. Give me a makeover and I'll leave in the morning, when I can hide among all the commuters."

With brown hair, sunglasses, and a little makeup, KC hadn't even recognized herself in Mandie's mirror. The disguise made her feel a little safer.

A few minutes later, KC hit the wall. Probably exhaustion from all the stress. She blanked out shortly after her head hit the pillow on Mandie's couch.

As big around as her calf, the powerful rattlesnake stretched out to least five feet long. Suddenly, it coiled. Its mouth opened, fangs protruded. The snake shot at her.

KC awoke with a gasp and sat up on the couch, holding a hand over her pounding heart. She hadn't had that dream in over a year—the dream about the rattlesnake ... and Brock. She could really use another hug from him right now. But that was silly. They had been two kids with a first case of puppy love, and it had all happened more than seven years ago. She had every reason to believe he'd forgotten about his childhood friend.

Friend? Who was she kidding? They were more than that. She didn't know what to call their relationship, but she would give almost anything to have it back.

Would you really?

Great. Another schizoid conversation between the two sides of her brain.

She still had two hours before Mandie's alarm went off at eight o'clock. No way would sleep come now.

Steady sounds of traffic came from the street. KC pushed the heavy curtain aside and peered out. The sun had just come up and the blue sky promised another warm day. Good. Wearing sunglasses wouldn't draw any attention.

People nearly filled the sidewalk, most headed toward Braddock Road Station. The commute was on and she should go.

KC threw on the only clothes she had. She could stop somewhere outside DC and pick up some more clothing.

She walked quietly to Mandie's bathroom, arranged her hair, put on the makeup, her sunglasses, and looked in the mirror. To herself, she didn't resemble KC Banning. But what about people who had seen that sketch shown on TV last night?

Please, God, I need You to hide KC Banning.

It had been a while. Would He even recognize her voice? It wasn't like she pestered God all the time with requests. But that would probably change. It needed to change. KC needed to trust Him more than she'd ever done before. Like Brock did.

There was a big bank in downtown Alexandria, about ten blocks away. Her maximum cash withdrawal had just been increased to $5,000. That should be enough money, but then came the dicey part, getting on Metro and quickly leaving the area before her account activity drew attention.

KC rehearsed the steps Senator Richards had insisted she take to get a new ID and a buy vehicle. Now it was time for KC Banning to get her cash and drop off the face of the earth.

She quietly slipped out of the apartment, locked and

closed the door, and turned toward Braddock Road.

KC froze when, a block away, a police car squealed around a corner, red and blue lights flashing, and its siren wailing.

The police car headed her way.

Chapter 4

Roberts Field, near Redmond, Oregon

The newly constructed terminal at the Redmond Municipal Airport had a rustic, western look to it, with large, exposed wooden beams and stained wooden walls. Rustic and western ... that was Brock, and the look of the terminal told him he was home.

He'd managed to get back without being drawn into any serious discussions with Julia. They had both slept most of the last leg of the flight home, exhausted from the stress of the Ebola incident—that's what the authorities had called it—and the resultant scrutiny they'd received at the airport in Guatemala City and when they cleared customs at LAX.

When he and Julia reached baggage claim, her suitcase tumbled onto the carousel. He grabbed it, set it beside her, and pulled out the handle.

She looked up at him, a pained expression in her eyes. "Brock, this is so hard, just going home with no way to find out about Itzy. We may never know what happened to her."

"Yeah. I know. This trip sure didn't turn out like we had hoped."

"No, it didn't." Julia smiled at him. As he had learned, her smile transformed her face, completely. She was a lovely young woman. "I ... I'd better go. My friend from church is waiting for me outside." Julia turned toward her suitcase and then swiveled to face him.

Before Brock could react, her arms circled him, giving him a warm hug. "Thanks again for staying behind to help me. Goodbye, Brock."

He returned her embrace.

Then Julia was gone.

What had he just done? For the first time in seven years, he'd hugged a woman who wasn't a relative. It didn't feel wrong. Maybe it was time for Brock to let go of his past and move on.

Brock's duffel bag came around the carousel. He pulled it off and looked through the glass doors to the passenger pickup area in front of the terminal.

Jeff's truck rolled to a stop outside.

Brock sighed. The hug didn't feel wrong, but it didn't feel right, either. Why?

The big TV monitor near the carousels flashed bright red letters. Brock glanced at the screen, then jerked as if someone had struck him. On the screen was a sketch of someone he recognized immediately, KC. The scrolling banner said breaking news, while the caption on the picture said Nationwide Manhunt Underway for Terrorist Accused of Murdering Senator Daniel Richards.

This was wrong. Had to be wrong. KC wasn't a murderer and she had one of the highest security clearances issued by the government. This was even more wrong than Gerald Carter showing up at a remote jungle clinic where they treated Ebola and sometimes infected people with it, little kids like Itzy.

Hannan had to be involved in the accusations against KC. Nothing else made sense. It had to be an evil man accusing an innocent, patriotic woman for some nefarious purpose.

Two inexplicable events had occurred within twenty-four

hours, both linked to the Hannan administration. Though they'd happened 3,000 miles apart, could the two events be related?

Regardless, KC was in trouble and he had to help her.

So much for moving on.

Brock hurried out to Jeff's truck, opened the door, tossed his duffel bag in the back seat, and climbed in.

"Bro, you look like you just saw a ghost. No. Your white face looks like a ghost. What happened?"

"Jeff ... I just saw KC's picture on TV."

"Who?"

"Remember the 'someone else' I mentioned at the village?"

"Sorta. That's about when Julia screamed and all heck broke loose."

"You don't know the half of it."

"I won't unless you tell me. Who's KC?"

"I hardly know where to begin."

A vehicle honked at them and Jeff pulled away from the terminal, heading back toward town.

"KC is KC Banning."

"Katheryn Banning, the dead senator's daughter? That's KC?"

"Yeah. But, Jeff, you don't know her, do you?"

"No. But I voted for the senator. First general election I ever got to vote in. KC, in those family political ads, brought him a few million votes. But weren't you going to move on? What about Julia?"

He ignored the question. "You didn't hear the main part of the story yet. KC's been declared a terrorist by Hannan, and there's a nationwide manhunt underway for her. They're saying she murdered a senator." Maybe God was bringing her back into Brock's life for a reason, correcting a mistake he'd made. Maybe they should have been together for the past three years. For Brock Daniels there were always too many maybes and too few answers. "KC needs me, Jeff, and we had a plan to meet at the ranch using messages buried there in a jar. I know she'll come back looking for that jar and looking for me."

"Bro, getting involved with anyone the law believes is a terrorist and a murderer could get you killed."

"There's no way KC is a terrorist or a murderer. She loves this country. That's why she went to work for DISA. The real terrorist is Hannan. He has to be the cause of this. But there's more, Jeff."

Jeff glanced his way with the crazy look in his eyes that Jeff reserved for people he thought were crazy.

"Don't look at me that way. Just listen for minute ... when Julia and I took little Itzy to that clinic, there was already Ebola there and the doctor said he had a cure for it. And do you know who else I saw at the clinic."

"Who? Elvis? I'll bet there was a UFO parked outside."

"Come on, Jeff. KC's in danger. Secretary of Defense, Gerald Carter, makes a secret visit to a jungle clinic where there's Ebola. Senator Richards, head of the Senate Intelligence Committee is murdered, and Hannan tries to blame it on KC. This all smells like Hannan, rotten to the core."

"That's a lot of surmising, bro. Do you really want to bet your life on it?"

"KC and I spent every waking minute together during the summer. Jeff, she was my best friend. That's just the way it is."

"You mean was."

"I don't know. But I've got to try to help her. She'll come looking for me and she'll go straight to the ranch." He had always protected her. KC would remember that, and she would come, unless they killed her.

It was silent in the truck for several minutes.

After Jeff turned west onto Highway 126, he glanced at

Brock. "Bro, you didn't answer my question. What about Julia?"

Jeff could be like a bulldog when he set his mind on something. But he wasn't getting the picture Brock had tried to paint about KC and him. "Julia's a wonderful woman. But I can't think about any woman but KC right now. You and Allie can explain it to Julia if she asks. Tell her KC and I go way back, thirteen years."

"What? You would have been about ... maybe 12? How old was KC when you two, uh, became attached?"

"She was almost nine."

"Almost nine as in actually eight?"

"Yeah. KC was eight."

"Hey, bro, what do they call that thing that comes before puppy love? Embryonic affection?" Jeff gave him that crazy look again, then it turned to a grin. "We should have brought Allie, the romantic, along. Soulmates at eight years old. You'd have her crying her eyes out."

Brock shot Jeff a glaring glance.

"Okay, bro. No more jokes. But what's the big attraction in an eight-year-old that would make a twelve-year-old boy hang out with her? I'd think that would be ..." Jeff gave him a palms-up shrug, "... well, boring."

"Boring? Hardly. She was a little Irish spitfire, complete with red hair and freckles. KC was so full of questions and ideas—she was smart. Really smart. Mentally a lot older than she looked. The stuff she thought of to do ... it was fun, even for a twelve-year-old boy."

"So she was your bud?"

"Yeah. I could talk about anything with her. I've never been able to do that even with—"

Jeff looked at Brock and a flicker of disappointment showed in Jeff's eyes. "As close as we are, Jeff, KC and I were closer. That's just the way it is."

"You mean was?"

Brock shot another frown at Jeff.

"Sorry, bro. So, what happened? Why aren't you married to this girl?"

"A couple of reasons. First, her dad was elected to the senate and he moved his family to DC."

He'd never told anyone about the letter. Not even his parents. Brock looked at Jeff. When Jeff looked his way, they exchanged that deep, intense, something-significant-is-coming look that male friends use to indicate the font is changing, that the next few words will be in bold italics. "That last summer, when she was 14, her dad cut the summer trip short. It broke KC's heart. I could forgive him for that, but after she kissed me and ran away crying—"

"Hold it, Brock. You, a seventeen-year-old boy, kissed a fourteen-year-old girl?"

"That's not what I said. *She* kissed *me* and ran away. I haven't seen her since. But there was a sealed letter waiting for me back at our RV. A letter from her father, the senator, saying that I was to stay away from his daughter, now that we weren't little kids anymore ... and that, basically, I didn't belong in his social circles, and never would."

"Ouch." Jeff shook his head. "But seriously, bro, would you want your fourteen-year-old, hormonal daughter running around with a good-looking, hormonal, seventeen-year-old guy? That's a disaster in the making."

"That's not what bothered me, Jeff. I mean it did, but it was the social strata thing that hurt. Both of our families came from middle-class America. The Banning's had a little more money than us, but still ..."

Jeff turned in at his house and stopped in the circle drive, behind Brock's truck. "Here's what we'll do. I'll tell Allie about you and KC. If Julia asks any questions, Allie can tell her a story that will have them both in tears, rooting for you and KC." Jeff paused. "And we'll also be praying for you two. If she feels like you obviously do, I think you need to start courting that girl, Brock."

Courting? If that were possible he would. But it wasn't. "Thanks, Jeff. You're the best. Tell Allie hello for me. I'd better get my stuff and head for the motel at the ranch. KC's coming. I'm sure of it, and I can't afford to miss her. Maybe I'll get a little writing in while I wait."

"But, bro, you need to be careful. Going against law enforcement and the will of a president like Abe Hannan, will put you in the crosshairs of people who will shoot without asking questions, believing they're doing the country a favor."

"Yeah. That's why I'm praying for KC. That she'll make it this far without Hannan's hounds tracking her down. She's smart, top of her class from MIT with a Master's in Computer Science. But, in her situation, one mistake is one too many."

Chapter 5

As President Hannan entered his private study, near the Oval Office, events of the past twenty-four hours rolled through his mind like storm surge waves, threatening to sweep away everything, his plans, plans others made for him ...

I won't let that happen. It's all under control.

Well, perhaps everything but Katheryn Banning. Her inspection of both his laptop and the private study worried him. She was regarded as the best network analyst in the network services group. How much had she deduced?

He closed and locked the door to the small carpeted room, the room he had declared off limits to all staff when Hannan closed the door.

Off limits? How many holes had the Secret Service drilled in the study's walls? He'd heard eighteen in the Oval Office and two in the private study, supposedly for observation. They couldn't hear him, only see him to determine if he was safe.

After Hannan opened his laptop and sat behind his desk, movement on his computer screen drew his attention.

A browser had opened and, within it, a chat window popped up.

He rolled his chair closer to the desk and placed his hands near the keyboard. The icon at the top of the chat window said it all. Just as he feared, Alexis.

As POTUS, Hannan was the most powerful man in the world. But one threatening word from Alexis, the Organization's enforcer, made him feel as helpless as a kitten facing a mountain lion. Hissing and spitting were futile efforts. And, if the organization thought their investment was in danger—he shuddered at the thought of the pain their remedy might cause him. He drew a breath and read the chat box.

U have a leak in/under the West Wing. Perhaps we should switch 2 plan B.

Alexis's accusation, tapped out by her fingers in Chicago, flew across 1,000 miles of fiber and wire and into the chat box. It had ended with a personal threat.

The Organization hadn't shared any details of Plan B with Hannan. But he had deduced that this plan, somehow, factored him out of their equation.

Surely they wouldn't kill POTUS? Maybe they would involve him in a serious scandal, one he couldn't brush off, and then try to remove him from office. But who would take his place?

Vice President Boring wouldn't cooperate with them. He remained willfully ignorant of the Organization and, though he hadn't officially resigned, the distance he maintained from Hannan had become the equivalent of a resignation.

Hannan typed his reply.

No need 4 drastic measures. Why do U suspect a leak?

Have U modified UR security S/W?

No. We are still hidden inside encrypted HTTP. My security suite will not complain. Let's continue.

OK. The Banning girl disappeared.

Disappeared? Explain.

Someone tipped her off and she fled. Disappeared completely.

Was it Richards?

Someone in the West Wing. Maybe her supervisor.

Nothing came back from Alexis for several seconds. He willed his breathing to slow and waited for something very unpleasant, certain that it was coming.

Find the girl, find the leak, and eliminate both. Blame Banning for everything.

His world was spinning out of control. Maybe it was an illusion that he had ever been in control. They had bought the White House for him. Twice. He owed them, but he also had limits.

By eliminate, do U—

Alexis had seized control of the chat, blocking his typing.

Find her and kill the little ...

He winced at the crude, graphic language that assassinated the character of Ms. Banning and the unknown leak.

The chat box returned to its normal state, waiting for his reply.

As POTUS, I cannot—

She had seized control again.

She's a murderer and a terrorist. Just do it! U have 36 hrs, then consider Plan B invoked.

The chat box disappeared and the browser returned to his home page.

Find two people and kill them in thirty-six hours? He must. If he crossed them, the Organization had the wealth, the power, and the complete absence of ethics to exact excruciating revenge.

When the wealthy elitists who had put him in the White House spoke, even the president had to jump. These were people who intended to shape the history of man. Bend it into their version of utopia, with them in total control and Hannan as their puppet. And if you gambled against them, you bet the proverbial farm on each roll of the dice.

At least 500 employees worked in the West Wing, or at

one of the many levels below it. Thirty-six hours. The questioning must begin within the hour.

Randall Washington, the head of DOJ, was ruthless, relentless and, as a member of Hannan's inner circle, knew enough to handle these interrogations. Randy could ferret out the leak. But who had warned Ms. Banning, the striking beauty who had tampered with Hannan's computer?

Alexis was probably bluffing about plan B. And as for plan B including his demise, presidential assassinations were frowned on in the USA. Not even the Organization could survive that kind of scrutiny.

But was he willing to bet his life on it?

No way. I've got to find the Banning girl.

Chapter 6

Bend, Oregon

Only thirty-five miles to go.

KC had to look in the jar. If it still lay where Brock had buried it, under the big Juniper tree, the jar's contents would tell her if she should leave Crooked River Ranch forever or run to Brock Daniels.

At 7:30 a.m., she mounted her silver-grey Honda in the warm, early morning sun and rode away from the cheap motel where she'd spent the night in Bend.

After three days of bonding with the powerful bike, KC's confidence had grown. She'd taken turns on a dirt road with the rear wheel spinning, spraying dust and gravel behind her. Once, she had taken the VFR800 up to 120 miles-per-hour on a straight desert highway. The exhilaration from the high speed was almost addictive. It gave her a sense of invincibility.

Now, KC and the 500-pound Honda were one. They moved as one.

Her oneness with the motorcycle reminded KC of her and Brock as they ran hand-in-hand through the desert seven years ago. And like the bike, Brock was incredibly powerful. At seventeen, he stood six-foot-four and had the build of an athlete. He had also made KC feel invincible.

Near the intersection of Highways 20 and 97, KC spotted a Dutch Brothers coffee shop. She turned in, swapped her helmet for the sunglasses, and drove through, grabbing an on-the-go breakfast consisting of coffee and two granola bars.

The regional coffee company, her favorite, was another reminder of all she had left behind when her father moved them from Oregon to DC. The desert, the rock formations, the canyons and rivers—she was a fool for staying on the East Coast, especially inside the Beltway. If she had only returned to Oregon after college, KC could have avoided all of this. If ...

Five minutes later, KC leaned into a sharp turn and merged onto Highway 97 North, heading toward Terrebonne, the turnoff for Crooked River Ranch. This was day four since she had fled from Mandie's place in Virginia and, for the fourth time, she retraced her steps since fleeing into oblivion. She had followed all of Senator Richards's recommendations for covering her tracks, but had she made any mistakes?

While in Virginia, she had taken the batteries from her cell and had eventually thrown the phone into the Potomac. She had withdrawn nearly all of the cash in her checking and savings accounts, $5000 on day one, due to the withdrawal limits, and another thousand on day two.

She used $50 to purchase a fake driver's license and then spent $3500 on the best used car she could buy for that amount of cash, using her assumed identity. But she only drove the car to Eastern Missouri. There KC traded the car for the Honda VFR800 Interceptor. Though the motorcycle was a few years old, it was worth more than the car, so she threw in a thousand bucks cash. The party selling the bike took it.

Hopefully, the authorities wouldn't expect a young woman to ride a powerful motorcycle two-thirds of the way across the country. And with her hair temporarily dyed brown, a dark faceplate on her helmet, and one of those protective motorcycle suits that circulated air through it, KC would not be recognized by anyone, even if they analyzed data from video surveillance cameras. But to be safe, she had taken the smaller highways, avoiding the freeways as much as possible. Whenever she stopped, she had replaced her helmet with a pair of large, dark sunglasses.

She had done her best. Made no obvious mistakes. If Hannan found her, it would be from something other than the obfuscated trail she had left.

Forty-five minutes later, KC approached the rim 400 feet above Crooked River Ranch. Below her, in the brilliant June sunshine, the golf course created a bright green oasis in the desert, extending a mile to the north. On the east edge of the golf course, the canyon plunged out of sight, a six-hundred-foot drop to Crooked River.

KC pulled the clutch, coasted down the steep road cut into the escarpment, and descended to Crooked River Ranch. After passing the golf-course entrance, she took the next right into the Ranch RV Park, slowing to an idle, letting the big Honda roll quietly around the grassy camping area. She stopped before veering right onto the trail to the basketball court.

This is where it had happened, almost seven years ago to the day. That day came storming back into her mind, vivid and brutal.

"I have to go now, Brock," she choked out the words through her sobs. "But, no matter what, somehow, someday, I'm coming back. Please, don't forget me. I'll never forget you. I'll write you." She kissed Brock, saw the surprised look on his face, then turned toward her family's motorhome.

"KC, I won't forget you either. And I'll write, too."

She ran half way to the motorhome, then stopped to look back.

Brock's gaze had locked on her, his body rigid, and his eyes blazed as intensely as when he fought the bullies for her. But KC's father, the senator, was a bully too powerful even for Brock.

When KC stumbled up the steps into the motorhome, her mom handed her a tissue.

Tears welled in her mother's eyes too.

KC shot a glaring glance at her father.

He returned it, filled with disapproval, and then pointed out the window at Brock, who still stood where she had kissed him. "KC, that's why I'm taking you out of here. I saw you kiss that Daniels kid. What did you think you were doing?"

Her mother laid a hand on his arm. "Justin, surely you remember when—"

"Stay out of this, Geneva." He turned back toward KC.

She wiped her cheeks and stared into her father's eyes, trying to match his intensity. "I just showed my best friend, someone who likes me for who I am, that I care about him."

"The Daniels aren't our kind of people. They—"

"They aren't good enough? That's what you think about me too, isn't it? Just show up for the political ads and smile, but keep my mouth shut, because I'm not good enough. If I was 18, I wouldn't go with you to DC. I would stay with Brock and—"

"If you prefer that country bumpkin to people like us, then maybe you aren't—"

"Justin! Stop it, right now."

"No, Mom. Let him say it. When I was born, he didn't get the son he wanted, only a red-headed girl with freckles. I wasn't good enough. I'll never be good enough for Senator Justin Banning." She ran down the hallway and fell across her bed, sobbing as the motorhome rolled out of Crooked

River Ranch.

No matter what she did it never earned her father's approval. If that's how it was going to be, she would earn approval. KC would impress everyone in DC with her accomplishments. She wouldn't do it for her father. She would do it for herself and for Brock. KC never had to earn Brock's approval, but she wanted him to be proud of her, because her father never would be.

KC's chest nearly exploded from the violent drumbeats inside. She took a deep, calming breath, pushed the past back where it belonged, then mounted her motorcycle, and veered right toward the basketball court, toward her future. KC was returning, three years later than she'd planned, but she was finally home.

When she stopped on the blacktop, the warmth of the morning sun already promised a hot day, evidently too hot for basketball. No one was on the court to see her dig up the jar.

After parking her bike near the big Juniper tree, she took off her riding suit, helmet, and then inhaled the Juniper's pungent, herbaceous fragrance.

She turned toward the east. From the far side of the Crooked River Canyon, a mammoth promontory dwarfed her, a seemingly unscalable rock cliff reaching upward nearly a thousand feet above ranch level until it intersected the powder blue of a summer sky.

Unscalable? If Brock had asked her to, she'd have climbed it with him.

One hundred yards ahead, the lookout's wooden structure overhung the six-hundred-foot-deep canyon, a canyon almost invisible until you reached its edge.

Whenever KC approached it, the earth seemed to drop into nothingness, leaving her exposed. The depths of the canyon pulled on her, as if drawing her downward to her death, yet leaving KC awestruck by the beauty of the rocks, the trees, and the ribbon of blue water flowing through the canyon.

She turned back toward the Juniper and located the large boulder near the tree's base. KC shoved aside the questions and doubts that assaulted her ... all but one. Had Brock ever come here on June twenty-ninth? Was the small glass jar still buried under the rock? Maybe all but two.

A stick with a sharp point stood propped against the tree trunk. It looked as if someone had whittled it for digging, then left it. The soil was loose, dry and crumbly. She stabbed it with the stick, easily penetrating the dirt. On her third stab, she hit the glass jar.

After working the jar free, KC's shaking fingers unscrewed the lid, and a paper inside fell into her open palm. Her heart started the steady acceleration that excitement always brought. She unfolded the paper and drew a sharp breath. There were three entries on three separate dates.

Knowing Brock had been here brought tears to her eyes. The first entry read June 29. Three years ago.

I guess Georgetown U is too far for you to come home. Maybe after you graduate. Miss you, KC.

Brock

Georgetown. So, after five years, Brock had still been tracking her. Not an easy thing to do, since she purposely kept a small footprint on the Internet. He had waited five years for her while she had totally neglected her best friend. At that thought, the depth of their childhood relationship came rushing back bringing all of its warmth, security, and sheer joy.

KC skipped to the last entry, then drew another sharp breath. It was dated June 29 of this year. Yesterday. Her hands shook so hard she could barely read the writing.

It's been a hard year. I miss you so much, KC. But, it's more than that. I need you.

I'm working on a novel, right here on the ranch, and trying to keep up my blog which is growing at an incredible rate. If all goes as planned, I'll be spending the next week at the Sun View Motel, writing. From my room, I can see the head of the Old Hollywood Road. It reminds me of you and of us. If you find this note, then please find me.

It almost sounded like Brock expected her to arrive while he was here. Had he seen her picture in the news and deduced the rest? Yes. He had known she would come here to hide and to find him.

He had written more, but there were eraser marks. What he had left on the paper was enough to start her tears flowing again.

Brock is only a quarter-mile away.

KC pressed a hand against her chest to contain the wild drumming her thought produced.

Brock missed her and was here alone. Like her, he had evidently not found anyone else. At least that's what she read into his words. But KC Banning, an "armed and dangerous terrorist," walking up to his door in broad daylight could endanger him.

KC faced the hardest decision she'd ever made. She could climb on her bike and ride out of Brock's life forever, or try to rendezvous secretly with him.

Should she try to reach him by phone, then play things by ear based upon their conversation? No. Katheryn Celeste Banning was like the rattlesnake Brock had killed when he saved her life. The nearly headless snake kept coiling and striking. Like the snake, she was still moving, apparently alive, but destined to die, certainly and soon. She had nothing to offer him but sorrow, danger, and death.

I miss you so much, KC ... I need you.

His words and her heart both said Brock needed her.

Probably not as much a she needed him, but still ...

KC reburied the jar, leaving a clean sheet of paper in it, stuffed the messages from Brock into her pocket, and rode her motorcycle on the small, dirt trail leading to the Ranch Chapel beside the Sun View Motel. She left her bike and riding gear in the church parking lot. Shoved her purse, and the .38 she'd bought, into the hard bags—along with any doubts about what she was doing—and locked them in.

Dressed in shorts, a badly wrinkled blouse, sun glasses, and tennis shoes, she walked toward the motel office, where there would be a phone. KC Banning couldn't turn around now ... even if she had wanted to.

* * *

After a breakfast of cold cereal and stale, bitter coffee, Brock sat at the table in the yurt named the Squirrel. His laptop lay in front of him, displaying its desktop.

The motel yurts were large, permanent structures split into two semicircular rooms. Each room had a king-size bed, multipurpose table with two chairs, and the obligatory stuff—microwave, small refrigerator by the door, bathroom, TV, phone, and Wi-Fi.

Best of all, two-thirds of the semi-circular outer wall was glass, a huge picture window displaying the spectacular scenery, including the golf course and the towering escarpment rising 400 feet above the west side of the ranch. He could even see part of the Crooked River Canyon less than 200 yards to the southeast.

He'd wanted peace and quiet, so he rented rooms 16 and 17, both sides of the Squirrel. Who was he kidding? He'd rented the adjacent room in hopes that KC would come. If she did, she would go straight to the tree, dig up the jar and—had he overstated things in his message? No. He'd probably understated them.

Brock looked out the window and scanned the top of the escarpment, lined with beautiful homes. His gaze swept across the golf course, stopping on hole number 5, near the canyon, a place fraught with memories of KC.

This setting provided an inspiring place to write, but Brock was a little short on inspiration this morning. He certainly didn't have enough for the bi-weekly blog post he'd intended to write.

Over the past year, his blog readership had grown much larger than he'd ever anticipated. His posts delved into the many problems in the U.S. He explored their roots, roots found in the false worldviews, relativism, and materialism that resulted from abandoning the absolute truths defined by the Author of Truth.

Brock combined politics, history, philosophy, and Christianity, inextricably blending them together to diagnose the country's and the world's problems. Once a month he would make a prognosis, his best judgment about some aspect of the country's future. Brock's predictions drew the most traffic, lately exceeding a million hits. These posts usually resulted in vigorous debates.

Most people appreciated his blog posts, many calling him a modern-day prophet. Brock Daniels a prophet? Hardly. But it was partly why he'd chosen the pseudonym, your voice in the wilderness. He *was* that pseudonym. A man crying out warnings from a remote, lonely place, his heart. It was a place that grew more isolated when radicals, from the far end of the political spectrum, assaulted him with vulgar, profane words, revealing a fierce hatred that had no rational basis.

Today, his fingers lay still on the keyboard. His heart seemed dried-up, empty, and his mind almost blank. After writing the note yesterday evening—the one he'd left in the buried jar—his words were all used up. He was alone in a dark and hostile world that—if he didn't buck up, tough man, Brock Daniels, the crusader for faith and freedom, was going to start tearing up.

Not gonna happen.

Brock grabbed his mouse and pulled down his favorites list, selecting a news website. If he couldn't write, at least he could read some news. It might make him mad, which was better than crying. It was also a good way to break through a mild case of writer's block.

When the news site's landing page came up in his browser, Brock sucked in a breath so hard that he choked. This time it wasn't a sketch. From his laptop screen, beautiful, smiling, and in full color, KC stared at him. But the caption above the picture ripped through his gut like a dull knife.

Nationwide Manhunt Continues for Terrorist, Katheryn Banning

When Brock refocused on those green eyes and smiling lips, someone twisted the knife. Before he recovered from the pain enough to unscramble his thoughts, his room phone rang.

Chapter 7

Katheryn Banning, where are you?

Abe Hannan sat behind the desk in his private study, staring at the computer Ms. Banning had examined far too thoroughly. No doubt she knew enough to recognize the military communications software installed on it. He'd been told she was brilliant. Adding two plus two would be no problem for her, but the sum of what she'd discovered created potentially lethal problems for Hannan's plans.

A familiar, anapestic knock sounded on the door. "Come in, Randy."

Attorney General Randall Washington dropped heavily into the chair in front of the desk, rubbed his eyes, and leaned forward against the desk in the study. "He's dead."

This wasn't the news Hannan expected. What was Randy telling him? "I thought you were going to give me some news about the Banning girl."

Randy released a sarcastic sounding chuckle. "Look, I just finished interrogating the last person on our list to find out who tipped off Katheryn Banning. Are you interested, or not?"

The Attorney General's impertinence had mushroomed lately, but he looked exhausted. Hannan chose to overlook Randy's attitude. "Alright. Who's dead and why?"

"The girl's supervisor in DISA, Major Grieve, may have had a chat with Ms. Banning, alone in his office, the day before she disappeared. He was stubborn. We used, shall we say, extremely enhanced interrogation techniques. His heart stopped. A major ... I'd have thought he would have been in better shape than that. Well, we don't know what the two talked about. He wouldn't tell us. But I think he might have told her too much."

"What did you do with the body?" Was Hannan actually asking a question that a common criminal might ask? That hindering voice of conscience again. Hannan hammered it into submission with rule number one. Abandon all morals and ethics, for the end justifies any means.

"You don't have to worry about the body. There was an accident and the major was badly burned."

So all Hannan's revamping of the military had still left some traitors among the lower ranking officers. He would have to deal with that later. "Despite the major's lack of cooperation, Randy, we may have a lead on the girl from another source. I hope to have her taken care of, shortly. You can resume your other tasks."

The Attorney General stood, gave him a curious glance, and turned to leave.

Hannan leaned across the desk and hooked Randy's arm. "On second thought, put this at the top of your list. Figure out how we find and deal with a thousand like Major Grieve when martial law is questioned within the ranks. Whatever you come up with should discourage any further dissention. Are you up to the task, Randy? If you're not, I can find someone who is." He gave Randall Washington the coldest smile Hannan could freeze on his face.

Randy's smile looked more like a grimace. "I can handle it. I didn't come this far only to back out when things get a bit dicey. But why me and not the Chiefs of Staff?"

"Because they take commands, not initiative. They're

politicians, wind-blown wimps."

"That's what you wanted, Mr. President. Yes men. And you've got them." Randy turned and left.

Randy was right and it galled Hannan. Every strategy has its downside, and controlling the military was by far the most difficult task.

After the door closed, Hannan pulled out his secure wireless phone, the one that had driven White House security crazy. He bypassed the security features added by NSA, using a technique Mitchell Dell had suggested, one of many ways Hannan had found to maintain some privacy.

And avoid the Freedom of Information Act.

He sat behind his laptop, directed his web browser to an obscure web site, and then keyed an obfuscated telephone number from the site into his secure phone.

When they found Ms. Banning, Hannan needed to know everything the nosey network geek had learned while she had the run of his study, absolutely everything, and who she'd told. Agent Belino had accompanied her, but was clueless about what she had actually done. Banning needed to be caught and forced to talk.

Abdul the Butcher, earned his name as an assassin by his brutality. He was a talented interrogator with a large arsenal of persuasive weapons. The man could control himself, for the most part, only becoming brute-like when he had opportunities that would not impact his paycheck. He was also the assassin Hannan used to exterminate another pest five years ago. It was often wise to select men for dirty work whose hands were already dirty, men whose dirty deeds one could hold over their heads.

Abdul answered on the third ring.

"I need a favor, Abdul."

"The last favor I did for you nearly got me killed. What is it this time, Hannan? Excuse me. I mean, Mr. President."

Hannan chose to overlook his impertinence for the

moment. "Look, I think you are really going to enjoy this assignment."

"I'm listening."

"You have the opportunity to be embedded with a black ops group, the most elite Special Forces in the military."

"That isn't saying much. You already riffed the best. In fact, you—"

"Abdul, you've got two choices. Would you rather travel to Oregon to help this group search for Katheryn Banning or be sent to Leavenworth, a one-way ticket?"

Silence.

Hannan sighed into the phone. "Maybe I should flip a coin."

"How do I join this group of *elite* soldiers?"

"They're currently leaving Eastern Colorado, headed for Central Oregon. Make reservations for a flight to Oregon. Captain Blanchard, commander of the group, will pick you up at Roberts Field, near Redmond."

"And what do I do in Hicksville, Oregon?"

"After we arrest the terrorist, Katheryn Banning, Blanchard's team will take custody of her. At the appropriate time, I'll give direct orders to Blanchard to hand Banning over to you. You interrogate her, using any methods needed. Find out everything she knows about unauthorized access to classified networks and whatever she learned from Senator Richards before he died. Report the information directly to me. I'll order the group to leave, then you kill her and ensure that her body will not found before it decomposes."

Abdul was silent for several seconds. What did that mean?

Hannan continued. "So how much will you charge for the entire job?"

"$200,000 plus airfare plus $1,000 per diem."

So Abdul had been calculating, not trying to back out. Now Hannan could sweeten the pot and probably save some money. "How much if I let you keep the girl for a few days, after you report your findings to me, and then kill her any way you choose?"

"This Banning girl ... she's the college-age kid whose picture has been all over cable networks and the newspapers, the one who looks like a model instead of a computer nerd?"

Knowing his subordinates proclivities tended to put them at a disadvantage in any negotiation, especially one like this. "Yes, Abdul. She's the auburn-haired beauty with green eyes."

"I'll do it for $100,000, my airfare, plus $1,000 per diem, starting today."

"Done. She's all yours, Abdul."

Chapter 8

KC's heart began its uncontrollable acceleration when Brock's phone rang.

From where she sat across the lobby from the Sun View Motel counter, the clerk couldn't hear KC, especially with the air conditioner running. Besides, once the clerk learned KC planned to call the "hunk" in room 17, the woman had agreed to keep KC's visit discreet.

"Hello." Brock's voice.

A flood of memories and emotions washed over KC like the twenty-foot waves on Oahu's North Shore. Beautiful and powerful, they swept her away to a time when she was safe, protected by the love of the truest friend she'd ever known.

"Hello?" His voice rose in pitch, questioning.

The backwash of a wave dropped her mind back onto the gritty shore of the present. She cleared her throat. "Brock, it's me. It's—"

"KC, is that you?"

"Yes."

"Where are you? That was brilliant. You dug up the jar, so you're here on the ranch. Does anyone else know you're here?"

She'd been trying to recover from the effect of hearing his voice. KC had to replay his words again to follow their logic.

Brock had obviously heard the news about her. Katheryn Banning, public enemy number one. What must he be thinking? "Only the clerk here in the motel office. She understands our meeting is supposed to be ... uh, discreet. And, Brock, I'm disguised. I ..." What would he think about how she looked? Her dark-colored hair? She could take the sun glasses off but—

"KC, listen. When you hang up, walk straight out the front door of the office, across the parking area, to the Squirrel Building, room 17. Don't do anything to draw attention to yourself."

He was inviting her. Inviting danger into his life. She shouldn't have come. But, after calling him, what could she tell him to make him understand why she must leave?

"KC, I know what you're thinking. You can't leave. If you try that, I'll just come looking for you. I want you to hang up the phone and walk across to my room, now. We'll sort out the rest after you get here."

Could she escape the motel area without Brock following her, without Brock further endangering himself? He would probably hear and see the motorcycle. And she needed the motorcycle.

"Please, KC. Come ... now."

There was fear and pleading in Brock's voice. She couldn't deal with that. "I'm coming. See you in a couple of minutes."

Doubts began their assault the moment she put down the receiver.

Please, God, whatever You do, don't let me endanger him.

KC stood and glanced at the middle-aged woman with graying hair, fiddling with a fax machine. "Thanks, Ma'am."

"Good luck. Oh, to be young again." The clerk gave her a warm smile.

KC wanted to ask if there was a restroom she could use, someplace with a mirror to make herself presentable. Brock had liked her auburn hair. He never said so, but his eyes told her that he was fascinated by it, especially when the sunlight set it on fire. Now it was dark brown, almost black. And, she was a ...

What was she doing? What was she thinking? KC had walked half way across the parking lot and could think of nothing but what Brock would see and what he would think about what he saw. Lives were on the line here, including the life of the nation she loved and sought to protect.

KC scanned the row of round, single-story buildings lining the lane that meandered through the motel's yurts. She walked up the steps and onto the deck surrounding the Squirrel Room, stopping in front of the door with the number 17. Brock's age when she saw him last. Now he was what ... 24, almost 25?

KC reached out to knock.

The door swung open.

Brock hooked her waist with a muscular arm and pulled her inside, pushing the door closed with his foot. Then, as he used to do so often, he took her shoulders, holding her at arm's length and studied her.

What were his eyes telling her? What were they telling *him*? Was it confusion she saw there?

Her eyes told her that Brock was even more handsome as a man than as a slender, athletic teenager. He was a bit taller, at least five inches above six feet. Bulging muscles flexed under his Polo shirt while he held her shoulders. His description in a single word ... magnificent.

She pulled off the sunglasses. "It's still me, Brock. I ... I colored my hair. It's only temporary. A disguise."

The confusion fled from his eyes. The look that replaced it stopped her breathing. If she stepped closer, Brock's arms would wrap around her in an instant. Then she would never be able to separate herself from him. Brock would die with her. This was a huge mistake.

"No, KC. Don't even think it."

There were no secrets between them. How could there be when they could read so well each other's eyes, facial expressions, and body language. The unspoken communication between them had always been uncanny, almost telepathic.

She should have contacted him during those long years. He had obviously wanted to contact her and had left notes in the jar. Brock needed to know how badly she felt, but words wouldn't come and wouldn't be adequate if they did.

KC pulled the paper from the buried jar out of her pocket, unfolded it, and held it up to show him she had kept it, valued it.

Brock looked at the note and—had he winced?

That she had never written had hurt him. The note only reminded him of it. Tears blurred KC's vision. She would not become a sobbing fool, but there was no way to shut off the tears. She closed her eyes. It didn't help.

Help came from the strong arms that pulled her close and held her. She couldn't move away, even if she had wanted to.

"You don't feel like an armed and dangerous domestic terrorist."

She wiped her cheek and looked up. "Brock, I shouldn't have come. I've endangered—"

"Then why *did* you come?" He peered into her eyes and waited.

She could never lie to Brock. "I couldn't help myself."

He smiled. "That's a good enough reason. You haven't done anything wrong, KC. I know you. But ..."

She shook her head. "Oh, I did a lot of things wrong. Not like morally or ethically, just stupid. Now POTUS ... uh, Hannan wants me dead."

Brock's smile faded away. "Presidents don't always get what they want. This one won't. Besides, if someone like KC

Banning is in danger from this administration, then I'm guessing every good citizen in America is in danger."

"And how would you know that?"

"You were working in the DUCC for DISA, right?"

"And how would you know that?

"I missed you, KC."

"You didn't answer my question."

"Yes, I did."

And he had answered. He wanted to know about her. *I miss you so much, KC.* The words from his buried note reinforced the message. Brock still cared deeply for her. But all she had for him was a reminder of that day seven years ago. "Brock, do you remember the last time we—"

He stopped her words with his finger over her lips. "Do I remember? How could I forget? That was the day I lost my best friend, my ..." Brock stopped talking with his lips, but his eyes continued to speak.

Their meeting, this exchange of words and feelings—KC knew this could only lead to that place and moment in time when they had parted. They had rewound the video of their lives, and it was time to press the record button. Time to create a new story where no one could ever again rip them apart.

Brock's eyes said he felt the same.

KC closed her eyes, moved closer, and relaxed in his arms.

Brock would kiss her. She knew that. And he did, softly ... on her forehead.

She tried not to look disappointed, but her face would betray her, so she hid it against his shoulder. Maybe she really was his best friend. That and nothing more. Did he still think of her as a kid? KC needed to say something, to change the subject, and her train of thought, or she would start crying again. "What am I going to do, Brock?"

"You're going to tell me your story, how you got into this predicament."

"Then what?"

His smile broke the pall that his kiss on the forehead had thrown over her. "I hear Hannan has a filthy vocabulary."

"He does. He just doesn't let the media hear it." Brock had certainly changed the subject. But where was he going with this?

"Kace, you need to do what you used to do to foul-mouthed golfers on hole number 5."

Number 5? The sharp dogleg left. The temptation to hit across the canyon to the green. A place KC had doled out punishment and rewards. "Number 5? Isn't that the hole where greedy golfers try to cut 220 yards across Crooked River Canyon?"

"Yeah. Tried to make it play like a par 3 instead of a par 4? Remember that duffer who started cussing when his ball clipped the trees after barely clearing the canyon?"

KC giggled. "He couldn't see his ball or us hiding behind the boulder by the canyon."

"He hit the tree, but the ball still rolled within a foot of the pin."

"But he couldn't see that. And he didn't deserve an eagle." She shook her head. "No one who talks like that should get an eagle."

"He didn't think he was going to get one either. Thought he'd come up short." Brock chuckled. "When he let out that string of four-letter words, you should have seen your face."

She threw her head back and laughed. "The dogleg hid us so, when they started down the fairway, I snuck onto the green and threw his golf ball into the canyon. His eagle turned into a double bogey. Served him right."

With a grin on his face, Brock's blue eyes peered into hers, "But when he couldn't find the ball, he really started swearing."

She poked her finger into Brock's chest. "And you covered up my ears."

He nodded. "Your innocent ears. That's what we're going to do to President Hannan."

"Cover up his ears? What do you mean, Brock?"

"You any good with computers?"

She grinned. "DISA thinks so."

"Then we're going to add some strokes to the president's game. A whole lot of them."

Whatever he had in mind could become dangerous. "You know, that could really make him angry."

Brock stared out the window at the golf course driving range. "That's what I'm hoping. Men who get mad lose control, and then they make mistakes. See that guy banging his driver on the ground?" He pointed out the window toward the driving range.

KC laughed. "He'll regret that if he bends the shaft."

So they were a team again, two friends working together. But being discovered now wouldn't result in the golf course marshal turning them over to their parents for discipline. "Sounds like fun if we don't get caught. So what do you have in mind?"

"First, you need to tell me why the president declared you a terrorist and what you think he's up to. Then we'll figure out how to throw his golf ball into Crooked River Canyon."

KC took a deep breath and released it slowly, like a deflating tire. Then she took Brock's hand, sat down at the small table in his room, and pulled him into the chair beside her.

He needed to understand the stakes. But where should she start? "This isn't a good story, Brock. Some of it is fact, part is conjecture, and the rest is a big jigsaw puzzle that I've been working on. Trying to throw POTUS's ball into a six-hundred-foot-deep canyon could get us both killed. And just being seen with me will put you on his hit list." She sighed again. "Now ... do you want me to continue, or should I leave?"

Chapter 9

Hannan's plans leading toward the declaration of martial law had proceeded smoothly with one exception, the Banning girl's interference. He still needed to catch her, but that was just a matter of a few hours. Perhaps a day or two, now that the military may have a lead.

Hannan's wireless phone rang. Blast it! He'd left the NSA features disabled after calling Abdul. No telling who this might be?

The caller ID was blocked.

Alexis.

She had a way of creating potholes in the smoothest of roads.

"How is our First Bachelor today? You know, you really should find someone suitable to marry. The Whitehouse was never meant to be a bachelor pad."

Her voice sounded far too pleasant. That usually meant trouble before the call ended. "Being single suits my purposes. Fewer people know my secrets. Now, why did you really call? It surely wasn't to draw more parallels between me and James Buchanan."

"Hannan, Buchanan. They rhyme. But no, when they look at your legacy, we don't want people thinking of Buchanan, the man whose gross negligence let the Civil War happen. However," she switched to her mocking, singsong voice, "... the mini-speech you inserted into the press conference, the speech about the outbreak of hemorrhagic fever ... such a weak statement."

"I'm not worried. Fear will motivate the people, but hope will lead them in the right direction. I'll hold another press conference, in a day or two, and reveal the government's vaccine. Hope will produce voluntary compliance with the martial law curfews, and certain other restrictions. No compliance, no shots, no hope."

"Then you need to start declaring martial law, now." No more singsong.

Alexis was right, but the way she often tried to twist his arm galled him. "I have it all under control."

"All of it? The food supply too?"

"Yes. As we speak, a terrorist attack is disabling the two largest oil refineries in the nation, forcing me to declare a critical shortage, leading to gas rationing. We'll then control the trucking industry, thus the food supply. On the other front, our Attorney General is putting the squeeze on certain businesses through their lending institutions—operation LVNR."

"What?"

"Just a euphemistic acronym for chokehold."

"Are all the lending institutions playing ball?"

Her continual pressing and questioning, was wearing on him. "They will. Against our recommendations, two banks made loans to some of our targeted businesses, in this case, ammunition manufacturers. We had those banks audited. Last week we fined them several million dollars for various infractions and threatened them with larger fines. The banking industry took notice and—"

"I see. Clever. We avoid any risk, the banks take it all. The people blame the banks, but they defend themselves by stating that they denied credit only to certain risky borrowers."

"That's right. They deny credit to the businesses we want to shut down."

"So, Abe ... how long until you initiate martial law?"

"Two more days for the areas already impacted by the outbreak. The rest of the U.S. will be handled area-by-area over the next three weeks as the unrest, violence, and fear spread."

Alexis sighed long and loud. "The second you catch that Banning girl, I want to know."

"Certainly."

"She comes from a long line of patriots, of which she may be the most extreme. Anyone like her, who has the potential to start an insurgency, should be considered a serious threat. Eliminate her and anyone else involved. Do you understand?"

"I understand."

The line went dead. Hannan enabled the NSA security on his phone.

So Alexis and the organization had concerns. Of course, some risks must be incurred when one seizes control of the most powerful nation on earth. But his grip on the USA had already tightened. It would continue to do so until his iron fist gained complete control for as long as necessary.

Hannan had needed more time. Eight years was simply not enough for immigration policies to make necessary modifications to the demographics, to appoint two or three justices to the Supreme Court, 450 judges total to the U.S. Courts of Appeals and the district courts, and then to create the stream of cascading executive orders and presidential memoranda that would turn a democratic republic into an autocracy when he pulled the trigger.

When it was all done, the Organization would have their version of utopia, complete with a neo-Marxian version of economic justice that would make Karl smile in his grave. The U.S. would pay for its economic and social sins, not that Hannan gave a rip about that.

Hannan would end all disparity and, in the process, become a wealthy, powerful man. That's what he cared about. No need to throw out or modify the Constitution, merely reinterpret it or, if needed, ignore it for a while when there were matters more important to the people; like staying alive.

When the smoke cleared, the greatest difficulty remaining would be repairing damaged relationships with former allies. If the relationship could not be recovered, he could vilify that nation until it repented or was no longer deemed worthy of being an ally of the USA.

The organization's plan, as implemented by Hannan, would work. He simply needed to tie up a few loose ends.

His wireless phone rang again.

He recognized the ID. Blanchard, the black ops commander. "Yes?"

"We have a lead on Ms. Banning. Thought you would want to know, sir."

Chapter 10

He had the key ingredients for a perfect day in the life of Brock Daniels. The sun shone brightly through the motel room window and KC sat beside him. But two spoilers had been stirred into the mix, Abe Hannan and thoughts of the letter from seven years ago. There was a third one, something he was reluctant to discuss. Why had KC never contacted him?

Maybe KC's father had been right and Brock didn't deserve someone like her. Maybe she really was out of his league. Maybe he didn't deserve her for a lot of reasons. Though these maybes had kept him from kissing her the way he wanted, he would never let KC walk into danger alone. Brock Daniels would keep that promise.

"Brock, are you listening?"

Was his distraction that obvious? He was letting KC down on all fronts. She had been telling him her story, and it would play a crucial role in determining what they should do. But his nagging question wouldn't go away. Brock knew why he hadn't contacted KC. But why hadn't she contacted him?

"Brock?"

"I ... KC ..."

She peered into his eyes, "Whatever it is, just say it."

"Why didn't you ever contact me or try to see me, Kace?" KC looked down at the floor, then wiped her tear-filled eyes and looked up at his. "I tried ... once. At the apologetics conference in Charlotte, where you were speaking. Brock, there were people there that I'd only seen on book covers, people so superior—I didn't belong there. I went out and hid until time for you to speak. Then I snuck in near the back of the room. But before you were five minutes into your presentation, I knew KC Banning wasn't good enough for someone like you. Never could be. And that broke what was left of my heart. I left."

Tears flowed freely now, but KC still looked into his eyes. "I at least tried to see you, Brock. But you didn't even try."

"No, Kace. I *did* try, but ..."

"I may not have long to live. I don't have time for buts, Brock. Only for the truth."

He emptied his lungs in a sharp blast and looked away. "Yeah ... only the truth." He could tell her part of it, but Brock Daniels had buried the rest too deeply to excavate the whole, painful truth in a moment's notice. "KC, when I heard about the plane crash, I wrote down the funeral date. Even checked airline schedules, but *he* was the reason I couldn't come. Your father didn't approve of me. It seemed disrespectful to attend his funeral."

"You're not making any sense. Brock, I looked for you at the funeral. I needed you, but you weren't there. It hurt." Tears streamed down her cheeks again. "That finally convinced me I was just a childhood friend, someone you got stuck with, and that those days were over."

He brushed the tears from her cheek. "That's not how it was. You and I were a lot more than just childhood friends. You know that, KC. We weren't whole unless we were together. That was true even when you were nine or ten, and all we did was have fun together. Without you, I didn't have any fun. Life was serious and full of disappointments. But when we were together, I came alive."

Brock looked down at his hands, wet with KC's tears. "I'm so sorry. I should have come to the funeral, if only for you, Kace. Will you forgive me?"

He had only hinted at the reason he couldn't attend the funeral. The same reason he didn't hold her and kiss her like he wanted to when she walked through the door of his motel room. When it came to the things he wanted most, Brock Daniels was never quite good enough. KC was beautiful, like royalty. Her father was right. Brock was a commoner, not in her class.

"I could forgive you for just about anything, Brock. How could I not." She took his hands, stood, and tugged until Brock stood with her. "Like you said ... we're not whole unless we're together." KC circled him with her arms and pressed her face into his chest.

He buried his face in her hair and returned the embrace.

"Brock, are we whole yet?"

"Yeah." Brock relaxed his hold on KC. The gloom their conversation had cast over them vanished, driven away by KC's beaming face and sparkling emerald eyes. As he studied that face, he ended up focusing on her full, red lips. It would be so easy to—no, he couldn't ... rather, shouldn't.

He looked over KC's shoulder to the king-size bed. Being here alone with her while emotions ran so high was a king-sized temptation. Even with danger lurking, he needed to be—

"Brock," KC whispered softly, "... I was a fool."

"Do you mean for letting me hold—"

"No, silly. Not that. And stop looking at that bed. You and I are not climbing into a bed together until, unless ... someday—" She stopped and blushed.

"Yeah." So KC was feeling it too. "Uh, I mean no. We won't. But why do you think you were a fool?"

After the redness faded from her cheeks, KC looked up at him. "Nearly four years ago, when I turned eighteen, I had done my duty. Dad had been elected to the senate. I was an adult and, no matter what anyone said or thought, I should have come back here."

"Kace, maybe I'm the fool. I should have gone looking for you. To see if you wanted to come home."

"Home. That's what it feels like being here with you. But we aren't safe here anymore. No more innocent times here for us. No more innocent times for anyone in the U.S." She paused and peered deeply into his eyes. "Maybe I should finish telling you why ... if you'll pay attention this time." She gave him her coy smile.

He gestured toward her chair. "Have a seat Ms. Banning." Brock imitated Hannan's voice of authority used in his speeches. "POTUS ... uh, POTSY, will hear your briefing now."

"You're no president. And Potsie? Wasn't he some nerdy character in a TV show?"

"No. P-O-T-S-Y, President of the Squirrel Yurt, wants to be briefed."

KC laughed the mischievous laugh of a little girl, a laugh etched indelibly on his memory. Then her expression grew serious. "I need your help, Brock. So listen carefully. I'll start with the facts, the things I'm sure of."

Over the next half hour, KC told him about her discovery of the president's unauthorized access to the classified networks and the events which followed; Agent Belino's text message telling her to disappear; her meeting with Senator Richards, Chairman of the Senate Intelligence Committee; the senator's murder.

"Brock, this president and his administration completely disregard the constitution, and nobody will confront him in a serious manner. I think he's trying to take absolute control of the country, maybe permanent control. And he'll remove anyone who gets in his way."

Brock stroked his chin. His conclusion was ... he hadn't shaved this morning. He would have if he'd known KC would—what was he doing? KC had just told him the USA was going down the tube and all he could think of was how he looked to her.

At some point KC had stopped talking.

"Go ahead. I'm ... listening."

"You weren't." She cupped his cheek and gave him a weak smile. "Me too, Brock." She pulled her hand back and waved it across her somewhat wrinkled blouse, then pulled on a strand of her newly colored hair. "And I wish this wasn't all happening. Especially, right now. Because ..."

He smiled at her. "Yeah. Because ..." After seven years, KC still read him well. "I really am listening, Kace."

"Alright, let's put the pieces into the big puzzle. Chaos is spreading through parts of the country from the deadly outbreak. The action by the Federal Reserve has caused the jittery stock market to go into freefall."

"Right after you called, before I turned the TV off, there was news about oil refineries being damaged in some kind of attack."

KC shook her head. "Hannan's doings. I'd bet on it. None of it looks like the president's fault, except perhaps his collusion with the Fed, and he can deflect that. If this president has any more tricks up his sleeve, he can destabilize the country until lawlessness makes it appear he must put the *entire nation* under martial law."

"And the people will beg him to do it. I've been blogging about that, Kace. The pattern of executive orders that Hannan has signed is scary. Taken individually, they each sound like prudent contingency planning. But if someone pushes the right domino over, the executive orders cascade, knocking all the dominoes down, putting him in absolute control. Well, all except for one potentially big problem for Hannan."

KC's eyebrows raised. "You mean the military?"

"Yeah. He's got to count on the military to be solidly on his side and loyal enough to turn their guns on U.S. citizens when things get violent. Five years ago, that would have been unthinkable. But now ..." He shook his head. "For my blog, I've interviewed several officers who are leaving the military after long, successful careers—some just short of retirement. They told me that, after the cultural changes Hannan's policies have forced on the military, many good men and women have bailed, while others are being selectively riffed using the $400 billion budget cuts as an excuse. It could happen, KC."

"I think that's why Hannan wants me out of the way." KC stood and paced the room. "I stumbled onto hard evidence that shows Hannan has illegally acquired private access to the classified warfighters' networks. He can break the chain of command and secretly give orders to soldiers who might not be keen on killing fellow Americans. But with the Commander-in-Chief giving direct orders ..."

"That sort of thing has been done before. Hitler found ways to use authority structures to coerce people into committing all kinds of atrocities."

"He's putting our nation at risk, Brock." KC's face turned red and her pace through the motel room grew furious. "When I took my job, I swore to serve and protect the U.S. against *all* enemies." Her voice crescendoed. "I won't allow it! Not to *my* country! I'll kill that arrogant little s—"

"Keep your voice down. Someone outside might hear you. And you're not going to kill anyone ... at least not yet."

"I wouldn't bet on that. And now he wants to kill *me*," she huffed.

"Kace, I wouldn't bet on that either. He'd have to come through me first."

"He's got a few million soldiers, including several thousand special ops types. And he can send a drone, or just write 'Brock Daniels' into the programmable memory of a cruise missile, and you're toast."

"Settle down for a minute. I've got an idea, but I'm going to need your help."

KC took a breath and exhaled like she was trying to calm down. But that red hair under the brown dye, and her Irish heritage, obviously weren't making it easy for her. She wasn't a girl you wanted to tick off but—Brock stopped and studied KC. Breast heaving, eyes flashing like emeralds, and the light shining through the large window highlighting full red lips on a perfectly sculpted face—even in her anger, her beauty was breathtaking.

Now those flashing emeralds had focused on him. "What are you staring at, Brock Daniels?"

He tried to give her his warmest smile. "Do you really want me to describe it?"

KC's huffiness deflated in an instant.

Brock took the opportunity to wrap her up in his arms. She relaxed against him.

Maybe she would listen now. He'd learned years ago not to try to communicate with her during her rants. She needed to be defused before he resumed conversation or everything he said was taken in the worst possible light, usually as incriminating evidence, against him.

"I do have an idea, Kace. And it really does require your help."

"I'm sorry. I feel so helpless. I need to do something." She pressed her cheek against his chest, squeezed him, and stepped back. "And I'm ready to hear Brock's brainstorm."

"Here's what I'm thinking. If we can put together some facts, including a fairly complete list of the triggers that Hannan will use to create the chaos—enough so that we can tell a credible story of how this president can take over the country—maybe we can turn the people against him. Start a grassroots resistance movement that will eventually stop him."

"Brock, if we create a resistance movement, and there's violence of any kind, people will be killed. Do you want that on your conscience?"

"No, I don't. But I'm not sure Hannan can stay in power if 300 million people oppose him. If we can win the war of ideas, maybe some ex-military types can stage a coup or something. We pulled it off in 1776."

"But a lot of people were killed then."

Brock started to use Patrick Henry's liberty quote, but KC would probably go off on him if he mentioned the or-give-me-death part. "If we can move quickly enough, maybe we can head this power play off before he gains complete control."

"Alright. So we plan to win the war of ideas." She peered into his eyes, with her mind-reading look, then a frown that said her mind reading wasn't working. "How do we do that?"

"We use my blog. I've already got a million followers. If the situation in the U.S. worsens, I'll get a lot more."

"You know what he'll do if that happens, Brock. He'll shut down your blog."

"But that's where you come in. Can you keep the blog up when his people try to take it down?"

"Gee. You don't ask much, do you? I'm a network monitor. I keep classified networks safe from world-class hackers. But I'm not one, myself."

"But you can do it, right? Isn't there a way?'

"Maybe ... for a while. But, eventually, they'll find out what I'm doing, shut us down, find us, and he'll kill us, Brock."

"But, if it buys us enough time, with 300 million people, we could defeat a would-be tyrant."

"*If*, Brock. That's a *big* if. And it will probably cost us our lives."

"Got any better ideas?"

KC took his hand in hers. "Why don't you sneak me across the border into Canada and marry me? We'll find a lake hidden somewhere in the Canadian Rockies and live off the land for the rest of our lives."

The look in her eyes said she was serious. "Kace, you don't realize how much you're tempting me."

"That *was* the general idea. I want you alive. What you're proposing will get us killed. If we could save the USA, it would be worth dying. But if this plan fails ..." She shook her head.

"Since we're not going to Canada today, let's piece together what Hannan and his cohorts have planned."

Brock jumped when his room phone rang. No one should be calling him. Certainly not on the room phone. He'd emphasized that he wanted privacy when he rented the room. "Kace, look out the small window by the door and check out the motel office and the parking area. Let me know if there's anything unusual happening." He picked up the receiver. "Hello."

"Mr. Daniels, this is Debbie in the office. My replacement, Caroline, just showed up for work. She said there's a roadblock on Highway 97 near Terrebonne. The police and some people who look like military are searching for Katheryn C. Banning. They believe she's in Central Oregon, because she was spotted at a coffee shop in Bend this morning. Caroline overheard someone say Ms. Banning has some ties to Crooked River Ranch. The government is calling her a terrorist and a murderer, armed and dangerous. I thought I should let you know."

"Thanks, Debbie." Brock hung up before he said more. The woman clearly knew who KC was and Debbie was trying to help. He just wished he had 300 million more like her. But, unfortunately, all he had was Brock Daniels.

"Brock, what is it? Tell me." White encircled KC's wide, green eyes, a look he used to see only when they ran across a rattlesnake.

Brock took her hands. "The FBI is at Terrebonne, along with some military personnel. They found out you were on a motorcycle in Bend. They've linked you to the ranch, and they may be coming here, as we speak. She knows, Kace. And she's trying to help us."

KC sucked in a sharp breath. "Brock, my Honda is parked in the church lot. It's a dead giveaway."

"I'll hide your motorcycle. I know some places they'll never find it. Since they haven't connected you and me yet, you should spend the night here, in the adjacent room. Tonight, I'm going to call in a favor from a friend who can get us out of here to a safe place."

KC's grip on his hands tightened. "What if they start searching the motel in the middle of the night?"

"I'll stand watch tonight. If they start any kind of search of the ranch, we'll make a run for the Old Hollywood Road, go down to Crooked River Canyon, and take advantage of those two days you and I explored it seven years ago."

"But we're talking military here. They have night vision goggles and scopes. Maybe even drones or choppers."

"You got any better ideas?"

"Yes. I've got one."

What had just popped into that brilliant brain of hers? "KC, that look in your eyes scares me."

"Me too, Brock."

Chapter 11

Why hadn't KC told him about her plan to hide them? For whatever the reason, she'd kept it a mystery, one Brock didn't have time to worry about at the moment. He needed to hide her motorcycle from whatever breed of dogs Hannan had sicced on them.

He moved to the window nearest the room door and pulled the curtain back. It wasn't completely dark yet, but this would have to do. "I'm going to hide your motorcycle, Kace. I'll be back in about twenty minutes."

She handed him the keys. "Please hurry, Brock. I ... I need you ... here."

"So Ms. Banning's plan doesn't work without Brock Daniels?" He shot her a questioning glance.

"Something like that."

Sometimes her stubbornness irritated him. He studied her eyes. The fear there was genuine. KC wasn't playing games with him, just reluctant to tell him something about a last-ditch plan. Hopefully, one they would never have to use.

He reached for the door knob, then stopped and looked back at her sitting on the end of the bed. Even with her hair the wrong color, she was so beautiful it created an ache inside just to look at her.

She looked up at him and blushed, her red cheeks visible

clear across the room.

Everything about her drew him in like a black hole pulls in asteroids. Everything but the one thing that kept him from telling her what was really on his heart. The letter. Though her father was dead, the message he left still spoke the plain truth to Brock. For someone like KC, he wasn't good enough. Not in her class.

Brock gave her a smile. A weak one. The best he could manage at the moment. "Listen, KC. If the worst should happen and they show up at the ranch before I get back, the instant you see them, run down the road into the canyon and go down the river. I'll enter the canyon at the north end of the ranch and head south. We'll meet somewhere on the trail."

KC returned his smile. Hers also weak. "Just a contingency plan, right?"

"Yeah. See you in a few." He walked out the door, praying he got back before anything happened.

In the motel parking spot, Brock opened his pickup, took out his leather hiking boots, and pulled them on. He leaned his pickup seat forward, moved his skateboard, pulled out his knee pads, and shin guards. Just as a precaution.

In the parking lot by the ranch chapel, he strapped on the pads, hoping they wouldn't interfere with riding KC's bike. He started the motorcycle, left the lights off, and tried not to rev the engine. With the Honda purring, he idled away toward the main road.

The place Brock had in mind lay about a mile north of the motel, off from Ranch House Road, the main road through Crooked River Ranch. The escarpment on the west side of the ranch rose nearly 400 feet and curved eastward, as one traveled north, until it bordered the road. Trees and bushes around the base of the cliff should hide KC's bike. The reputation of this location would almost ensure it wouldn't be searched.

In a couple of minutes, Brock approached the hiding place for the motorcycle. He'd not passed any vehicles on the road and the lights were out at the convenience store a quarter mile ahead. With the store closed, it was unlikely there would be any witnesses.

When the shadowy outline of the thick grove of trees appeared on his left, he downshifted and veered off the road. After dodging rocks and desert vegetation, he gunned the motorcycle toward the stand of trees.

A mound of rocks lay near the center of the trees. A stream nearby, fed by irrigation runoff, made this prime rattlesnake habitat. No one intentionally ventured into the rocky, wooded area at the base of the cliff ... except Brock Daniels.

Praying his armor worked, he flew between the trees, then cut the engine. Before the motorcycle sputtered to a stop, Brock pushed out the kickstand with his toe and propped his feet up on the gas tank. The bike stood without falling.

Thunk.

Something struck the front wheel of the motorcycle. Buzzing and rattling sounds seemed to surround him, but most came from the rocks in front of him.

Brock scooted back on the seat and stepped off the back of the bike. He whirled and leaped from the rocky area. Something pounded his right leg below the knee as he sprinted out of the stand of trees. Fortunately, it hit his skateboarder's kneepad.

He reached down and felt the pad. A cool, wet sticky substance clung to his fingers. Brock shivered at the thought of those fangs coming within an inch of his leg.

The motorcycle keys. He'd left them in the ignition. For now, that's where they would stay, with rattlesnakes guarding them.

Maybe he shouldn't tell KC about the rattlesnake striking

his pads. She was more afraid of the little vipers than him. But he would tell her what Hannan's posse would get if they tried to search where he'd hidden the motorcycle. Rattlesnakes biting rattlesnakes. The irony of that possibility brought a sardonic smile.

With at least half the nation in a state of panic and the other half intently watching events unfold, most people had cancelled their vacation plans. Crooked River Ranch had grown quiet over the past 24 hours. Brock didn't have to worry about traffic—not as much as he worried about rattlesnakes in the dark—so he walked back toward the motel down the centerline of Ranch House Road, keeping his distance from any grass and bushes on the shoulders that might hide the slithering demons.

When he reached his truck, Brock put his pads and boots away and walked back to the room. He opened the room door with his key and found KC with her nose pressed against the glass of the big picture window, looking out to the southwest.

"See something fascinating out that window, KC?"

Her head pointed in the general direction of the road descending from the plateau down to ranch level. "I've been watching the road where it passes the lookout at the turnoff—where they would first appear and ... Brock ... I see several headlights. Looks like some vehicles pulled off the road and stopped at the lookout."

Brock stuck his head against the window, beside hers. "The lights all went out, almost simultaneously." His heart shifted to a higher gear.

"It's them, Brock. I know it." KC curled an arm around his waist. The arm tightened.

The pounding rhythm in his chest accelerated to allegro. "Time to go, Kace. We'll take the Old Hollywood Road into the canyon." He tried to turn away from the window.

Her arm constricted, holding him against her side. "No.

We can't go outside. From up there they can see the whole ranch. With their night vision goggles, they would spot us and trap us in the canyon ... or, just shoot us with those guided sniper rifles. They can kill a person three-quarters of a mile away."

"Guided rifles? Where did you hear that?"

"I work with the military, you know."

"So, we just wait here for them to find us?"

"Sort of." She looked down, away from his face.

They didn't have time to waste, but KC still wasn't telling him what she had in mind. Maybe goading would help. "Kace, I really thought you were smarter than that. I figured, by now, you'd have a good plan for this scenario."

"If you'd stop calling me a stupid woman, I'd tell you my plan." She pulled the large curtain back a few inches and looked out. "Vehicles are coming down the hill. Eight or nine of them." KC stepped away from the window.

"We're out of time. Why haven't you told me what we're doing?"

She shot him a corner-of-the-eye glance. "Because you're not going to like it."

"Great." As he expected. Brock stepped back to the window.

She took his hand and pulled him toward her. "Have you ever played poker?"

"What kind of question is that?"

"Well, have you?"

"A few times, just for fun."

"Were you any good at bluffing?"

"No. Don't have a poker face." Where was she going with this? Crazy?

"Well, that had better change, fast." KC pulled back the curtain a few inches and looked out again. "Brock ... two vehicles just turned in at the motel."

"They could be all over this place in another minute.

90

You'd better tell me what we're doing."

KC walked to the far side of the king-size bed, kicked off her shoes, and began unbuttoning her blouse.

"Kace, what in heaven's name are you doing?"

"It *is* in heaven's name ... well, sort of. It's from the Bible."

"David and Bathsheba?"

"No. More like Rahab's—"

"The prostitute? Hannan's people are gonna break down our door and we're—"

"They won't break it down if you'll unlock the deadbolt and the doorknob. I checked the door. They can open it from outside."

Footsteps pounded the pavement outside.

With the tempo of his heart now thumping out presto, Brock unlocked the door. He turned toward the bed and saw KC's blouse floating to the floor.

She had thrown the covers back and had already slid beneath them. "Brock, pull off that shirt and get into bed."

"With a prostitute?"

"I can be your bride if you prefer."

"KC, if it's the last thing I do, I'm going to—"

"Just do it, Brock, or it might be the last thing. And, by the way, Rahab's going to keep her face covered. You have to do the lying." KC pulled the bedspread up to her eyes.

"Hence the reference to bluffing." Brock ripped off his shirt, shucked his shoes, and jumped into bed.

"Brock ... since you're doing the lying and I'm hiding in your room, I guess I'm the spy and you get to be Rahab."

"Great. I'm a bluffing liar and a prostitute."

"Right now, you need to be my husband. Just hold me, Brock, and tell them it's our honeymoon."

The door flew open.

Chapter 12

Three men burst through the door. Two in tactical gear held their assault rifles in firing position. The third man, in street clothes, carried something that looked like a voice recorder. His eyes quickly scanned the room.

KC pulled the sheets up, nearly covering her eyes, while she kept her face in the shadow of Brock's shoulder, hoping the men couldn't see the color of her eyes.

Voice recordings. Voice prints. How many other ways did they have to identify her? KC would keep her mouth shut, her eyes mostly hidden, and hope Brock could do that thing he wasn't so good at, bluffing. But if the men threw back the covers and saw them wearing most of their clothes—she prayed that wouldn't happen.

"FBI." The man with the recorder flashed a badge. "Identify yourselves."

KC kept the covers at eye level.

"Guys, I'm Brock Daniels and we're here on our honeymoon. If you're looking for some bad guys, you got the wrong room."

"Check out the bathroom." Mr. Badge Flasher pointed toward the closed door.

One of the gunmen pushed the bathroom door open and used his rifle to slide the shower curtain to one side.

"Nobody here, sir, and there aren't any other hiding places in these rooms."

"The other gunman moved toward the door. "These two don't fit the profile."

The FBI guy studied them for a moment. "Sorry to have bothered you."

"Well, at least you gave us a story we can tell our kids."

Was Brock actually smiling at the men?

All three hurried out the door.

Brock pulled his arm from KC, the arm that had encircled her bare shoulders. "Sorry, Kace."

"Sorry? Not any good at bluffing? I don't know what to believe about you. They had four aces and you didn't even have a pair of deuces."

"Wrong. I had a pair. But you and I are a lot more than a pair of deuces. KC, I ... I ... want ..."

For once, Brock, the writer, had run out of words. What was he trying to say?

"Kace, I want you—

The room phone rang.

"Saved by the bell," she muttered.

Brock answered the phone and seemed to be just listening to the person on the other end. He hung up and turned toward KC. "It was the lady in the office. She said we were the last room they searched and the men are gone. But on the way out, one of them stopped by the office and asked her about the couple in room 17. She told them you and I were here on our honeymoon. She knows, Kace. That makes me uncomfortable. But she *did* cover for us."

So, they were safe for the moment. KC remained under the covers with sheets pulled up around her neck. "Honeymooners. What do you think about that?"

"KC, this is no time to be thinking about that. We might be killed tonight. It could still happen if we—"

"My point exactly. There are things I need to know, Brock, before it's too late."

Brock looked at her face and winced, visibly. "If we don't get out of here pronto, it *will* happen tonight. If they were to find the motorcycle, they'd turn over every rock on the ranch looking for you."

He was deliberately avoiding her. Trampling on her feelings, and he obviously knew it.

Tears blurred her vision. "One of these days, Brock Daniels, you'll have to stop changing the subject, stop avoiding issues and—" Tears trickled down her cheeks. "Darn!"

"What?"

"Nothing."

Brock had noticed her tears. But he just pulled on his shirt and fiddled with his cell.

"Go ahead and make your precious phone call, but keep your head turned the other way. I'm putting on my blouse."

* * *

KC was right. He *was* avoiding talking about the issue of *them*, of his true feelings for her. He loved the girl he remembered and was sure he loved the young woman she had become. But he couldn't tell her that. Maybe, in time, he could tell her why. Sometime beyond that he might be able to tell her everything, if it wasn't too late.

KC's father was right. KC was above him in social standing. She could have been a world-class model had she chosen. She was brilliant, a major leaguer, while Brock never even made it to Single A in the minor leagues. He wasn't even drafted.

"I said you can look now."

He turned toward her. As it had happened every time since she showed up, her innocent, girl-next-door beauty captured his mind every bit as completely as the person she was had captured his heart.

"What are you thinking? I wish you wouldn't stare at me like that. You know, it wasn't wrong, Brock. And we didn't do anything wrong. Is that what you're thinking?"

Brock sighed, still at a loss for words, afraid of what he might say and afraid to say what he wanted.

"Well, say *something.*"

He fumbled for the words, any words that weren't, themselves, a fumble. "I've only kissed a girl once in my life, and now I've crawled into bed with one. Just you, Kace, for both. And, no, you didn't do anything wrong. But we need to get out of here now. I'll call Jeff after we're off the ranch."

Brock had just dropped the ball in the red zone, an unforgivable fumble. Time was running out, but all he could do was put his defense on the field and hope for the best. He shoved his laptop in its case.

"Here we go again." She shook her head.

"Get your things, KC."

"My things are on my motorcycle."

"Everything?"

"Well, no. I have my fake ID and some money in a flat fanny pack around my waist. Obviously, you didn't peek or you would've known that."

Brock stuffed his writing materials into his duffel bag. "Do you need anything from your bike?"

"If you hid it where I think you did, it can wait."

"It's in the snake den, Kace."

"Then it can *definitely* wait."

Brock grabbed his bag and computer case. "Let's go." He turned and tossed the room key on the table, pulled the door closed, and stepped into the darkness toward his truck.

She followed him, lagging far behind.

His failure to respond when she clearly wanted to hear his feelings had hurt KC. Now her mood had changed. But this was not something Brock could easily fix. And now was not the time to try.

When he approached his truck, he unlocked it with his key fob, the truck lights flashed in response.

Her hand gripped his shoulder and pulled him to a stop. "Brock, look. Between the church and the office. Vehicle lights just came on at the RV Park down by the store."

"That's a half mile away, but they might have spotted my truck lights." If the FBI had searched both RV parks after hitting the motel and still came up empty, they would be frustrated, possibly desperate, and ready to follow any clue. Like any moving vehicle.

KC hurried to the passenger door. "If they're leaving the other park, they'll be headed back up the main road in a couple of minutes. We need to clear the top of the hill and get off the ranch before they see us. Otherwise, we're trapped here."

Brock jumped into the driver's seat.

KC slid in beside him and curled her fingers around his right hand. "Do you know if this Jeff guy has a good hiding place in mind?"

"All I know is he owes me a big favor."

The instrument lights in his truck lit her face dimly, a face that held a deep frown. "It's midnight and he owes you a favor? That's it? That's encouraging, Brock. Really encouraging."

Chapter 13

Brock drove with the headlights off as his truck climbed the steep hill leading out of Crooked River Ranch. He downshifted to avoid hitting the brakes as he rounded the sharp right turn at the top.

He and KC were off the ranch now, and in a few seconds they would be completely out of sight of the searchers. "Can you see them behind us?"

"I see their headlights," KC said. "They're following us."

"Following us? KC, you should've said something."

"I would have, but they're moving slowly, shining lights on both sides of the road. They wouldn't be searching that area if they'd spotted us." She paused. "You know, Brock, we can't go through Terrebonne or to Highway 97. That's where they had the roadblock."

Brock didn't reply.

"So, where are you taking me?"

"Out into the boonies. I'll pull off somewhere near the alpaca ranch and call Jeff."

"You mean, the man who's going to hide us but doesn't know it yet?"

KC had never directed her sarcasm at him. What was happening here?

"Jeff and Allie have a small cabin on a lake about an hour's drive south of here. Actually, it's his dad's cabin, but he lets them use it."

KC looked out her window into the darkness. She didn't reply. Evidently didn't want to.

Probably for the best. Things had gone sour between them. He didn't like it and didn't want to say anything to make matters worse.

Ten minutes later, when he turned off the road at the big alpaca ranch, KC still hadn't spoken. Her head hung now, chin nearly on her chest, just above her folded arms.

This rift was a first in their thirteen-year relationship. The fiery nine-year-old had sometimes spewed hot lava at him for a few seconds, then curled her fingers around his and gave him her warm smile. But this was not a nine-year-old girl sitting beside him. And it was easier to give a young girl what she wanted than a grown woman, much easier.

Brock stopped on the side of the small country road opposite the alpaca ranch and pulled out his cell.

"How do you know they're not tracking your cell?" Her first words in ten minutes questioned his judgment. Not a good sign.

Brock hit Jeff's entry on his contact list. "They don't know who I am yet. No reason to track my cell."

"You can bet Hannan's people know who Brock Daniels is, the man who pounds the Hannan's administration, mercilessly, from the Internet. They might be tracking you right now."

KC had mentioned something that had crossed his mind. Scrutiny would come, eventually, because of his blog. "I'll buy another phone as soon as I get a chance."

He pushed the call icon and waited while Jeff's phone rang. Brock stared into the darkness around them. Only a single pinpoint of light shone in the distance. A light from the alpaca ranch. Just like his life. One pinpoint of light, KC, and the light was fading. He was turning it out like a dimmer switch, twisting it, unspoken word by unspoken word.

Jeff's voice startled Brock. "Hey, bro. What are you calling me at midnight for?"

"Sorry about that. But I need to call in a favor."

"Now?"

"Yeah. Right now. It's ... important."

"Tell me what's up, and I'll see what I can do."

"Let's not talk about this over the phone."

"Sounds mysterious. Double O seven stuff? Oh, I've got it. You've changed your mind about Julia and—"

"No, Jeff. My life's in danger."

"She must have showed up at the ranch."

Brock wasn't going to make any reference to KC over the phone. Thankfully, Jeff hadn't said her name. "Where can we meet to talk?"

"What's going on, sweetheart?" Allie's voice. She sounded sleepy.

"Tell you in a minute, hon. Brock, you know the twenty-four-hour restaurant a mile toward Redmond from my place?"

"Yeah."

"Meet you there, bro. Fifteen minutes."

"Jeff, it'll take me a little longer." They would need to take a circuitous route to be safe, halfway to Sisters, then circle back toward Redmond. "How about thirty minutes?"

After he ended the call, a hand came to rest on his shoulder. "I'm sorry, Brock. I wasn't questioning your judgment." Her words, her eyes focused on his face, and the warmth in her voice all said she hated the icy chill in their relationship as much as he did. "I trust you. I always have and ... suppose I always will."

When her fingers left his shoulder, they found his hand.

Brock's reserve evaporated. "Kace, I trust you too ... and suppose I always will."

Now both of her hands wrapped around his right hand. "Then why won't you trust me with your feelings ... about me? We don't even know if we'll be alive in the morning."

How he felt about her—that he loved her—the one thing he couldn't tell her now. But the reason for his reluctance was the one thing that would destroy their relationship. And the demolition had already begun.

"Brock?"

He didn't reply.

* * *

KC wiped an unshed tear from her eye as she looked down the road at the distant lights of Redmond. Brock hadn't said a word in the past fifteen minutes. If he would only tell her what she needed to do or change to fix things, she would do it. He liked her, was obviously attracted to her, but there was some problem he refused to discuss.

The lights of Redmond grew brighter, obscuring the stars. Now, streetlights lined the highway. One of them lit a large yellow and red sign marking the entry to the restaurant.

KC's heart started its slow acceleration when Brock turned in to the parking lot, a lot nearly empty at 12:45 a.m. Who was this guy, Jeff? Could he really help them when the government sought them, including law enforcement and probably the military?

Brock pulled the wheel hard left and parked on the right side of another pickup, a newer and nicer truck than the ten-year-old Dodge that Brock drove. He killed the engine and rolled down his window.

The passenger-side window of the other truck slid down.

A woman by the window leaned back in the seat and the driver leaned toward Brock. "Hey, bro." A strong confident voice sounded from the adjacent truck. "Follow me."

"Where we headed? Your cabin?"

"Nah. This place is a lot better. Trust me."

"Jeff, I still need to know where we're going. There are certain roads we can't drive on."

Jeff didn't answer. Had "we" surprised him? KC Banning was certainly going to surprise him. At that thought her pulse shifted to a higher gear. She squeezed Brock's arm which rested on the steering wheel.

He glanced her way, then looked back at Jeff and the woman.

"Bro, I got you a mansion at Crooked River Ranch, and you—"

"We can't go back to the ranch. No way."

"This place isn't *on* the ranch. It's on that bluff that overlooks the ranch. You interested or not?"

KC quickly iterated through the advantages of that location: several routes of escape; birds-eye view of everything on the ranch; close enough to the ranch that anyone escaping from the ranch would probably not choose it as a place to hide. She squeezed Brock's arm again. "Brock, take it. It's perfect."

"Yeah. I see what you mean. Hannan's hounds will be following other trails." He leaned his head near his window. "Lead the way, but keep us away from Highway 97."

"Will do." Jeff's truck window went up and his truck started.

Twenty minutes later they rolled along Rim Road, on the high plateau above the ranch.

Brock was talking again, but still avoiding the discussion she desperately needed. However, KC had learned the woman with Jeff was Allie, his wife. Brock said KC would like her. Jeff had been a world-class decathlete, and Allie had immigrated to the U.S. from Mexico.

Brock's friends were interesting and unusual. Would they become her friends too? Would she even live long enough for that to happen?

Jeff turned in at a house with a long circle driveway.

From its dark profile, the house looked like a large, multilevel home ... as in mansion. Whose house was it?

Jeff jumped out of his truck and rushed to Brock's now open window. "She's running a bit late. Said she had a migraine."

"She?" Brock asked. "Who are we talking about, Jeff?"

"Julia. Don't you remember, while we were in Guatemala, she told us about the place she inherited?"

"Maybe I wasn't listening."

"So we noticed. You were miles away, bro."

"Yeah. Guess I was."

So, was there something going on between Brock and this Julia? Had KC's sudden appearance disrupted a budding relationship? The note in the jar didn't sound like that was the case. Brock's note said it had been a hard time for him and he missed her. And the way he held her, looked at her, certainly indicated there wasn't another woman.

To the south, headlights appeared, moving their way.

KC would soon find out.

"That's probably Julia. She'll give you a tour and the keys. Now that we've driven out here in the middle of the night, Allie and I would like to see the place too."

Everyone but Jeff waited in their vehicles until Julia arrived.

When Julia slid out of her midsized sedan, she stopped, clutched her chest and coughed a couple of times, wiped her forehead, then turned toward the door of the house.

Jeff was right. Even in the dim light, she didn't appear well and seemed to have more than just a migraine.

"Brock," Julia stepped onto the front porch and pointed toward the row of bricks lining the flower bed stretching across the front of the house. "The spare key is hidden under the seventh brick from the porch ... in a Ziploc bag. Would you get it, please? You'll need it. Excuse me. I'm going to freshen up a bit. Not feeling well. But come on in. I'll be out in a minute. You can check out the great room while you wait."

Julia unlocked the door and left it open. After hitting the lights, she disappeared down a hallway to the right.

Jeff and Allie went inside.

KC waited for Brock, who was replacing the brick with one hand and holding a key in the other.

She followed him into the house where, beyond the entry, Jeff and Allie appeared to be admiring a spacious, somewhat rustic room with a gleaming hardwood floor, perfect for hosting gatherings.

Brock stopped in the edge of the great room and scanned it. "Wow. We needed a place to hide out for a while, but I was thinking cabin in the mountains, not a mansion on a hill."

KC stepped into the light of the great room and stopped beside Brock. She tensed, waiting for the coming reaction.

Brock motioned toward her.

Jeff's mouth opened, but nothing came out.

Allie studied her with curious eyes.

"Jeff, Allie, meet KC. She's the girl I told you about."

Jeff's gaze darted back and forth between her and Brock. "KC, as in Katheryn Celeste Banning, domestic terrorist?"

KC blew out a blast of air. "That would be me."

Jeff's index finger now pointed at Brock, wagging between Brock and her a couple of times. "So, she did show up. It's pretty plain to see why you couldn't forget her, but could forget—" Jeff stopped and glanced toward the hallway where Julia had gone.

Brock had been talking to Jeff about her while on a trip. Couldn't forget her? And no relationship with Julia. Maybe

KC had misinterpreted his reluctance to answer her questions. If so, why was Brock holding back?

Allie walked across the room and gave KC a quick hug. "It's so good to finally meet you, KC. We, rather, Jeff heard a lot about you."

"Hi, KC. Yeah, good to meet you."

KC nodded to Jeff.

"I need to change the subject a bit." Brock moved beside her and circled her with an arm. "There's no easy way to say this. Jeff, Allie ... our illustrious president has some really bad things planned for the American people."

Jeff and Allie looked at each other with wide-eyed stares. They didn't realize the degree of danger.

KC waited for Brock to tell them.

He continued. "KC stumbled onto some of it and was promptly declared a terrorist so she couldn't—"

"But he can't do that." Allie's eyes blazed. "Certainly not to a U.S. citizen."

"You ought to read some of the executive orders and memoranda Hannan has written. He's given himself the right to do that and to hold KC indefinitely, outside of the justice system, if he chooses. Allie, I'm asking you and Jeff to keep KC's whereabouts secret. Mine too, since they will probably want to kill me once they realize why they didn't find KC at Crooked River Ranch."

"You can count on us," Jeff said. "But, bro, are you saying the FBI searched the ranch and couldn't find you? They must be slipping."

"KC came up with a plan that tricked them and saved our lives." Brock glanced her way.

She could see it in his eyes. Brock cared, but for some reason he wouldn't tell her.

Jeff whistled through his teeth. "That must've been *some* deception."

Brock grinned. "It was. One of biblical proportions, you might say."

Allie had cooled off a bit. At least her face wasn't red. "You mean like Gideon when he tricked the Midianites?"

"Not exactly." Brock squirmed.

KC took his hand. If he wasn't going to change the subject, she would. "Brock they need to know what Hannan has planned for all of us."

"Yeah. You're right, Kace." Brock sighed. "Stock market falling, interest rates jumping, the outbreak—"

"Hannan's doing?" Jeff's eyebrows pinched. "I thought the guy was just incompetent, but you're saying he—"

"I'm saying he caused it all, intentionally. And he has more triggers to pull until he can put the entire U.S. under martial law, making it look like he had no choice. The worst thing is ... once he has complete control, KC and I believe he'll never give it up."

Allie's naturally tanned face turned red again. "How could any man be so cruel as to cause an outbreak of hemorrhagic fever among the very people he swore to protect?"

A crash came from the hallway.

"Julia?" Allie broke toward the sound.

Brock stepped in front of her, cutting her off from Julia. His face went pale. KC had never before seen true fear in his eyes. What was Brock thinking?

KC took Allie's arm. "Let's go check on her."

Brock's arm shot out, blocking their path. "Don't touch Julia. At least not until—"

"She could have it." Allie gasped. "Hemorrhagic fever. The incubation period is about right. Brock, you and Julia both helped Itzy."

Itzy? The picture came into focus. KC stared into Brock's eyes. "Were you exposed to this in Guatemala?"

"Maybe. But Julia was with Itzy, a Mayan girl, before we suspected what she had."

Jeff joined Allie and KC in the hallway, where Julia sat on the floor. "But how?" Jeff asked. "After you and Julia caused the big commotion at the airport in Guatemala City, you said they called the CDC, and they cleared you both to fly."

"Yeah. These days, the CDC does a lot of things it shouldn't do." Brock's voice had turned cynical. "Little things like losing vials of smallpox and letting people infected with a deadly disease on commercial flights."

"It's all my fault." Julia's voice was weak. "I wasn't careful enough when Itzy first got sick. That was—" she coughed. It turned into a coughing fit. Her hands clamped to the sides of her head. "It was about eight days ago. My head." She moaned. "I've never had a headache like this, and I'm burning up. A while ago I was freezing."

Allie hooked her husband's arm. "Jeff, we have to get her to the hospital in Bend. That's the best medical care within 200 miles."

Julia fought off another coughing spasm. "You'll only expose yourself. I'll drive myself ... to ... Bend." She leaned over onto the floor. "I feel like I'm going to throw up."

"She can't drive herself. She might pass out," Jeff said.

KC ran into the bathroom and grabbed two large towels and a washcloth. "Julia, can you hold this washcloth over your mouth so you don't cough on us?"

"I ... I think so." Julia sat up and then struggled to her feet.

KC gave her the washcloth then draped a towel around her arms and shoulders. "Guys, help her to the car, but use the towels. Don't touch her body or her clothes."

"I'll drive her in my truck." Jeff said.

Julia nearly fell, but caught herself. "Put me in the bed of your truck, Jeff. Don't expose yourself."

"But I can't let you ride—"

"You have to!" Julia's voice ripped at KC's heart. This young woman, facing death, was still selfless, more so than KC could have been.

"I'm going to get in the bed of your truck now." Julia stumbled toward the front door.

Five minutes later, Jeff's truck roared out of the driveway on the way to Bend with Julia wrapped in blankets in the bed of pickup.

KC opened a phone book she found by the telephone in the great room and flipped through the pages until she reached the H's. "Here's the number for the St. Charles Medical Center in Bend."

"Just a sec. May I use your cell, Allie?" Brock asked. "You know, just in case Big Brother is tracking me?"

Allie pulled out her cell phone and handed it to him.

He keyed in the number as KC read it to him. Brock's voice grew intense. "I need emergency, please." He paused. "Yes. A patient is on the way to your emergency room, and we're almost certain she has Ebola."

From the look in Brock's eyes, KC could see that chaos had erupted at the other end of the call. Good. Maybe Julia would get the care she needed.

Brock ended the call.

KC took his hand and motioned for Allie to come closer. A lump formed in KC's throat. She swallowed hard. It didn't go away. "You learned something about this disease during your Guatemala trip. Brock, is Julia going to die?"

Brock sighed, a sharp blast of air. "Unless Hannan is willing to distribute some of his precious vaccine, she probably will. The disease has about a 90% kill rate."

Allie's large brown eyes focused on Brock, intense and questioning. "How do you know the government has a vaccine? There's no vaccine for Ebola."

"Allie, you don't modify and weaponize a deadly virus unless you can protect yourself from it. This is just one more thing Hannan can use to control the people. Kowtow to me and you can have my vaccine."

For the third time, Allie's face grew red. "Hannan has to go. If Julia dies, I'll kill him myself!"

KC took Allie's naturally tan hand.

Allie's face contorted like she was on the verge of tears. "This frightens me, KC."

"Me too, Allie. Let's pray for Julia."

The virus, and the disease it caused, were completely out of KC's control. For the second time in months KC was going to seek help from God instead of relying on herself. She prayed He would answer her prayers ... this time. But was she really praying for her *prayers*? What kind of convoluted reasoning was that? It was the reasoning of a person who still did not trust God, at least not the way Brock trusted Him.

"What about us?" Allie looked from KC to Brock. "We didn't touch her, and she didn't cough on us."

Brock took Allie's hand, completing the circle. "I was around Itzy more than you and Jeff. But we're all at risk. For us ... we wait seven to fifteen days and see if we get sick."

"If this virus was genetically modified," KC peered into Brock's eyes, "it could be airborne. You know that, don't you?"

"Yeah. I hate rattlers, but at least you can see and hear them. These microscopic demons are invisible. They just come in and take over your body one cell at a time until all your organs turn to—"

"Stop it, Brock." KC glanced at Allie's face. Tears streaked her cheeks. "That's enough. We need to pray now."

When they finished praying, Allie walked out of the great room, headed toward the kitchen. "I'm going to find something to disinfect the bathroom and every other thing that Julia might've touched. I've got to do something to occupy my mind while we're waiting to hear from Jeff. I'll check the cupboards and make a grocery list for us too."

"Good idea," Brock said. We need to get settled in here for what might be a long stay. And I need to get on the computer network. KC, when you get a chance, would you check out the news on TV. Not the liberal networks. I've had enough of Hannan's propaganda. We've got to know what we're up against as the landscape changes."

* * *

Brock headed down the long hallway, leading to several bedrooms, and looked into the first room on the right, a study. At the far end, on the exterior wall, a window opened to the front of the house. Sparsely populated book cases lined the walls on both sides. A desk sat by the window. Two reclining chairs were aligned, side-by-side, midway between the desk and the doorway, with a small table against the wall by the doorway on his left.

Perfect for working, both for KC and him.

Five minutes later his laptop had awakened and quickly connected to the house Wi-Fi. While his browser opened, KC walked into the room, her face devoid of color.

Brock stood and turned toward her.

She circled him with her arms.

His protective instincts on high alert, Brock pulled KC close and held her. "What's this all about?"

"You need to see the news, Brock."

"That bad?"

KC looked up at him with concern in her eyes and her chin pressed against his chest. "Watch it for a few minutes, then you tell me."

Chapter 14

Whatever had left KC so visibly shaken could not be good news. Brock followed her onto the polished hardwood floor of the great room. When KC stopped and pointed the controller at the TV, he wrapped an arm around her shoulders.

At the far end of the room, the head of an attractive woman filled the screen of the large flat-panel TV. The scrolling banner at the bottom read, "Hemorrhagic Fever Crosses Mexican Border." Brock looked away from the mesmerizing, scrolling message and tried to focus on the woman's words.

"The disease hit San Antonio and Houston and has now spread to other cities. Though the cases are still few, the incubation period for the virus is one to two weeks, so we are seeing only the tip of a very deadly iceberg—a hemorrhagic fever that kills 90% of its victims.

"Meanwhile, rumors have spread of the existence of a government-developed vaccine. People in the affected areas of Texas are demanding that the government make the vaccine available. As fears mount, demands have turned to riots, spreading from Brownsville northward to San Antonio and eastward to Houston. Because this pattern suggests the disease came across our southern border, Texas Governor, John R. Ewing, has called in the National Guard to secure the entire Texas border with Mexico. With National Guard troops spread thin, one has to wonder if President Hannan will declare martial law and deploy the U.S. military."

KC changed the channel. The news camera panned across a crowd of people demonstrating outside a supermarket, while the word "Live" blinked at them from the upper right corner of the screen. Soldiers in tactical gear stood between the angry crowd and the entrance to the store. Several objects flew through the air at the uniformed men.

"What is this about, Kace?"

"This is in LA. The grocery store is one of many that have closed because of the disruption to the food supply. Trucks aren't getting through. Shelves are empty. People are desperate and angry."

"How did this happen in just a few days?"

"EPA policies have finally begun impacting people where they live, taking us to the ragged edge of an energy crisis. What appears to be a terrorist attack on two large American refineries pushed us over the edge. A gas shortage. The West Coast is feeling it first."

"They're firing, Kace."

"I can't watch this." She turned away from the screen, burying her face against his neck.

Brock couldn't stop looking at the scene. It held him spellbound with horror.

The shooting stopped. Several civilians lay motionless on the ground, blood pooling around them. The soldiers still pointed their weapons at the crowd, a crowd now pushing and shoving in panic-filled retreat.

The media had, in effect, broadcast a snuff video. Radical Islamists did this sort of thing, intentionally, to terrify. But why did the U.S. news media? And why had they shown it to the viewing audience with no warning about graphic violence?

Only one reason came to mind. The government had wanted it, maybe ordered it, to intimidate others into compliance with the administration's policies, policies now moving rapidly toward martial law. The message was clear, resist and you die.

KC wrapped her arms around Brock and leaned against him. "We shouldn't be surprised." Her words came wrapped in a hoarse whisper. "Shooting a few people seems like a heavy-handed response until to you compare it with wiping out a million people using a weaponized, genetically altered virus. Before you came in, I heard Hannan has already invoked martial law in several metropolitan areas."

So he was right. Brock seethed inside, his stomach cramping into a huge knot. "I'm with Allie. I want to kill that dirty little s—"

KC slapped her hand over his mouth. "I agree, but don't say it, Brock."

He took her hand in his strong grip and slowly removed it from his mouth. "Excuse me. I think I've got a blog post to write."

KC studied him, frowning.

Brock peered deeply into her eyes, wanting to read her response to his question. "Kace, are you ready to help me when they try to shut me down?"

"I've got a plan, but I still need a day or two to implement it. And I hope there's another computer in this house, because I'll need to spend a lot of time online each day to keep your blog going."

"KC ..." Allie's voice came from behind them.

KC turned toward Allie.

"There's a laptop on the counter in the kitchen. It's plugged in and a little blue light on it is blinking."

"Thanks, Allie. Hopefully, we're in business. But, Brock ... let me read your post before you publish it, please."

Always looking out for him. KC didn't like to see him out of control. "Don't worry. I'll keep it clean ... unlike Hannan's vocabulary."

"Be sure you do or it's *you* I'll be throwing into the canyon this time."

Allie's cell rang, playing a familiar old love song. "It's Jeff. Pray for good news. We need some."

KC's hand reached for Brock's.

Brock thought of Julia in Guatemala, so full of life and love for the Mayan children. He took KC's hand, pulled her close to him, and listened.

"Jeff, how's Julia?" Allie sucked in a sharp breath. "Oh, no ... But what about you? ..." She waited, listening intently to Jeff's news. "Hold on while I tell them." Allie looked from KC to Brock. "Julia coded in ER. She seems to be stable now. They've got her quarantined in a special room. St. Charles is talking to CDC, demanding vaccine from the government to save Julia and stop an outbreak here in Oregon. And ... they've quarantined Jeff and kept his truck."

Brock draped his free arm around Allie's shoulders. "Tell Jeff not to worry. KC and I will take care of you."

Allie gave him a weak smile. "Thanks."

A loud voice came from Allie's cell. "I want to talk to Brock. Now, Allie."

Brock pulled his arm from Allie's shoulders and put his palm next to her cell phone.

Allie's brown eyes welled as she dropped the cell into his hand.

"You there, bro?" Jeff's voice.

"Yeah. I'm here."

"I'm counting on you."

"Don't worry. After tonight I owe you one, maybe three or four. We'll keep Allie safe until they let you go."

Jeff's voice grew soft. "What if they don't?"

"We'll keep her safe for as long as she needs us."

Jeff sighed. "Brock ..."

Silence.

"Yeah?" Brock waited.

"What if Hannan's army comes after you and KC?"

"Can anyone there hear you, Jeff?"

"No. I'm in an isolation room. They watch me via video, but the camera's at the far end of the room, and it doesn't have a microphone."

"Okay, listen. If things start looking dicey here, KC and I will make a run for it. We'll find another place to hide. Allie will just be Julia's friend, housesitting for her. Nothing more."

"Thanks, bro. You're the best. But you guys need to pray for Julia. It's touch and go right now. Without the vaccine ... well, it doesn't look good."

"We'll pray, Jeff." He handed the cell back to Allie.

She put it to her ear. "... Love you too. Take care, sweetheart ... Call me when you can."

KC whispered into Brock's ear. "Jeff's questions didn't cover all the bases."

"You thinking of one in particular, like—"

"Like what do we do if you or I develop symptoms?"

"There's nothing we could do, KC. If we go for help, we're dead. We don't go, we're dead anyway. Don't wanna think about that right now. I think I'll go write that blog post while I can still feel my fingers around Hannan's neck."

KC set the TV controller down. "I'm angry too. But please be careful, Brock." She wrapped both her hands around his and held it near her heart while she looked into his eyes. "It's not just you. There are three of us in this house."

"Yeah. I know, Kace. But there are some things I need to say to Mr. Hannan ... and to the world about him."

Chapter 15

Hannan's Vice President, James Boring, had paled, then bailed at the first mention of Hannan planning to over stay his second term. Boring had lived up to his name, indicating he would resign if events began to test his queasy political stomach. He was a liability Hannan would have eliminated by now, but his replacement would be the ambitious President Pro Tem of the Senate, Hank Redding, an opportunist who would sell out his own mother for a shot at the White House. And, as vice president, one carefully aimed shot was all it would take.

Abe Hannan rolled his chair around to the front side of his desk in the Oval Office. Placing his shoes on the presidential seal woven into the carpet, he sat facing the three men in the room. They were his inner circle for the work of securing his hold on the government and the nation.

Attorney General Randall Washington, the only African-American in Hannan's cabinet, and Secretary of Defense Gerald Carter, a sixty-something political veteran, sat on the couch on his right side. Super geek, Mitchell Dell, Whitehouse Cyber Security Coordinator, and youngest member of the group, sat alone on the couch on Hannan's left. The rest of his cabinet knew they were outsiders looking in at the inner circle. But they had no idea what lay inside that circle, at least not yet.

Randy shoved a sheaf of papers at him. "Brock Daniel's latest post. You'll want to read this."

Hannan took the papers, looked at the title, skimmed the article, then focused on the last portion.

He's our modern-day Nero, playing golf while America burns.

I seldom quote Shakespeare, and never anything from Macbeth. But, today, the old bard's words seem fitting. Hannan's just a walking shadow, a poor player that struts and frets his hour upon the stage and then is heard no more— his words a tale told by an idiot, full of sound and fury, signifying nothing, nothing unless we allow his words to define our future.

Fellow Americans, we cannot allow that.

As you look ahead to tomorrow, what do you see by the dawn's early light? Is it the star spangled banner still waving? She may wave for a while yet. The larger question— what does she wave over? "O'er the land of the free"? Hardly. What we see around us is no longer the land of the free. How about home of the brave? That's the salient question, the question you have to answer.

If your answer is yes, then join me as, once again, a group of American patriots declare our firm reliance on the protection of divine Providence, and mutually pledge to each other our lives, our fortunes, and our sacred honor in order to secure our independence.

We must do whatever it takes. Sacrifice whatever is needed. If we do not, fellow countrymen and women, then it's good night America.

So what's it going to be for you? Reveille or Taps?

May God grant you wisdom as you choose this day whom you will serve, Abid Hannan, or our Creator and the people of this once great nation.

May God bless and protect you all.

Your voice in the wilderness,

Brock Daniels

Abid Hannan? How had Brock Daniels learned his birth name? Only his father and mother knew the ethnic origin of "Abe." Hannan's anger grew until hot lava spewed out his mouth in a string of profane, derogatory names."

Randy scanned the faces of his peers. "Daniels sure got the sound and fury part right."

Hannan shot his Attorney General an angry glance. "Mr. Daniels will feel my fury and eat his words, even if it's the last thing this president does." Hannan continued to curse Brock Daniels and his ancestry.

Mitchell Dell winced at his words.

"Don't flinch from the truth, Mr. Dell. Daniels is all that and more. Can't you see he's inciting open rebellion? I want him tried for treason." But Hannan decided not to draw attention to the use of his birth name. He would not offer any explanation, simply let it pass as a slur.

Randall Washington nodded. "Yes, he's probably given us enough to indict him for treason. But he's also rallying the people, and this guy's good. When I first read it, he almost had *me* in tears."

"I'll have you in tears if this right wing nutcase isn't—"

"Pardon me for differing with you, sir." Gerry Carter shook his head. "This guy is anything but a nutcase. He knows exactly what he's doing, and he's very effective."

Hannan shoved an open hand at Carter. "Which means?"

Mitchell Dell cleared his throat. "His last blog post had five million hits on just the servers we counted."

"What do you mean by 'the servers we counted'?"

Mitchell sat up straight on the couch. "He's popping up on servers all over the place, using numerous existing blogs. We've shut some of them down, but somehow his posts continue to rank high with all the major search engines. Anybody who wants to find him can ... at any time. And we don't know where he'll pop up next."

117

"Then shut the search engines down." Hannan wadded up the printout and slammed it down on the Presidential Seal. "Shut them all down, starting with Google."

Attorney General Washington cleared his throat. "Mr. President, you don't want to do that. Right now people are— well, the one's that aren't looking at Mr. Daniels—they're looking at you as their savior ... your vaccine, trying to keep law and order, promises of reviving the economy. That could all turn on a dime if they believe it was you who cut off their source of information."

Hannan turned toward his Cyber Security Coordinator and waited until the man's eyes acknowledged Hannan. "Can you stop him?"

Mitchell Dell slumped in his seat on the couch and looked down at the floor. "Not right away. We'll keep after him. If we find a pattern to his posts, we can eventually put him out of business."

Gerald Carter leaned forward, placing forearms on his knees. "Our best bet is to go straight for the source. Capture Brock Daniels, interrogate him, and dispense with him, once and for all." Carter looked up at Dell, sitting across the coffee table from him. "I suggest you throw all of your cyber resources into trying to locate Mr. Daniels. When you find him, I'll send some of my special forces after him—a black operation."

Hannan watched Mitchell, looking for any sign of reticence. The leader of the nerds had, at times, proved to be a gutless geek. "Mitchell, can I count on you to handle this task of finding Mr. Daniels?"

"May I use NSA and—"

Hannan swore. "Use whatever resources you need, and tell any reluctant geeks that you're acting under my direct authority. Just do it, Mr. Dell, and let me know the second you find him."

Chapter 16

At noon, Brock sat at the desk in the study, staring out the window at the front yard. The July mid-day sun beat mercilessly on the grass, turning the edges of Julia's lawn brown. The sun slowly, inexorably, incinerated the grass while Hannan's political inferno did the same to Brock's country. He pulled his hands from his laptop keyboard, leaned back in the office chair, and stretched.

Today was July 5 and the past five days at Julia's house had been a blur of activity.

Late in the evening of July 2, the second day at the house, Brock and Allie had driven to the Super Walmart in Redmond. Brock bought a cell phone that wouldn't broadcast his location via GPS, and Allie had filled their grocery list.

On day three, Jeff called. Allie said he sounded bored, but he did have good news. Julia was holding her own, maybe getting a little better. An unconfirmed rumor, making the rounds at St. Charles Medical Center, said that some high-ranking official had ordered the CDC to give her the vaccine. If so, Hannan probably knew about it.

Just having Hannan think about Bend, Oregon and Julia, only an hour's drive away, sent shivers down Brock's spine. He prayed Hannan's people wouldn't link Julia, KC, and him.

July 4 had come and gone with only Brock's patriotic blog post to celebrate. Hannan's address to the nation had obviously been meant to give hope to the people. But the man had no real hope to offer, unless he offered to resign.

Today was day five in Julia's mansion and the study had become his and KC's work room. He'd given her the choice of desk, table, or one of the chairs. KC took the biggest easy chair, leaving Brock at the desk, facing the window to the front yard.

It was probably a good thing to have KC sitting behind him. Just having her in the room was distracting enough. She preferred to lay crosswise, knees bent over one arm of the chair, with her computer in her lap. In another ten or fifteen years she would feel that in her back.

Ten years. Where would they be? *Would* they be?

Right now, KC was beautiful and barefoot, in dark green shorts and a light green tank top. But her relaxed posture had changed a few minutes ago. She'd started performing a post.

KC had managed to post all of his blogs using some clever tricks. She created a long list of existing, but abandoned, blogs. When he finished a post, she would upload it to three or four blog spots, using her Internet savvy to ensure that each post ranked high on the search engines' lists. It had worked, and readers seemed to be finding his posts easily via search engines.

Brock's right wrist was killing him from hours of pointing and clicking with little rest. For the remainder of the day, he would abandon the desk and sit in a comfortable chair to write his post out on paper. After finding a thick notepad and some mechanical pencils in the small desk, he moved to the recliner, near KC.

She had swiveled into the chair seat and now sat upright, rigid, as if one errant key stroke or mouse click could end in disaster. KC needed a break, but he couldn't tell *her* that. She wouldn't listen. At best, he could start a conversation that slowly drew her away from her stressful work.

Brock leaned toward her and tapped her shoulder. "Kace, how many hits are we getting today?"

KC glanced his way. "Your posts are on multiple servers, so I can only estimate the hits. But I wrote a script, which I have to tweak daily, to give us a rough estimate."

"Are we up to two million yet?"

She looked at him again and smiled.

KC had no clue how that affected him. Maybe someday he could tell her, if they survived Hannan's power play.

"Would you believe fifteen million hits yesterday? Maybe being the Fourth of July helped. The worse things get the more hits you get. You don't realize how much power Brock Daniels wields these days, do you?"

He focused on the notepad in his hand, leaned back into the big chair, and finished the sentence he'd been writing. "You know what they say about the power of the pen."

"You mean pencil." KC stood and approached him.

It had worked. She would at least get a short break.

She sat down on the arm of his chair. "I know you haven't wanted to do this, Brock, but I think you should allow blog comments. You know, give people a way to contact you."

He looked up at her. "Seriously, Kace, how do I respond to ten million comments a day?"

"You don't. Not individually. Somewhere in your post you can thank people categorically for their comments. But what if somebody wanted to contact you with information you really needed to know?"

"Even if they did, we can't go looking for a needle in a haystack every day, a needle that may or may not exist."

"Let me worry about that. I'll write a Perl script to filter the comments. It may take a little tuning, but I think it could become an important source of information."

"You're on that laptop at least sixteen hours a day. When do you have time to write this Perl script?" Brock shook his head and returned to his writing.

"If we allow comments, I would work on the script after ... after you kiss me goodnight."

He looked up.

KC studied him. She was reading his mind ... or trying to.

"But I haven't—"

"Exactly. You *haven't*." She laid her hand over his. Hers was trembling.

"Brock, we don't know if we're going to be alive tomorrow. This isn't the time to be holding back words, hiding feelings. I see Allie waiting for Jeff, worrying while they're apart. And we're here, together—" Her voice broke. KC turned her head and wiped her cheeks. Then she was back, waiting.

He looked away. There were issues. First there was the letter, then there was the girl, rather the woman, sitting beside him, the one he didn't deserve. He turned his hand over and curled his fingers around hers.

"Well, are we going to allow comments on your blog or not?"

An intentionally loaded question. He looked at their interlaced fingers. Then at KC's face. "Yeah."

"Yeah, what?"

"Start the comments."

"Good. I already have ... well, as soon as you give me your next post."

"So how long until the comment filtering script is done?"

"It's already written." She gave him her impish grin, the one he'd first seen thirteen years ago.

"What am I going to do with you?"

"Brock, you don't have to do anything with me that you don't want to do."

"I've only done something I didn't want to do once. I watched you turn and run away seven years ago."

KC's grin had vanished. Her eyes stared at the wall, with a blank expression on her face, the look he'd come to recognize as fear.

Brock stood. "What's wrong, Kace?"

"Will you just hold me for a minute?" Tears welled and flowed down her cheeks.

He pulled KC into the big chair with him and waited. She would tell him when she was ready. She always had.

With her face against his neck, she struggled to stifle her sobs. "I'm afraid that ... I ... I'll make a mistake and get us all killed. It would only take one slip while I'm hacking blog servers and they could trace me."

"We all know what we're doing isn't safe. You always take too much responsibility on your—"

"Brock, I went back to the last server I'd transferred your post to." She pulled her head from his neck and wiped her cheeks. "It was just a feeling I had ... that I should check. When I did, there was a strange process running. I logged in as super user and studied it for ... probably for too long. Several times this process accessed the HTML and cgi-bin directories of the webserver. It had also opened up a port and communicated through it to another server. I traced the communications to an IP address located in Maryland. I think Hannan has NSA looking for us, and I might have just encountered them."

"Not good. But is there any way they can trace you to our location?"

"I hid behind other computers to disguise my location, but we're talking about NSA. If they throw enough resources behind their effort, it's only a matter of time until they locate our router and identify this house. Just like he did with Senator Richards, Hannan will kill you, he'll kill me, and he'll kill Allie who isn't even involved in—"

"But I am involved." Allie's voice came from the doorway to the study. "If I wasn't before, I am now."

Brock released KC and they both turned their heads toward Allie.

She waved him back to KC. "Brock, keep holding KC. She needs it. She's been carrying too heavy a load." Allie's voice was commanding, and her eyes blazed with fire.

He draped his arm around KC's shoulders and held her.

"Hannan is a monster." Allie continued her rant. "I've been watching the news while you two were here working. Today the CDC declared the outbreak an epidemic. The food shortage caused by the gas shortage has people rioting all across the nation. A third of the country's population is now under martial law and Hannan's flying troops back to the U.S. from overseas as fast as he can to enforce the expanding martial law. We've forgotten our allies and most have turned against us, even Israel, because we're no longer trust—"

"You've made your point, Allie. So, what do we do now?" He looked from Allie to KC sitting beside him.

Allie clenched her fists and stared at him. "I want you and KC to keep doing what you're doing until they force us to run and find a new place to hide."

Brock gladly broke eye contact with Allie's intense brown eyes and focused on KC. "What do you think?"

"I'll take more precautions. Try to remain anonymous when posting blogs. That's when we're most vulnerable. But we need to know if our router is being accessed. That's the signal to run. I'll turn on router logging and set up a utility to pull the router log in real time. I can run a Perl daemon on the laptop to monitor IP addresses. The daemon will look for our NSA friends—anyone in DC, Maryland, or Virginia."

"What if they come in from some other area?"

"My kludge of a system wouldn't detect them."

"Kace, if it *did* detect them, how long would it take you to ID them?"

"We'd know, or at least suspect who it was, within a couple of minutes."

"Hannan could put a team of special ops troops on a Gulfstream from Georgia and they could be landing at Redmond in a little over four hours. They could be breathing down our necks in less than five."

KC shook her head. "They could be breathing down our necks in two hours if they came from Joint Base Lewis-McChord."

He hadn't thought about Lewis-McChord. "Okay, then we need an emergency evacuation plan that gets us out of here and well hidden in one hour."

KC's eyes widened. What had she thought of now? "Brock, if Hannan wants us badly enough, we could be under satellite surveillance within minutes, or under air surveillance from a nearby airport in less than an hour."

Again, KC was a step ahead of him. But there was a way around this danger. "Satellite surveillance wouldn't detect us at night. I don't think we've deployed infrared satellite surveillance that can detect people. Those satellites can only see rockets, fires, big sources of heat. So, Kace, only upload my posts at night then, if you're detected, it'll happen at night"

"That means we'd be escaping under the cover of darkness. Brilliant, Mr. Daniels."

The look KC gave him contained a lot more than mere admiration. It completely destroyed his concentration. "But

... uh, Hannan's got a lot of other things to worry about besides us. Surely he won't take any extreme measures."

"If he wants to look like a savior to the people, he can't have me running loose, telling people what he's up to. I know too much, Brock. And so do you. He'll take any extreme measures he thinks are needed. If his people locate us, he could have police helicopters from Bend hovering over us in less than an hour. And *their* sensors *would* pick us up at night."

KC was right. Hannan could use the police, the military—any local or federal government resources to find and apprehend them. "Okay. Our plan needs to get us a safe distance from this house and hidden from any surveillance in less than forty-five minutes. Any ideas?"

Allie, who had been silent for the entire technical discussion, cleared her throat. "I have one.

* * *

As KC anticipated, blog comments started flowing in immediately after she turned on commenting for Brock's posts. People were thanking Brock and begging him to continue giving them hope in what they described as their darkest hour. Some called it the nation's darkest hour.

If we still have a nation.

Near the end of day six in Julia's house, KC's Perl script had nearly finished its run, when text scrolled across the script's window, displaying three blog comments. She copied the text directly from the window into a file on her laptop. Now, log off this server, ASAP. Good. She had gotten in and out with no signs of detection.

Her approach to comment collection was risky, because KC had to return to the servers where she'd uploaded Brock's posts, each time exposing herself to possible scrutiny and detection. If she didn't go back after several hours elapsed, they might miss important comments. But going back doubled or tripled their exposure to NSA, or whomever Hannan had sicced onto them. There had to be a better way.

Modify the script and schedule it to run automatically, as a cron job. Then have it spit the comments out as an obscurely named html file in the webserver's HTML directory. She could visit all the servers from her web browser and view the harvested comments. No logins. No file transfers. She would just be one among hundreds of thousands of people visiting the web site, reading Brock's blog.

KC raised her hands high. "Eureka!"

Brock gave her a curious glance. No, more than a glance. He was ogling her.

She stared at him until he returned the stare. "So ... satisfied with what you saw, Mr. Daniels?"

He looked away. "Kace, what's gotten into you lately? No. Don't answer that. Just tell me what Archimedes found."

"What *did* he find, Brock? Surely *you* know."

"Well, he discovered the law of buoyancy. But—"

"And I just discovered the law of boy see."

"What?"

"B-O-Y as in you, Brock Daniels. You ogled me. Seven or eight years ago you would have threatened to punch a boy out for looking at me like that. What gives you special privileges where I'm concerned?"

"Because I ... because I'm ..."

"When you can answer that question without tying your tongue in a knot, then maybe you've earned some privileges."

"Changing the subject, Kace ..."

"I could have predicted that." KC's gaze dropped to the floor and she folded her arms.

* * *

Brock had hurt KC again. But giving in to what she wanted would, in the long run, hurt her even more.

He shoved the troubling thoughts aside. "Seriously, what do you think about Allie's last-ditch-escape plan, hiding in the Ranch Chapel? It's a big facility. Probably a lot of hiding places."

"We can't even plan to do that until someone talks to the pastor, finds out if we can trust him—that'll be risky—and sees if he's willing to hide terrorists." She looked up at him. "I can't be seen on the ranch, so that's up to you."

"Okay. But the chapel only works if we can climb down to ranch level. So, first, I want to try the spot we picked to get off the escarpment. The wild goat trail we saw suggests it's climbable."

"Climbable for goats, you mean."

"Are you saying a goat's a better climber than me?"

"Well, yes. The ones I saw in National Geographic climbed places people couldn't go without ropes and pitons."

She must be trying to irritate him. "Come on, Kace, this is just one little escarpment, not K2 or Everest."

"One little *400-foot* escarpment."

He chose to ignore her comment and avoid an argument. "I'll time myself on the descent. Then, from the base of the cliff, it's only about a six or seven minute walk to the Ranch Chapel. If I can climb down in eight minutes, we can make it to the chapel in about fifteen. Faster if we run."

"Assuming nobody gets hurt on the climb."

"You're just a little ray of sunshine today." Brock regretted the cryptic tone of his voice the moment his words slipped out.

KC didn't reply. The shock and hurt on her face said it all.

She had practically begged him to tell her how much he cared for her. He had dodged her question and then made his sarcastic remarks while she was hurting. As kids, the trust between them had always run deep. Her face said it had just grown shallow. Probably not enough left to keep him afloat.

But something ran deep. Whatever it was, KC, sitting in her chair staring at the floor, was drowning in it.

"I'm sorry, Kace. I didn't mean—"

"I want you to listen to me carefully, Brock." Her voice grew soft, almost inaudible. "I never thought I would be saying this. Not to you." She sniffed, wiped her cheeks, and raised her voice. "If there was anyone else here who could fill in for me, I would leave, Brock. I wouldn't be here after today."

Her words hit him like a blow to the head from a heavyweight boxer, the kind of punch that puts another boxer down and out. But even a dazed Brock Daniels knew better than to approach a ticked off KC, especially when ticked off had morphed to hurt deeply and angry.

He wanted to wrap her up in his arms, tell her he loved her, beg forgiveness, plead insanity—anything to remove the torment and tears from her face.

But she unplugged her laptop and left with it tucked under her arm, walking down the hallway toward her bedroom, wiping her eyes with her free hand.

He couldn't feel any lower than right now.

Correction. Allie stood in the doorway of the study glaring at him. "Brock Daniels ..." Allie crept toward him, with an index finger pointed at his face. "I don't know what you did to that girl, but if you know what's good for you, you'll march down that hallway and undo it." She stopped in front of him waving that finger in front of his nose. "Have I made myself clear?"

"Yeah." He backed away, afraid the accusing finger might actually poke his nose. "But, Allie, I didn't realize—"

"Well, now you do, so fix it!" She whirled and strode out of the room.

Now what? The two other people in the house hated his guts. The present administration, law enforcement, and the military, all wanted him dead. Not a good time to write an uplifting blog post.

Who was he kidding? How could he lead a grassroots effort to take back this country when his life was a total mess? He needed KC or he couldn't do this, and he needed her for a lot more than her technical abilities.

When KC cooled off a bit, he would approach her. But what could he say? He hadn't a clue, but the insanity plea was looking better all the time.

After twenty minutes of hearing Allie banging things around in the kitchen like she was doing a major remodel, Brock made his move before Allie showed up in the study with a frying pan in her hand. He pulled a large sticky note off the pad on his desk and wrote in large letters, "INSANE" and stuck it on his forehead. Brock took a deep breath, exhaled slowly, then headed down the hallway toward KC's room.

Chapter 17

When Brock's hand reached for the doorknob to KC's room, the door flew open and she stepped out, bumping into him.

"Oh. It's you." She stepped back and her eyes focused on his forehead. KC stifled a giggle.

That was a good sign. "Someday, Kace, I promise to tell you why I acted insane today, but I need to get my sanity back first."

"That was lame, Brock. Even for you it was totally lame."

He circled her with his arms.

KC didn't move away. She didn't move at all.

He pulled her close.

She let him.

He kissed her forehead.

"Back to that stuff again?" She whispered. "You could aim a little lower, you know."

KC had offered herself, unreservedly. He couldn't accept. Not now. Instead, he sought words that were true but without promising things he couldn't give and didn't deserve. "Kace, I need you. I can't do this without you, not just because of the technical stuff. Unless you're with me, I just don't have the heart for it."

"So, Brock Daniels is finally admitting I have a place in his heart?"

"Yeah. So deep that it scares me to think about losing you." He pointed to the sticker on his forehead. "Makes me go insane."

Another giggle slipped out. "You're not off the hook yet, Mr. Crazy Man. But I need to tell you something about the blog comments."

"Okay. But you do realize you're changing the subject?"

"Temporarily. Brock ..." She took the sticker off his forehead and stuck it on hers. "I did something really stupid. I was angry, not thinking about anyone but myself, and I contacted someone."

Taking risks that could impact others. This was not like KC. She would risk her own life and limb, but ... "What kind of someone are we talking about?"

"Someone who left three blog comments for you, all containing veiled requests for direct communication. One provided a slightly disguised phone number."

"Got any ideas who this person might be?"

"I did some simple checking on the Internet. The phone number was for a cell phone recently purchased somewhere around Fort Benning, Georgia."

"A military dude? Maybe he's one who still puts some stock in that oath people take when they swear in." Brock's mind sorted through a dozen different scenarios. Two-thirds or more were threatening.

Her free hand found his. "I know. You're worried. I can see it in your eyes."

"Shouldn't I be?"

"Listen. This person, more likely a group of people, is somewhere in Central California, moving northward. I heard on the news today that a group of men broke into the Fort Irwin Ammunition Supply Point a couple of days ago. That's in the desert east of Barstow. They took ammunition and class A explosives." KC stopped and waited.

"Might be related. But, Kace, this person, or group, could be coming to help us or to kill us."

"Brock, Fort Benning is the headquarters of the 75th Ranger Battalion. You know, Special Forces, Rangers. They sometimes conduct joint training exercises near Fort Irwin. Like you said, maybe these guys take that oath seriously and have broken away from a bad commander, like the Commander-in-Chief. Rangers are capable of training a whole battalion of locals. What I'm saying is maybe we have the makings of an effective resistance force."

"So what do you think we ought to do? They could be coming to take us out, to take us into a bloody insurgency, or ..."

"I know it's a risk. But there's only one way to find out, Brock. Here's the cell number. Do you want to text them, or should I?"

Chapter 18

Just when Hannan thought they had contained the hemorrhagic fever, it seemed to be surging out of control, even after he'd relaxed all restrictions on distribution of the vaccine.

Something strange was happening with this genetically engineered disease. Pondering the possibilities made his skin crawl.

Hoping his Health and Human Services Secretary could explain the recent outbreaks, Hannan asked her to attend the first part of a meeting with his inner circle, in the Oval Office.

Dr. Patricia Weller was a slender, attractive, single, middle-aged doctor who had gotten involved in politics shortly after she completed her residency. She was now a veteran politician that Hannan trusted, for the most part, a woman who evidently did not like geeks. She sat as far away from Mitchell Dell as the couch on the left side of the office would allow.

"Ms. Weller—"

"Patricia, please, Mr. President."

"All right, Patricia. What's this I hear about a case of Ebola in Oregon? A case we evidently treated."

She had no problem meeting his gaze. A woman with confidence. He liked that.

Patricia nodded. "I did authorize a young woman to be vaccinated. She was brought into emergency at St. Charles Medical Center in Bend ... that's Central Oregon. She coded in ER, but they stabilized her, recognized the symptoms, and called the CDC, begging for the vaccine. The CDC called me."

"Please answer this for me, Patricia. Up until this time, the spread of this disease has followed a pattern that wouldn't lead me to believe someone in Central Oregon would contract it. Not at this time. The worst possible scenario is that real Ebola—" Hannan stopped when Ms. Weller's eyebrows raised.

Real Ebola. He had said more than he intended in her presence. A serious blunder. "Did you determine how she became infected?"

"Maybe *you* should tell *me*?"

A snarky remark? So his miscue hadn't gone unnoticed. "No ..." He softened his voice, "... Patricia, *you* tell *me* what you know about her."

Ms. Weller folded her arms across her chest. "Alright. It seems she went on a short-term mission trip, chaperoning a church youth group. About two weeks ago, the group worked with Mayan villagers in Central Guatemala."

Hannan's mouth twitched at her last two words. He faked a smile to cover it up.

But his Health Secretary had been studying his face. Her sagacious smile said she had read his reaction and had developed her own opinion of it.

Now, he had two choices. Trust her or kill her. Maybe there was a third alternative. He would have her monitored for a while, then make the decision. "Thank you for your help, Ms. Weller. You're excused."

She turned toward the door that Randall Washington already held open.

When she stepped out, Randy closed the door and locked it. He gave Hannan a long, questioning stare.

Hannan waited until Randy sat down. "Call the hospital in Bend, Randy. Find out everything they know about the girl. Don't let them stonewall you with patient's privacy excuses. Use my name if you need to."

Hannan turned toward Mitchell Dell, seated alone on the couch, as usual. "*You* will get me the names of everyone on that mission trip to Guatemala. Tell the State Department the President needs the information." He paused. "Something smells rotten here and I want it dealt with. Report back to me in thirty minutes. You too, Randy." Hannan shot the Attorney General a glaring glance. "Do you both understand?"

The two men nodded.

"Okay. That means we all meet back here at 2:30 p.m."

What were the odds of KC Banning—the KC Banning who knew far too much—being last seen precisely where an unexpected, but quickly diagnosed and treated, Ebola infection had occurred? An infection caused by the genetically altered virus. At least he hoped it was the created version of the virus, or his whole plan could be jeopardized, along with a million more lives.

The clock in the Oval Office displayed 2:28 p.m. Three of the four men were seated in their usual places, but where was Dell? The geek must be having problems with the State Department.

Impatience with Mitchell Dell sent Hannan's fingers drumming out a snappy, anapestic rhythm on his desk.

At 2:29, the White House Cyber Security Coordinator stepped into the room and locked the door behind him. He wore an annoying smirk on his face.

So, he thought he had good news. But, Randall Washington also displayed a crooked smile. Maybe things were finally looking up.

Hannan waited until all were seated. "You seem happy, Mitchell. Would you care to share some of that with the group?"

"Certainly." Mitchell Dell sat up straight on the couch. "Four adults accompanied ten teenage kids on a mission trip to a village near Chisec ..."

Chisec. Hannan flinched when he heard the location. The landing strip, the clinic, both lay only a stone's throw from Chisec. No American tourists should have been allowed near the clinic.

Dell continued. "... the married couple, Jeff and Allie Jacobs, live near Redmond. The young lady who got sick, Julia Weiss, lives between Redmond and Bend, and the fourth adult chaperone was ... Brock Daniels."

Daniels! Hannan swore, rose to his feet, and paced across the Oval Office. He stopped on the Presidential Seal. "Daniels knows far too much. But—"

"Mr. President ..." Randy stood, "... the young lady who is recovering from the disease, had helped a sick child, one who had gone to the clinic near Chisec."

"Too many coincidences!" Hannan couldn't restrain his anger. Everything seemed to be going to blazes in a hand basket. Or it would if they couldn't stop Brock Daniels and catch Katheryn Banning.

"I'm afraid there are more coincidences." Randy leaned forward on the couch.

Hannan started to swear again, but swallowed his words when he noticed the confidence on Randy's face. Hannan leaned back against Oval Office desk. "Go ahead."

"As I was leaving my office to return, one of my assistants handed me the FBI report from the agents who interrogated several people who knew Katheryn Banning and her deceased parents. It seems that, as a child, Ms. Banning spent a lot of time each summer on Crooked River Ranch, just north of Redmond, Oregon. She had a childhood friend then, a very close friend ... Brock Daniels."

Hannan pounded his fist on his desk. "They're working together, somewhere in Central Oregon. We stop them and our plan is on track. Mr. Dell, have you had any luck locating the source of Brock Daniels's blog posts?"

"Some. We know that someone has very cleverly posted them and hidden themselves while doing so."

Hannan's frustration became a knot in his gut. "That *someone* is Katheryn Banning. I'd stake my life on it."

Dell continued. "This person was careful until they went back to a couple of servers and spent a little too much time on them. We were able to trace them back to the originating router. It's in a house just west of Crooked River Ranch. Some of my people located it about an hour ago."

So the FBI had searched the ranch but neglected to look outside the ranch. A mistake Hannan would not allow again. They should already have Brock Daniels and Katheryn Banning in custody.

Defense Secretary Carter, who had been silent for most of the meeting, cleared his throat. "Give us the location and I'll have a team of Rangers from JBLM in their backyard in two hours."

Hannan shook his head. "No, Gerry. We've already used the military far more than we had planned. People are getting nervous about that. I think it would look better if law enforcement officers arrested these criminals. Let's use a police SWAT team with helicopters—any resources they need, from ... what is the nearest large city?"

"Bend, Sir," Mitchell Dell said.

"From Bend. Tonight while they're sleeping. They should take the prisoners to a remote area in the vicinity, where they will hand them off to a black ops team, with an embedded interrogation expert, a team I authorized and which is already in Oregon. Once we learn how much Banning and Daniels know, and what their plans are, they will be killed trying to escape. I want you to oversee this effort to its completion, Randy. And let me know the minute they are confirmed dead."

"Mr. President ..." Secretary Carter leaned forward on his forearms. "... you realize there will be a steep price to pay. Brock Daniels is loved by millions and is considered a patriot."

"Then perhaps we should change that perception before we kill him. Anyone have a suggestion?"

Randall Washington stood and paced behind the couch where he'd been sitting, pinching his chin and staring at the floor.

Hannan watched Randy and waited.

He stopped and looked up at Hannan. "I have a suggestion. We will expose the *real* Brock Daniels. Certain writings will be found showing clearly that he is a white supremacist whose hatred, not his patriotism, fueled his desire for a larger platform to indoctrinate the masses. And now he's involved with that terrorist, Katheryn Banning."

That could work if they planted the right evidence and carefully revealed it, building a thoroughly condemning case against him. And dead men cannot defend themselves. Neither can their dead friends.

"Splendid. Do it, Randy. And show that the DOJ has had a file on Mr. Daniels for months, because of the evidence you are about to create. We'll cut off most of the negative reaction to his death before it occurs."

"What do we do with Jeff and Allie Jacobs?" Randy asked.

"They are the dead friends I referred to. Interrogate them, and then they should have an unfortunate, fatal accident."

Chapter 19

As Brock and KC walked down the hallway from her bedroom toward the study, he mulled over the possible contact she had mentioned. For as long as he had known her, KC's gut instincts had been right on target. If she was right this time, they might soon have some help in their effort to give CPR to a dying USA. But, if she was wrong ...

KC hooked her arm through his. "I don't know what else to do but to contact these people, and pray they can help us."

She looked up at him, studying him. The soft, longing look in her eyes said she had forgiven him, but was not yet satisfied with the state of their relationship.

Playing the role of dearest friend was killing him while ripping his heart to shreds. KC obviously wanted much more and would soon either explode in a fiery eruption or stuff her feelings until her heart broke, permanently. It was a lose-lose situation.

"Well, what do you intend to do?"

Running away to Canada with KC was growing more attractive by the minute. But they would probably never make it across the bor—

"You didn't answer my question." She looked up at him, dazzling Brock with her green eyes.

Time to get his head back into the game. "I'll text them, Kace, but I don't want to do it from the house. There's no GPS on this new cell I bought, but the FBI could still estimate our position from the cell towers around us. Why don't you and I drive about fifteen or twenty miles away, a little south of Redmond, and do our texting from there? If they detect my call, it will give them a big area with a lot of city in it to search."

"You go. I should stay and monitor the router, just in case."

"Then I should leave now." And get away from her questioning eyes that were driving him to distraction.

Ten minutes later, Brock approached Terrebonne on Northwest Lower Bridge Way. The risk of being spotted on Highway 97, where there had been roadblocks a few days earlier, stopped him a quarter-mile short of the highway. He pulled off on the corner of Northwest 19th, cut the engine, and pulled out his cell.

Brock unfolded KC's printout of the blog comment containing the ten digits they believed were a phone number. He entered the numbers and then entered part of the blog comment to help validate himself as the author of the text message.

He held his finger over the send button, then stopped. The second guessing began, fears that he would endanger everyone. The what if's continued, assaulting him until he recalled KC's words, "There's only one way to find out, Brock."

He sighed, pressed send, and prayed.

In less than a minute, he received a reply.

Is this B. Daniels?

B4 I answer, 2 whom am I speaking?

Captain Craig, 75th Ranger Reg. Have my det with me.

He was tempted to celebrate, but suspicion doused his enthusiasm. The supposed captain had revealed a lot in those ten words. Why would he do that? He could be spoofing, revealing information to gain trust.

Brock would proceed, but with caution and without full disclosure of the location of Julia's house.

Do U want 2 RV with B. Daniels?

Thought you'd never ask.

Being cautious 4 various reasons.

Understand.

Call me on voice when U reach OR border.

Already in OR.

I-5 or 97

97

Call me when U reach Sunriver and will give U RV pt.

Roger that. Calling from Sunriver in approx 4 hrs.

Four hours. A little after five o'clock Craig would reach Sunriver, then another ninety minutes to the ranch. The Rangers, if that's who they really were, could arrive as early as 7:00 p.m. And, so far, Brock had not disclosed their location. Cell tracking using towers could only place him near a point fifteen miles from Julia's house. It was the best Brock could do to protect them, at this juncture. If this turned out badly, they would still have enough time to run.

Brock started the engine and drove his truck back to the house.

He found Allie standing by the kitchen sink, staring out the window that overlooked the ranch, below.

Near Allie, KC sat working on her laptop at the breakfast table.

When Brock entered the room, KC stood, her eyes asking him a thousand questions with one glance. Then her expression relaxed and a smile stretched those full red lips across her incredible face. As usual, KC read him well. She pulled Brock into a warm embrace. "I knew it. Finally, some good news."

He tilted his head down, she looked up, their faces now only inches apart. "How do you do that, Kace?"

"What?" She whispered.

"Read my mi—"

"Brock Daniels, you idiot." Allie's voice. "Kiss her. Then give us the details ... about the phone call, I mean."

This wasn't the time to argue with Allie. It wasn't a time to let KC down again. And he had the perfect excuse to do what he'd wanted to do since the first moment KC had walked into his motel room a week ago.

Her kiss, the sweetness of KC's soft lips, her body pressed against his—nothing like the brokenhearted kiss of a fourteen-year-old girl. This kiss came full of promise, passion, and a sense of inevitability, like the fulfillment of some ancient prophecy. And Brock Daniels would not be the one who ended this kiss.

Eventually, KC broke it off. She pulled her head back and peered into his eyes, while Brock studied hers.

Eyes full of surprise, cheeks pink, and breathing heavily, she looked like he felt. Like, maybe they should try that again.

When Brock pulled KC closer, an irritating alarm sounded. KC's laptop screen lit up.

"Someone's on our router, Brock." She slid from his arms and sat in front of the laptop.

Allie's cell phone rang. She pulled it from her shorts pocket.

It took only two seconds to turn cloud nine into complete chaos.

Brock moved behind KC, looking over her shoulder, "What have we got?"

"I'll tell you in a minute. Let me locate their IP address." She pasted a string of numbers into another window. "I'm querying the DNSDB ... Brock it's coming from—darn it! The machine froze. I'll have to reboot." KC pushed the power button and took the laptop down hard.

Allie slipped her cell into her pocket. "That was Jeff. The results of his blood work just came back from the lab, and they cleared him. He could be home in a couple of hours."

"That's good news," Brock said.

KC looked up at him and Allie. "I only glimpsed the IP address before the laptop froze. I think it was from the general DC area, but I'm not sure where. To be safe, we've got to assume they've found us and that Hannan will send someone. Probably soon."

"Kace, it's only 2:00 p.m. here. When do you think they'll come, today or tonight?"

"I'd bet tonight. It gets dark around ten o'clock. Sometime after that."

"Okay. Now for my news. The guy I texted says he's Captain Craig, commander of a detachment of Rangers. They're in Southern Oregon, headed up Highway 97."

In a split second decision, Brock bet everything on the Rangers and rolled the dice. "I'm calling Craig, now. We have no choice. Maybe they can tell us what to do. According to what he said, they should be here around 7:00 p.m. our time."

"Jeff should be here around four or five o'clock, unless he has problems getting approved for discharge. We'll have another person to help us," Allie said.

Or one more person to hide.

Brock redialed Captain Craig's cell, on voice this time.

He answered on the third ring. "Hello. This is your friendly blog commenter."

"Craig, the router here was just compromised by someone in the DC area. We're expecting some unwelcome guests, soon."

"Doesn't surprise me. It was only a matter of time until they sicced NSA on you. We're just north of Klamath Falls, coming in two motorhomes and an SUV that we borrowed from friends. Is there an RV Park nearby?"

"Yeah. There are two on Crooked River Ranch. But what about the folks coming to visit us?"

"What's your assessment, Daniels?"

"They're not just gonna shoot rockets and kill us. We believe they want to interrogate us first."

"Okay. I have two ideas. The one we actually invoke depends upon who comes to arrest you. You'll have to trust me to spring the appropriate trap. It's best that I not tell you more at this time."

The cramp forming in Brock's stomach tightened. "You're asking for a lot of sight-unseen trust."

"I guess I am. But the operation—let's call it Operation Spoof—if it works, we can begin to divide and conquer."

"Whatever that means." By trusting Craig, he could be getting everyone killed. Now, everyone included Jeff. "And how do I know you aren't spoofing me?"

"Because I took an oath to defend the Constitution. It wasn't an oath to obey the Commander-in-Chief when he violates it. And I swore to fight against all enemies, foreign and domestic. I think the CIC is of the domestic variety."

"Okay, we'll wait until nine o'clock. But, if anything happens before that, or if you're lying, our blood is on your hands. If you're lying, and I'm still alive, I'm coming after you, Craig. Do you understand?"

"Loud and clear, Mr. Daniels."

When Brock ended the call, he looked up into KC's questioning green eyes.

She shook her head then stared at him like she questioned his sanity. "Do you realize you just promised to go after a special ops guy, someone trained to kill you in at least four dozen different ways?"

"Yeah. But he got the message that I would go after him, Kace ... you don't look impressed. So, it wouldn't worry you if I were coming after you?"

"Brock Daniels promising to come after KC Banning? I would be totally impressed." Her lips curled into her coy smile before she returned to her laptop. "Bring it on, Brock. But you might get more than you bargained for."

He would get exactly what he wanted. But could he do that to KC? Every time he asked that question, war broke out between his heart and his head. After the events of this day, Brock wasn't sure which would win.

Brock and KC moved back to the study to work. But he hadn't gotten anything written since Allie incited that kiss. He doubted that KC had either. For nearly five hours they had played a game of hide and seek with their covert glances, each pretending not to notice the other stealing mental snapshots.

Watching KC, laptop in hand, stretched out across the easy chair, barefoot in her green shorts and tank top, was far more pleasant than wondering who Hannan would send after them and when his goon squad would show up.

Brock's cell phone rang. The time on his cell was 7:30 p.m. and the caller ID displayed Craig's number.

"Daniels, we're passing through Sunriver. Had some holdups. A flat tire and needed gas."

"So you'll be here about nine o'clock?"

"That's the plan. But we'll go directly to the ranch and park our RVs. Call if anything happens, otherwise, see you a little after nine o'clock ... once you tell us where you are."

"All in good time, Craig."

By 9:00 p.m., the sun had set over the Cascades. Several small wildfires on the eastern slopes of the mountains provided enough smoke to turn the western sky blood red. Brock hoped it wasn't prophetic of the evening's events.

The low rumble of an engine sounded from the front of the house.

"It's Jeff, finally." Allie scurried to the front door.

Jeff burst into the entryway, wrapped his long, strong arms around Allie, and kissed her. After the second kiss, she pulled her head back.

From thirty feet away, Brock recognized that flash of fear on Allie's face.

Jeff held her shoulders and smiled. "It's okay, hon, I'm clean. No Ebola."

Brock gave them a few minutes alone, then briefed Jeff on the detection of the router and the imminent arrival of Captain Craig and the Rangers.

Jeff's smile had long since vanished. "So, we were detected. You know, the arrival of someone other than Rangers might be imminent, bro. Down the ridge a couple of miles, a helicopter landed in a field. I couldn't see it very well as I drove by. It was about 300 yards off the road, behind some trees. At the time, I had no reason to be suspicious. But now ..."

"Did you see a logo or anything indicating who it belonged to?"

"Sorry. All I know is the color was dark. Dark blue, maybe black."

"Brock ..." KC's hand came to rest on his arm. She looked up at him with fear in her wide eyes. "They're already here. I think it's time to call your Ranger friend."

"Yeah. Guess it is. Listen up, everybody. Roundup what you need in case we have to run for it." Brock hit Captain Craig's number in his call log.

One ring, two rings ...

"I'm sorry, but the person you called has a voice mailbox that has not been set up yet."

Chapter 20

KC grabbed the small pack containing the few belongings she'd brought to Julia's house and returned to the kitchen where Brock stood with his cell to his ear, pacing the floor.

He yanked the phone from his ear. "Blast it!"

She wanted to put a hand on his shoulder, to hold him, something to show concern for the man she loved. KC stepped to his side instead. "He's not answering?"

"I think Craig turned off his cell. There are at least a dozen reasons he might do that and eleven of them aren't good."

Allie and Jeff strode into the kitchen carrying their bags.

Jeff's frown deepened. "Bro, you don't think the Rangers are coming, do you?"

"I don't know. But we've only got about three options here." Brock rubbed his chin and stared at the wall as if the answer to his dilemma was written on it. "We can run for it in our vehicles, but they're out there somewhere in the area. We'd be spotted and caught. That would leave us farther from the Rangers and maybe dead."

"Is hiding in the chapel still an option?" Allie asked.

"Not a good one." Brock dropped his phone into his shorts pocket and plopped into a chair at the breakfast table. "The chopper landed too close, meaning whoever came in it is too close. If we tried to go down to the ranch, they'd spot us from the ridge and we wouldn't be hidden, just trapped."

KC looked at Jeff and Allie both anxiously fidgeting, but holding hands. She looked at Brock's hands on the table and started to reach for them, then stopped. "I vote for staying here, out of sight in the house, and waiting for the Rangers."

Brock stood. "All in favor of KC's suggestion."

All four raised a hand.

"I'll try Captain Craig again at about ten o'clock."

After fifteen minutes of nervous chatter, Brock pulled out his cell phone. "I'm calling Craig now." He keyed in the number and put the phone to his ear. "Same message. His phone is off. Well, it looks like we're on our own."

"No we're not. Somebody's out there," Jeff pointed toward the kitchen window. "Someone just activated the infrared sensor on the patio light. I saw him jump back behind the trees when the light came on. He had a rifle."

To think that Hannan's people were on the property, armed, coming for them, sent KC's heart racing.

"Great." Brock shook his head. "We don't have anything to hold them off with. Anybody know if there are guns in the house?"

Allie pointed toward the stairs. "There might be. I looked yesterday. There's a gun safe in the master bedroom, where I've been sleeping. It has a funny kind of lock on it. And a scanner thingy."

"Well, that scanner thingy means we probably can't open it to see if there's a gun inside," Brock said. "And that rifle Jeff saw is probably an automatic. That's what we need."

The wild look in Brock's eyes turned KC's racing pulse into panic-filled pounding.

"It's what we need, and I'm going to get us one."

Brock's final words sent a jolt of electricity through her. "You're not going out there, Brock. No way."

He circled her with his arms. "Kace, I've got to. At least we would have a fighting chance."

This was crazy, but she could read his eyes. Brock was serious. KC slipped from his arms. "Over my dead body you're going out there. Don't make me fight you, Brock." She looked at Jeff. "Grab him, Jeff. And ..." KC pulled out a frying pan from the cupboard. "I'll brain you before I let you get yourself shot. Maybe it'll knock some sense into you."

Brock leaped to her right, sprinted through the kitchen door, and hit the light. The kitchen went dark. He flung open the door leading to the garage, circled an SUV parked there, and disappeared into the darkness.

KC chased after him. She had to reach the side door to the garage before Brock went out. If he made it outside, she would never see him again. Not alive.

She rushed into the garage, closing the kitchen door behind her.

The small door on the far side of the garage creaked.

Too late. He was outside.

If Brock was going to die out there, he wouldn't die alone. KC scampered across the garage, dropped to the floor, and crawled out the door onto the landscaping rocks lining the side of a large concrete patio.

Brock wouldn't have gone to her left. His body heat would trigger the patio light. A fatal mistake.

A movement to her right. Another straight ahead.

Ahead to her right, a shadowy figure rose from the rock landscaping and stood. Brock's profile stood out dimly against the stars.

Directly ahead of her, another figure turned, swinging a long object around toward Brock.

Brock's body twisted, then shot forward.

A thud sounded. Then a grunt.

The person ahead of KC dropped to the ground.

Brock ran and pounced on the fallen man.

Movement erupted from trees and bushes further out on both her left and right.

Whether Brock got the gun or not, someone would shoot him. A few feet to KC's right, near the side of the garage, the silhouette of a large boulder blotted out part of the night sky.

Brock scooped up what looked like the man's weapon, then sprinted toward the garage.

The belching of automatic weapon fire broke the silence. Light flashed to her left.

Brock dove to the ground. He landed only four feet from KC.

She grabbed his arm and yanked.

Brock swung the rifle wildly at her head.

She ducked. "It's KC." She jerked Brock's arm again.

Off balance after his wild swing, he landed beside her in the temporary shelter of the rock.

"Sorry, Kace. Didn't mean to—"

More gunfire. Bullets ricocheted off the rock, whining through the air. Others thwacked against the side of the garage.

"What were you thinking, going after them with just a rock?" KC whispered. "I ought to kill you."

"Then I wouldn't be here to cover you. Kace, I'm going to pull this trigger in a minute. When the gun shoots, stay low and get into the garage as fast as you can. Hide behind the SUV parked there. Stay behind the wheel, if you value your legs."

"No way am I leaving you, Brock. Never again. Get that through your thick—"

Bullets shattered small rocks near them. They both hugged the big rock as rock fragments peppered the garage wall.

"I spotted the two shooters by their gun flashes. Go, KC. Before any others arrive. I've got you covered."

Brock was right. But who would cover him?

KC took off when he sprayed the shooters positions with a long burst. She dove through the garage door and crawled on all fours behind the big SUV, parking her body behind the driver-side front wheel.

Another burst of gunfire sounded, then stopped. Brock must've run out of ammo while trying to cover himself.

KC prayed he would make it. Prayed more intensely than she could ever remember.

When the small garage door opened, the staccato barking of the automatic rifles lasted for at least fifteen seconds. How could Brock *not* be hit? Then she realized he was kneeling beside her.

His arm circled her waist and pulled her tightly against him.

Tears filled her eyes and streamed down her cheeks. She pulled his head against hers. "Are you okay, Brock? So help me, you better tell me the truth."

"I'm all right, Kace. Truth is, I almost, uh, you probably don't want to know ..." There was almost a chuckle in his voice.

"How can you joke when—the real truth is, I'd kill you right now, Brock Daniels, if I didn't—I care about you ... more than you realize."

"It's a fine time for bringing up that subject, KC."

"I'm not sure any time would be fine with you. Now, how do we get back into the house without getting shot?"

"Follow me. They can't see us and they're not going to rush us when they know I've got an assault rifle."

"Brock Daniels. Katheryn Banning. Toss your weapons outside and come out with your hands up." An amplified voice sounded from somewhere near the front of the house.

KC followed Brock through the door and into the dark kitchen.

Several bright lights hit the house simultaneously, coming from different angles. The entire area around the house was nearly as bright as day.

A man's voice repeated the amplified message.

Brock fiddled with his gun, popped out the clip, and replaced it with another one he pulled from his pocket. "Just loaded my last clip."

Crouching low, Jeff and Allie moved into the kitchen from the great room.

"You two fools okay?" Jeff asked. His voice sounded a bit shaky.

KC blew out a blast of air. "I'm okay. The fool with the stolen assault rifle can speak for himself."

"Seriously, bro? How did—"

KC broke in. "How do you think, Jeff? He took out a guy with one of his hundred mile-per-hour fastballs—a three-pound rock—and then stole his gun."

"I'm all right, Jeff. And, Kace, it was just another rattlesnake."

Tears came again at the reminder. Brock had saved her life once more. But this one had been coiled to strike Brock, not her.

Evidently Allie noticed her reaction. She gave KC a quick hug. "Now what do we do?"

"For the next few minutes, we're probably safe. But after that ..." Brock shrugged.

"I don't think they'll be anxious to rush us after Brock took out one of their men, and then stole an assault rifle." KC said.

The bull horn blasted another message at them. "Throw out your weapons and—" the message stopped. Several of the spot lights went out in a span of three or four seconds.

"Something's happening out there." Brock said. "Let's just sit tight for a few minutes until we know—"

A different voice came from the bull horn. "Daniels, this is Craig. The area is secure. We need to talk."

"Is this Operation Spoof?" Brock's voice took on his rarely used sarcastic tone. "How do we know you aren't one of them, Captain Craig, if that's who you really are?" "

"Okay. Mr. Daniels, in about sixty seconds, take a peek at your front yard."

Chapter 21

Brock crept to the left side of the drapes covering the living room window.

Two hands clamped on his shoulders like vise grips. "Don't even think about opening those drapes and putting your head in front of that window." KC's voice of authority, a voice she seldom used.

"I'm not exactly stupid, Kace."

She huffed a blast of air. "Not exactly, but close."

"Well ..." Jeff moved toward the window. "Somebody needs to look out there."

Allie grabbed his arm. "But it's not going to be you, Jeff."

Brock had to do it. He had consented to communicate with Craig, so this whole situation was his responsibility. "Make sure all the lights in the house are off. I'll go into the last bedroom down the hall and see what Craig is up to. He won't know which window we're using, so I'll have enough time for a quick look."

The four scattered and soon the house was dark.

Brock hurried down the hallway and positioned himself beside the bedroom window. A tug on his shirt told him KC had followed him.

"Daniels …" Craig's voice came through the bullhorn again. "My team just risked their lives for you, and you still don't trust me? That hurts, bro."

"Not as much as that ammo in your assault rifles would hurt me," Brock whispered as he crouched beside the window in the bedroom. He felt for the corner of the drapes. KC's hand clamped on his wrist. "Let me do it, Brock."

"Not gonna happen, Kace." The thought of a bullet ripping into KC felt like a knife in his stomach, hara-kiri. It's what he would feel like doing if he let anything happen to her.

Brock pushed the edge of the drapes back until a narrow gap revealed lights outside. When he slid his face forward, KC gasped.

He pulled his head back. If he was right about what he'd glimpsed, some of the SWAT team had restraints on their wrists and others lay on the ground. It appeared one was getting CPR. "Craig's men have the SWAT team under control."

"So we're safe?" The tone of her voice said KC didn't feel safe.

"Safer than we were fifteen minutes ago. I'm going out to talk with Craig." Brock waited for a protest.

It didn't come. Was KC conceding? She would bear watching. KC's desire to protect, something she'd had as long as Brock could remember, was getting out of hand. Probably because she felt responsible for their predicament.

Brock took KC by the wrist and held her tight enough so she couldn't pull her arm free. He led her into the great room where Jeff and Allie joined them.

After he parked KC beside Jeff and Allie, Brock moved to the entryway door. "It looks like Craig's telling it straight. They've got the SWAT team under control on the front lawn."

He turned the doorknob and slowly pulled open the front door.

Craig's silhouette in front of the lights remained still. His hands hung by his sides. All good signs.

Brock walked out the door.

Footsteps sounded from the porch, behind him.

"It's the Banning girl." A voice came from one of Craig's men.

Brock turned, saw KC, and tried to cut her off.

She shook her head and glared at him.

Trying to stop her was futile. He stretched out a hand. She took it.

He pulled her close. "One of these days, Kace, you're going to listen to me."

"Tell me what I want to hear, Brock, and I'll listen."

Her remark was *way* off the subject.

You gotta stop ignoring her comments, Dude. Maybe for her it's the main subject.

He thought staying alive was the main subject.

To KC, knowing that you love her might be even more important.

This was no time for a schizophrenic attack from the right side of his brain. But Brock had a sudden urge to kiss her. That would really impress the Ranger commander, wouldn't it?

Still holding KC's hand, Brock turned and walked toward Craig.

"Daniels, what's with you two?" Craig moved his hands to his hips. "We have urgent business to discuss and you're ... well, look at you."

Brock needed to change the subject.

A body dressed in SWAT team gear lay on the front lawn, while two Rangers worked on him.

Brock pointed at the downed SWAT team member. "It looks like someone got hurt. Are they giving him CPR?"

"Yeah, CPR. He really needed a defibrillator. But they're too heavy to carry." Craig glanced at the man on the ground. "His heart went wacko. Almost stopped."

"Where did you find him?" KC's voice dropped to her soft alto—feminine and alluring.

Just thinking about her voice in those terms told Brock he was still a distracted fool.

Craig motioned toward the corner of the garage. "We found him near the bushes on the garage side of the house. You know what happened to him?"

"I know he got hit in the chest by a two-pound rock going a 100 miles an hour. I also know Brock could've pitched in the majors."

"He's coming around." The man administering CPR stood.

Craig pointed a finger at Brock. "You attacked a SWAT team member with a rock?"

"Yeah. We needed the gun. Got one too."

Craig studied Brock's arms and shoulders. "I thought you were a writer, not a warfighter."

Brock shrugged. "Back to the subject at hand. Now that you've got them, what are you gonna do with the SWAT team?"

"Daniels ... these men aren't our real enemy. They were just doing their job, following orders."

"Yeah. Orders to kill KC and me." Brock wasn't ready to pardon anyone on the SWAT team after the shots they'd taken at KC and him.

"It's time to ..." Craig paused and glanced toward the house. "Can you and I go inside for a moment?"

"Do it, Brock," KC said. "We need to hear his plan. The longer we stand out here, the more danger we're in. Somebody's going to wonder what happened to their SWAT team and will probably pay us a visit to find out."

Craig studied KC for a moment. "Something tells me you would make a good Ranger."

KC met Craig's gaze. "The way things are going, something tells me I might get the chance." She walked across the lawn to the house and opened the door. "Come on in."

Just like that, KC had taken over, made the decision, and implemented it. And he had let her. She was beyond smart, had good instincts. Though it scared the heck out of him when she was in danger, he should probably let her lead more than he'd been doing.

Brock followed the two inside, closing the door behind them.

Jeff's and Allie's anxious eyes stared back at Brock.

He gestured toward Craig. "Meet Captain Craig, U.S. Army Ranger. Craig, this is Jeff Jacobs and Allie, his wife."

Jeff shook the man's hand.

Allie simply nodded to him.

"This is quite a crew you've got here. Two beautiful women and two obvious athletes. Wait a minute ... Jeff Jacobs." Craig rubbed his chin, then pointed at Jeff. "Decathlon, 2012 Olympics. Was that you?"

"It was."

"Two *incredible* athletes. So, you four, unarmed—well, to start with unarmed—were holding a SWAT team at bay when we arrived?"

KC hooked Brock's arm with hers. "We couldn't have held out much longer with one assault rifle and only two clips."

"Maybe it's a good thing for the SWAT team you didn't run out of ammo and start throwing rocks again." Craig gave them his easy-going smile, a smile that exuded confidence and seemed to build it in those around him.

"Craig, you never called us back after you got here. How did you find the house?"

Craig's smile came again. "It was the only house in the neighborhood with a firefight going on in the back yard."

KC gave Brock a corner-of-the-eye glance. "Duh."

"Daniels ..." Craig grinned at him. "Do you always let her insult you like that?"

Brock looked at the impish grin on KC's face. If he could look forward to seeing that face every day, he'd let her do more than insult him. But he wasn't going to tell Craig that.

Brock shook his head and stuck out a thumb toward the front yard. "So what's the plan for the SWAT team?"

"As I said, the administration's the enemy, not those guys. But if we can't restrain them, they'll give us a major headache. So, we invoke Operation Spoof."

Craig was trying Brock's patience. "That's about the fifth time you mentioned this spoof gig. Would you care to elaborate?"

"Yes." KC said. "I'm rather curious how you'll dissuade a group of men, armed to the teeth, men with orders to capture or kill Brock and me."

Craig looked from Brock to KC. "I'm going to tell them the truth, just put a little spin on it, increasing the FUD factor."

KC frowned at him. "A military acronym? Does that involve some four letter word?"

Brock grinned. "If it does, Craig, she'll slap you silly."

"Fear is the only four letter word; fear, uncertainty, and doubt—FUD. I'm going to tell them that there's some sort of coup going on in Washington. It's the truth. I'll say the channels of communication have been compromised."

"I can testify to that," KC said.

"And I might ask you to. Then we tell them the chain of command is being violated so that we don't know who's telling us what."

KC nodded. "That's partially true. But, you know, if any orders are coming from Hannan, we'll know it because—"

"That's the part I won't tell them. Instead, I'll get them to agree to obey no orders that jeopardize the lives of American citizens, because that could be enabling the coup. In addition, it's morally and constitutionally wrong. I'll advise them to sit in a holding pattern until we can make sense out of what's happening. And I'll tell them to leave Brock Daniels and KC Banning alone."

KC's twin frown lines deepened. "But I've been declared a terrorist."

"And according to Hannan, I'm preaching treason," Brock said, still arm-in-arm with KC.

Craig nodded slowly. "I understand your concerns. If they don't buy the spoof, we'll let you two talk to them, telling enough of your story to show them that you're innocent."

"What if they still don't buy it?" KC pursed her lips.

"I was afraid you would ask that. In that case—"

KC cut him off. "Do I really want to hear this, Craig?"

"Probably not. Let me just say Rangers don't kill innocent Americans, no matter how deceived and misled they are."

The tension left the muscles in KC's arm. She sighed. "That's all I wanted to know. We can't stoop to Hannan's level."

"And we won't." Craig's eyes glanced repeatedly at the door. Obviously, he was anxious to get outside. "But, we will defend ourselves as necessary. With most of the country under martial law, my men, and some others like them, plus you two, could be the USA's last hope. I've got a plan that I need to talk to you about, later. But for now, let's go outside and use Operation Spoof to neutralize a SWAT team. And you two stay behind me until I motion you to come alongside."

Brock slid his hand down KC's arm and took her hand. They followed Captain Craig out the front door.

Immediately, several lights hit them.

Craig stepped off the front porch and stopped. "Daddy-O, what's our status?"

A tall man in tac gear stepped in front of the group. "All accounted for and under control."

"And the downed ninja?"

"Heart's beating strong. He'll be fine," Daddy-O said. "But, sir ... the SWAT team's been getting comms like crazy the last five minutes. Someone wants to know their status."

"We don't reply," Craig said, then turned to Brock and KC, motioning for them to come alongside him. "We need to speed this up, because we could soon have another chopper overhead, and I'm pretty sure there won't just be a SWAT team on the next one."

Brock looked at KC.

Her wide eyes said she understood their growing danger.

"Captain Craig?" Brock leaned close to him. "How fast can you spoof?"

Chapter 22

What in the blazes did Captain Blanchard think he was doing in Central Oregon? He hadn't sent Hannan any updates since the Oregon Police SWAT team flew off in a chopper more than two hours ago. Were they still waiting for darkness on the West Coast? Had there been problems? Regardless, this growing drama surrounding Ms. Banning, and now Brock Daniels, had dragged on far too long.

The tension in his shoulders and neck had given Hannan a major headache. He leaned back in his chair, trying to relax, and propped his feet up on the Resolute Desk in the Oval office, while concerns about the two people he feared most continued to niggle.

He pulled open the drawer on the left side of the desk and picked up the phone stashed inside. The light indicated it was plugged in. Hannan keyed in the contact number for the commander of his black ops group.

"Captain Blanchard here."

"President Hannan. What happened to status every hour on the hour, Blanchard?"

"Sorry, sir. But I've been waiting too. The SWAT tactical dispatcher has the only direct contact with the team. But, Mr. President, there have been no comms for the past ten minutes."

He had a bad feeling about this. "Are there any problems?"

"No, sir. No *known* problems, and we wouldn't expect comms during the most critical part of the assault, anyway."

"At what point does 'no comms' become a problem?"

"Sir, if we don't hear anything in the next twenty minutes, I would interpret that as a problem."

Hannan swore. "How much trouble can it be for a trained SWAT team to apprehend two civilians who probably aren't even armed?"

"One would think it should be a simple operation, sir. Even a barricade situation with a weapon in the house wouldn't—"

"Captain Blanchard ..." Hannan cut him off, "If we don't hear something in the next fifteen minutes, I want your team to fly in and end this situation. Use whatever force you deem appropriate to eliminate the threat of those two escaping."

"Mr. President, 'whatever force' includes a transport helicopter with a special forces detachment onboard and a heavily armed Apache helicopter. People on the ground—the Central Oregon SWAT team and the two, uh ... perpetrators—could *all* be killed."

"If that's what it takes to stop Daniels and Banning, then so be it. This is a serious national security threat. Under no circumstances can we allow those two to escape. Do you understand? Under *no* circumstances?"

"We understand. I'll relay your orders."

"And I'll stay on the line until you do."

Another communication device squawked noise and spit static. "Apache 01, dispatch here. By order of the Commander-In-Chief, if you hear no comms from SWAT team CO in the next 15 minutes—that is by 0020 hours— destroy both targets on the ground, using whatever force deemed necessary."

Another voice came through the line, weaker and tinnier, after its relay through two microphones. "Apache 01 here, please confirm orders. If dispatch receives no comms by 0020, we are to ensure both targets are destroyed, even if it results in collateral damage, such as—"

"Yes!" Hannan yelled. "Blast it! Use your missiles if necessary. Do you understand?"

"Apache 01 here. Was that the CIC?"

"Dispatch here. Yes, Apache 01. The Commander-In-Chief. Did you copy?"

"Roger. Orders for conditional attack with assured target destruction came through loud and clear."

Chapter 23

Faint, in the far distance, over the murmur of voices on the front lawn, another sound reached KC's ears, the wop, wop of a helicopter's rotor. She knew Craig needed to win over the SWAT team using Operation Spoof, but if he didn't hurry, or didn't succeed on the first try, they could be in a literal world of hurts.

Craig positioned himself at the center of the line of men, the SWAT team seated on the lawn, and the Rangers standing behind them. "I want you to know this, SWAT team members, you have nothing to be ashamed of. There was no way you could have known you were flanked by a group of Rangers. I'm Captain Craig, commander of this detachment of the 75th Ranger Regiment. We're thankful everyone is safe. Now, who's your commander?"

No reply.

"Will the SWAT team commander, IC, or whatever he calls himself, please stand?"

A short, powerfully built man rose. "Deputy Ramirez here. I'm the team leader." The man stood still, as if at attention, staring at Craig.

"Remove Deputy Ramirez's restraints."

The Ranger standing behind Ramirez deftly cut the heavy duty ties from the man's wrists.

Captain Craig approached Ramirez and extended a hand.

Ramirez studied Craig's hand for a moment, then shook it. "Craig, you've got some explaining to do. We were sent here by—"

"I know who sent you. But there's something you and your men need to know, as it impacts everything we're doing out here, including the two good citizens standing behind me."

"Good citizens?" Ramirez spat the words back at Craig. "That's not what we were told."

"Nor us, Ramirez. But now we understand part of the why. The rest is still a mystery, a very curious and dangerous mystery."

"What mystery? Our orders, and the reasons behind them, seemed crystal clear."

"The problem is ..." Craig paused. "We don't know who any of our orders are actually coming from."

"What?" Ramirez's eyes widened.

"As we speak, there's a coup attempt in progress in DC."

"What the—" Ramirez swore loudly. "A coup? In the USA? And how do you know that?"

KC realized the chopper sounds had grown louder. No aircraft were visible in the half of the horizon she could see, but, the other half ... She needed to do something to speed up the spoofing. "Craig ..." KC moved alongside him. "We need to hurry here. I hear choppers in the distance."

"Men, this is KC Banning. She discovered a security breach, including a violation of the chain of command. Instead of kudos from POTUS, it got her branded as a murderer and a domestic terrorist."

Ramirez pointed at Craig. "But it was the President who declared her a terrorist. Are you saying that Hannan—"

Craig cut in. "Ramirez, I suggest you listen for a moment, before choppers swoop down and open fire on all of us."

Ramirez stopped his probing questions. "Okay. We're listening."

Craig gestured toward KC. "You've got the floor, Ms. Banning. But don't keep it too long."

KC gave the SWAT team a brief summary of the computer and communications breach, as well as the events that followed the murder of Senator Richards and her becoming number one on the FBI's most wanted list. She had to be careful about implicating Hannan. If it seemed unwarranted, it could break the trust that seemed to be growing between them and the SWAT team. "But though it seems like Hannan is involved, we can't be sure. Maybe he doesn't know who to trust either. In the meantime, I've got a suggestion." KC looked at Craig.

He stared into her eyes, shuffling his feet. As a commander, he wasn't used to giving up control, and he was probably worried about letting her take the lead at this critical juncture.

Finally, he gave her the open hand, go-ahead signal.

"Until we know who the bad guys really are, I say that we follow one simple principle. Do no harm to innocent American citizens. And we do that no matter who seems to be giving us orders. We must continue doing no harm until we've identified the coup members."

Ramirez gave her his intense stare, the one previously reserved for Craig. "Which means, for us?"

Brock stepped beside KC and hooked an arm around her waist. "Which means that the SWAT team, the Rangers, KC and I, as well as the other two civilians, are on the same team. If we keep fighting each other, I believe whoever is after KC will kill all the survivors of the fight."

Another member of the SWAT team rose to his feet. "And why should we believe someone who's been preaching treason?"

Two helicopters came into view near the Cascades to the west. One turned and headed eastward, directly at them.

Brock gestured toward the choppers still several miles away. "There's your reason."

Craig barked out orders. "Blaine, is that an Apache?"

If KC remembered correctly, Apache helicopters could hold enough armament to blow a small town off the face of the earth. Hopefully, this one wasn't armed to the teeth, but ...

"Listen to it." The man called Blaine paused for a moment. "I'd bet my life it is."

"We're all about to bet our lives." Craig turned to another Ranger. "Steve, get the RPG-7 ready."

"Sir, are you sure about that? The only way an RPG can stop them in time is—"

"I know, Steve. It's a long shot. No pun intended. But, we've got no cover here, so we don't have a choice."

Craig turned toward another one of his men. "Dan, give me the laser rangefinder. I need a precise firing distance if we don't want to become literal toast."

"Or Swiss cheese," Daddy-O added.

Craig shot Daddy-O a glance. "I was getting to that ... when the pilot sees the laser, he might start firing his M230, hence the Swiss cheese. Our shot needs to get there before that event, Steve."

"Understand, sir. Needs to arrive at, or near, RPG self-destruct range. That's 920 meters."

Craig turned to Brock. "Are there any large boulders nearby?"

"Only one. Around the side of the garage."

"You and Ms. Banning get behind it, and stay there. Now!" Craig turned back to the man resting a long, strange looking gun on the top of his shoulder. "Steve, I'll give you a ready at 2500 meters and the fire command at 1200. If you believe in prayer, I would suggest you start praying this works."

KC pulled Brock to a stop before they disappeared around the corner of the garage. "Craig, what if it doesn't?"

He shot her a glance as he raised the laser. "If the M230 chain gun doesn't get us, then the house, yard, and all of us disappear in a big fireball from a Hellfire Missile. But, behind the boulder, you two might survive."

Craig pointed the laser at the incoming chopper. "2500!"

A stream of gunfire started.

"1200, fire!"

A line of exploding vegetation rushed straight at them.

A bright flash from the front yard lit up the entire area.

Brock grabbed KC's arm and dove toward the boulder that had protected them from the SWAT team's assault rifles. But what bore down on them now made an assault rifle look like a Nerf gun.

Chapter 24

KC's breath blasted from her mouth when Brock landed on her. She drew a breath that sounded like asthmatic wheezing. She tried to move, anything to resume breathing, but Brock's body pinned her to the ground, covering and protecting her.

A flash lit the area.

A boom sounded.

The concussion shook her body. She finally drew a full breath.

No more shooting.

A brighter flash. Everything turned white.

The whine of the helicopter's engine stopped.

The ground shook from a deafening explosion that seemed never ending as the noise reverberated between the sides of Crooked River Canyon.

Still pinned by Brock's large frame, KC couldn't see the source of the light to the west, but the bright light had faded to a red glow.

A hush settled over them, broken only by the soft crackling of flames.

She could breathe normally now, but the pungent smoke, like that of a wildfire, burned the inside of her nose.

Several of the men cheered.

Brock raised his head.

She tried to pull his head down. It was a feeble attempt, because one of her arms was still pinned to the ground. "Brock, get off me, or so help me I'll ... I'll—"

"It's okay, Kace. Getting off now. Craig's men sound happy, so I guess we survived." He peered over the top of the rock.

KC pulled her legs and other arm free, then stuck her head up beside his. A small fire to the west burned in a spot directly on the line the helicopter had flown. Somehow, Craig's man, Steve, had brought down the chopper. Maybe all that praying had something to do with it.

Pain shot through her rib cage. Brock was a big, strong guy. She would probably have bruises after he landed on top of her. "Brock, I'm not a quarterback you can sack whenever you get a chance. That hurt."

He curled an arm around her shoulders." Sorry, Kace. Never sacked a woman before."

"Sacked a woman?" Despite the aches and pains and their precarious situation, KC almost laughed. "I should hope not, Brock Daniels."

"Should not hope what?" He pulled her to her feet. "Forget it. Come on. Let's hear what Craig has to say. I've got a feeling we need to get out of here, ASAP."

When she and Brock reached the rest of the group, Craig was speaking. He looked toward the fire then back at the men. "An Apache has a crew of two."

At his words the men became silent, staring at the place where two men had died.

Craig gave them a few seconds, probably to process the deaths of two American soldiers.

Who knew what the helicopter crew thought they were actually doing? Killing two terrorists? Intentionally supporting an evil commander-in-chief?

Ramirez shook his head. "It's sad that we had to kill two of our own."

"I wouldn't feel too badly, Ramirez," Craig said. "They're now meeting their maker, and I wouldn't want to be in their shoes."

Ramirez cocked his head. "What do you mean? They were just following orders."

The tall man Craig called Daddy-O spoke. "No. They were violating both their oaths of office and the U.S. Constitution by trying to kill innocent Americans. No matter how you slice the issue of Banning and Daniels—innocent until proven guilty, or, as I believe, completely innocent—those two are murderers, along with whoever gave them their orders. No trial for American citizens. That's not legal. And that Hellfire Missile they were going to shoot at us—they might be finding out about the real thing right now."

"Well said." Craig slapped Daddy-O on his shoulder. "But we just took out an Apache attack helicopter. Whoever sent it isn't going to be happy with us. We'll have more visitors soon and, as you just saw, they may have been coming for Ms. Banning and Mr. Daniels, but they don't give a rip who they kill in the process."

"Craig," Ramirez pointed to his men still in restraints. "What about my men?"

"As Mr. Daniels said, we're on the same team now, fighting for our lives. Free the SWAT team and give them their weapons."

Restraints were cut from each man.

Craig continued. "Now we need a plan to get away from this house, off this mesa, and down to the ranch. We can't rappel down the cliff, or we'd be sitting ducks."

"What about Jeff and me?" Allie stood behind Craig with Jeff by her side.

Craig turned toward them. "I assume that's your pickup in the driveway."

Jeff nodded. "It is."

"Well, they located this house while it was still light, so they can identify your truck. Don't drive it unless you want another chain gun shooting at you and your wife. I'm afraid you'll have to come with us until we figure out a way to get you home. Now, is there a way off this escarpment that minimizes our exposure?"

"Maybe," Brock said. "There's a deep notch in the escarpment about 200 yards north of here. An animal trail goes down it. I had planned to use it to escape the house if we needed to. Unless the chopper flies directly at the notch, they shouldn't be able to see us as we go down. But getting to a place to hide on the ranch is—"

Craig cut in. "You let me worry about that last part, Mr. Daniels." He paused for a moment, apparently considering Brock's suggestion. "You and Ms. Banning grab whatever you need from the house to continue your work and meet us at that trail."

KC hooked a hand around Brock's arm and yanked. They both sprinted toward the front door, while the others circled the house, headed toward the cliff.

KC bounded through the door, then trotted down the hall toward the study, where she'd left her laptop.

Brock followed close behind her.

As she stepped into the study, the realization that she had just come within a second or two of being blown off the face of the earth hit her like a blow to the head. Thoughts of facing death without knowing Brock's true feelings toward her created an emptiness that drove her to him. She had to know, now. "Brock?"

"Yeah." He grabbed his laptop's case.

She closed her laptop and unplugged it. KC fought to steady her shaky voice. "We were nearly killed." She coiled the computer cord around her hand. "We might not have much longer to live. There are things I need to know."

He dropped his laptop into its sleeve. "Kace, this isn't the time for—"

"But we might not have any more time." Tears now blurred her vision. "Just tell me what's wrong with me, and I'll try to fix it so you'll—"

"Kace ..." Brock whirled and wrapped her in his arms. "There's nothing to fix. I ... I ... want you just like you are." He kissed her forehead and released her. "Here, use my laptop case, since yours doesn't have one. I'll just use the sleeve for mine."

"You're doing it again."

"I'm sorry, Kace. But we've got catch up with—"

"No." She clamped a hand on his shoulder. "I might be dead fifteen minutes from now, and I don't want to die like this. I've got to know about you ... about us."

Brock dropped the computer case and held her again. "No matter what, I'll always love you, KC. I may not deserve someone like you, but I'll always love you."

His love was all she wanted. But what did he mean by not deserving her? What caused that kind of twisted thinking? Right now, she didn't have time to explore, or unravel it. Knowing he loved her, and always would, had to be enough.

She had always believed Brock didn't keep secrets from her. They talked about everything. But he evidently was keeping something from her now. She couldn't believe that anything Brock had done would make him unworthy of her. KC had trusted him completely since that summer they first met. But now, for the first time, something had begun eroding that trust.

KC sighed sharply, trying to blow out the disturbing thoughts, then slid her laptop into the shoulder case Brock had given her. She pulled the wireless router from a bookshelf, unplugged it, and stuffed it in the side pocket of the laptop case.

"Come on." Brock took her hand and pulled her toward the study door.

A familiar sound sent her heart galloping out of control. "Brock, is that a helicopter?"

Brock stopped moving. The room grew quiet except for the wop, wop of a helicopter rotor.

"Kace, let's go out the back door."

They left the study and rushed toward the rear door that exited from the kitchen. KC reached the door first and gripped the doorknob.

Brock grabbed her shoulder. "Wait. We've got to assume that chopper has nighttime surveillance capability. We don't expose ourselves if it's close enough to see us."

This was not a good development. She turned and looked up at Brock. "Then we might be trapped in the house while Craig and the others get away or ..."

Brock dipped his head. "Yeah, or ..."

Either scenario wasn't good. While Brock peered out the back door, KC prayed that the chopper would remain out of sight until they could catch up with the others. She turned one last time and looked behind them, checking to make sure they'd turned off all the lights.

Brock opened the back door and stepped out into the darkness.

With a whoosh and a roar, a large helicopter leaped up over the escarpment and bore down on the house, lighting the area around it.

Brock jumped back, banging into her. He yanked the door closed.

Had they spotted Brock and her? They would find out soon, unless it was another Apache attack helicopter. If it was, then she and Brock might never know. And Julia might never get to enjoy her recently inherited mansion.

* * *

The big helicopter's pulsating roar passed over the house.

Brock ran to the guest bedroom window and looked out.

The chopper circled the area where the Apache lay burning on the desert floor.

KC's chin slid onto his shoulder. "They're checking out the Apache."

"Yeah. We need to go now, Kace. Before they focus on the house."

They ran to the kitchen and slipped out the back door.

Trees had been planted along the ridge to serve as a windbreak. Beyond the windbreak were the sparse Juniper trees, providing some cover all the way to the deer trail.

"Let's use the house to block their vision as long as we can, then the windbreak. We'll go tree to tree after that using the Junipers. Ready, Kace?"

Sirens sounded in the distance. Probably local firefighters coming to contain the small, but growing desert wildfire.

"Let's get out of here, Brock."

They ran through the Junipers, dodging small bushes.

The chopper turned toward the house.

Brock pulled KC behind a large Juniper, praying it was dense enough to hide them. He circled her waist with an arm and held her firmly.

"I'm not stupid, Brock. I'm not going anywhere."

"Can't I hold you because I want to?"

"You're only doing it because it's safe to hold me here. You won't have to finish anything you start."

Her accusation cut him. The fact that she was right cut even deeper. But, at the moment, the helicopter was a bigger concern. "He's landing on the front lawn. As soon as he drops below roof level, we—"

"He's down, Brock. Let's go."

* * *

They caught up with Captain Craig and the rest of the group halfway down the escarpment, on a deer trail. KC thought it might be a treacherous descent in the dark, but deer weren't goats. These animals obviously knew what they were doing when they started using this path to go down to the ranch for grass and water.

"They just caught up with us." Daddy-O's voice came from somewhere ahead.

Craig moved to the back of the line of people.

"This chopper was bigger, Craig," Brock said.

Craig stopped them on the trail. "Did it have one main rotor, a small vertical one in back, and a wide body?"

Brock nodded. "That sounds like it. It circled the Apache, then landed on the front lawn. That's when we ran."

"It's a Black Hawk. And it probably has a special ops team onboard. That means we need to get to the RVs while the team on the chopper is examining the downed Apache and searching the house." Craig motioned toward the edge of the escarpment. "If they get to the ridge line and scan the ranch with their NODs—"

"Their what?" Brock asked.

"Nighttime observation devices. And twenty people running to the RV Park at 0100 is going to look mighty suspicious."

But there was a way to avoid that risk. KC pointed to a spot on their left, at the base of the cliff. "There's a trail through the trees that goes by a pond where Brock and I played as kids. I think there's enough vegetation to keep us covered all but the last two hundred yards to the RV Park."

Brock laid a hand on her shoulder. "She ought to know. KC used that trail when she adjusted the lie of golf balls. The old duffers never did catch her."

"Sounds good," Craig said. "When we get to the road, I'll cross with KC. She'll lead the way."

"What about the RV Park?" Brock said. "Won't your motorhomes stand out like sore thumbs? The park's probably empty after everyone left to protect their homes."

"The park was filling up when we arrived," Craig said. "I guess people are fleeing the violence in the cities to safer places. The ones who came here didn't realize they were coming to a war zone. We had to take the last two spots at the south end."

"That'll help," KC said. "We'll only have about a hundred yards to run from the trees to your RVs."

Craig stopped them at the bottom of the escarpment, near the road. "Blaine, scan the ridgeline for any Hannanis."

Soft laughter came from several of the Rangers in the group.

"We'll cross in fours, as long as you—"

"Two Hannanis on top at ten o'clock." Blaine spoke softly.

"Okay, everyone. Ease slowly behind the nearest vegetation, then don't move."

"Captain, they turned and walked toward the house. Disappeared over the ridgeline."

"Watch our 6, Blaine. I'm sending the first group across."

Jeff, Allie, a SWAT team member, and a Ranger scurried across the road, stopping under a dense stand of trees.

"Still clear, Captain."

In another five minutes the entire group had gathered under trees near the pond.

Craig pointed into the darkness ahead. "Lead the way, Ms. Banning."

A dark area, the pond, lay directly ahead of them. "First, we need to circle around the pond using the driveway to the golf course. From there on we'll be under cover."

"You've got our 6 again, Blaine," Craig said.

"Still clear. Haven't seen anyone since the two Hannanis a few minutes ago."

"Hannanis?" Brock said softly.

"Just a pun, Daniels," Craig said. "We use a similar word for the enemy in Afghanistan."

"I like it." Brock chuckled.

KC couldn't hold back a smile, despite their circumstances. Brock would make a good soldier. But she prayed he would never have to be one.

In another two minutes, KC led the group through the dense vegetation she had played in for several summers.

Blaine had their 6, which she deduced was their rear.

And, hopefully, she had their 12.

She sighed in relief as they approached the end of the trees at the road by the RV park. Being responsible for one's own safety was nothing like the burden of twenty people relying on you. How did men like Craig do that every minute of every mission?

KC held up her hand for them to stop. "There it is." She pointed to the motorhome a hundred yards ahead. "But what do we do when we all get there?"

Craig pointed at the open space ahead. "Let's worry about getting there first. Blaine, anyone on the ridge?"

"All clear, sir. But I can only see part of the area of concern from here."

"I'll be able to see it all once we're in the motorhome. You all know the drill. We cross in fours, but this time I'll go with the first group."

Blaine said he couldn't see all of the locations where Hannan's men might be hiding, watching them. Twenty people moving around at this time of night would bring their enemy down on them in minutes. KC's heart started its fear-induced acceleration when her group of four stepped from the cover of trees and began their run toward the two motorhomes.

Chapter 25

At 2:30 a.m. KC sat beside Brock on a large couch that also accommodated Jeff and Allie. Two large sliders made the living room of the motorhome feel large and comfortable.

A Ranger sat in the driver's seat, peering through the windshield, watching the ridgeline above him.

KC prayed the ranger would see no one on the ridge and that she could simply relax beside Brock for a while.

In a few minutes, Craig joined them, taking a chair across from the four. "Ramirez is a good guy now that he's seen the light. He's answering the comms from his dispatcher to keep the cops off our backs. So, here's our plan. We can't sit here with Hannan's Special Forces combing the area. Once it's daylight, they'd probably be able to track us. So, we leave at first light, dropping off Jeff and Allie near their house and the SWAT team near their chopper."

Allie's eyes widened. "But what do Jeff and I do if they come to our house?"

Jeff straightened on the couch. "And what about my truck?"

Craig listened intently to their concerns. He had a way of showing people their questions were important. He was a good commander, a good leader, and a good man.

"Allie, if they come to your house, you were just watching your friend's place while she was in the hospital, that's all," Craig said. "And about the truck, you left it because it won't start. And it won't, because we disconnected a cable when we arrived. Didn't want anyone getting away at that point." He paused for a moment. "But now we need a new hiding place and I'd like to stay on the eastern side of the mountains. Less population."

Jeff leaned forward, forearms on his knees. "I've got a cabin about an hour's drive south of here. It's near the base of Broken Top by the big Three-Creek Lake."

"Jeff," Brock said, "It's not really a cabin, it's a—"

"I know. It's an old trailer house. But it's clean, weatherproof, and private. Only one problem, no Internet access."

Craig's nod said he was interested. "Internet access is no problem. We'll set Brock and KC up with satellite access for their laptops. The U.S. Army will be your ISP."

"Hannan's army?" KC wasn't comfortable with that arrangement. "Military computing security specialists, NSA, using a military satellite link, isn't that a bit risky?"

Craig shook his head. "Not as long as you stick to protocols that are used within a web browser. Isn't that right, Commo Guy?"

The ranger sitting in the driver's seat swiveled around facing them. "That's about the size of it. It's more secure than where you were operating from the house."

"I'll take your word for it. My DISA experience didn't teach me much about what happens after the uplink to a satellite."

Craig looked at Jeff. "Are there any RV parks in the proximity of your cabin?"

"There's one a couple of miles from the cabin, near Sisters."

Craig slapped his hands on his knees and stood. "Sounds like we have a plan. We'll pull out just before sunrise, that's 0600. Jeff, you and Allie can use the bedroom in the back. You've got almost three hours to grab some sleep."

KC stood. "And Brock and I?"

"You're not married, Ms. Banning. You get the living room. But I'm guessing you'll both be on the park's Wi-Fi the rest of the night."

"They have Wi-Fi here?"

"Sure do. It's not secured so no posting blogs tonight. Just to be safe."

After Jeff and Allie left for the bedroom, Brock and KC pulled out their laptops and connected to the Wi-Fi.

KC went to a news site. Tonight, she and Brock were conspicuously absent from the headlines.

"If the comments are any indication, my last post had a lot of hits, Kace."

"That's great. You and I aren't on the front page today. I guess that's good too. It looks like some metropolitan areas are stabilizing with FEMA supplementing the food and water supplies, while the military's throwing undesirables and looters into those prisons they deployed."

"National Defense Authorization Act, the subsection on counter-terrorism lets him do that. If he declares any of those people terrorists, he can detain them forever, with no right to charges, a trial, a lawyer—"

"Enough. Don't remind me. That's probably what he has in mind for us."

"Kace ... I don't think we'll survive what he has in mind for us."

"I've got enough on my mind without—I'm sorry, Brock. But I do need to devise a better scheme for posting your blogs. One that is nearly impossible to trace back to our location."

"Make it a scheme that permits daily posts." Craig's voice came from the passenger-side front seat.

"Why daily posts?" She wondered what Craig had up his sleeve. He'd only implied that he had some plan.

He slid out of the passenger seat and took another at the dining table on the edge of the living room. "Because I've got a plan that just might save this nation. But it won't work without you two."

"Of course we'll help." KC sighed. "But seriously, like how can a blogger, a so-so hacker, and one detachment of Rangers take over the United States when the president has the entire nation under martial law and is dead set on killing us?"

Craig grinned. "Because it's not just you two and a ranger detachment. How about adding some Navy SEALs?"

"How do you know we can trust anyone, especially if they're trying to contact us?"

"Someone did try to contact me by radio. I was cautious. Told them I'd get back to them. Only made a vague reference to a plan to right some wrongs. They took the bait. I think they're for real, but I haven't tried to reach them again. I was waiting to find Mr. Brock Daniels." He looked directly at KC for a moment. "And I found a whole lot more than I bargained for."

What was Craig referring too? Rather who? Surely not to her.

Evidently Brock had the same question. His eyes shot a scary looking glance at Captain Craig, icier than any she'd ever seen from Brock.

Maybe she needed to calm things down a bit. "What makes you think this plan will work, Captain Craig? And how will it work?"

"And where do I come in?" Brock asked, his eyes still fixed on the captain.

Craig looked from KC to Brock. "How sleepy are you two?"

KC tried to grin at him. "Keep talking, you'll know if you're putting us to sleep. Brock snores."

"And how would you know that?" Brock's chilly stare froze on her.

Craig slapped his palm on the dining table. "Do you two want to hear this plan or not?"

Evidently he caught the bad vibes Brock had been broadcasting.

KC nodded.

Brock finally dipped his head.

Craig took a breath and let it out slowly. "First, you need to realize that most of the Rangers and other Special Forces in the military take their oaths of office and their allegiance to this country seriously, very seriously. Over the past seven and a half years, Hannan has tried to emasculate the military. Just look at the Army Chief of Staff, General Dean. He's played politics his entire career. He's Hannan's yes man and he's a first-class wuss, just like the other chiefs of staff. Hannan has riffed most of the best officers over the last four years, under the guise of budget constraints. Now our military is mostly a bunch of wusses. Sure, they can kill you with their weapons, but if the fight gets tough, they'll cut and run. I'd stake my life on it."

Craig wasn't painting a very bright outlook for their plan, but KC chose to reserve judgment until she heard more.

"We'll be joined by more Rangers, Navy SEALs, maybe some Raiders. It won't take many to do the job. But our activities will need to be coordinated across the nation to be effective. That's where your blog comes in, as does KC's IT skills. We'll need a coding scheme to pass information through the blog to coordinate our movements and attacks. Hannan has control of all the national media, either directly or indirectly, and nearly everything else we might want to use."

"But not the Internet," KC said.

Craig nodded. "Thankfully, not yet. But Hannan's already painted a bull's-eye on it and handed the FCC a McMillan sniper's rifle. KC, can you come up with a nearly undetectable way to pass information through the text of Brock's blogs?"

"Give me a few hours and you've got it."

"Good. As we begin to threaten Hannan personally, he'll turn paranoid. I'm counting on that. He won't trust anybody's judgment but his own. Without advisors, he'll make mistakes. And when he gives mistake-riddled commands to his wussy yes men, they'll obey them."

Craig stopped.

KC looked at Brock. "Are you sleepy, Brock? I didn't hear you snoring."

"I'm not sleepy, Kace. Come on, Craig. We need to hear the rest."

"Well, as soon as Hannan makes a major mistake, and I know he will, we go for his jugular. He'll hide when he realizes that's what's happening, because—"

Brock cut in. "Because he's a wuss too."

"He'll probably hide in the DUCC," KC added.

"When that happens, he'll stop leading. He'll only be trying to escape with his life. That's when we'll need to stabilize the nation. We'll need to call Congress to convene, dispense with Hannan in an appropriate way, throw out the entire Hannan administration, and schedule an election for a new president, if we're past this year's general election."

"We will be," Brock said. "The conventions were scheduled for August, five weeks from now. They won't happen."

Was Craig's plan a violation of the constitution? "What about line of succession?"

"Yeah. I thought about that," Craig shot her a glance. "If he doesn't cut and run when he's tagged for the job, we can use the Speaker of the House. If he turns tail, succession goes through the cabinet, a bunch of political thugs. Number seven is head of the DOJ, Randall Washington, worst of the lot. We have to toss them *all* out. Unfortunately, that violates the Constitution. I don't know how to avoid that. But, when we do start again, with the election of a president, we start from scratch, adhering strictly to our Constitution. If the House and Senate had the guts to stick to it, and we could trust SCOTUS to uphold it, we wouldn't be in this mess."

Craig stopped and studied both of their faces. "Well that's the short and sweet of it, how to establish justice, insure domestic tranquility, and promote the general welfare in five minutes." He paused. "So, what you think?"

KC shook her head. "You're relying so much on Brock and me. Are you sure that's a good idea?"

"Brock Daniels has a huge platform with the American people. Keeping the spirit of America and the people's hope alive is critical, as is coordinating our moves on the military chessboard in order to put Hannan in checkmate. So, we need to keep you two alive at all costs."

Craig looked from Brock to KC. "With you two, we can do this in a few months. Without you, we're talking years, and that's too long. The nation would never recover."

"Best case, Craig, what do you think our odds are of taking this nation back?" Brock sat lips tightly pressed. He was ready to take his marching orders. KC could read that loud and clear.

"With you and KC, plus a few patriotic special forces teams ... about 60-40 in our favor. But without you, Brock, 20-80 against us. Without KC—we could try to replace her with a Special Forces geek—I'd say 30—70 against us."

KC squirmed in her seat on the couch. This looked good on paper, but there would be casualties. It wasn't a full blown civil war, but ... "What about loss of life?"

"Regardless, it won't be a bloodless takeover. Hannan's mindset and his current activities guarantee that."

KC looked at Brock. He wasn't going to ask the question, so she would. "What about collateral damage?"

"Little or none," Craig said. "Our thrusts will be surgical in nature, carefully planned and executed. Innocent civilians will only be endangered if they're somewhere they shouldn't be in the first place."

KC had heard all she needed to hear. "Then I'm in." She looked up at Brock.

He took her hand. "I'm in too."

Craig looked at their clasped hands for a few moments. "It's pretty obvious there's some kind of relationship between you two. I haven't needed to ask before, but in planning for all contingencies, I—"

"KC's mine, Craig. And you can make that clear to *all* your men." The intensity in his voice surprised KC, but saying he owned her pushed one of her hot buttons.

"You don't own me, Brock Daniels." Even as she said the words, KC knew there was a half-smile on her lips. Two hours ago, she practically begged him to tell her that he loved her. Maybe a little jealousy went a long way. And maybe there were things about Brock she only thought she knew.

"No, I don't own you, Kace. But you and I go way back. Are you forgetting—"

"I'm not forgetting anything." She smiled warmly. "Brock's right. Since I'm the only single woman among twenty men, you can tell your men to stand down, Craig."

Craig grinned. "That's all I needed to know. Now, it's after 0300, so maybe we should all—"

"Captain Craig," the weapons man, Steve, stepped to Craig's side. "Daddy-O just spotted warm bodies moving along the ridgeline near the house."

"Great. I didn't think they could track us until daylight, when we planned to be gone. Tell him to keep two people watching at all times, and let me know if anyone tries to come down to the ranch."

"What do we do if that happens?" Brock asked.

"We have to go out and fight them before they get to the RV Park. If we don't, innocent people camped here will be killed."

"What do you want KC and I to do if they come?"

"Stay inside the motor home. If we don't return by morning, slide in the sliders, unplug the power, and drive away, just like we planned. But leave us the other motor home and the SUV."

The tall sergeant they called Daddy-O entered the room. "Two men carrying lights just stopped on the ridge above the trail we came down. They appear to be following our tracks."

"Tell our men in the other motor home to be ready to move out in two minutes." Craig picked up his assault rifle and headed toward door.

Chapter 26

The silence outside the motorhome seemed to grow deafening, drowning out KC's thoughts. She pulled her hand off the touchpad on her laptop and plopped it in her lap. "Not knowing what's happening out there, I can't concentrate on anything else."

Brock leaned back on the couch beside her. "It's been quiet the whole time they've been gone. I'd say that's a good sign."

"It probably means that the chess match in the dark will go on for a while."

He draped an arm over her shoulders. Brock didn't realize how that made her feel. Like when he had held her after killing the rattlesnake. Like maybe she really was Brock's. But he had probably claimed her as his just to protect her from any overly curious, testosterone-driven Rangers.

"It can't go on in the dark for much longer. It's 4:30 a.m. Dawn's early light is coming. I think they'll wrap things up before then."

"But what are we going to see by the dawn's early light?"

Brock chuckled. "Kace, I'd bet all my money on Craig's group of Rangers. His flag will be the one still waving."

She laid her head on Brock's shoulder and nestled it into a comfortable position against his neck. "I hope you're right."

The living room door opened with a pop and the lights in the motor home went out.

KC tried to jump up, but Brock's strong arms pulled her closer to his rigid body.

"Craig here. We cut the lights so we wouldn't be seen."

Two shadowy figures crept into the living room. A dim light came on in the kitchen area.

"Well, what have we here?" In the dim light, the white teeth of Steve, the gun guy, showed through the grin on his face.

Brock finally released her.

KC sat up on the couch. "We didn't hear any shooting. So, what happened?"

Craig put down his gun and pulled off his black gloves. "Let's just say that even Hannan's hand-picked, special operations guys are cowards. When it came down to an actual encounter, they ran instead of fighting."

Brock sat up beside her. "But being wimps, won't they try—"

"Yes. It wouldn't surprise me if they tried to sic another Apache on us. We need to get out of here before that happens. Wake up Jeff and Allie so we can move the sliders in."

"Did I hear my name?" Jeff shuffled down the hall into the living room.

"Get your wife up, Mr. Jacobs," Craig pointed his thumb at the hallway. "We're pulling out in fifteen minutes. And, Jeff, while the men unhook our two motorhomes, you can write down directions to your cabin, in case we get separated along the way. Here's a pen and a pad."

Allie walked into the living room, looking much more awake than Jeff.

KC stepped around the coffee table to Allie's side. "We're leaving in fifteen minutes. You and Jeff will be home soon."

"What about you and Brock?"

"Brock and I have decided to help Captain Craig and the Rangers. The only way we'll ever be safe is to stop Hannan. I'm sorry we got you involved in this."

KC's words brought a pained expression to Allie's face. "No, KC, don't be sorry. Jeff and I want to start a family soon. But I wouldn't want to raise my children in the nation Hannan wants to create. We'll pray for you both ... for the Rangers, and for more good people to join you."

"Move to the center everybody. The sliders are coming in." Craig's voice.

With a hum and a whine, the living room narrowed to two-thirds its former width.

Craig stood at the front end of the living room. "Find a comfortable seat, everybody."

Allie and KC sat on the couch. Jeff and Brock took seats on the floor beside the two women's feet.

Craig looked at the two men on the floor and grinned. "You'll be riding without seat belts, so find a way to brace yourself in case we have to brake hard."

Jeff hooked an arm around Allie's bare legs. "I've got two fine looking legs to hang onto."

Brock looked at Jeff, then at KC's bare legs beside him. He reached for her legs.

"Only in case of an emergency, Brock." KC rapped his head with a knuckle.

"Ouch. But Jeff—"

KC leaned forward and looked down at him. "Jeff and Allie are married."

"You see, bro, marriage does have its privileges." Jeff grinned and stroked Allie's shin. "I told you what you needed to do, Brock. Obviously, you haven't done it."

What had Jeff told Brock to do? With guys, who knew? It was a subject she intended to pursue later, when she and Brock were alone.

Craig cleared his throat much louder than was necessary. "We're leaving now. The other motorhome and the SUVs, delivering the SWAT team, will leave in about twenty minutes, and we'll rendezvous after we deliver Jeff and Allie."

Craig headed toward the passenger seat, but stopped and turned back to face the two couples. "You know something? This is exactly why we haven't put men and women together on combat teams." He grinned at Allie and KC, then took the passenger's seat beside the driver, Steve.

"Craig?" Brock swiveled on the floor to face the front.

"Make it quick." Craig turned to face Brock.

"Just thought of something that might be useful. KC's motorcycle."

"We don't have time to pick up a motorcycle."

"What about the guys in the other motorhome? I hid it about 300 or 400 yards from where we're sitting. Keys are still in the ignition."

Craig rubbed his chin and nodded. "That could work. The other motorhome has a toy compartment on the back. It can hold an ATV or a couple of motorcycles."

"Her bike's 200 yards north along the road from the RV park turn-in, where the road swings alongside the escarpment. Off to the left is a thick grove of trees. In the middle of the trees is the motorcycle, on top of a pile of rocks … which is a den of rattlesnakes."

Craig slid out of his seat and stood. "Rattlesnakes we can handle, as long as they're not the kind Hannan allows to slither into his cabinet. We'll pick up the bike if we can. No promises, though." Captain Craig hurried out the door.

In a couple of minutes, Craig was back, and the big motorhome rolled out of the RV park.

When they approached Jeff and Allie's house, Craig had Steve stop the motorhome about a quarter mile away. Evidently he didn't want anyone to associate the RV with the Jacobs's house.

Craig slid out of the passenger seat and shook Jeff's and Allie's hands. "You two, remember what I said to do if anyone comes around asking questions. Plead total ignorance. You were victims, helping a friend look after her house. People in the wrong place at the wrong time."

Jeff nodded.

Brock stood and shook Jeff's hand as he and Allie stood by the door. "Thanks for everything, Jeff. How can I ever repay you?"

"Bro, just don't ever call me again asking for me to help you find a hideout. Now you be careful and take good care of KC. Oh yeah, remember what I told you to do. After seeing her, I was right, bro. Like obviously and totally right."

KC gave Allie a hug. "We'll be praying that no one bothers you and Jeff."

Allie's welling eyes overflowed a few drops. She brushed them away. "Take good care of Brock, KC. He's a good man. And, we'll be praying for you, the Rangers, and our nation."

Before the door closed behind Jeff and Allie, Brock turned toward them. "Jeff, be sure to tell Julia we're sorry her house got a little shot up. Don't even mention the Hellfire Missile scenario. Oh yeah, tell her it was KC who stole her laptop."

KC looked from Brock to Craig, who still stood by the door. "Men. How can they just joke about death and destruction while it still threatens them?"

Captain Craig gave her a crooked smile. "What do you want us to do, cry?"

"You ... you, oh." She wadded up a piece of paper that had managed to remain on the coffee table during the drive, and threw it, hitting Craig in the back of the head.

"We're under attack, Steve. Get us out of here." Craig buckled into the passenger seat.

Craig was still joking.

KC looked at Brock, who had taken Allie's seat on the couch, expecting to see more mischievous, male humor on his face.

Evidently Brock had been watching her, maybe studying her. And what she saw in his eyes before he realized he'd been caught, took her breath away.

Brock had been keeping the depth of his feelings for her mostly hidden. But why? And what had Jeff recommended that Brock do? It was something to do with her. These would have to remain mysteries until Brock was ready to reveal them. But she would give him some gentle reminders.

An hour later they rendezvoused with the rest of the group. Daddy-O joined them and pulled up a chair behind Captain Craig and Steve. The three spoke in hushed tones, a long, private discussion that took most of the hour's drive to Jeff's cabin.

Brock's head leaned against her as he dozed most of the way.

Despite her life being in danger, she had Brock beside her and a team of men protecting them that she and Brock could trust with their lives. For the first time in months, KC took time to thank God for all she had. Her prayer regarding Hannan, however, was far less gracious, one which she probably should ask for forgiveness.

The winding route to the cabin was lined with Junipers and, closer to the mountains, some tall Ponderosa pines. They took several national forest roads to reach Three Creek Lake. If KC had estimated correctly, the RV Park was a little farther away than Jeff described, more like eight miles instead of two.

Jeff's cabin, actually an old trailer house, sat 100 yards from the southern shore of Three Creek Lake, near the end of National Forest Road 16. Dense timber lined the western shore. The eastern side was more desert-like but with some timber on a hill rising to the southeast.

The lake was deserted today. A trailhead, complete with a parking area, lay at the north end of the lake. It might have been a popular spot under normal conditions, but people didn't go to the mountains to play when the entire nation was sick and hemorrhaging.

The only other building she had spotted on the way in sat on the eastern shore of the lake. It had been recently used, but she saw no one there today.

It's strange how observant one becomes when picking a place to hide to save one's life, a place that, if not chosen and used wisely, might end one's life. It was also strange to think that, in a place so remote, they would use satellite communications to start an insurgency to remove from office POTUS, the most powerful man on the planet.

After they had skirted the eastern shore of the lake, Brock woke up. He swiveled toward Craig when the RV stopped. "I know the RV park is farther away than we thought, but we're pretty secluded. There aren't many ways in. My cell has a strong signal, so I would say we don't need to tie up one of your men with guard duty. KC and I will be fine here."

Craig stood and stretched his arms from the hour-long drive with the AC running full blast. "Let me think about that while our commo guy, Sergeant Meyer, gets you connected via satellite."

Though the temperature outside was probably approaching 90, KC felt chilled. She leaned against Brock for warmth.

He wrapped an arm around her. "Are you cold?" He rubbed the goosebumps on her arms.

"I was." She reached for his hand.

He took hers. "Come on, Kace. Jeff's cabin is probably sweltering inside. It'll warm you up."

Would Craig leave them here without a guard? And Brock was the one who suggested it. If they were left here unchaperoned, Brock would have a hard time avoiding the conversation KC needed. Could he really be that clueless? Maybe something was changing in that male mind of his. *A girl can always hope.*

In another hour, Commo Guy had both her and Brock's laptops connected wirelessly to the internet, using the router she had borrowed from Julia's house to create their LAN in the trailer.

KC started enumerating all the things either they had taken or had been damaged at the house. She soon stopped, realizing that the brief firefight and the items they had confiscated probably represented losses to Julia totaling at least $20,000.

Craig opened the door and stepped into the small living room of the twelve-foot-wide trailer. "We're leaving you the generator in case the power goes out. You'll need to keep your laptops charged and the router and antennas powered up or you'll have no Internet access. We're headed for the RV park, now. Good luck blogging. See you tomorrow."

"I'll have an info encoding scheme worked out by then," KC said as she looked around for a guard. She didn't see one.

Craig had watched her scanning the area around them after the other men loaded into the motor home. "We're not leaving a guard unless that becomes necessary, so call us on your cell if anything comes up." He handed them a slip of paper. "Memorize these numbers and destroy the paper. You can reach us at any one of those cell numbers. We gave you a three-day supply of food and water. The food's by the fridge. We'll bring more after we do some shopping. Oh, yes."

He looked at KC. "Your motorcycle is in the toy compartment in the other motor home. Thought you'd like to know."

"Thanks. That bike cost me $4500."

"Any questions before we take off?" Craig stood on the entry steps.

"No questions. See you tomorrow, Craig." Brock's eyes focused on his laptop screen, and his fingers resumed their furious attack on the keyboard.

KC sat in an easy chair at one end of the coffee table. Her chair sat at right angles to the couch where Brock hunched over his laptop.

The door closed and KC was alone ... in a house ... with a man. Living with a man. The thought wouldn't go away. What did Brock think about that? "We're all alone here, Brock. We'll be here hours at a time without a chaperone."

He looked up and studied her face. "Does that bother you? I mean, even in this situation it might not—"

"I know you. Otherwise, it would. Remember our last summer together, seven years ago?"

He nodded. "Two and a half days I'll remember for the rest of my life."

His openness now, compared to his guardedness over much of the past thirty-six hours, surprised her. Maybe she should test the waters. "I practically hung onto your arm the whole time we explored Crooked River Canyon. You were 17. It would've been easy to take advantage—"

"Kace, you were only 14."

"I was old enough."

"Yeah, I guess you were. The most beautiful teenage girl I'd ever laid eyes on."

"And you did a lot of that. But, I didn't mind." She smiled at the memories. "I knew I could trust you because of what you believed, and because I knew Brock Daniels."

"All right. We've established that you're the most beautiful woman I've ever seen and that you can trust me. Where else does this conversation need to go?"

Brock had changed girl to woman, and that meant he still viewed her as special, at least regarding how she looked. "Nowhere. We have work to do ... for now."

"Kace, are we playing some kind of game? You need to tell me if we are." Brock's frown and stare said he was becoming exasperated with her.

"No. No game." But was that the truth? Somehow it felt like they were playing fox and geese checkers, and she had just cornered the fox. But that wasn't what she wanted. The father who never had time for her had left KC with a need, a need that no one but Brock had been able to meet. But did he really *want* to meet it?

Her question immediately led to another. As Brock had told her seven years ago, God could also meet the needs of a person's heart. But in the years since her family moved to DC, and since her parent's death, KC's trust in Him had waned.

"Kace?" Brock studied her face again.

"Huh?" She had missed something.

"I said we need to get back to work now."

She nodded. "Yes. We haven't been online since early this morning. And I need to check out our new satellite connection, for speed and security."

Brock looked up from his screen. "And I want to see what Hannan's been up to, now that his assassination plans for us failed."

KC rebooted her laptop. It came up in less than a minute and found the router. At the router passkey prompt, KC typed in the passkey Sergeant Meyer had given her.

The laptop connected in a few seconds. Now, she was sending HTTP through a dish to a satellite in geostationary orbit, a little over 22,000 miles above the earth, back to a downlink and across the Internet to—she typed the national news broadcasting website URL into her browser and pressed enter—to New York City. And then data took the reverse path back to her laptop.

KC waited for the busy home page to load. When it did, she recoiled from the screen like someone had slapped her face.

Brock's head tilted up from his laptop screen. "What is it, Kace? Your face just lost its tan."

"Come here, Brock, if you want to see what Hannan's up to." Staring at her from the screen were side-by-side portraits of her and Brock. She read the caption.

Domestic Terrorists Join Forces, Shoot Down US Army Helicopter

Brock circled the coffee table and crouched, peering over her shoulder. "A liar and the father of it. That's where this came from. What else does it say?"

Read it, Brock.

Two domestic terrorists have joined forces, creating a well-armed militia that shot down an army helicopter, killing the pilot and the entire crew last night in Central Oregon.

This terrorist organization, known as the Restoration Army, has taken advantage of the national crisis to begin carving out territory for itself in the same manner as Islamic Jihadist groups in the Middle East. If you believe you have seen them, or have any information about them, call 800 – SAVEUSA, immediately.

Brock laid his hand on her shoulder. "Like I said, straight from the father of lies. They didn't mention that it was an Apache attack chopper trying to murder us and that the 'entire crew' was the pilot and one other person. Where did Hannan's press secretary do his internship? With the tabloids?"

"Brock," her voice had grown soft, and unsteady. "He'll turn the nation against us. How much will this affect your blog readership?"

"I don't know." Brock leaned down and kissed the top of her forehead, then turned toward his laptop on the coffee table. "But I'm about to find out."

Chapter 27

"What do you mean you encountered heavy resistance?" Hannan pulled his feet off the desk in the Oval Office and sat up. From the moment the communication sergeant established the secure connection, Hannan's black ops commander had been feeding him excuses, half-truths, and outright lies. "Were you shot at?"

"Not exactly."

"What in the blazes is that supposed to mean? Did someone shoot at you or not?"

"No, Sir. But they were out there. Several of them."

"Several? She's barely 21, still a girl, and he's what, 24? That's two young, inexperienced civilians, Captain Blanchard. Can't you handle them?"

"There were others, possibly as many as ten. They moved like a well-trained team."

"I know that the Central Oregon SWAT team disappeared, but you're not saying that some deputies became outlaws and tried to take you on, are you?"

"No, Mr. President. I believe this is a military group."

"How would the military have gotten involved?"

"Sir, some people and equipment went missing in California ... Fort Irwin."

"How many men?"

"One detachment of Rangers."

Hannan swore again. "Suppose they were Rangers. If you can allow one detachment of men to deter you from completing your mission, then maybe you aren't the man for this job, Blanchard."

"Not just men, sir. These are special forces."

"And you're *not?*"

"We are, sir. But—"

"But what? Look, Captain Blanchard, tell me what you need to guarantee that these two domestic terrorists disappear in the next 24 hours, and I'll try to get it for you."

Silence.

"Well?"

"Mr. President, we have to locate them again, and—"

"That's it, Blanchard. I'm sending your replacement, and until then consider—"

"Mr. President, let me finish, please, sir. We've associated this group with a motorhome that left the area this morning, around sunrise. If you can get us two Apaches, one with a drone and a drone controller, we'll eliminate the whole lot of them in 24 hours."

"Blanchard, we have looters and dissidents locked up in every metropolitan area in the nation. The whole country's under martial law, and I don't have enough troops to secure it. I can't free up resources like I could two weeks ago. And, about the drone ... if you fly it anywhere near a populated area and it starts a panic, I'll have your bars and your head. Is that understood?"

"Yes, sir. Completely."

"I'll get the Apache and a drone to you as soon as I can. In the meantime, use law enforcement to help you track that motorhome. They have traffic video, don't they?"

"Yes, sir. We'll find them and then take them out when we get the chopper."

Hannan ended the call with Blanchard's words still echoing in his head, "When we get the chopper." That's when Blanchard would take them out. The captain was afraid to engage these people on the ground. He wanted a Hellfire Missile to do his job for him, while he remained a safe distance away.

If Blanchard got his missile, there would be no interrogation of Ms. Banning or Mr. Daniels. Whatever wheels those two had set in motion, might continue rolling even after their deaths. And the secrets Ms. Banning took from his study might continue to spread like a cancer.

Maybe it had just become impossible to free up two Apache's and a drone. Yes, it had. And Captain Blanchard would have to earn his hazardous duty pay the old-fashioned way, with boots on the ground. Why were his best men turning out to be—what was the word—wusses?

Chapter 28

To Brock it had seemed as if last night might never end. But now, the morning sun lit the living room of Jeff's cabin. It lit the blue water of the lake, visible through the living room window, painting Three Creek Lake a deep cobalt blue. And KC, sitting in the easy chair by the couch, lit his life. But he didn't have the right to tell her that or a dozen other incredible things he thought each time he looked her way.

"Well, what did you find out Brock? Did Hannan's lies cost you any readers?"

Watching KC was a pleasant diversion from his laptop screen. His eyes burned and his vision had gone fuzzy after reading at least a thousand comments from his last post. But, even with blurry vision, he could see KC's face.

Brock *knew* KC's face even without seeing it. He'd memorized every freckle, every wave in her hair, the shape of her chin, the way her full, red lips turned up at the corners of her mouth, and—

"Didn't you see anything? Or, are you and I not talking now?"

He would have been cut deeply by the "not talking" barb, but KC had a smirk on her face. She knew where his eyes and mind had been focused, and that look in her eyes said she liked what she knew.

Time to answer her question. "Hannan's lies? Some people bought them, Kace. Others didn't."

"You haven't told me how you plan to respond."

"I'm still thinking about that." He turned back to his laptop screen and rested his hands on the keyboard. It was a rough draft, not ready for her scrutiny. "Let me work on it a bit, and then I'll show you what I've been thinking."

"You've already done that." KC's lips formed her enigmatic smile and her head tilted down to her laptop. Her smile faded, her eyes grew intense, focusing on the laptop screen. KC was gone. She'd vanished into a world where computers spoke arcane languages known only to them and the geeks who loved them.

Geeks? KC didn't fit that mold. Certainly not the stereotype.

Every time Brock stopped typing and came up for air, he glanced at KC. Each time she'd been deep in thought, studying something on her laptop for a few seconds then resuming her furious typing. Probably developing the coding scheme she'd promised to deliver to Craig.

After two hours of typing with only a few breaks, Brock leaned back on the couch, hands clasped behind his head, and stretched the kinks from his neck muscles.

KC looked up from her laptop screen to the opposite wall. The intense look in her eyes gradually softened.

Over the last few days, Brock had come to recognize this part of her, a part that was new to him, as the period of adjustment, the time when her mind extricated itself, layer by layer, from the world of pure logic, computer code, until she was mentally with him again.

She looked at him and smiled. KC was back. And, as he had just written in his blog post, she was beautiful.

Maybe he had poured too much of his heart and too much raw truth into this post. But it needed to pack the punch of a sharp right jab to Hannan's nose, a jab of truth that brought blood and fury. In his attempt, Brock had trodden on dangerous ground, both with Hannan and with his readers.

KC would know if he had gone too far, if he'd pushed the right buttons. She was an expert pusher of people's buttons, often preferring confrontation as her method of communication.

If KC could draw a person's feelings out into the open, where she could examine them, she considered her communication successful. If that didn't happen, she pushed another button, looking for an emotional reaction. Push, examine, and repeat, until the desired result was achieved. It was a brutal, but effective communication method, and Brock enjoyed seeing it in action as long as he wasn't the object of her button pushing.

He met her warm gaze. "Does that smile mean you finished Craig's blog encryption scheme?"

"I have several reasons to smile. But, yes, that's one of them."

"And the others?"

"How about ... we're together. We're safe, for now, and well hidden."

"Well hidden? Yeah. But we're not two kids hiding from golfers after messing with their golf balls. We're hiding from—"

"Brock Daniels, you love making me miserable, don't you?"

She was pushing his buttons and leading the conversation her own direction. He'd never figured out how to stop her once she started, even when she was only nine. "Making you miserable wasn't my intent."

Her eyes widened, becoming green emeralds that seemed to hold the sum of all knowledge, especially knowledge about Brock Daniels. "Then suppose you tell me what your intent was."

"Suppose I don't want to." Evasion never worked with her, but ...

"Then I'll draw my own conclusion, which is—"

"KC, you win." Brock flung his hands up in surrender. "Whatever it is you want, just tell me." He shook his head. "You're gonna get it anyway. You always do."

"I've never taken advantage of you, have I?" Her mischievous smile was back.

"No. Like some wizard, you just have this mysterious way of making me want whatever you want, like that old song about a love potion. Number 10 or number 5."

"Sounds like a win-win situation to me."

"What do you want, Kace?"

"It was number 9."

"What was number 9?"

She got up from her chair and sat beside him on the couch. "Do you know how many hours of sleep I've gotten in the past 6 days?"

"Not much. Is it 9?"

"Fifteen, Brock. Less than three hours a night, not counting a few ten-minute cat naps. Yes, I worked the wrinkles out of my method for posting your blogs. Craig's encoding scheme is done. I'll show it to you later. Is your blog post finished?"

"It's written. But I wanted your input before—"

"You can have it, later." She scooted close, wrapped an arm around him, and laid her head on his shoulder. "I'm exhausted. My brain's fried. It's been a week since I felt safe. Will you hold me while I take a nap? Just a short one? Make me feel safe? Keep all the rattlesnakes away?"

"This isn't what we did when we were kids. Not even when we were *tired* kids."

"Like you said, 'we're not two kids anymore'." She nestled against his neck and closed her eyes.

No doubt she was tired. And what male on the planet could resist the sweetness of KC begging for something she needed, something he could easily give?

He brushed her hair from her face. "Can I use your head for my pillow?"

"Mmhmm." Her voice softened to a whisper. "Whatever ... you ..." Her breathing became slow and regular.

The girl who had grown into the woman he loved was sleeping, safe in his arms, for the moment. Brock laid his cheek on her head. Who knew what lay ahead of them in the next day, the next hour? If only he could freeze time. If only ...

But KC's reference to the rattlesnake reminded him of the time when KC's life had depended on his throwing ability, the time he'd first noticed she was no longer a little girl. That incident was etched indelibly into his memory. He could replay the scene anytime he wanted, anytime like the present time.

After nearly eleven months, Brock couldn't wait another minute to see KC, but she wasn't anywhere to be found.

"Brock?" A soft, alto voice came over his right shoulder, familiar sounding but also strange.

He stepped away from the big Juniper tree by the basketball court and into the hot sunshine. Brock turned toward the voice, looked, swallowed, and nearly choked. "KC?"

"Well, yeah. Who did you expect?" She stood, studying his face. KC was dressed in a pair of snug-fitting, pastel green capers or caprios—whatever women called those knee-high pants—and one of those blouses that tied above a woman's waist.

He was staring. Brock knew it, but he couldn't help it. Because it *was* KC, but it *wasn't* KC. Certainly not the KC from last summer.

At least four inches taller. Hair now a darker auburn, but still blazing in the sun. Eyes a deeper, darker green. She still had the freckles sprinkled across the cheeks and nose of her tanned face, but there were curves in places where she had never had—

"Brock Daniels!" Her eyes turned to glaring green emeralds as her hands went to one of those new curvy spots, her hips. "If you make even one remark, so help me I'll—"

"KC, I'd never do that. You know—"

"I only know what your eyes are telling me, and ..." She didn't continue.

He sighed in relief. It wasn't a good thing to tick off KC.

Over the last eleven months, this girl, his buddy, maybe even soul mate, had morphed into a young woman. Brock tried to reply, but was too confused by the contrast between the girl he expected to see and the beautiful young lady standing—

A piercing buzz jolted his nervous system. Every muscle in his body went rigid.

KC drew a sharp breath and froze.

Brock spied the source of the menacing noise. Under a bush, two feet from her bare leg, laid a coiled rattlesnake. "Kace, don't move a muscle."

Head erect now, the three-foot rattler had given its warning. It wasn't going to wait much longer. If she moved, it wouldn't wait at all.

"Please, Brock, I can't just stand here while—"

"Then close your eyes and think about something else."

"Something else? You've got to be kidding." Her voice was barely audible now above the agitated snake's buzzing.

Brock lowered a hand to the ground and curled his fingers around a baseball-sized rock. He could throw hard and he could throw strikes. But could he stop a strike with KC's life on the line?

The snake's roving tongue had sensed the large, warm-blooded threat only twenty-four inches away. Its head began the tell-tale back and forth motion. The rattler wasn't going to stand down. Its mouth opened wide, fangs extended. That little demon would strike even if KC didn't move.

From the stretch, Brock let both a prayer and the rock fly.

The triangular head shot toward KC's leg.

He tried to correct the trajectory as the rock spun off his fingertips.

KC's scream pierced his ears.

But the head of the striking rattler veered off course. A foot behind KC's right leg, the snake now lay writhing in the dirt.

She leaped from beside the bush, nearly knocking Brock off his feet when she collided with him.

He wrapped KC up in his arms to keep her shaking body from falling, but kept his eyes focused on the snake. Its mangled head hung limp from its neck, if a snake really has such a thing as a neck. The loud buzz dropped off to a feeble rattle, but the snake kept coiling and striking.

KC swiveled in his arms, pressed her back into him, and shivered as she watched the nearly headless snake striking at nothing. "You nailed him, Brock. I thought I was dead, but ..."

"Couldn't afford to miss, Kace." Brock's heart finally caught up with the desperation of the previous few seconds. Now it pounded out his full realization of the danger to KC. Anger at the rattlesnake surged through Brock and flew out his mouth. "No way would I let that darned little s—"

"Don't say it!" She slammed her open hand over his lips. "No swearing, Brock. That's what he is alright, but I don't want you to ... why's he still striking?" KC looked up into his face with terror in her wide green eyes. "He still wants to kill me, doesn't he?"

Aware now that this wasn't a little girl in his arms, Brock loosened his hold on her.

But KC continued to stare at the striking snake.

"No, Kace. He's not trying to kill you. Snakes are stupid. They don't have much of a brain, and half of it is distributed along their backbone. That half still thinks he's in danger. He's so dumb he doesn't even know he's dead yet." He cupped her chin and pulled until her eyes left the snake and focused on him. "Are you okay?"

"I am now." She turned, stood on her tiptoes, and softly pecked his cheek. "Now that you saved me."

That had never happened before. Now what was he supposed to say?

Before he could come up with an appropriate response, KC grabbed one of his hands. "Come on. Race you to the lookout." She flashed him her smile, but it seemed to speak a different language than it used to.

By the time he got his mind in gear, she nearly jerked him off his feet. Then they were off, running hand-in-hand toward the canyon rim.

So just like that, the snake was history. That was vintage KC. Using fun to conquer or forget her fears. But, in reality, there were people in the world a lot like that snake. People programmed to do evil because they believed evil lies. Someday he wanted to help fight against such people, maybe with his words, his writing. But he hoped he never had to fight *them* to save KC's life.

But here he was, seven years later, trying to do that very thing, save KC's life. And it would take more than a well-aimed, one-hundred-mile-per-hour rock. Was Brock Daniels, the man who had never been quite good enough, up to the task? He knew the truth and it frightened him.

Chapter 29

KC's dream receded, rushing away from her down a long tunnel. She tried to grab the scene in her mind and hold onto the picture of Brock running across the desert with her, laughing, carefree. But it faded away, replaced when her eyes opened by—

Pain!

Her right arm had cramped from wrapping around Brock's sturdy frame for ... she didn't have a clue how long. She straightened her arm and flexed her hand.

Brock's slow, regular breathing tickled the stray wisps of hair on her forehead every time he exhaled. The couch didn't feel nearly as soft as when she sat down on it beside him. His heavy head, compressing her neck and adding to her weight on the couch, also added to her discomfort.

But Brock still held her snugly with both of his strong arms, safe from every rattlesnake in the world, human or reptilian. If only she could freeze time. If only ...

Brock's head moved. He drew a deep breath and raised his head from hers.

She could endure whatever lay ahead if only she had some time like this each day to rest, secure and, she suspected, loved. But she sensed Brock still wasn't ready to have a serious discussion about that.

"You awake, Kace?"

"Just let me pretend I'm not for a while longer."

"Sorry. Can't let my ... uh, you be delusional."

KC sat up on the couch and studied his eyes for a moment. Confusion. That's what she'd seen in them. Or perhaps reluctance. "Since I showed up on your doorstep at the motel, you haven't quite figured out what to call me, have you? You've called me KC, shortened it to Kace, but ..."

"I called you mine, Kace." The look in his eyes morphed from confused to serious.

"Yes, you did."

The words that would force Brock to discuss the issue foremost on her mind moved out to the tip of her tongue, where she stopped them. He wasn't ready for those words or the discussion. And she worried about the outcome. She worried about not living up to his expectations. That was the specter left by her dead father. Why wouldn't it go away?

Brock was also holding back for some reason. Could it be Julia? Or was this another case of KC simply not being good enough? Regardless, until Brock was ready to tell her why he held back, she wouldn't push him beyond the point where their relationship had stalled, somewhere between a hug and a kiss.

"Kace, how soon can I post to my blog?"

"Be glad that I don't have a frying pan in my hand, Brock Daniels." How could he, in a few seconds, jump to a subject so unrelated?

"Be glad you don't have a frying pan? We missed lunch, KC. At this point, I don't care if you *are* a bad cook."

Bad cook? The urge to tweak his nose came, then went when she saw his mischievous grin. She stood, intending to see what Craig's men had left for them in the refrigerator, and perhaps to burn to a charred, inedible brick whatever she heated in the microwave for Brock.

He stood too, pulling her into a close—now closer than close—intimate embrace, an embrace she found herself returning and delighting in.

KC's face grew warm, too warm. And Brock had squeezed the breath out of her. "I can't breathe, Brock. You don't realize how strong your arms are. I guess a girl should expect to get squished by an arm that throws a hundred miles an hour and tears the heads off rattlesnakes."

Brock's arms went limp, the smile on his face faded.

What had just happened? "Brock, what is it?"

"That was then. Now is now."

"What do you mean? Last night you took out one of the SWAT team members with a throw. I bet you could be pitching for the Mariners if you wanted to."

Brock's body tensed and he released her, completely.

She'd only seen this reaction from him when she ventured too near their relationship, something Brock didn't want to discuss. But baseball? "So what happened with you and baseball?"

"Nothing." His one word conveyed a lot, but not nearly as much as the pain in Brock's eyes.

"So that's the problem." As kids they'd never kept things from each other, not that KC knew. Brock already had one secret he wouldn't talk about. If she could prevent it, she wouldn't let him have another. "Baseball was such a big part of your life. Much more than football. Please, Brock, tell me what happened."

"Kace this has been a good day, so far. Do we have to ruin it?"

"If you don't tell me, I'll just start asking questions, like always, and you'll end up telling me … like always." She took his hand, pulled him to the couch, and sat beside him. "Something happened. Was it your senior year?"

Brock took her hand and interlaced fingers with her. "Something did happen my senior year, but it wasn't bad. The Royals offered me a contract, but I turned it down."

"Turned it down? You hadn't changed your mind about baseball, had you?"

"Kace, you know me better than that. I had declared for the University of Oregon. Some guys take a contract when they're too young. They're still developing and they get overlooked. They never make it out of the minors. I hoped to be drafted higher after playing college ball."

"So how did you do as an Oregon Duck?"

"It turned out to be a nightmare." Brock's body tensed beside her. His clenched fists and shuffling feet said he was antsy and agitated.

She had opened up a painful subject. But Brock needed to tell her about it, not keep it bottled up inside. She rubbed his arm with her free hand, wishing she could absorb part of his pain.

Brock glanced at her hand, relaxed, and draped an arm around her shoulders. "I injured my elbow and missed half of my freshman year, then injured my shoulder my sophomore year and missed my junior year while I rehabbed it."

Brock was so strong and young. These couldn't be pitching injuries. She looked up trying to read his eyes. "You didn't injure your arm throwing, did you?"

"You're good, KC. Maybe I should let *you* tell the rest of the story."

"No. I want *you* to tell it to *me*. All of it. So, how did the rehab go?"

"The injuries weren't from throwing pitches. Both were freak accidents. First, hit by a broken bat. The next year I injured my shoulder diving for a ground ball on a cold day, a stupid thing to do. It was the second baseman's play, not mine."

He paused and shook his head. "But my senior year I was back, throwing harder than ever. I didn't think of myself as damaged goods, but when I went to talk to one scout, while waiting in his office, I saw a report on his desk, a report on me. I can quote it almost verbatim. 'Maybe one or two years in the minors is all his arm will hold up for. Doesn't matter that he can crank it up to over 100 miles-per-hour. He won't be throwing 70 in a couple of years. Don't waste your money on Brock Daniels.' I was never offered another contract."

KC laid her head on Brock's strong right shoulder. One stupid scout had ripped Brock's dreams away and she had made him relive it. "I'm so sorry. They were wrong, so wrong. Did you ever try out for a team?"

"No."

"Brock, you would have proved that scout wrong."

"Kace ... sometimes a person just has to accept the truth. I wasn't good enough. Like some other things in life, major league baseball players are out of my league."

Brock's words brought tears to her eyes. The man sitting beside her was meant for greatness, and he couldn't even see it. A thought jolted KC like an electrical shock.

He thinks he's not good enough. Out of his league. Is that why Brock won't pursue me?

She had to change his mind, had to make him see. "You're wrong, Brock. I know because I've got proof. Your arm saved my life, first from a striking rattlesnake and then from a man armed with an automatic rifle. No major league pitcher would attempt that. They couldn't do it if they wanted to. But you did. If you hadn't, I wouldn't be sitting here beside you. Is that good enough for you, Brock? It's good enough for me."

"Kace, I ..." He stopped.

She wouldn't let him off the hook this time. "Maybe striking out major league batters is more important to you than saving my life."

The pained expression on Brock's face said she'd struck a nerve.

KC wanted her cruel remark back. Brock had revealed a deep wound from his past and she had minimized his pain and inserted herself into the issue, an issue where she didn't belong. "I'm sorry, Brock. You didn't deserve that."

"Maybe I did. I've been ..." He stopped again.

"Been holding back?"

"Yeah." His blue eyes peered into hers, intensely, warmly. Something had changed in the last few seconds. "Listen to me, KC. If I lost baseball, my writing, everything else, but still had you in my life, I'd consider myself a lucky man. I'd be a happy man."

"How do you want me in your life, Brock? As a little sister? Your friend?" Finally, the issue she'd wanted him to discuss was on the table.

Brock looked away. Instead of peering into her eyes, he scanned the room, finally focusing on the bar between the living room and the kitchen. "How do I want you? Can I show you?"

"You should know the answer to that without asking, Brock Daniels."

He stood, carried his laptop to the bar, and set it next to a set of speakers. "The sound in these little things is incredible. Jeff leaves them here for when he and Allie come up and ... well, you get the idea."

"No, I don't. Maybe you should show me."

"Kace ..." Brock's cheeks reddened and he focused on the speakers.

"At least tell me what you're up to." She stood.

"Come here." He opened his web browser and clicked a couple of times.

KC stopped beside him and saw the home page for a web radio station. "Billy Joel Radio? We're going to listen to music?"

"Yeah, sort of."

"Don't I have any say in the matter?"

"Okay, you pick the song."

KC clicked on some song called "This Night."

Brock nodded. "That works, I think." He selected repeat.

"Come on, Brock. You mean we're going to listen to this song forever?"

"Kace, if you'll remember I was going to show you something."

How he wanted her? That's what he said.

Music started. Brock adjusted the volume until a slow rhythmical melody filled the room with incredible sound and the unmistakable voice of Billy Joel. He hooked an arm around her waist and pulled her to an open space on the living room floor. "We've had nothing but danger and distractions since you came back home. I want to change that. Dance with me, KC."

"I should warn you, I don't do this very well." KC took a ballroom dancing posture, placing a hand on Brock's shoulder and reaching for his other hand.

"No, Kace. You're not my little sister and not—here, let me show you." Brock wrapped his arms around her waist and pulled her snugly against him. "Just follow me."

She circled his neck with her arms. When the music swelled in some vaguely familiar melody, KC laid her head on his shoulder and swayed with him to the music. She listened to the lyrics, words about two people promising to be friends but—she glanced up at Brock.

He peered into her eyes as the words told about two friends becoming something more ... lovers. This was what Brock wanted to show her?

Her cheeks grew warm. KC hid her blushing face against Brock's neck.

The chorus again crescendoed in its romantic melody. This time she recognized it, a beautiful Beethoven Sonata. The music, Brock holding her, words that seemed to describe them and their relationship. How could Brock have planned this? She had picked out the song. So why did it all seem orchestrated, specially for them?

Too many questions. KC shut them off, laid her head on Brock's shoulder and danced, two people who completed each other, moving as one. This was what their childhood friendship had been leading to all along.

Like the Beethoven sonata, composed by the old maestro, their lives had been composed by another Master, the composer of life, and He'd intended for theirs to be a song played in two-part harmony. She was beginning to sound like Allie. Again, KC stopped thinking, stopped trying to explain everything, and flowed with the music to Brock's lead.

Was the song playing for the fourth or fifth time? KC didn't want this moment to end, but it would at some point. Then what? That depended on Brock. Was he feeling all that she felt?

Brock pulled her gently to a stop and lifted her chin until she looked into his eyes, but he said nothing.

"Brock, I guess I'm not just your little sister."

"No, Kace. You're not."

"Is that what you wanted to show me?"

He moved his hand to the back of her neck and nudged her forward. "It's part of it."

"I wouldn't want you to do something you didn't want to do."

"I've been doing that since you showed up at the ranch. And I'm tired of doing what I don't want to do. So ..."

Brock pulled her closer, slowly, allowing her to opt out.

That wasn't going to happen. KC closed the remaining inch between their lips, as her dearest friend became something much more.

Several seconds later, she pressed her cheek into Brock's chest while he held her. His heart was beating rather fast too. Knowing Brock, his racing heart might be the only feedback she got about their kiss. But a girl can always hope. Mandie's favorite phrase. KC smiled.

"Kace ... that's what I've wanted to do from the moment you walked through the door of my motel room."

Her vision blurred with tears as she smiled at Brock.

"You are so beautiful when you do that."

"Red hair, freckles and all? I'm glad you think so."

"I know so. But, you know what?" He looked across the room to the kitchen.

"Maybe you'd better tell me."

Brock released her from his embrace. "I'm hungry."

"How could you just—Brock Daniels, I ought to—"

"Kace, you can't live on love. At least that's what I've been told. Right now, I believe it." He walked to the refrigerator, opened the door, and peered in. "Where's all the food Craig left us?"

"He said *by* the refrigerator, Brock. What's in that box with the red top, sitting on the floor?" What had just transpired between them was incredible, but Brock evidently didn't want to discuss it. He still had some secret too deep in his heart for her to pull out. For now, she would wait.

Brock shut the refrigerator door and looked at the box beside it. "It says MRE's. Meals ready to eat. "He ripped the box open and several shrink-wrapped packages spilled onto the floor. Brock grabbed one. "Says it's a chili and macaroni meal. Let's see, it's got chili and macaroni, raspberry applesauce, grape jelly, crackers, an oatmeal cookie, tropical punch mix, and Starbucks."

"Starbucks in army rations?"

"Just kidding. It's instant coffee. But you won't have to worry about your figure. Only a thousand calories."

"Who's worried about their figure?" KC stretched to her full five feet seven inches, putting hers on display.

Brock had noticed. "Well, you don't want to be a—" He stopped.

She could see the realization in his eyes.

He'd stepped onto a minefield and he knew it.

"So when I'm middle-aged, with a midriff bulge, you won't like me anymore?"

"That's so far away, Kace, that I'd like to, uh ..."

"Yes?"

He didn't reply. Instead, he picked up two bags and took them into the kitchen.

She folded her arms and watched him move rather efficiently around the small kitchen, dumping the food from the bags onto plates. "You didn't even ask me what I wanted."

"Doesn't matter." Brock slid the plates into the microwave.

"You're really considerate today, you know."

"Realistic. They're *all* chili and macaroni. They'll sustain us, but I wouldn't expect much more than that."

Brock had kissed her because he wanted to, but he wasn't ready to talk about their future. Just as well. They needed to refocus now, because they needed to survive Abe Hannan's assault, or they would have no chance at a future.

"Brock, how long do you have to heat them?"

"For two meals, it says about five minutes."

"Come here then, and I'll show you how my information-embedding scheme works. You need to understand this because it impacts your writing."

"Kace, please don't tell me the computer will generate my blog posts. Computers don't know how to write. I know how to write." He sat down beside her on the couch, while the microwave whirred and buzzed.

"It's not that bad. You just have to accommodate certain letters, you know, make sure they appear somewhere in your blog. And, yes, it may cramp your style a bit, but it's necessary to communicate a hidden message. Besides, you're good with words."

"Yeah, but the computer isn't."

"Don't be a grouch potato. You can handle this, Brock." She slid her laptop in front of them on the coffee table. "Look. You put your written blog post in one text file, the message we need to communicate in another, then run my Encode Perl script. The script finds all the characters in your post needed to create the message and indexes them as an array which is written into JavaScript embedded in the page source of your posted blog."

"What if you need letters that I haven't used?"

"Not a problem. A list of the letters the message still needs is printed to the screen. It will usually be a small list. You just add a few words to your blog, wherever you want, so that the missing letters and digits are somewhere in your post and rerun the Encode Perl script to index them. Then I take the output and post it to the blog as HTML, and we're done. See, that's simple enough."

Brock stared at the HTML KC's script had generated. "Okay. So, now the message is there, but how do our SEAL or Ranger friends get it out?"

She brought up a web page. "Pretend this was your post. They visit your blog, then view the page's source ... like this. The page's source opens in another browser window. Then they save it and run my Decode Perl script on it. It reads the JavaScript array embedded in the page, builds the indices as a Perl array, and uses the array to reconstruct the message."

"KC, couldn't NSA figure out what the index in the code is used for?"

"Maybe. But it just looks like embedded JavaScript. Even if they did figure it out, they don't have the Decode script."

Brock popped back to the window with her script output. He studied it and rubbed his chin for a few seconds. "But if they suspected what you were doing, couldn't they, by brute force, come up with a way to decode the message?"

"Maybe. But my Perl script changes the way it encodes information every time you use it. It does this by hashing on a date-time string that's read from the computer's clock and embedded in each post. That string changes every millisecond, making it very difficult to decode, especially when you don't even know what you're looking for."

More chin rubbing. "Given enough time, couldn't a group like NSA still figure this scheme out?" He looked up at her, frowning.

KC sighed sharply. "Yes. But think about it for a minute. First, they would have to figure out that we're coordinating operations between military units. Then they have to guess how. Are we using radios, cell phones, or something else? If they ever began to scrutinize your blog posts, we would still have weeks before they figured out what we're doing. Then they would have to solve the index hashing scheme by brute force, and relate it to the seed, the date-time string. That could take a while. So, I'm guessing we can use this for two months with no worries. Maybe even six months. But I get the impression Captain Craig wants this whole operation to be completed in less than six months. If you and Craig are both worried about discovery, I'll devise another scheme and keep it in my purse."

"Kace, don't you mean in your hip pocket?"

She looked down at the side of Brock's hip. "I don't carry a big, bulging wallet in my hip pocket, like some men I know."

Brock reached down and felt his wallet in his back pocket.

She stared at his rear for a couple of seconds. "Men look deformed when they do that. Is that how you want me to look?"

"Uh ... no. I rather like the way you're formed."

KC shook her head. "Now that we've established your thoughts on my posterior, what do you think about the encoding scheme?"

"There's only one problem, Kace. You've got to give the Decode Perl script to everyone who needs to use it."

"I know. I'm going to let Captain Craig deal with that. But I don't think it's an insurmountable problem because, if I was him, I'd want a face-to-face meeting with the commander of any military group before I joined them in pledging my life, my fortune, and my sacred honor. I can prepare a flash drive with a Perl installer, my script, and anything else on it a new member of the Restoration Army would need."

"Restoration Army? I'm not going to use any name that lends credibility to Hannan's lies."

"Just a joke, Brock."

"But you're probably right about Craig meeting with someone before trusting them. That's what he did with us." Brock sighed. "Now that we've reviewed your homework, I'd like you to review mine.

Brock brought up the text of his post on his laptop and turned it so KC could see the screen.

In light of certain lies being spread about me and one of the most patriotic women you could ever meet, Ms. KC Banning, I want to set the record straight by presenting the truth. Not conjecture, not conspiracy theory, but things I know first-hand or that I have verified through eye witnesses that I trust.

Bluntly stated, the truth is that President Hannan is a liar who, with a ring in his nose, is being led down a destructive path by the father of lies. Hannan is also a murderer who has

*slaughtered men, women, and helpless children in an attempt
to reach his selfish goal. He doesn't want to be our president.
He literally wants to be our king.*

*On top of all that, Hannan is a craven, power-crazed, little
wuss.*

"A wuss? Brock, you poked his ego right in the nose.
Hannan thinks he's almost God, but you painted him as
satanic. He's going to be furious."

"That's the idea. We need him really angry. Angry and
careless. These are just the charges, Kace. You need to keep
reading to hear the evidence."

KC picked up Brock's machine and set it in her lap.
Where was I?

*… a craven, power-crazed, little wuss. A wuss who
surrounds himself with other wusses who are afraid to say
anything but yes. For example, look at Army Chief of Staff,
General Dean. He has a long and uncolorful history of playing
politics and spouting political correctness, most of that right
out of Hannan's little red book.*

*The same can be said of the other chiefs of staff,
including the chairman. Ask them to plan and fight a real war,
and you'll see their rear ends disappearing in the distance.*

*They are all yes men. A leader is supposed to find safety
in the multitude of counselors, but not with this group. All
Hannan gets is affirmation, so much affirmation that it has
led to delusions of grandeur. And now we have a psychopath
in the White House, a malignant Narcissist.*

After Brock's insult-laden opening, KC continued reading
through his description of finding the clinic in Guatemala
where children were intentionally given Hannan's genetically
altered, airborne version of Ebola, the disease that had
already claimed the lives of hundreds of Americans who
didn't have access to the vaccine, a vaccine Hannan used to
further control U.S. citizens.

She couldn't suppress a smile when Brock introduced her, doting on her as a "beautiful, sweet, patriotic, young woman who only wanted to protect her country", a dream she'd had since Brock met her when she was eight years old.

Brock attributed all of the current chaos in the nation to Hannan's scheme to force martial law before the political conventions, effectively cancelling the general election. Without specifically mentioning the Army Rangers, Brock included a description of the failed Apache helicopter attack on Brock and her, an attack ordered because Hannan's men, like their boss, were all pantywaists.

Brock ended with a quote.

What's a patriotic American to do with a man like you? The words of Dietrich Bonhoeffer sum the situation very well, "If I see that a madman is driving a car into a group of innocent bystanders, then I can't as a Christian simply wait and comfort the wounded and bury the dead. I must try to wrest the steering wheel out of the hands of the madman." So, hang on tight to that wheel, Mr. President, because here I come.

Your voice in the wilderness,

Brock Daniels

"So what do you think, KC?"

"This guy's been catered to most of his life." She tapped a few times on her laptop's touchpad, then popped up another window and typed in it. "Other than some rare bad press for the media's darling, he's probably never been insulted like this before. Coming from someone he's tried and failed to kill, someone who's exposing that failure, he's going to lose it when he reads this."

"We probably should let Craig take a look it this before we post it, don't you think?"

"Uh ... too late. I just ftp'd it."

"Kace ... seriously?"

"Yes. It's live."

A knock sounded on the door of the trailer. "Captain Craig here. We need to talk."

"Something's going to hit the fan for sure."

She nodded. "Probably so. In the West Wing and at Three Creek Lake."

Chapter 30

What would Captain Craig's reaction be to Brock's inflammatory blog post? Brock opened the door, fearing the worst.

Craig entered the trailer house and took a seat in the easy chair at one end of the coffee table. He glanced at the two laptops sitting side-by-side on the coffee table, like their owners now sat on the couch. "So, how's the new digs?"

Where was this going? "They're fine. Right, KC?"

She nodded. "And our Internet connections are better than I expected."

Craig grinned. "Our specialty. Rangers' lives depend on comms."

Brock took KC's hand. "But there is the issue of us being together 24-7, largely unchaperoned."

"Ordinarily," Craig sighed, "... we wouldn't do this. But this is war and my men are spread as thin as—well, too thin. You two are upstanding, moral adults. Believers too. Any problems I should know about?"

"I wish." KC gave Brock her coy smile. "Changing the subject—about the information encoding scheme. I developed one that allows groups to coordinate through Brock's blog, but it's a one-way broadcasting scheme. You can send multiple messages each day, simply by having

Brock make minor edits to update an existing blog and, voila, a new message. Captain Craig, you do realize that there are drawbacks to this method of communicating, don't you?"

Craig nodded. "You mean no feedback loop and the person with the blog posting authority, probably Brock, becomes a bottleneck?"

"Yes." KC sighed. "There's just no way we can safely use this for two-way communication."

"But I can broadcast to a large audience, so we can live with that. I've got other plans for feedback. But, speaking of updates, have you tried to post from here yet?" Craig focused on Brock.

"Uh ..." How should he say this? "Yeah. When we read what Hannan fed the media about us forming the 'Restoration Army' and killing the 'whole crew' of a helicopter, I got a bit angry, and so I tried to get a rise out of him with my post."

Craig's eyes narrowed as he stared at Brock. "Just how big a rise did you try to get?"

KC set her computer in her lap, "You can decide for yourself." She read the part of the post calling Hannan a wuss and his whole crew pantywaists.

After a chuckle, Craig's brow furled. "From now on, I want you to clear with me anything that impacts our strategy to defeat Hannan's coup, including any provocative statements. Is that clear?"

"Yes, sir," Brock slumped back onto the couch. It had gone better than he thought and he didn't have to implicate KC.

Her fingers flew over the keyboard. "Let's see if Brock's pantywaist post has drawn any comments. I'm running the script to scrape them. It'll only take a minute or so."

"Part of the reason I came up here is to let you know I made contact with a team of Navy SEALs," Craig said.

"That's great," Brock sat up on the couch.

"Do you think we can trust them?" KC looked up at Craig, giving him her squinting frown.

"I do. But, to make sure, I'll have to travel about 300 miles to meet with them. I'm uncomfortable with leaving you two defenseless."

KC set her laptop back on the coffee table. "You've got the road in here covered at the main highway. Are you going to leave anyone there while you're gone?"

"I am. I'm also leaving you an assault rifle. So, I need to give you both some OJT on the use of this weapon and go over strategies for using it to defend yourselves against an assault. It shouldn't happen, but we need to be prepared."

Brock grinned. "On the job training. So, we finally get to be Rangers."

"Not exactly." He reached into a long bag he'd brought with him and pulled out a clip. "Here's an empty magazine. I want to see you load, unload, reload and, if there's no one around the lake, we'll put in a full magazine, and you can both shoot one short burst to get a feel for automatic mode."

At the words, "automatic mode," KC jumped up, beating Brock to the door. "This should be fun."

The eight-year-old adventurer he'd met thirteen years ago was back.

"Craig, I shot an AK-47 in automatic mode the night you showed up."

"Well, you're going to shoot an M4 today ... my way."

"I wasn't complaining, you know."

Craig grinned. "From the look on your face, I gathered that."

After the preliminaries, with an empty magazine, they went outside. KC took her turn first. It ended with a smile when she pruned a small bush off near the ground. "Makes you feel almost invincible." Her smile faded. "Sure hope I don't have to do that to a real live person."

When Brock shot in automatic mode, he noticed the barrel tried to rise more than when he'd fired at the SWAT team.

"You two should do fine, if need be." Craig nodded toward the trailer. "Let's go back inside."

Captain Craig sat in the chair by the coffee table and pulled a small pad of sticky notes from his pocket. "Okay, here's the plan. We leave you two at Three Creek Lake with an M4. Steve will be at the Sister's RV Park. If any danger should arise you can call Steve's cell. Here's the number." He pressed a sticky note onto the coffee table.

"Steve's the guy who took down that Apache helicopter, right?" Having that guy around would make Brock feel better about this.

"Yes. He's our gun man. But we don't anticipate a repeat of that Apache helicopter incident." Craig stood and turned toward the door.

"Wait, Craig." KC set her laptop on her legs. Her fingers flew over the keyboard for a few seconds. There's something here you need to read. It sounds like some riffed Air Force pilots want to know if there's any way they can help us."

"They could be useful." Craig rubbed his chin. "But they could also be bait." Craig sat in the easy chair. "Show me how to reply to their comment."

KC put the laptop in his lap and moved the cursor to the comment reply box. "Just start typing. But remember this is in the clear. No encryption."

Craig typed, then paused. "I need to say something that's subtle, but provides a cell number." He finished typing. "We have several disposable phones only trackable by triangulation on cell towers. I guess we can risk one of them as long as we don't use it near our home base. Remember, I'll handle any further communication with the pilots."

KC stood and pulled a small flash drive from her shorts pocket. "In case you bring the SEALs into our group, this has a complete Perl installation for a PC or Mac, and it has our decode script on it along with instructions."

Brock stood beside her.

Her hand found his.

"Thanks," Craig said. "I'll see you in two days. Be careful." He glanced at their hands. "I can see you're enjoying the digs and each other's company. Just don't enjoy it too much. Be back in a couple of days."

The door closed.

"Why do I feel I just got a lecture from my dad?" Brock turned toward KC. One look at her answered his question.

She shrugged. "That kind of lecture is the last thing *you* need."

KC didn't have a clue about the depth and intensity of his feelings for her. Their dance and the kiss had exposed only a fraction of what he felt. Though he had tried to warn KC about his tendency to fail, to always come up short, he hadn't mentioned their differences in social strata or the letter that had so graphically portrayed them.

If KC and Brock survived Hannan's assault on democracy and on them, they would return to American society where Brock would eventually fail KC. Just like he'd failed at everything he tried. It would end their relationship. Until then they would fight Abe Hannan together and Brock would pray for a miracle, one that turned him into a man suitable for the woman who had won his heart as a girl and still held it. But the odds were they'd be killed in the battle. If so, at least he would go down swinging and could be thankful that he had KC by his side for whatever was left of his life. If Hannan's men were to locate them now, with Craig gone, there wouldn't be much left.

Chapter 31

"You're not serious about going to Europe are you?" From the far side of the desk in Hannan's private study Secretary of State, Eli Vance, gave Hannan Eli's patented, bug-eyed stare. It came through glasses so thick they magnified Eli's eyes until the old man's narrow face resembled that of a grasshopper.

Hannan shook his head, but couldn't shake the impulse to stomp on the grasshopper. He wouldn't, because the crusty old goat still had an incredible ability to deal with most of the leaders in the Middle East. Besides, he would make an awful mess on the carpet.

"Well, say something, Mr. President, Abe."

"No. With the crises here, I've decided against going to Europe. How can I go with Katheryn Banning still running loose with that blogger, Daniels?"

"It's just as well. You're not the most popular man in Europe right now. Or Israel for that matter. Somebody would probably shoot you." Vance gave him a crooked smile that lifted one corner of his wide mustache.

That was Vance's comment on any trip he didn't think was necessary. Somebody would shoot Hannan. This time the old geezer might be right. "Look, Eli, we knew we'd have to rebuild some trust after—"

"Rebuild? You destroyed the foundation. NATO is voting right now to exclude us from meetings until they see how the dust settles in DC. And the UN wants us out of the Security Council until—Abe, they're treating the U.S. as if a coup were underway."

It wasn't exactly a coup, but Vance was right about the storm waves battering foreign relations. "We'll ride this out and when we emerge with a strong, stable, central government, we'll renew the treaties, offer some placating promises, foreign aid, and whatever else is needed until all this is forgotten." He looked at his watch. "Eli, I've got to go now."

"I know ... to meet with the young whippersnappers in that tight little circle of yours."

"You know you're invited to attend, like always."

Eli chuckled. It ended with a coughing spasm.

"You should have quit smoking years ago. It's going to kill you."

"I know. I know. But, like always, I'm not coming. And you should be worried about the people who might kill you, Abe. Nearly every country with a significant military has put it on high alert while the most powerful nation on earth is in crisis. No, you don't need me at your meeting. I need to go and smooth some ruffled feathers." Eli Vance stood and stepped toward the door of the study. "We wouldn't want the boys in Europe to do anything rash, would we?"

Boys in Europe. Eli was an anachronism, born too late. "No, Eli. We wouldn't want that."

After Vance ambled down the hallway, Hannan followed behind him, stopping at the Oval Office door.

They were all there. Good. Because the matter at hand could be far more urgent than being kicked out of NATO or off the UN Security Council.

This new Ebola outbreak was more than disturbing and Hannan needed to understand what had caused it. That's why he'd asked his Secretary of Health and Human Services, Dr. Patricia Weller, to come, once again, and provide an update.

Randall Washington, Gerald Carter, and Mitchell Dell sat in their usual places. Dr. Weller, forced to sit beside Mitchell Dell, sat at the far end of the couch, clearly distancing herself from the nerdy-looking head of cyber security.

Putting people on the defensive was often an effective way to get them to disclose more than they intended. Hannan drew Dr. Weller's gaze and glared at her. "Dr. Weller, I thought you said we had this Ebola epidemic under control. I want to know what's happening."

"Despite your ... uh, the delay implementing ESF #8..." She shot Hannan an angry glance. "We *did* have it under control."

He overlooked her impertinent remark because Hannan had deliberately hindered Dr. Weller with a series of excuses for not initiating this Emergency Support Function for medical disasters. He wanted the outbreak to become an epidemic before taking aggressive action. "Go ahead, Ms. Weller."

"After we declared the ESF #8 emergency, we had just gotten all the wheels of our response turning when a visitor brought the Zaire strain in from Africa. There's a small, ongoing outbreak in Sierra Leone, Central Africa. This person was exposed to the U.S. strain of Ebola in a hospital here in the U.S. As you may know, viruses mutate by gene swapping. A nurse at the hospital is now dying from an Ebola strain for which our vaccine is ineffective. We fear that the original Ebola has acquired from the U.S. strain the ability to go airborne. This means we have airborne Ebola in the U.S. and no vaccine to treat it. It's a formula for disaster. In Africa, the kill rate of the Zaire version is ninety percent. I believe it will be only marginally better in the U.S."

Hannan's plan had been to stay in control, even during the chaos. He hated not being in control. That was why he hated Alexis ... and Dr. Weller's news.

Gerald Carter, his secretary of defense, should never have created a biological weapon that could not be controlled. "You told me, Gerry, that our genetic—" Hannan caught himself, but not in time.

Pat Weller's eyebrows raised.

She may be an outsider, but she wasn't stupid. If the ready availability of a vaccine for U.S. Ebola had raised her suspicions, a vaccine normally years in the making, then the blunder he'd just made would confirm them.

He took a calming breath. "So now, Secretary Weller, how do we handle this threat?"

She wasn't making eye contact. Not a good sign.

"We quarantine the victim and everyone that came in contact with him. Quick and radical isolation of all who might be infected. It's our best approach, and we need to get on that, immediately. Of course, we can look for a quick path to a new vaccine, but that's a longshot."

The thought of that bug floating along through the ductwork in the West Wing sent a chill up his spine. "Let's cut to the chase. What do you think our chances are of actually containing this new strain of the virus so that it does not become an epidemic?"

Dr. Weller sat, hands folded, tapping her thumbs together for nearly a minute. Clearly she was calculating. "The Ebola virus should not spread as easily in the United States as in Africa, but this virus is airborne, and we have no statistics to calculate the base transmissivity. This is only a semi-educated guess, but I would say odds of containment are 50-50."

Hannan stifled a gasp. There might not be a country left to govern if this strain were to become epidemic. "That's not acceptable. You've got to tip the scales in our favor. I'll give you whatever resources you need." If a few people needed to die to squelch this disease, then so be it. "You are excused Ms., uh, Dr. Weller. I want you to start your work on containment, immediately."

Hannan waited until the door closed behind her, then spoke. "I asked you to come here prepared to discuss the biggest threats we face in finishing the mission of centralizing control of the nation. After hearing Secretary Weller, what are your thoughts?"

Attorney General Washington cleared his throat. "That new version of Ebola has got to be our biggest concern. If it spreads rapidly, we lose everything—the government, all our social structures, and possibly our lives. And, Mr. President, Dr. Weller knows we created the U.S. version."

Hannan nodded. "But we need her. I'll have her followed, her workplace and home bugged. If she lets any secrets slip, we'll take appropriate action, quickly."

Defense Secretary Carter leaned forward in his seat on the couch. "You want to talk about big threats? Brock Daniels is still influencing a lot of people, with Katheryn Banning's help. We believe a group of Rangers has linked up with them in Central Oregon. The results of analyzing the Apache crash told us it was brought down by an RPG–7. Only a knowledgeable person, with a little luck, could do that, someone with access to an RPG like those stolen from Fort Irwin in California."

"Can someone tell me why we can't take care of two civilians and one detachment of Army Rangers?" Hannan stood, walked in front of his desk, and paced across the Presidential Seal on the carpet.

"Mr. President," Gerald Carter spoke slowly and distinctly, "... these are Rangers, men who can survive indefinitely in any known environment and who have mastered nearly every type of weapon and explosive we have. They have the capability to train local civilians, creating a militia regiment within a few weeks. If you don't get them, they most certainly will get you. They can move undetected among us, penetrating into secure areas."

Carter's description made the Rangers sound as threatening as the modified Ebola virus. Thoughts of two types of unseen killers stalking him brought an icy chill that gripped Hannan's heart. His plans could be all for nothing.

Was his fear reflected in his eyes? He looked away from his circle of men, trying to regain his composure. "What resources will it take to guarantee we eliminate Daniels, Banning, and the Rangers?"

Mitchell Dell's face lit up and he pointed his index finger at the ceiling, the signal that the geek thought he'd had a brainstorm. "NSA hasn't been able to locate them, but based upon what we already know, maybe there is a way. We know there's cooperation at some level between the missing Rangers, Banning, and Daniels. We've interviewed everyone around here that knows Katheryn Banning. We've done the same for Brock Daniels in Oregon, including a brief chat with Jeff and Allie Jacobs."

Hannan interrupted. "Please get to your point, Mr. Dell."

"Mr. President, if you'll just listen for a moment, I think you'll like the point I get to." Mitchell Dell scanned everyone in the room, looking a bit smug.

This irked Hannan, but he was desperate to rid himself of Banning and Daniels and certainly of the Rangers.

Dell continued. "We know this ... Ms. Banning and Mr. Daniels are both loyal to a fault. We believe Jeff and Allie Jacobs know more than they are telling. Also, Julia Weiss, the young woman who contracted Ebola—by the way she's ready to be released from the hospital in Bend—she was part of the close-knit missionary group that went to Guatemala. It was in Julia Weiss's recently inherited house that Banning and Daniels hid, and it was also there where the Rangers shot down our Apache helicopter."

"The plan, Mr. Dell."

"Okay, here's my plan. Suppose, instead of discharging Julia Weiss, we take her into custody and leak to the Jacobs that she'll be interrogated, using enhanced techniques, until she tells us where the two perpetrators are. Ms. Weiss is still weak from the disease. She probably wouldn't survive the interrogation. They will know that and I think they'll cooperate."

You are an idiot Mr. Dell. But, perhaps only half an idiot.

"Dell, Julia Weiss won't have a clue where the two are. She's been in the hospital with Ebola. Take her and Allie Jacobs. Threaten to interrogate them both and hold them indefinitely as terrorists. Mr. Jacobs will do whatever we tell him in order to save his wife. Since Mr. Jacobs is Daniels's closest friend, at the very least, he'll contact Brock Daniels. We track Mr. Jacobs, using all the technology available, and the two perps will be ours."

He glared at Mitchell Dell. "I shouldn't have to do your thinking for you." Hannan scanned each face in the room. "I shouldn't have to do it for *any* of you."

Gerald Carter sat up and slapped his hands on his knees. "But what about the detachment of Rangers?"

Carter was questioning him again, trying Hannan's patience. "If we're lucky, they will try to save Banning and Daniels, and we'll get the whole lot of them. We can abort the insurgency before it's even born."

Secretary Carter shook his head. "If you're lucky? Don't you remember what happened the last time this team of Rangers got involved? We lost an Apache helicopter and your black ops team played retreat. I agree, it's a plan, but you'd better enhance it to account for the Rangers."

Hannan gestured toward Secretary Carter. "So what do you recommend? Overkill?"

Defense Secretary Carter's eyes turned to cold blue steel. "Yes. Something like the final scene in Butch Cassidy and the Sundance Kid."

"Great." Hannan's voice grew caustic. "So now we're using Hollywood movies for our battle strategy? My Secretary of Defense, no less. You are pathetic, as was your guarantee that we could control your little virus, which now might make the Bubonic Plague of the Middle Ages look like the common cold."

Carter pulled his head back like he'd been slapped in the face. "I've had about enough of your arrogance and your mouth, Hannan, and your sloppy management of this whole operation." Gerald Carter stood to leave the room. "It's your fault this happened. You delayed our response, just like Secretary Weller implied."

If Carter couldn't keep his cool ... Hannan opened the drawer on the right side of his desk and pushed a button.

Two secret service agents rushed into the Oval Office.

Hannan pointed at Carter. "Arrest this man for treason. See that he does not get Miranda rights. Lock him up with the other terrorists we've captured."

"But you can't ..." Carter blubbered.

"I just did."

After Carter had been taken away, Hannan looked at the two remaining men. "You're either with me or against me. Is that clear?"

Both heads nodded.

"Good. Now, Mr. Dell, you and Randy finish planning the arrests of Julia Weiss and Jeff and Allie Jacobs. Make sure Jeff Jacobs tells Daniels about our hostages. I believe the chivalrous Mr. Daniels will offer himself in exchange for his best friend's wife. But, in case I'm wrong, make sure we're tracking Jeff Jacobs. With a little luck, we'll soon have them all."

Chapter 32

With Craig 300 miles away meeting some Navy SEALs, Brock had concerns. Even having Steve's cell number to use in case of an emergency didn't remove Brock's angst. As long as nothing unexpected happened, they should be okay, but ...

Brock and KC sat side-by-side on the couch in Jeff's trailer, the spot they had become most comfortable with, the spot that placed them so close he could feel the warmth of KC's bare leg against his. Sometimes the spot was downright distracting.

She looked his way smiling, then giggling.

"Alright, what's so funny?"

"It's not funny. More ironic. No, satisfying. Do you remember that first summer we met?"

"I remember. Almost like it was yesterday."

"Do you remember what we talked about?"

"KC, we talked about everything under the sun. You told me how you tried to bleach off your freckles and got nothing for your pain."

"And you said it doesn't work. That everybody's got to live in whatever kind of skin they're born with, so I had to learn to like mine."

"Then you got mad at God for giving you freckles. But, Kace ..." he lifted her chin until she looked into his eyes, "... a girl's face without freckles is like the night sky without stars."

"Cheesy, Brock. Kind of nice, but still cheesy." The corners of her mouth turned upward as she took his hand. "That's not what I was referring to. Even back then, you and I dreamed about doing the same thing when we grew up, protecting our country. You through your writing, me through—well, I hadn't figured that out yet."

"We got our wish."

She looked at their clasped hands, intertwined fingers. "More than that. Neither of us could do this alone, not with Hannan's hounds running amok. We're a team, a good team."

Brock's cell played its tune for an incoming voice call. He glanced at the caller ID and didn't recognize the number. "Kace, it's a local area code. Should I answer it or not?"

"Go with your gut."

Brock pushed the icon to pick up the call.

"Brock, it's Jeff. I wouldn't call you except this is an emergency. A really bad emergency."

"It had better be an emergency. Because you called me here, we're going to have to find a new place to hide. But what's up?"

"Julia was discharged today." Jeff's voice sounded shaky, like he was about to choke up. "Allie and I picked her up from the hospital to take her home. Before we left the hospital, all three of us were arrested by the FBI."

"What?" Brock turned on the speakerphone so KC could hear this.

"Bro, it gets worse. They turned us over to some other people who threatened to interrogate Allie and Julia— interrogate as in torture—to find where you two are. These other people said Hannan can hold Allie and Julia as terrorists, indefinitely. Their spokesman said if I would contact you, and get you to turn yourself in, they'd set the women free. I don't believe them, bro, but I had to call."

"Where are you calling from, Jeff?"

"It's a public phone. They aren't listening, but I'm afraid they might somehow be able to trace the call, or get the cell towers your cell is using and ... well, you know."

"Yeah. But we need a plan. Do you know where they took Allie and Julia?"

"No. But I caught a glimpse of people dressed like the Rangers. So I think special ops types have them. Maybe it's those guys that landed at Julia's house in the Blackhawk. They drove westward, toward the mountains, not toward any of the cities."

Brock knew what driving away from the cities meant. For what Hannan's people had in mind for all five of them, they didn't want any witnesses. He and KC needed some time to plan and then needed another discussion with Jeff. "Can we call you at this number in two hours, Jeff?"

"Bro, I'll have to tell them something before that. What do you want me to say?"

Brock was putting Jeff in a horrible position, trading off the safety of his wife with that of his best friend. In reality, Hannan would likely kill them all. Brock knew what he had to tell these people. He glanced at KC.

She was staring at him. Fear grew in her emerald eyes. She grabbed his arm. "No, Brock. You can't do that."

"It's okay, Kace. They're only words to placate them. It's not what we're actually going to do."

Tears welled in her eyes. "But they'll manipulate you, using Allie and Julia, force you to ..."

Brock shook his head. He touched her cheek. "Don't worry," he whispered.

"It's Julia, isn't it?" KC whispered back.

Julia? "Kace, it's both of them. Hannan's men will kill them."

Brock lifted the phone to his ear. "Jeff, tell them I'll surrender to them in exchange for Allie and Julia. But I need to be sure the women are safe, so there will be conditions."

"Thanks, bro. I'm sorry. I'm really sorry."

"It's okay. Hey, forget going back to that phone in two hours. Come to the RV Park here in Sisters, the one by the turn off to your cabin and, Jeff, tell them I demanded that you report their answer to me, *in person*, or the deal is off."

"Will do. Pray for me, bro."

"You can count on it." Brock ended the call and set his cell on the coffee table.

Had he pushed Hannan too far with his blog posts? Maybe. But Hannan had finally learned enough about them to set a trap. And because Brock had called Jeff about a place to hide, Brock had brought danger to Jeff, Allie, and Julia.

Once again, Brock Daniels had come up short. But if he died, it would happen trying to save his innocent friends.

KC clung to his arm. "Hannan finally found a way to get to us. He's been studying us, scheming." Tears streamed down her cheeks. "I'll kill that arrogant little s—"

"Stop, KC."

"I wasn't swearing."

"But you were getting there. We need to contact Steve and form a plan. And I think it's time to pray. We're going to need—"

"Pray? I've done that, Brock. He lets us down most of the time. Some things you just have to do yourself."

"Kace, of course we'll do everything we can, but think about it. It was no accident that brought you to me when I was at the motel on the ranch. No accident that we escaped from the motel and took out that Apache chopper. He's been with—"

"You mean God? No, *we* did the right things. Craig's man, *Steve*, brought that chopper down with his skill. Hannan's men are going to kill you, Brock, unless I can come up with—"

"It's not all on your shoulders. We've got you, me, Steve, and Jeff, too."

She shook her head. "Against Hannan's black ops team that's executing a plan, an evil, insidious but finely tuned plan."

"I'm going to text Steve now. Less chance of compromising our location that way. Then we'll figure out how to throw a monkey wrench into their plan."

KC sat beside him, leaning forward, hands on her forehead.

When Brock reached for his cell, a tear splattered on the coffee table.

Chapter 33

Hannan's black ops team has Julia and Allie. Wants to trade for me. 2 hrs. We need a plan.

Brock

Brock stood and pressed send, as if standing would hurry the delivery of his text message to Steve at the RV park. Brock's mind seemed like a blender full of puréed thoughts, a messy goop from which he couldn't grab anything solid.

"Kace, help me here. Jeff's my best friend. I can't ..."

KC stood beside Brock and put her arms around him. After he texted Steve, her mood had changed. She seemed calmer. "You're not going to surrender to them, and Steve will help us, just like when he took down the helicopter. So, it's going to be okay, sweetheart."

She drew a sharp breath and pressed her fingers over her lips.

It was the first term of endearment that had ever passed between them. KC must have used that word in her own mind for a while or it wouldn't have slipped out as it did.

KC looked up but avoided his searching eyes. "I mean ... that, uh, Steve will know how to handle, what do they call it, a hostage extraction?"

Brock lifted KC's chin and peered into her eyes. The warmth in them said she had meant her words. How long had she thought of him as sweetheart rather than closest friend? Years or days?

Brock shut off the spigot of questions flowing from his mind and focused on KC's upturned face, on her inviting eyes ... on her lips. She was so beautiful.

So out of your league.

She waited, inching closer to him.

Brock kissed her forehead and held her. "I'm so glad you're here, Kace, and I don't have to face this alone."

KC pressed her cheek into his chest. "Just say the word, Brock, and you'll never have to face anything alone."

As Brock sought an appropriate reply, his cell jingled its message-arriving tune.

KC released him. "It's got to be Steve. You'd better get it."

"Kace, I—"

"The message, Brock. We need to know what Steve said."

Brock opened the text and read it aloud. "On the way. Grab what U need. Be there in 15."

KC picked up her laptop, charger, and shoved them into the case. "Who knows what we'll need for planning or if we'll be coming back here? Who knows anything anymore?"

She had said the words for his benefit, because she was hurting.

That raised another question. Was Brock hurting KC more by leaving her hanging than by telling her he wanted a life with her, regardless of her dead father's wishes? That question had haunted him for several days. But Brock couldn't deal with it until there was a lull in this war. At the present, they were marching into battle.

An engine roared as a vehicle topped the hill northeast of the lake. Brock turned toward the window behind the couch. "It's Steve and he's really moving. Come on, Kace. Let's meet him outside. We can talk on our way to the RV Park." Brock grabbed his computer case and the rifle Craig had left them.

KC followed him out the door, computer case on her shoulder.

He locked the trailer as Steve's SUV slid to a stop in a cloud of dust.

Brock opened the back door of the SUV for KC, and then entered behind her.

She gave him a surprised look and slid across the seat to make room for Brock.

"Let's beat it for the RV Park, Steve. We need to pick Jeff's brains before we finalize any plans. He should be there in fifteen minutes."

Steve hit the gas, spun a half doughnut on the dirt road, and glanced back at Brock when they flew down the short straight stretch by the lake. "Do you really think they'll give us that advantage? Actually free Jeff to come back instead of just having him call?"

"I emphasized no deal unless Jeff delivers the message in person."

"You can be sure they'll throw a wrinkle into this, a wrinkle we didn't expect." KC took Brock's hand.

She had no idea how that symbol of their closeness, her hand on his, calmed him.

Steve accelerated to a speed slightly below Brock's panic threshold. "We need to do a weapons and ammo inventory, get the layout of this place from Jeff, and plan our strategy."

Steve described an arsenal in the back of the motorhome, enough munitions to blow a crater in the ground the size of a city block, if something set it off. Too bad they didn't have enough trained warfighters to make use of it all.

KC didn't speak during the rest of the ride. Brock didn't know how to interpret that, but at least she kept his hand in hers. That was a good sign. No way did he want to go into a deadly situation with bad feelings between him and the woman he loved.

Some of the Rangers were married. They must have strong marriages with strong women; otherwise, warfighters would never survive their first battle. How could a man concentrate on war if he's afraid of losing his woman?

Brock looked up at Steve in the driver's seat. "You single, Steve?"

"Yeah. Runnin' solo through life, so far."

Just as Brock thought. "So no fiancé or girlfriend?"

"Not yet. It's not like I'm not looking, but things are a bit dicey for forming relationships these days."

KC studied Brock.

He wasn't going to step on the landmine Steve had inadvertently planted.

"RV park ahead," Steve said. "I'll slow down as we enter."

Brock's cell sounded the tune for an incoming call. He pulled it out. "It's Jeff's number." Brock picked up the call.

"Jeff here. Listen, bro, one of Hannan's men gave me a cell and told me to call them back on it to negotiate the details."

"Then they're tracking it," Steve said.

"Who was that?" Jeff asked.

"Steve. You remember, the gun man."

"I remember. Brock, it's probably best if you come to my place. They already know where it is. They don't need to know where you're staying, not if we can help it."

Steve glanced back at Brock. "How far is that?"

"Fifteen minutes. Turn right at the main highway and ignore the speed limit," Brock said. "We're gonna lose fifteen minutes of planning time here."

Steve slowed the SUV and reached back over the seat. "Brock, give me your phone for a minute."

Brock pushed the cell into his hand.

"Steve here, Jeff. Are you at home?"

"Yes, I'm at home."

"They didn't take you with them to where they're holding the women, then turn you loose?"

"No. They left me here."

"Then get out a pencil and paper and write down everything you remember about the men, the vehicle that took the women, and which way it went."

"I'm on it."

Steve gave the phone back to Brock.

"How were Allie and Julia doing when they left?"

"As good as could be expected. They were scared, but not losing it. But that supposed FBI guy, a Middle-Eastern looking dude, couldn't keep his eyes off them. He scares me, bro."

"Then we'll make special plans for him. See you in fifteen, Jeff."

On the highway, Steve accelerated to above eighty. "When we get to Jeff's, leave everything in the SUV except what you need for planning."

They reached Jeff's house in less time than Brock thought possible.

Steve turned in the circle drive and stopped near the front door of the ranch-style rambler.

KC grabbed her laptop, then climbed out of the SUV.

Steve brought the assault rifle he'd stashed in the back.

Brock brought his laptop and the M4 Craig left with them.

Jeff flung the front door open. "Man, am I glad to see you guys."

"Got the paper?" Steve pointed at the sheet of notebook paper in Jeff's hand.

"Right here."

"Put it on the coffee table and sit beside me while I scan it." Steve looked up at KC and Brock. "Watch over our shoulders and chime in if you have something to contribute."

"I'm going to get on Jeff's Wi-Fi in case we need maps." KC said. "Is that okay?"

"Yeah. The passkey is ..." Jeff paused. "Uh ... AllieBaby. But don't tell her I told—" A cloud darkened Jeff's face. Fear showed in his eyes. It stopped his words.

Normally, Brock would've ribbed Jeff about that AllieBaby passkey. But this wasn't a normal time.

Steve scanned Jeff's list. "Good eyes, Jeff." Steve was obviously trying to move Jeff beyond any disheartening thoughts. "You say it was a late-model, black Chevy van, and it turned on Whitted Market Road?"

"Yeah. They weren't taking Allie and Julia to any jail around here. In fact, I don't swallow the whole FBI impersonation thing. They were headed into the desert, or toward the Cascade foothills north of here."

Brock's train of thoughts turned to words. "They turned north on Whitted, which becomes Northwest Helmholtz."

Steve stopped what he was doing and watched Brock.

"They would need a secluded place for what they have planned and also to hide their team. That road takes them north toward the ranch, but the only secluded places are—"

Jeff cut in. "Along the Deschutes River."

"You mean like Steelhead Falls?" KC pointed to her laptop screen. "I've got the parking area at the trailhead up on a satellite map. You can see a lot of detail here."

Brock patted KC's shoulder. "Good job. That fits perfectly. It's west of the ranch, the direction the chopper came from when they attacked us at Julia's house. It's got to be the place."

He glanced at the time displayed in the corner of KC's laptop screen. "We've got less than one hour until I'm supposed to surrender. I think I should surrender here at

Jeff's house. I'll tell them Jeff ran off so they wouldn't recapture him."

Steve shook his head. "Brock we can't let them have you. So we're going to jump the men who come to get you, leave them here incapacitated, if they're still alive. That way, the three of us can drive right up to where they're holding the women before the rest of their group gets suspicious."

"What about me?" KC looked up at them, eyes blazing. "You're not cutting me out of this."

The determination in her voice pushed a knife into Brock's gut. KC would be in danger. But she wouldn't back down on this issue. Not KC.

Steve studied Brock's eyes. His expression said he understood Brock's concern. But what would Steve do about it? Steve placed a hand on KC's shoulder. "KC, we'll double back to the RV Park and go north to Steelhead Falls from there. Your motorcycle is in the toy box on the back of the motor home. Are you comfortable riding it on off roads?"

"I rode it two-thirds of the way across the country. I'll be fine."

Steve dipped his head. "That's settled. Now zoom in on that parking area above Steelhead Falls ... right there. Are any of you familiar with this area?"

"We all are," Brock said.

"Good. Let me study the layout for a minute. I can make an educated guess how Rangers would set up camp there." He pointed to the hill above the trailhead. "How high is the hill? Can we watch the entire area below?" On KC's screen, Steve circled the area around the trailhead to Steelhead Falls.

Brock traced the hilltop with his finger. "Yeah, all along there it's high enough"

"What's this building?"

"It's a glorified outhouse. Has both a men's and a women's side."

"Okay. When we arrive, we stop short of this hill. I'll climb it, take out any sentry they may have put there, and then we'll survey the camp to finalize our extraction scenario."

Brock laid his hand on Steve's shoulder. "Guys, I think we need to finalize that plan for jumping the men here. They'll be arriving in fifteen or twenty minutes."

"He's right," Steve said. "If we can lure them into the house to take you, they're ours, even if they leave the driver in the van."

"Steve, they've got Allie and Julia for security. Are they really going to be worried about anything when they pick me up?"

"Daniels, Rangers, even bad ones, are trained to be paranoid about unknown enemies, and to prevail in spite of Murphy's Law. These guys won't just stroll into Jeff's house and let us jump them. So we need some bait."

KC sat up on the couch and scanned the faces of the three men around her. "Who is it they really want here?"

"No, Kace—"

"Brock, just listen for a minute. You're not getting off free here either." She paused and looked at Steve.

"Go ahead, Banning."

"Okay. Here's how my plan plays out. Jeff moves his car to the far end of the circle driveway. That forces them to drive in and circle to the house with the driver on the side nearest the front door. After they stop, Brock opens the door and, if nobody tries to shoot him, he just stands in the doorway waiting. They'll get antsy at that point. Before they start yelling at Brock, I walk up behind him and let them get a good look at me, then I disappear back into the house."

"Banning," a smile spread across Steve's face, "that's brilliant. Everyone they need to capture to finish their mission is right here. So they—"

"Yes. But it has to look like my appearing was a bit of an accident, and Brock has to look like he's totally ignorant of my appearance or they might not take the bait. That's when Brock says he's not going out until they prove that Allie and Julia are safe. He says he needs to talk to the women on the phone."

Steve raised his hand, "You da man, KC."

Didn't she realize this was a men's high-five ceremony? Brock nudged KC's shoulder.

Finally, KC slapped Steve's hand.

She was an incredible woman. But the danger to her twisted Brock's gut into one big knot.

"Okay," Steve said. "Here's where we go from there. Brock's stuck in the front doorway, so I need somebody who can handle this M4. Jeff?"

"Don't look at me?"

"Craig showed Brock and me how to use it, Steve," KC said.

Steve studied KC's eager eyes for a moment. "Alright, KC will pick up the M4 after she retreats into the house. The driver will get out, stand by the door, brandishing his weapon, and cover the men, probably two, who come to the door for Brock. KC slips out the back door, quietly around the corner of the house, hides behind that bush at the corner, puts her gun in automatic mode, and gets ready to shoot."

KC's eyes widened. "So I just gun the driver down? No warning or anything?"

Steve laid a hand on her shoulder. "KC, they tried to gun us all down with an Apache helicopter. They plan to kill you all, Brock, Julia, Allie, Jeff ... and you. If it's any consolation, your shots probably won't kill this person because of his body armor. But you've got to make sure he can't fire his gun."

Brock tapped her shoulder. "Kace, look at me."

Her eyes glared like two green laser beams. "I can do this, Brock." She spat the words at him. "No filthy li—"

Brock covered her mouth. "She's ready, Steve. What's next?"

KC pulled Brock's hand from her mouth and huffed a sharp sigh.

Steve took a deep breath. "Brock puts out his hands in surrender. When the Hannani reaches for him, Brock yanks the guy inside. The man at the vehicle will tense, then raise his gun. That's when you open fire, KC. Shoot until he stops moving. I shoot the number two man before he can get a shot off, while Brock and Jeff whale on the man we pulled inside. Then we make mummies out of them with duct tape, unless they're not breathing. In that case, we just use a little less tape."

"Then we all hop in the van and get my motorcycle?" KC looked up at Steve.

Steve nodded to her.

A hard side of KC Brock hadn't seen before showed in the determination on her face and in her rigid posture. This was the mental and physical toughness that had allowed her to escape DC and make it safely to Oregon. He prayed it was the last time in her life she would have to draw on it.

"Listen up." Steve walked toward the front door. "Let's assume our places and walk through this exercise. They could be here in another ten minutes. Remember, perfect practice makes perfect. Let's get it right."

Seven minutes later, a black Chevy van slowed as it rolled down Highway 126.

Brock stood near the front door, looking out a window. He glanced at KC behind him.

She gave him thumbs up.

It didn't slow his accelerating pulse. When Brock thought about what these men were intent on doing, anger surged through him. He squelched the anger with logic. Putting things in perspective, this was only one small battle in a war, a battle in which he *would* do his part.

He glanced at KC again.

She checked her gun, leaned it by the back door, and returned to her spot in the living room as the black van rolled around the circle drive. It stopped with the driver's window only ten yards from the front door.

The sliding door on the opposite side opened. The driver didn't get out. Not two, but three men in tac gear scurried around the back of the van to the house side.

Murphy's Law. Which one of them would be its victim? He would make sure it wasn't KC ... no matter what that required.

Chapter 34

"Four men," Brock whispered to himself.

Steve's voice came from behind Brock. "Only one change. KC takes whoever stands nearest the van. I've got the extra guy."

Brock shot a prayer up through the blue summer sky, as he slowly opened the door. He waved a white towel, then flinched as several metallic clicks came from guns now trained on him. They didn't fire, so Brock moved into the doorway.

Footsteps sounded on the carpet behind him. KC.

The men outside stiffened as if jolted by electricity. The apparent leader motioned one man toward Brock and waved the other around the house, opposite the direction KC would be moving.

The hair bristled on the back of Brock's neck. KC would be the victim.

The back door creaked. KC was outside, unaware of the man circling the house behind her.

For a few seconds, Brock fought the strong urge to forget the plan, grab a weapon, and run to the back yard to protect her. He shot another prayer up for KC ... and for himself not to completely lose it with worry.

He had to continue with the plan or they might all be killed. Brock took a deep, calming breath. "Prove to me that Allie Jacobs and Julia Weiss are safe, and I'll go with you. But I need to talk to them on the phone."

The leader pointed his gun at Brock. "That's no longer part of the deal. You can see them for yourself, soon enough. Cuff him."

The man nearest the door only carried a handgun. He holstered it and pushed a set of police-style, zip-tie handcuffs toward Brock. "You know the drill. Slide your hands in these, Daniels, and no—"

Brock grabbed the man's wrist, yanked with all of his arm strength, jumping backward with his powerful legs. He flung the man six feet into the room, rolled to one side, and sprang to his feet.

Gunfire erupted. Multiple locations.

Was it KC?

Steve shot through the living room window. Then jumped to the doorway.

The guy on the floor reached for his holster. Brock gave him a vicious kick.

Jeff put him out with a baseball bat to the head.

Steve fired another burst.

More shots behind the house.

The van driver slumped over the wheel.

The leader went down on the lawn.

Brock ran to the back door. A trail of blood sent his heart drumming, wildly.

He followed the trail across the back lawn to a body. A body dressed in tac gear.

KC flew around the corner and lowered her gun when her intense green eyes focused on Brock.

She pushed the safety lever and practically leaped into his arms.

"Secure in front." Steve's voice.

"Secure in the house." Jeff.

"Secure back here. Hannani down." Brock yelled.

"And not moving," KC whispered in his ear as she clung to him.

"Kace, when he broke for the other side of the house, I just about blew the whole plan."

"When I looked around the corner and one man was missing. I knew, Brock."

"Yeah. I guess you did."

"Would you hold me for a few seconds? Steve said we're secure."

"Kace, I'd hold you for a lifetime if I could."

She looked up at Brock, her questioning eyes peering deeply into his. "*If* you could?"

Maybe someday she would understand.

When he released her, the tough look had disappeared, and the KC he knew so well was back.

Brock walked out onto the back lawn and felt the man's pulse. As he expected, there wasn't any.

In the house, Jeff and Steve were rolling bodies up in duct tape.

"Brock," Steve waved toward the van. "Driver's dead. Drag his body in here. Get the guy in back too."

Jeff ripped off a length of tape. "More blood? Come on, you guys. Allie and I will have to get new carpeting after this."

Brock stopped beside the van and looked back at Jeff near the doorway. "If you tell Allie you stashed dead bodies in here, you'll have to get a new house."

"That's better than having to get a new country," Steve said. "Now let's hurry. We've got a motorcycle to pick up and two women hostages to rescue. Toss all their weapons and phones into the back of the van."

"I'm on it." KC scooped up several guns.

After securing the man Jeff had clubbed on the head, Steve stood. "Jeff, do you have a flat file, one you can grab quick like?"

"Yeah. In the garage. I'll get it."

"Brock, where are those cuffs they were going to put on you?"

He looked around the living room door, then outside. "They're on the front steps."

"Grab them. Use Jeff's file to smooth off the ridges on one side. You'll be able to pull the cuffs off at the right time."

"When's the right time?"

"We'll decide that when we're sitting on top of that hill overlooking their camp." Steve motioned toward the van. "Come on, everybody. They think their mission is on track. Let's hurry so we don't lose the element of surprise."

Steve took the driver's seat of the Chevy van. Jeff rode shotgun. Brock rode in the second row of seats with KC pressed against his side.

He had nearly killed a man. KC had. He had experienced a furious gun battle. KC loved him. The list went on as countless emotions wove a tangled mess in his mind.

One thought emerged from the confusion and rose to the forefront of his consciousness. He loved this incredible woman who sat beside him, clinging to his arm. One moment a tantalizing woman who could've been a model, the next a computer genius, then the stereotypical Irish woman with red hair, freckles, and a temper hovering near the boiling point. Now, she was a warfighter, a reluctant one, but not one any sane member of the human race would want to face as an opponent because, on top of all her qualities, KC had a heart that simply would not quit.

Brock glanced at her.

She caught and returned his glance, a glance that turned into something much more tender and longing.

How could he even think of life without her?

Life. Somehow, they had to hold on to it through the events of this day, or it wouldn't matter what he thought.

Before Brock realized it, they approached Sisters.

Steve turned in at the RV park and stopped the van, placing the sliding door near what he called the toy box on the rear of the motorhome. "Each of you grab an M4, and I'll dole out the ammo. We don't want anybody getting stuck with the wrong magazine ... or an empty one." He lowered the back door of the motorhome, creating a ramp.

KC ran up it and checked out her Honda motorcycle. "Keys are in the ignition. The tank's three quarters full. But how am I going to carry my gun?"

"I'll give it to you when we stop. Remember, everyone, we stop at the place KC showed us, about a quarter mile east of the hilltop."

KC rolled the Honda to the ramp, jumped on, and coasted down, stopping beside the van. She hit the starter twice and the engine revved, then slowed to a purr.

Steve closed the motorhome door. "Let's go, before one of those cell phones we confiscated starts ringing. And, KC, stay behind us. That's an order, Ms. Banning." Steve waited for her response.

"Yes, sir." KC gave him a salute that was all wrist and no arm, then pulled her helmet on, carefully tucking the curls of her long hair inside.

Within 60 seconds, they were flying down the highway with KC a safe distance behind.

No worries about getting speeding tickets these days. With the societal chaos Hannan had created, even the police in rural areas focused on the higher priority tasks.

Brock glanced at the confiscated cell in his hand. It said 3:15 p.m. Even after speeding, with the delays required by their cautious approach to the camp, they were probably going to arrive at Steelhead Falls about ten minutes later than the four men would have. Maybe it wouldn't arouse suspicion. Maybe ...

As they neared the falls trailhead, the pavement ended and Steve slowed.

Brock glanced behind them. Not much dust for KC to eat.

Not that it would have mattered. She sped up and passed them, then pointed to a small side road, a two-tracked trail winding through a forest of Juniper trees, a place she'd spotted on the satellite photo. She turned onto it.

Steve followed her and parked the van in a spot hidden from the road. "Come on, Rangers. Time to check our weapons and ammo again."

Steve was doing a lot of handholding to make sure their inexperience didn't get anyone killed.

KC took the M4 Steve shoved at her. "How do I carry this on the motorcycle? Put the strap over my shoulder?"

"Just hang on to it for now, Banning ... in case anything goes wrong. See the rock formation near the hill?"

She nodded.

"The sun's still up high enough, so I'll signal you with a mirror after I make sure there is no sentry, or ..." He paused. "If you hear shooting, keep your weapons handy, but leave. Ms. Banning, in that case, you leave your motorcycle and go with the guys in the van."

"So after you signal us, what then?" KC asked.

"The men will bring their weapons and spare clips. We move quietly until I meet you on this side of the hilltop. Do not go to the top. Understand?"

"Yeah," Brock replied. "We won't expose ourselves."

"What about me and the motorcycle?"

"This gets a little tricky, but I want you to idle along the road, keeping the engine as quiet as possible. About halfway up the hill, cut to the left into the trees. From there, I'll help you push the bike nearly to the top of the hill. That's where we spy on the Hannanis and finalize our plan." Steve looked at Brock. "Still got that cell you borrowed?"

"Yeah." Brock patted his pocket.

"Keep it, but keep it turned off. We're overdue, so they might try to call. We don't want the cell playing Reveille as we go into their camp. If our plan starts falling apart, I want you, Banning, to pull the magazine from your rifle, toss it, along with the rifle, into the bushes, and ride hard back to the motorhome. Got it?"

She nodded.

"All right, Rangers. I'm going now. Look for my signal in about five minutes."

Brock watched Steve's controlled movements as he traversed the sparse forest, silently, keeping himself covered by trees from anyone looking down the backside of the hill.

"Bro," Jeff stepped to his side. "He still hasn't said anything about Allie and Julia."

"Nothing to say yet, Jeff."

KC rested a hand on Jeff's shoulder. "He knows what he's doing. This stuff is Steve's life, Jeff. He'll tell us how to free Allie and Julia once we see what we're dealing with. We'll get them out."

KC was a nurturer. Brock hadn't noticed that before. Another good quality of a wife and a mother.

He sighed and tried to focus on their task. "Captain Craig said a detachment of Rangers consists of twelve men. We took out four. They might have only eight left."

Jeff still looked worried. "So, we're outnumbered two to one."

KC tapped his shoulder and shook her head when he looked her way. "You forgot Julia and Allie. Eight to six. With Steve leading, I like those odds."

A dark cloud seem to cross Jeff's face. Fear showed in his frantic, darting eyes. "But there's that crazy Middle-Eastern guy who only wants Allie and Julia for his own purposes. He didn't look like he belonged with the other men."

"Okay. It's nine to six," KC said. "I still say we win."

A light flashed from the rock formation on the next hill. "Steve's ready for us. I'm with KC. Right is on our side. God is on our side. The enemy's evil. In the end, they lose. And today they lose. Let's go."

KC started her bike and idled away.

By the time Brock and Jeff reached the rock formation, KC and Steve had pushed her motorcycle up to their stopping point.

Steve located a small, level area with an animal trail leading over to the main road. He parked the bike there.

KC locked the Honda and tucked the keys in her shorts pocket.

Occasional bushes, Juniper trees, and a few Ponderosa Pines lined the hilltop. Near the crest of the hill, Steve crouched behind a large bush, motioning for the others to join him. "Here's what I see." He spoke barely above a whisper. "Sleeping tents for about fourteen, all situated in the parking area, on the north side of the camp. The large tent on the south side of the parking area, about fifty yards from the others, must be where they're holding the women."

KC shoved her head between Brock and Steve. "So how do we extract Julia and Allie?"

"This all has to happen in a short span of time, before they get overly suspicious. But we can't rush it. It needs to look like everything is under control when we roll in. So, Brock, Jeff, and I get in the van. Jeff drives. We go right through the parking area and continue to the opening in the big tent, where Jeff will pull in, leaving the sliding door toward the tent. We'll use the van to block the view from the tents on the other side of the camp. That's where I think the gunfire will come from."

"What if they challenge us as we go in?" Jeff said.

"Just keep going. If any shooting starts, I'll cover us until you stop the van in position. But, I'm guessing there won't be any shooting until we go for the girls."

"And what do I do?" KC gave Steve her bug-eyed glare, the look she reserved for exasperation.

"Let me finish with the van, then we'll cover your part."

She shuffled her feet. That KC was antsy and feeling slighted was understating things. This did not bode well for what was coming.

Steve continued. "Here's the rest of our plan. The van stops. I shove a handcuffed Brock out the sliding door, barking commands to him and showing the barrel of the gun we borrowed. At this point we should be able to see Julia and Allie. This is when the Hannanis will realize something is wrong. So I pitch an M84 flashbang grenade into the tent. Brock, you hit the ground and cover your head when I say *now*. The grenade temporarily disables everyone there except Brock. But you might be a dazed for a second or two. Shake it off as quickly as you can. Jeff and I start firing on any visible Hannanis. Brock carries the two women one at a time into the van, slams the slider shut, and jumps in the driver's seat, while Jeff and I shoot the place all to heck so we can get out of Dodge."

"How fast can we do all that?" Jeff asked.

"From the time I shove Brock out until he's in the driver's seat headed out needs to be less than 60 seconds. I hear Brock's a quite an athlete. I'll bet he can do it in 45."

KC gripped Steve's shoulder. "And my job is?"

Brock could see what was coming. "Kace, we need you for this. If anything goes wrong, you're our last hope. Maybe this nation's last hope."

"Brock Daniels ..." her voice grew a little louder than was prudent. "You're a manipulative—"

Steve gave her the finger-on-lips quiet sign.

She huffed a blast of air. "Just tell me what you want me to do."

KC had backed down. And she would be away from the gunfire. Maybe he wouldn't worry about her so much this time.

Steve pointed down the deer trail to the road. "Strap the rifle across your back and ride your motorcycle up the road stopping shy of the top of the hill. But don't go to the top until you hear the grenade, or until shooting starts. Watch us from there, but keep your head down. Don't shoot unless you have to protect yourself. This won't happen, but if for some reason we don't get out ... here's my cell and here's Captain Craig's secure phone number. Call him as soon as you're safely away and hidden. He should be back early tomorrow. Here's the key to the motor home."

"But you guys are going to get away, so—"

Steve cut in. "So you beat us back to the motorhome. Go as fast as you can. If we're chased, we'll have to lose them. It might be a while before we get there. We'll call you on one of the cells to keep you posted. Keep a gun ready until we arrive. Got all that?"

"Got it." KC stared at Steve with her hands on her hips. "Don't like it, but I've got it."

Steve pointed back toward the parked van. "Okay, guys, it's back to the van for us."

Brock brushed KC's cheek with his lips as he moved by her. "Love you, Kace."

He wanted another good look at KC, one to take with him to keep, just in case. Brock looked back.

KC brushed a tear from her eye, her gaze locked on him.

Two kids facing danger again. How he wished it were only from some angry old duffers.

How did these Rangers do this? They faced death over and over again knowing loved ones waited at home, hoping and praying their men would return.

Brock looked ahead at Steve's broad shoulders and stealthy movements through the bushes and trees. It was more than training. It was something God placed in the heart of those called to be warriors, called to defend the innocent against aggressors. Brock didn't have it, not the calling. But today, this hour, he had to be a warrior. If he failed, Allie and Julia would face the crazed man Jeff feared, and probably something worse than death.

When they reached the van, Brock climbed in the back, slipped on the cuffs and pulled with his right hand. It slid free. He placed his gun to the side of the sliding door where he could grab it quickly, if needed.

Jeff steered the black van up the hill. Brock drew a sharp breath as he surveyed the camp. Under blue skies and the hot Central Oregon sun, the camp in the Steelhead Falls trailhead parking lot didn't look dangerous. Behind it, nearly thirty feet below, the clear blue water of the Deschutes River flowed through a dark pool to a rock-infested rapids where blue turned to white. That this beautiful scene would soon become a battlefield seemed surreal.

Brock breathed a soft prayer for all of them, especially Allie and Julia, then mentally rehearsed his role over and over in an endless loop that would only stop when the van stopped beside the big tent.

Three or four men stood near the soldiers' tents as the van passed. Maybe the others were away somewhere. But, with the exchange imminent, Brock doubted it.

Jeff cut diagonally across the lot and headed straight for the target, the big tent thirty yards beyond the graded, graveled parking area.

With the tinted windows hiding them, the van rolled beyond the parking area.

One man stopped, turned his head, and watched with what looked like mild curiosity.

Jeff slowed the van and circled to bring the sliding door beside the tent opening.

The van stopped.

Steve stood beside the passenger's seat and shoved Brock through the open door. "Get in there, Daniels."

Brock faked a stumble and glanced ahead. Two women in chairs. A man beside them.

"Now!" Steve's voice.

Brock fell to the ground, pulling his right hand free from the cuffs, covering his ears, slamming his eyelids shut, and pushing his face into the dirt.

Noise slugged Brock in the head like a boxer's punch. The flash felt like it burned the skin on his hands. He jumped up, shook his head a couple of times and stumbled forward toward the empty chairs. Three people lay on the floor of the tent.

The tat, tat, tat of M4 rifles sounded behind him.

Brock reached the women. He picked up Allie first. Looking at Julia, helpless and unconscious after braving a battle with Ebola, he felt guilty. But Allie was his best friend's wife. He half ran and half stumbled toward the van.

More gunfire. All of it came from the direction of the van and beyond. Good. The vehicle would shield him as he loaded Allie.

She groaned and put her hands to her head as he laid her down inside.

"Stay down, Allie. We're under fire." He turned to go back for Julia.

* * *

On top of the hill, KC sat on the idling motorcycle, ready to go at a moment's notice. She eased off the clutch and rolled to the right side of the road. The flap on the big tent was open. From where she positioned the motorcycle, KC could peer into the semidarkness of the big tent.

Brock ran out carrying Allie.

Thank goodness. They were going to get the women out.

Brock turned to run back in, then he stopped.

From inside the tent, a big brute of a man moved toward Brock. The man had a limp body hanging across his arm. Julia. He pressed a gun against her head.

There was no way Brock could survive this.

KC had only one option.

She slipped the Honda in gear, revved the engine, and popped the clutch.

Brock would give himself for Julia. He'd do whatever the man said.

KC speed shifted through second, ending up in third gear at the bottom of the hill. The speedometer hit 60 miles-per-hour as she crossed the parking area. She flew through the line of fire. Thankfully, her roaring engine drowned out the sound of gunfire. One less distraction.

A loud crack sounded near her ear. KC flinched. Maybe the engine couldn't drown out everything.

She looked at her helmet bouncing wildly where she'd strapped it on the handle bar. A stupid mistake, but not nearly as big as the one she might be making now.

KC braked hard, shifted down, and rounded one end of the van with the rear wheel spinning, spraying one corner of the tent with dirt and gravel. She entered the tent at an angle.

The man dropped Julia's limp body and moved to KC's left. His eyes widened when she aimed the motorcycle straight at him. He raised his gun.

She was in far too deep to back out now. KC twisted the throttle wide open.

The Honda's engine roared as it shot forward.

Chapter 35

Though her VFR800 Interceptor could generate nearly 100 horsepower, the powerful bike seemed to move in slow motion as KC bore down on the gunman inside the tent.

With her chin nearly on the handlebars, KC flew by Brock.

The gunman stood only a step from Julia's body.

Please don't move toward Julia.

KC pointed the front wheel at the center of the man's body and held the throttle wide open.

Would he choose to shoot or try to jump out of the way?

He hesitated.

KC squeezed on the handle bars and locked her elbows.

The bike slammed into the big brute.

The impact pitched her body off the seat.

The back wheel went airborne.

KC's body shot up into a handstand over the handlebars.

Just stay on the bike.

She managed to hold onto the handlebars until gravity slammed her butt onto the seat.

Again she squeezed the grips, anticipating the coming acceleration.

The back wheel hit the ground spinning.

The bike shot forward, bursting through the tent fabric like paper.

KC backed off on the throttle.

What lay beyond the tent? The river? Trees and rocks?

She laid the motorcycle on its side and crouched on top of the bike. With one foot peg digging a trench in the dirt, KC rode out the slide.

The big Honda slid to a stop in a cloud of dust. Her heart still pounding out panic, KC focused on the drop-off, only two steps in front of her, then on the river thirty feet below.

Behind her, the continuous tat, tat, tat said the firefight still raged.

What had happened to Brock? Had he gotten Julia? What about the gunman?

KC picked up her bike, jammed it into first gear, and skirted the parking area away from the fighting. Between the trees to KC's left, Brock climbed into the van, without Julia.

He slid the door closed. The window by Brock's head shattered.

The shot came from the tent. KC had hit the gunman. The motorcycle dealt him a devastating blow, but he was evidently still alive and shooting. What kind of a brute was he?

KC shifted down at the base of the hill and turned left, toward the roadway.

Brock was okay, wasn't he? He had to be. She had done something stupid. Risked her life, yet managed to survive. Surely God wouldn't let it be for nothing, would He?

KC climbed the hill, weaving through the Juniper forest, until she hit the road.

The van carrying Brock, Jeff, Steve, and Allie trailed KC by fifty yards. Behind it a cloud of dust obscured everything. Hopefully, they weren't being chased.

Regardless, they were fortunate to come out unscathed after the brute of a man had recovered so quickly from the flashbang grenade. They had planned to meet back at the Sisters RV Park rather than go to Jeff and Allie's house, but their plan had included having Julia with them. Now, they would need another plan, a plan to free Julia, a plan where the element of surprise had been eliminated.

Since the men at the camp still had Julia, maybe they wouldn't try to chase KC and the van. Regardless, KC led the van at speeds far above the legal limit until they approached Sisters.

The van rolled into the RV park, hugging the rear wheel of her motorcycle.

Steve stopped the van and jumped out. "You've got the keys. Quick, we need to get your bike stowed away and hide this van. They might send someone after us."

"Did you see anyone following?"

"No. But we need to be prepared." Steve unlocked the door and lowered it.

KC ran the Honda up the ramp, parked it, and ran back down.

While Steve closed the rear door, Jeff drove the van onto the National Forest road, headed toward Jeff's cabin.

Steve rushed her, Allie, and Brock inside the motorhome. "Jeff's going to hide the van about a quarter mile away. Said he'd be back in about five."

Steve paced the floor, agony etched into the lines on his face. On his fifth or sixth pass, he stopped, facing KC and Brock. "There was a side flap on that tent. After KC ran the gauntlet ..." He paused and stared disapprovingly into her eyes, "... I moved down to it and slipped inside. I saw Julia. Held her hand. Her eyes opened and I saw trust. She knew I wasn't one of Hannan's men. That's when the big, ugly dude jumped up and put a gun to her head. I dove for the door, tucked, and rolled out of the tent. He didn't shoot. But I left her behind." His voice grew more intense. "I saw the fear in her eyes when that man grabbed her, and I just left her behind. Rangers don't leave anyone behind! Not ever!"

KC had never seen Steve this close to losing it. He was a man in total control. Maybe she hadn't seen enough of combat life to make judgments about these incredible men. In fact, she would pass on the whole thing, combat life and understanding the men who volunteer to do it, if she could.

She glanced at Brock.

He nodded. Evidently, he knew what had happened in the tent.

KC stepped to Steve's side and gave him a quick hug. "Come on. Let's make a plan to get Julia out of that creep's hands."

Steve's eyes widened. "You saw him too?"

KC nodded. "Gave me the creeps even though I was about to run him down."

"Run him down?" Brock waited for her to look his way. "Kace, your guardian angel was all over you today or you wouldn't be standing here."

"I know. And you know me, Brock. I blame God for things, then don't thank Him when He comes through for me."

Brock gave her his all-knowing nod that could sometimes be infuriating. His nod stopped when the cell he carried played a tune. He pulled out the cell and glanced at the display. "I think we just got a plan. The plan is Brock surrenders and Julia goes free. It says I have to surrender to them at the camp not later than 9:00 p.m. this evening, or they're going to ...."

"To what?" KC asked.

Steve leaned down to read the text.

"I deleted it, Steve. He's not going to get the satisfaction of anybody else reading it. He's not just a creep. This guy's demonic."

Chapter 36

President Hannan sat alone in his private study, his secure cell planted in his ear, a place it had spent far too much time over the past 24 hours, thanks to Katheryn Banning, Brock Daniels, and some uninvited guests, apparently a Ranger detachment.

Captain Blanchard, the black ops commander was about to repeat himself for the third time. "Julia Weiss knows nothing. Her only use to us is for a bargaining chip."

None of these people could live. Hannan couldn't afford to let them tell their story to anyone, or have Brock Daniels tell it for them. "Once this incident is over the girl dies, too. Then you need to move your camp."

"Mr. President, they can't go to the police. They would be arrested. The camp needs to stay where it is for now. We've got things set up to interrogate Brock Daniels and any of the others we deem necessary. Since we have the girl, we'll get Daniels."

Maybe Hannan should give on the camp issue. The team was safe there and Blanchard said they had set up a portable jail. That could prove useful. "Alright, Blanchard. Keep your camp and your jail. But after you get Daniels, keep him, too. At least for a while. If we have him, we'll get Banning. Those two are tight. Then, we'll lure the Rangers who've taken their side. The Rangers must have been busy elsewhere since they didn't help in the rescue attempt."

"So you want us to hold Daniels for a while?"

"Yes. Don't let Abdul have him until a while after you get Banning. Let the two commiserate for a while. And when the Butcher starts his work, I want Ms. Banning to hear it, and know what's in store for her. She will pay for all the trouble she's caused us. Don't let Abdul kill Banning until we've attracted the Rangers. When they come, spring the trap we've set. Now, if you'll pardon me, I've got an Ebola outbreak to deal with."

Chapter 37

At 6:00 p.m., Brock, KC, Allie, and Steve sat around the small dining table in the motorhome. Jeff stood nearby, watching out a window for any unwelcome visitors.

KC could see Brock's resolve growing. Bit by bit, Brock retreated into himself, blocking out everyone, even her. He was steeling himself for what would come when he surrendered to Hannan's men to gain Julia's release. Seeing that, ripped KC's heart to shreds.

Julia's release? They wouldn't actually release her. The demonic man was obsessed with Julia. But Steve had experience with hostage situations. Surely, he could find a way that didn't involve Brock actually surrendering.

"Steve?" KC waited for him to come back from wherever his mind had wandered.

Slowly his eyes returned to their usual state of alertness, then they focused on her.

"You've dealt with hostage situations before. There's got to be some other way than Brock surrendering. Can we make another plan?"

Steve didn't reply.

Brock stared across the table at the wall. No eye contact with anyone. "The only plan we need is the one that ensures Julia's safe release when I surrender."

"But Craig and the other men will be back in twenty-four hours." KC looked from Brock to Steve. Neither would look at her. "Can't we stall?"

"In twenty-four hours, Julia will be dead. Craig can't help us with this." Brock sighed and stared at the wall. "Think about this for a minute. Julia has gotten the worst of everything that's happened since we went to Guatemala and Hannan created all this chaos. She went to Guatemala wanting—"

Jeff cut in. "Wanting a relationship with you, bro."

"But she got Ebola," Brock said. "She inherited her grandparents' mansion, loaned it to us for a hideout, and we got it shot up for her. Nearly destroyed by a missile."

KC tried to speak, but Brock spoke over her. "Julia survived Ebola, but who knows what long-term effects it might have on her health, and on the very day she was discharged from the hospital, Hannan's black ops team abducted her, a team with a demonic dude who apparently wants her."

Steve had only listened up to this point, but the agony on his face said he wasn't going to remain silent. "Then we flash banged her with an M84 and knocked her out. That was my idea, and she's *still* a hostage."

Brock continued staring at the wall, avoiding KC's face. "I could've gotten Julia out, Steve. But I chose Allie first." Brock glanced at Jeff. "I had to."

Brock must not be thinking well. He shouldn't have said that. Not with Allie present.

Tears overflowed Allie's eyes and spilled onto her cheeks.

"It's not your fault, Brock," Steve said. "You did your best and you risked your life."

Brock gave Steve a glaring glance that revealed the anger and turmoil raging inside him. "Well, maybe now my life will actually save Julia."

It was a losing battle. Tears threatened to trickle-down KC's cheeks. When one did, she quickly wiped it away.

Steve noticed. "Let's rethink this surrender gig. May be there *is* another way to—"

"They're waiting for us!" Brock's voice grew angry. "The only other way is to go in guns blazing. Then we die. Julia still dies. It's suicide."

KC laid her hand on his. "Brock, what you're proposing is suicide too. Please don't do it."

He pulled his hand from hers. Refused to look at her.

KC continued. "Listen to Steve. We can come up with a—"

"No, Kace." He finally looked at her.

But she wished he hadn't. The love in Brock's eyes was missing, replaced by a haunted, emptiness.

"I think it's time for you to trust God, KC. You know, like you've never trusted Him before. I have to surrender. There's no other way, and I'm not willing to just let them kill her."

Brock had pointed out her biggest weakness, not trusting God, only trusting KC Banning. Had he done that to hurt her? If so, he'd succeeded. "I hope sacrificing yourself for Julia makes you feel good enough, Brock, because it won't make you good enough. Not enough for ..."

KC stopped and wanted her words back, desperately, but she had opened the box and unleashed a world of evils that could never be contained.

The horrific hurt on Brock's face and in his eyes said it all.

It was over between them. She stood, shoved her chair aside, and walked out the door.

She should have known better than to come looking for Brock. After all, he didn't care enough about her to keep his promise to write to her. He didn't come when her parents died. Then Brock's rant and Jeff's words confirmed her suspicions about Julia. KC's feelings for Brock were mostly one-sided. Still she couldn't bear to stay here and see him taken.

As KC walked toward the back of the motorhome, reality came into focus, and it ripped apart what was left of her heart. If Brock wanted someone who trusted God more, Julia was the better Christian, a better fit with Brock's life. And Julia didn't come with all of KC's baggage.

KC had never met her father's expectations, and she hadn't met Brock's. She wasn't good enough for anyone or anything, except for getting Brock killed. And that's what coming back had done. Because of her, Brock would die.

But maybe there was a way to save Brock, to make KC's life worth something. If Brock wanted Julia, KC would get Julia for him. And she could do that without Brock's help or God's help.

She swiped at her tears, then looked up at the door handle for the toy box on the back of the motorhome. In their hurry to get the motorcycle inside, they hadn't locked the door.

* * *

Brock watched KC walk toward the door. Heard her softly crying. It was better this way, especially after KC's stinging words had made it clear that, just as Senator Banning had said, Brock wasn't good enough for her. He stared at the floor until he heard the door close.

KC was gone.

The way it had ended for them would make it easier for her to accept that he was gone from her life and was never coming back. But watching her leave again nearly broke his resolve. He wanted to tell her he loved her, that he'd never forgotten her. Not for one day. He'd kept the reminder of her in his pocket since that day seven years ago.

Brock looked up at Steve and, for the first time, saw confusion in the man's eyes. Brock also felt the vibes coming from Steve. They weren't good. Bad vibes from Jeff, too.

Allie left the table and went out the door, probably chasing down KC.

"Steve, you still need to come up with a plan, one that ensures Julia is safe when I surrender. Got any ideas?"

Steve gave Brock a frown, then blew out a blast of air. Steve's blue eyes returned to their usual bright, intense look. "This is where Hollywood got things right. In the old Westerns, each side would start their hostage walking toward the other side, a slow, simultaneous exchange. It's not one hundred percent but it—"

"Not a hundred percent? You got that right," Brock said. "It's not like we have one of *their* people. They'd be happy killing us both."

Jeff took Allie's seat at the table. "We can threaten them, tell them we have a—what is that antitank RPG?"

"An AT4," Steve said. "Doesn't work, Jeff. That's like telling China and Russia we have a first strike capability. Their reaction would be to strike first. It would immediately start a firefight. We wouldn't win and we couldn't save Julia."

Brock slapped his hand on the table. "So, it's settled. At 8:00 p.m. you take me to Steelhead Falls and we do the exchange before nine o'clock. I don't want to hear any more about it."

The front door opened. Allie stepped in, looking like she might cry. She pulled the door closed and folded her arms across her chest.

Another door closed. Or had it opened?

Steve stood, then froze as a motorcycle engine revved. He moved toward the door.

"No, Steve." Allie blocked the door with her body and brushed away the tears that trickled down her permanently tan cheeks. "It will only make things worse. I tried to persuade her not to go, but KC said she couldn't stay and just watch Brock ..." Allie's voice broke. She didn't need to say any more. They'd all gotten the message.

Jeff stood, hooked Brock's arm and tried to pull him toward the door. "Come on, Brock—"

"Leave me alone, Jeff. Please. Just leave me alone."

When Jeff stopped pulling, Steve put a hand on Brock's shoulder. "If you've got anything to say to her, you got to do it now, man."

Brock didn't move from his chair.

"Don't let it end like this." Steve's voice crescendoed. "You've got to stop her, now!"

Jeff drew Brock's gaze. "It's the letter again, isn't it? You're not good enough for her."

Allie glared at Jeff. "How could you say a thing like that, Jeff? Especially now."

"Jeff's right. I'm not in KC's league. Not socially. Maybe not in any way. Everything I've ever dreamed about is ... out of my league." He was never good enough. People and circumstances screamed that message at him. KC stayed away, even after college. She only came to hide. His dreams had always been out of his league, whether it was baseball, blogging, or KC. Who was he to think he could help save the USA. His words weren't good enough. Brock Daniels was not the voice crying in the wilderness to save his country, only a whiny little voice, complaining about a world he was powerless to change.

Jeff slapped a hand on Brock's shoulder and spun him around. 'Not in her league? Bro, that's crazy talk. You and KC were meant for each other. The minute I saw you together, I knew that. You're more than good enough for her."

"It's more than KC. I'm not good enough for—I'm a joke. My words can't save the USA. All I can do successfully is get people killed in a failed insurgency. At least this way it will only be me who gets killed." In the end, all his hard work came to nothing, every time. He was just the son of a blue collar worker. Nothing extraordinary about him at all ... except his failures.

"Your words got us to come." Steve studied Brock for a moment. "Craig isn't a man to do anything rash. He knew what you were capable of and wanted to be a part of it. Just because we're between a rock and a hard place here doesn't detract from anything you've accomplished."

Steve was right about Craig. "I certainly pulled the wool over Craig's eyes. But my words only get people killed. Now, the only words left to say are prayers, prayers to a God I don't even want to talk to."

Steve huffed out a breath. "No one fools Craig. And you can't fool fifteen million or more Americans who relied on you for hope. Your words mattered to them, to Craig, and to everyone in this room. And, though she left, they mattered to KC, too."

"Brock ..." Allie's voice came softly over his shoulder. "You've saved KC's life several times. Armed with only a rock, you saved us all when the SWAT team attacked. And your words have a power I've never seen in any other writer. If you've got words for KC, at least tell me. Please. I'll make sure she hears them."

Brock's words in the jar. The only honest words he'd said to KC. The words saying he needed her. When he kept his words bottled up, because of fear of failure, of course they failed. When his words about his feelings for KC remained bottled up in a jar, they accomplished nothing. Only when KC took them out of the jar and read them did they bring his dream, the woman he loved, to him.

Even his writing was mostly putting words in a jar, bottling them up. Half of what he wrote Brock was afraid to post. Afraid his words said too much or too little. Too weak or too strong. Those words were bottled up in unused files on his hard drive.

And when he posted his words, *he* was bottled up, hiding behind a computer screen and two thousand miles of fiber and wire. If Brock was going to have an impact, his words needed to be said face to face. Maybe it was time for him to let his words out, to stand up to this president and his men. In a few hours, he would face some of them.

Allie was right. God had given him the gift of words and a powerful arm. Twice that arm had saved KC's life, and his words—maybe he was born to use his gifts for such a time as this. Maybe KC was born for this time too, just as Mordecai had said to Esther. But what they appeared to be born for required both Brock and KC ... *together*.

The years they had spent together as children had all been preparation for this very time. To give up on KC was to give up on what God had intended, and it meant Brock would be giving up on the nation he loved.

KC. Her last words and the pain on her face came into sharp focus. She wasn't trying to hurt him. Brock knew her so well, he should have known that. KC couldn't stand to see him die because ... Because?

"Because KC loves me!" The words exploded from his mouth.

He should have listened to her, not pushed her away.

Allie grabbed his chin and turned his face toward her. "Brock Daniels, you're a fool if you didn't know that. Please, don't let it end like this. You are a great man, one who's willing to save Julia by sacrificing yourself."

Allie's words touched something deep inside him. Maybe he had made a difference.

Sacrifice! The word shook Brock to the very core of his being. When he put the events of the past few minutes into context, he knew what would come next. KC would try to free Julia by offering herself before Brock could surrender?

285

That would be pure foolishness. But KC loved him. She *would* sacrifice herself, even to that brute of a man.

"How could I have been so stupid?"

Jeff poked Brock's shoulder. "You want me to answer that, bro?"

"No. But I have to stop her."

Brock had always let other people and circumstances stop him from going after anything he really wanted. A letter from Senator Banning, a letter from a baseball scout. That wasn't going to happen again, ever. He wouldn't allow anything stop him from going to save the woman he loved.

"Stop her? Bro, what are you thinking?"

"Allie ..." Brock's heart drummed out his panic. "Did you see which way KC went?"

Allie's eyes widened, full of fear. "She pulled out onto Highway 126, headed east."

"KC." He groaned out her name. "Hannan wants KC in the worst way. Steve, she's going to try to bargain with them. Give herself for Julia before I get there. We've got to stop her."

* * *

KC turned onto Highway 126 and rode eastward on her bike.

What she wanted most was to protect the people she loved. But she had failed to protect Brock, failed to protect the others, and failed her country. That was KC Banning, a total failure.

There was a way to redeem herself. She could be the one to sacrifice her life. She seemed to have lost Brock, but she could save his life. Without him, hers wasn't worth very much anyway, except to Hannan. To him, KC Banning was worth far more than Julia Weiss.

KC only had, at most, twenty minutes to spare if she wanted to be certain she reached Steelhead Falls before Brock could stop her. He knew her. Brock would soon figure out what she was doing. She might need all of that time buffer for negotiating with Hannan's black ops team.

She couldn't let go of the last, small measure of hope without making a desperate attempt to end this nightmare. But she had very little time left.

KC leaned low, almost to the handlebars, kicked the bike into high gear, and opened the throttle. The Honda responded, pushing her back on the seat and accelerating up to 100 miles-per-hour. KC backed off to 90. She needed to reach Jeff's place safely. There, she would quickly do her work, then go on to Steelhead Falls to negotiate Julia's release.

Nine minutes later she rolled in to Jeff's and Allie's driveway. KC rode across their lawn to the backyard. She could only afford five minutes here. If her first attempt failed, she would abandon this part of her plan. It was a long shot anyway, a desperate attempt to get Craig and his men to return.

Jeff had locked the front door. KC tried the back door, hoping ...

No such luck. It was locked.

She picked up one of the lava rocks lining the flower bed and smashed the glass slider, reached through, and unlocked the door. Her laptop still lay on the table. They'd left in such a hurry she hadn't even logged out. It was still connected to the network.

After one quick glance, KC turned her back on the gruesome scene in the living room and focused on the laptop screen. She logged into Jeff's original blog as administrator and quickly found a draft blog that Brock had never posted. She prayed it was a good one because she had no choice but to use it.

KC wrote out her message.

Black Ops team took Julia as hostage, forcing Brock 2 surrender at Steelhead Falls. Need your help ASAP. KC

She composed a couple of sentences, adding them to the blog and encrypted it. The encryption succeeded and KC logged in to one of the blog sites she was currently using.

The mouse cursor hovered over the icon to post the blog, but KC stopped. Something niggled.

What was she thinking? She wasn't thinking. She was stupid. So incredibly stupid!

She clicked on the icon to post the blog, then ran out to her motorcycle and opened the hard bags. Right where she had left it was the secure cell Steve had given her to use in case of an emergency. This was their only phone for contacting Craig. Evidently, they'd all forgotten she had it after the rescue attempt failed.

She pulled the slip of paper with Craig's number on it from her pocket and prayed that he was ahead of schedule, maybe on his way home right now. She keyed in the number.

"Hello."

No military jargon or anything. But it was Craig's voice.

"This is KC. Just listen, I've only got a few seconds."

"Listening. Go ahead."

"The black ops team took hostages, Allie and Julia, and are forcing Brock to surrender. He's going to do it, but I'm going to try to offer myself first. We need your help."

"We're on our way back, about six hours out. Where is this taking place?"

"Steelhead Falls trail head. About seven miles west of the ranch, along the Deschutes."

"Got it. Listen ... rely on Steve and do everything possible to stall. Push your stalling to the limits. We'll arrive in Sisters around 0300."

"Thanks, Craig. Got to go now."

"Praying for all of you."

She ended the call and dropped Craig's cell into her shorts pocket. She'd lost another minute. KC had used six minutes of her buffer here at Jeff's and nine minutes in route. A total of fifteen of her twenty minutes were gone. With only five of her twenty minutes left for negotiating Julia's release, KC needed to hurry. If Brock arrived during those negotiations, they might both be killed in the chaos that would erupt.

She mounted the Honda, hit the starter, and headed back to the highway. When the wheels hit blacktop, KC speed shifted up through the gears until she hit 110 miles-per-hour.

Which was the fastest way through the maze of roads? Uncertain, she opted for the straightest road, shifted to high gear, and cranked the throttle wide open, holding it there until the tach hit the red line at 138 miles-per hour.

A few minutes later, KC idled up the hill above the encampment and parked her motorcycle behind a bush on the right. She stripped off her riding gear, tossed it behind some bushes, and slipped the key she would give Julia into the pocket of her shorts.

KC's first glimpse over the top of the hill revealed one surprise, a new tent behind the large tent. As she scanned the camp site there was another surprise. The black van they had stolen from Hannan's men sat behind a cluster of trees on the near side of the camp.

At the edge of the parking area, a lone figure stepped out of the shadows and into the yellow rays of a setting sun. A familiar figure. Brock. He knew her, just like she knew him. And he had beaten her to the altar.

If she had remembered Craig's cell before heading for Jeff and Allie's house, this would never have happened. Her stupid mistake would kill Brock.

There was only one thing for her to do. Get her .38 and die trying to rescue Brock, because living had lost its appeal. She turned toward her bike and reached for the handle on the hard bags.

Two thumps sounded behind her.

Before KC could turn, an arm wrapped around her neck and a hand clamped over her mouth. The arm bent at the elbow, squeezing KC's neck. Her vision went fuzzy and gray just before it went black.

Chapter 38

As Brock crouched behind a rock on the northeast side of the Steelhead Falls parking area, he tried not to think of what lay ahead. If he focused on that, he would probably back out.

"Show us Ms. Weiss." Steve barked out his command from behind the far side of the large rock.

"After we see Brock Daniels." A raspy voice replied from across the parking area.

This was going nowhere fast. He hadn't gone through the agony of losing KC for nothing. "Julia, this is Brock. Are you all right?" He waited.

"Brock, is that really you?" Her voice barely carried the 100 yards between them.

"Ask me a question, Julia. Any question."

"What was the native language spoken in the village?" Julia may sound weak, but her mind was sharp.

"It was Qeqchi."

"I'm all right. They haven't ... hurt me. Not yet, anyway. You don't need to do this, Brock."

"Shut up, you ..." A vile string of names cut off Julia's words. It wasn't the raspy voice this time.

"Are you still okay, Julia?"

"Yes." Her word ended in what sounded like an epiglottal stop. Probably a hand slapped over her mouth. They weren't going to let her speak anymore.

Brock looked to the far end of the rock where Steve stared back at him. "She's okay, Steve. Let's do this, now."

Brock stood up and stepped away from the rock. His body fully exposed, he would soon find out whether they really wanted him or just wanted him dead.

"Release Julia Weiss." Steve's voice echoed through the river canyon, loud and angry.

Julia stepped in front of a barricade consisting of two vehicles side-by-side, enough metal to stop anything but perhaps the AT4 Steve told them about.

"We have several guns on Ms. Weiss. One stupid move by you ... no more Ms. Weiss."

This was the weakness of the whole exchange. Steve and Brock had no equivalent hostage. No one they could threaten to kill in retaliation.

The success of the exchange depended on these men's understanding of how badly Hannan wanted Brock. After the insults and exposing Hannan's schemes, he probably wanted Brock even more than Hannan wanted KC. Hopefully, he'd made that clear to these men.

Brock moved slowly toward the barricade, trying to match Julia's speed. He would not move within grabbing range of their grubby hands until Julia was safely behind the rock by Steve.

Fifty yards to go.

Julia approached on his left.

"Jump behind the rock when you get close enough, Julia," he whispered.

She nodded. "Praying for you, Brock. I ..." Tears on her cheeks, Julia apparently failed to find words. But her tears and the anguish on her face said more than enough.

A noise sounded from the trees on the hill about fifty yards to Brock's left. Was some trick about to be played on them? An attack from their left flank?

He stopped forty yards from the barricade.

No shots. No more sounds. Something didn't feel right. But none of this felt right, especially not getting to say goodbye to KC. That was his biggest regret. And where was KC? They hadn't seen her in their frantic drive to Steelhead Falls.

Her motorcycle wasn't at the camp. But that didn't mean she was safe.

"Keep moving, Daniels, if you value your life." Raspy voice again.

Brock almost laughed. Value his life? They were going to take it, regardless. The value a person placed on their life was a relative thing. Relative to Julia's. Relative to KC's. Relative to a successful effort to dethrone Hannan.

He glanced back at Julia. His stop had given her a slight lead. If they didn't shoot Julia, this would work.

At about ten paces from the reach of anyone behind the barricade, Brock looked back.

Julia appeared to be the same distance from the shelter of the rock.

He stopped and folded his arms.

"What kind of game is this?" Raspy voice again.

A gun jutted out, pointing at him.

Another, off to Brock's left, appeared to aim at Julia.

"It's no game. I'll finish my stroll as soon as Julia is safe. We both know I have no possible means of escape. So—"

Another voice spoke softly. "Maybe they've got antitank weapons."

"Idiot." Raspy voice said. "They would be killing Daniels too."

At that moment, the last sliver of the sun slipped below the mountains to the west. In the twilight, Brock saw Julia leap to the rock.

He walked to the barricade and into the grip of evil.

Several hands clamped his arms. Two men threw him to the ground.

Brock managed to twist as he went down, throwing one of the men off balance.

The man stumbled, cursing.

Brock hit the ground on his back.

"Cuff him," Raspy voice said.

Brock looked up into an icy stare. Two bars on his chest. This man was the equivalent to Captain Craig, the detachment commander of the Rangers.

No. This man epitomized all the evil Hannan stood for. In a fight between them, Craig would kill this man.

The man who stumbled, pulled out a set of zip cuffs. Since Brock was on his back, the man cuffed his hands in front.

Brock would take any small advantage he could get, at this point.

As they jerked Brock to his feet, he saw the taillights of the SUV clear the hill. Steve and the others were gone. Safe for the moment.

Brock felt an urge to break free and run after them, despite the likelihood that Hannan's men would shoot him. If they didn't shoot him, they could run a cuffed man down easily enough. He would let the men take him and then hope Craig returned early ... or hope for a miracle.

As they paraded him before the men in a brief victory celebration, Brock scanned this crew of men. Even at a glance, it was obvious that this scurvy crew was no match for Craig's men.

Brock had been right in his blog rant about Hannan. His emasculation of the military had left him with mostly pantywaists. Evil men who could still kill and maim, but morally and emotionally, they were depraved. Nothing but men without courage who would only fight when they had an overwhelming advantage.

Brock opened his mouth to state his opinion, but when the demonic dude stared at Brock, grinning at him, he thought the better of it. This guy wasn't a wuss. Just evil incarnate, like the one who controlled him.

"Welcome, Mr. Daniels." Even his monotone voice exuded evil.

Brock looked into the man's eyes. There was no life in them. Dead in trespasses and sins became more than just words on a page.

With a man on each of Brock's arms, they pulled and shoved him past the opening to the large tent. Near the right side of the tent, Brock saw an inclined board and what looked like Velcro straps laying on it.

Waterboarding? Did they really think he knew some precious secret they had to torture out of him? He had said everything on his blog. Everything except things related to the Rangers.

The two men continued their brutal escort toward the newly erected tent pitched on a flat piece of ground thirty yards behind the big tent.

Brock struggled against them. He wasn't anxious to see what lay beyond the tent door.

When one man pulled back the tent flap, the tent's purpose became clear. A portable jail on wheels sat inside, the kind used at big events with rowdy people. Not a cell for prolonged confinement. No water. No toilet facilities. No bed. Not a cell for prolonging life. Only a holding place until the torture began.

The bed was next door, the inclined board. A place where people would be forced to lie down. A place where sleeping would be the last thing on their mind.

As they shoved him inside the cell, a commotion broke out near the barricade at the far end of the large tent. Loud, excited voices.

One word rose above the cacophony. "No!" It wasn't uttered as a protest. It had been given as a command. It was a voice he would recognize anywhere. KC.

But he had to be mistaken. He needed to be mistaken.

The noises quieted. "Cuff her and take her to the jail." Captain Raspy's voice.

"We have them both. Shall I start with Mr. Daniels now?" Demon dude's voice.

"No. Hannan said to wait a while."

"But—"

"Abdul, I said we wait. As long as you are attached to this group, you are under my command. Do you understand?"

"Abdul the Butcher only understands the fine art of torture." A mocking voice. "Don't turn your back on him, Captain."

Abdul the Butcher? Where had Brock heard that name? He couldn't remember, but it fit the man.

Two things were certain. KC would be a prisoner with him for a while and Abdul would take Brock first. He had to do something to buy time. He had to endure the torture, to drag it out.

At some point, Steve or Craig would attempt a rescue. No. Steve couldn't do it alone. Jeff, athlete that he was, wasn't trained for an assault, especially against such odds. They would wait for Craig.

Brock needed to pray that Craig came back early, and that Brock could endure whatever Abdul the Butcher had planned for him until then. Needed to pray? He needed to do a lot of things, but it all seemed so futile.

Had Brock Daniels come up short again, despite his valiant effort to reach Steelhead Falls ahead of KC? Or was something else happening. Was he being given a chance to pull all his words for KC out of the jar and unleash their power? If so, at least KC would know the truth. And if Brock could endure the torture long enough, maybe they wouldn't both die here at the hands of Abdul. Brock would save KC's life if it was the last thing he did on planet earth, the very last thing.

Someone yanked the tent flap open.

Another man pushed KC inside.

In the twilight, their gazes met and locked on their targets.

KC stopped. She mouthed the words, "I'm so sorry."

She was sorry? He had been the one who failed. If only they could start this day over again, he would've told her everything. Told her what she wanted to hear. What he wanted to say.

Please, give me that chance.

KC's escort shoved her in the back to get her moving. She stumbled and crashed into the cell door, unable to stop herself with her cuffed hands. One small groan escaped before her eyes grew fierce and angry.

KC turned and kicked the man who shoved her, a vicious kick to his groin.

He doubled over, cursing.

KC was going to spit on the guy.

"Kace, no!"

She turned to look at him.

The man grabbed a handful of her hair, hair that was showing its auburn color through the brown dye.

The second man pulled his accomplice back. "Captain Blanchard says to lay off until he gives the word."

The hurt man with the injured pride wrenched free. "Nobody does that to me and gets—"

"What's going on here?" Captain Blanchard entered. "You ..." he pointed to the man she'd kicked, "... lock her in and get out of here you ..." Words crafted to demean flew out of Blanchard's mouth.

A captain cursing one of his men? Calling them vile names? What had become of our once proud military? Men who fought and faced death as brothers.

The door to the cell opened.

KC placed her foot up on the trailer bed, the cell floor.

The indignant man shoved her hard in the back.

KC stumbled forward.

Brock stepped in front of her and stopped her from falling.

Blanchard grabbed the guy who'd pushed her and shoved the man out of the tent. "I'll deal with you later."

KC pressed her back into Brock, staring out of the cell at Captain Blanchard.

It was the rattlesnake scene from seven years ago. But there were no rocks to throw. Brock's hands were cuffed and Blanchard wasn't headless. His strike would be deadly.

"What a nice looking couple." Blanchard's raspy, mocking voice continued. "See you later ... if I can manage to hold Abdul off for a while. He's an anxious man." Blanchard locked the cell and left, closing the tent flap on his way out.

KC turned toward Brock, her tear-filled eyes questioning him.

He spread his elbows as wide as his cuffs would allow and circled her shoulders. "Why, Kace?"

"Because I still love you. I was so angry that I tried not to. But, I couldn't. Just like that rock you threw into Crooked River said, KC plus BD. And, now I guess we die together unless ..." She stopped.

"Unless what, Kace? This isn't a time to be holding out on me."

"Before I got here, I called Craig on the secure cell Steve gave me. Nearly forgot I had it with all the ... well, you know."

"Is Craig coming?"

"Yes, but he's ... I'm guessing over four hours away."

"I heard Blanchard, this group's illustrious commander, tell his men to leave us here for a while, KC. I don't know how long they'll wait. We need to stall them as long as possible. But first ..."

She closed her eyes and pressed her cheek against his chest.

"KC?"

She looked up at him, with tear tracks on her cheeks.

Please help her understand.

He wiped her cheeks again, then cupped them. "There are some things I need to tell you. I should've done this a long time ago."

"You mean things like why you don't love me like I love you?" Her voice dropped to a whisper and she looked away from him.

Brock gently turned her face toward him. "No. There's a reason I didn't tell you how much I loved you, how much I needed you."

"I know. Because Brock Daniels doesn't tell lies."

"We don't have time for arguments and misunderstandings. Just listen to me for a minute, please. Then you can say anything you want."

Fear showed in KC's eyes.

Didn't she know she had nothing to fear from his words? "That day you left in tears, seven years ago, I was devastated. I lost the most important person in the world to me."

KC studied his face. She was trying to anticipate where he was going.

She usually read him well. But this time she wouldn't be able to read his mind. He had buried this truth so deeply no one knew all of it but Brock Daniels, and it had haunted him every day for the past seven years.

"After you left and I got back to my parents RV, there was a sealed letter waiting for me ... a letter from your father."

KC frowned, then gasped. Realization flickered in her eyes and her face contorted in horror. "Oh, Brock. I—"

"Wait. Let me finish. He said now that we were teenagers, I had to stay away from you. You were too young for me and ..." Brock swallowed hard, "... I wasn't good enough for you. He meant the wrong-side-of-the-tracks sort of not good enough. The kind that never goes away."

The horror had vanished. Fire blazed in KC's green eyes. "How could he do that to me and never even tell me. I hate him!" She looked down at the floor, struggling to stifle her sobs. "I never met his expectations. I wasn't the son he wanted. He never loved me ... then he took the best thing in my life away from me ..." She looked up at his face, "... you, Brock."

"Kace, maybe you should rethink that. No matter how wrong he was, he *did* love you."

"You don't lie very well."

"In his own way he *was* protecting you. If I was him I'd be concerned about a 17-year-old boy spending time with my 14-year-old daughter. I think your father loved you, he just didn't know how to show it in the ways you needed."

Realization of the truth of his words flickered in KC's eyes, barely visible in the last moments of twilight.

Soon he wouldn't be able to see those eyes at all. He had to tell her the rest now. He needed to see her reaction before light and life expired.

Brock spread his arms and put them around her again. "I love you, KC. I guess I have ever since that snot-nosed eight-year-old with tears on her face started swinging at those twelve-year-old bullies. It was a different kind of love than it is now. Even then, every time I looked into my future, I saw you in it. But, after the letter, I only saw what I could never have. If I still have a future after today, I want you in it."

KC's eyes still questioned him. Couldn't she see that he was finally pouring his heart out to her, unbottling all his words and feelings?

Chapter 39

Why had Brock waited until now to tell her this?

"Brock, I begged you to tell me that several times. Even tried to manipulate you into saying you loved me. Today, when you ranted about all the bad things that had happened to Julia and wouldn't change your mind about sacrificing yourself for her, I gave up. I can never be the person Julia is."

"There's nothing between me and Julia, if that's what you're thinking. She's a sweet woman, but we're barely friends. It's you, Kace. Only you that I love."

She looked into Brock's eyes and saw the truth. He loved her, only her. Why couldn't she see it before?

KC couldn't stop her tears. Though they blurred her vision, the truth about her relationship with Brock came into sharp focus. God had put two kids together, a perfectly matched pair, and allowed them to bond, forming something so special words couldn't describe it.

She buried her face into Brock's shirt until she managed to stop crying. "Brock, there's no way you and I could have *not* loved each other. I should have known that and clung to it. When I turned eighteen, I should have gone looking for you." KC looked up. "Then maybe we ..."

Brock cupped her cheeks again, leaned down, and pulled her face toward his. Then he kissed her, softly, sweetly.

She returned his kiss with a fierce passion, trying to compress seven years of pent up emotion into a few seconds.

This time, Allie hadn't ordered it and KC hadn't initiated it. Brock kissed her because he loved her. In that moment, all the present danger fled. She was a girl again, running carefree with Brock through the desert, their whole lives and untold adventures ahead of them.

Footsteps from outside the tent grew louder.

Brock pulled his lips from hers. "I love you so much, KC ... I—"

The tent flap flew open, ending their moment, ripping away her dreams.

KC gasped.

Evil slithered in like a snake. Blanchard. "What have we here?"

Brock put his mouth beside her ear and whispered. "I love you, Kace. Always will. Pray for me. Pray for both of us. Stall them. Keep stalling them until Craig gets here. It's all we can do."

Another person stopped beside Blanchard. Abdul. "How touching. Soon it will be my turn, Ms. Banning. Or should I say KC?"

Brock's body stiffened at Abdul's words. "Tonight will be the night you die, Abdul." Brock glared at Abdul and spoke in a low menacing tone. "You won't live to see morning."

Abdul recoiled at Brock's words as if he'd been struck. Slowly, a toothy grin spread across Abdul's face. "So the prophet is crying in the wilderness. Yes, soon he *will* be crying, begging for his wretched life ..."

When KC looked up, Brock glared at Abdul with a fierceness far beyond the menacing look Brock gave the bullies who had tormented her as a child. His body shook, but not from fear. Hannan's men had no clue what Brock could do, even in cuffs. He was powerful and fierce in a fight. But, if he acted on his anger, they would be forced to kill him. She couldn't let that happen. Couldn't let go of her last shred of hope. Not yet.

Blanchard unlocked the door. Two more men entered the tent and stepped up into the jail.

Brock tensed as if he would lunge at the men.

KC gripped Brock's hand and pulled him back, until one of the approaching men knocked her hands away.

Anger erupted from somewhere deep inside her, molten lava that would burn everything in its path without regard to the consequences.

The two men each grabbed one of Brock's arms.

"No! You can't have him!"

No one paid any attention to her.

KC drove her foot up toward the back side of the black-haired man, kicking him so hard the impact slammed her body onto the floor.

The man howled when her vicious kick hit a vulnerable spot. He slumped forward, cursing.

KC bounced up from the floor and drove her shoulder into his rear end sending the man sprawling onto his face. She backed away from her prey, ready for another assault.

But the black-haired man had turned toward her roaring obscenities.

Brock wrenched free from the other soldier.

The dark-haired assailant launched his body, head-first, at KC.

Brock's right foot delivered a ferocious kick that caught the man under his chin with a loud crack.

His head snapped backward, and his body flipped end for end, then lay limp on the jail cell floor, his neck at an unnatural angle.

For a few seconds the tent went silent as everyone stared at the lifeless body.

Brock clasped his hands together and raised them to club the man beside him.

KC turned to charge the man.

A deafening shot left her ears ringing.

"Stop! Nobody moves!" Abdul's booming voice. "Or the next shot goes into your pretty little face." He stood in the doorway of the jail with a big gun trained on KC's head.

She turned toward him, clenching and unclenching her fists, then stepped back with her right foot, ready to charge Abdul.

"No, Kace." Brock stepped between her and Abdul. "That's enough. You've made your point."

Blanchard moved past Abdul and faced Brock. "That's one more charge against you, Daniels. You just murdered one of my men."

Brock gave him a mock laugh. "Murder? No, Blanchard. That's Abdul the Butcher's specialty."

The two soldiers wrestled Brock toward the jail door.

KC reached out and touched his shoulder.

The soldier on the left backhanded her.

KC tasted blood as the blow to her mouth knocked her to the dirty, wooden floor.

"Don't touch her again or I'll kill you where you stand, Johnson," Abdul growled. "She's mine, and I don't want her beaten."

The soldier, Johnson, held a staring contest with Abdul. It ended when Abdul raised the barrel of his gun to Johnson's face.

"Come on, Daniels." Blanchard yanked Brock toward the cell door.

Brock resisted as much as he could without them resorting to beating him. He was doing what he'd told KC to do, stalling.

A million words she wanted to say streamed through her mind. But anything she said would only make matters worse for Brock.

Brock—had she told him she loved him in those last moments? She hoped so, but she didn't remember.

Blanchard handed off Brock to a uniformed man standing in the tent doorway, then came back, locked the cell door, and left.

Brock was gone.

KC would never see him again, not in this life.

Abdul stood outside the locked door staring at her, all of her ... inch by inch.

She turned away from his insolent, leering eyes.

"So this is Katheryn Banning, the woman who tried to run over me with a motorcycle. Look. Do you see what you accomplished? Nothing. When I am through with Brock Daniels, he will be nothing ... quite literally. But you are mine, KC. In the most general sense." The man's eyes roved over her again.

She shivered, looking into the face of evil.

Her shivering stopped when KC realized what she must do. Whatever happened, she would die fighting this man. He would never touch her except to kill her in a battle that ended her life. She would be cunning, calculating, cruel, brutal, whatever it took to hurt him so badly that he *had* to kill her.

"Yes, you will be mine." He sneered at her. "But first I must persuade Brock Daniels to answer my questions. Then perhaps I should put him down for a long nap." Abdul turned and left the tent.

KC had been told that human beings can live without food for weeks, without water for days, but not one second without hope. Was there any hope at all? Craig and his men couldn't get here for at least four more hours. Brock would be dead by then and she would be—KC couldn't let her mind accept that conclusion.

She couldn't help Brock. With the camp closely guarded, Steve and Jeff wouldn't stand a chance if they tried to rescue Brock and her. KC shoved all the things she couldn't do from her mind and sought something she *could* do, but could think of nothing but impossibilities.

All of the computer abilities in the world could not help her now. Her worst fear, not being able to protect the people she loved, had come true. Brock would die. Abdul would come for her. The nation wouldn't be saved. Game over. KC fails. Evil wins.

Once again, for the final time, KC Banning simply was not good enough, always falling short of expectations ... hers, others', and God's.

At the end of herself, and of her hopes and dreams, there was only one place to turn ... to the One who never seemed to answer when she needed Him most.

Pray for me, Kace. Pray for both of us.

Brock's words. Those words and his final kiss were all she had left of him. KC slumped to the floor on her knees. But it wasn't low enough for someone like her. After all the time she had shoved God aside, would He even listen? She laid face down on the floor and poured out her heart, the heart she'd only allowed Him to have partial access.

How long had she lain on the jail floor, face pressed into it, arms outstretched, crying, and praying? It might have been five minutes or an hour.

KC rolled onto her side. Through the floor of the jail cell she heard footsteps.

She listened.

They sounded closer.

They were coming for her now. Brock must be dead.

The tent flap flew open.

And now it was her turn.

Chapter 40

Still lying on the floor, KC drew a sharp breath when four men entered the tent, all wearing strange uniforms, hooded so that only their eyes showed. They had an assortment of weapons. Some she didn't recognize.

This didn't make sense. A firing squad? Had they decided to shoot her? That would be better than being given to Abdul.

KC pushed herself to her knees.

One of the men approached the cell door. He stopped, his eyes studying her.

She backed away from him to the far side of the jail cell.

"Katheryn Banning?" The man spoke softly in unaccented English.

"That depends." She wasn't ready to tell them anything. Not yet.

"It's her." One of the men whispered. "I'd recognize her anywhere."

"You *are* Ms. Banning, aren't you?"

"Who are *you*?" She spoke softly.

"We are Israeli, mostly Sayeret Matkal."

"Sayeret Matkal?" She'd heard the name, but ...

"The special forces of the IDF. But we assembled a special team for this mission, comprised of members of the Kidon, Mossad, and Sayeret Matkal." The man shoved something into the jail cell lock. It clicked and he pulled the door open.

This didn't compute. Why would Israel help her? Israel hated Hannan. But how did Israel even know about KC? "Israeli intelligence and special forces?"

"Close enough." The man nodded as he pulled something that looked like a cutting tool from a pocket in his uniform. When he pushed it toward her cuffs, KC gave him her hands.

He cut the cuffs from her wrists.

"I don't understand. How did—"

"We don't have much time." He leaned close to her and spoke softly. "We must hurry. Suffice it to say, we read your message asking for help."

"What message? The blog post?"

The man nodded and took her arm.

"I thought the Rangers might see it. But *you* read it?"

He nodded as he led her to the edge of the tent.

Realization hit her. KC thought she was clever, a computer genius, but … "You solved my encryption scheme." It wasn't a question. She knew they'd done it, and it humbled her.

With that realization, the shock of the men arriving vanished. She had poured out her heart, begging for help, and this time help *had* come. God had heard her blubbering, incoherent prayer, and answered it.

These men had been making their way here for days, maybe weeks. That meant God had provided for her even before she'd asked. Maybe she didn't have to be perfect or good enough to be accepted. That raised a question KC had never asked herself. Had she been expecting things of herself that no one, not even God, expected of her?

The answer came softly from deep inside her mind or heart.

You are loved. And you only need to be the person God created you to be. Nothing more.

It didn't matter what her father thought about her, only what God thought. And Brock had told her what he thought about her. He had loved her since she was just a girl. But God had loved her from eternity past.

Believing the truth, that she was deeply loved, removed the chains from her heart, chains that had bound her with their lie since she was a young girl. KC was free. Free to pursue Brock and to draw close to God. Neither would reject her. They both loved her and had proven it.

"Ms. Banning ..."

Her name yanked KC back to the jail cell. To a reality that no longer seemed completely hopeless. "Brock Daniels is in the other tent. Hurry. You've got to help him. They're torturing him."

"Daniel, take Ms. Banning south of the camp and make sure she's protected from any stray bullets. If we get separated, go to our designated rendezvous point." He turned to KC. "Do exactly what Daniel tells you to do. You'll be safe. Now to free Brock Daniels."

What if this was some kind of trick? "Why are you doing this?"

"Because Hannan is a liar and he's destabilizing the entire globe, not just the United States. Israel cannot afford to lose the best ally it's ever had. If Hannan has absolute power, we fear for our nation. And the U.S. will not be our ally again until Hannan is gone. Your efforts to take back this nation have not gone unnoticed. But, for you to complete your work, we need you and Brock Daniels alive."

The man gestured to several others. Shadowy forms moved silently in a mesmerizing sequence of advances toward the tent where Abdul held Brock.

Please let him be alive.

Daniel pulled KC further away from the camp, leading her along the route she had taken with the motorcycle when she escaped. After they reached the trees, he pulled her into a fast jog, heading up the forested hill above the camp.

Alarm shot through her mind when KC remembered the guard that captured her. She stopped.

"It's okay." Daniel said. "The sentry is dead. I'm taking you over the hilltop where you will wait by your motorcycle. If all goes well, Brock will be there shortly."

A loud explosion sounded. It lit the entire campsite. The concussion hit like a blow to KC's head. When she turned to look, blazes engulfed the cluster of small tents.

Gunfire erupted in the camp.

Daniel pulled KC behind a large Juniper tree. They crouched, sheltered by the tree and a small boulder and listened to the war, a constant tat, tat, tat coming from the camp, punctuated by explosions.

How could Brock survive all the violence and the chaos? Had he even survived his time with Abdul? She didn't even know how long that monster had Brock in the big tent. If Brock lived through it, would he be emotionally scarred for life?

Two more explosions lit the entire river valley and left KC's ears ringing.

Silence.

It was over, for better or worse.

For Hannan's men, it would be far worse. Weak, selfish, undisciplined men like them stood no chance against these Israeli Special Forces.

More gunfire. It came from near the Steelhead Falls trailhead.

Daniel gripped her arm. "Ms. Banning, this is not a good development. I need to contact—"

Running feet crunched through the forest, climbing the hill toward them.

Another explosion.

In the flash of light, KC saw a silhouette approaching. A tall man, Brock.

Daniel raised his weapon.

"No." She shoved his gun barrel down. "It's Brock Daniels."

Daniel stepped away from KC and raised his weapon again. "Are you sure?"

"Yes." She called out to Brock. "Identify yourself."

"KC?"

She smiled at the sound of his voice.

"It's okay, Daniel." KC broke away from Daniel and ran to Brock.

Daniel's feet rustled softly on the hillside behind her.

More gunfire.

Then everything that wasn't Brock ceased to exist.

His strong arms pulled her to him. He was wet. His shirt drenched. Was it water? Blood?

"You okay, Kace?" Brock seemed out of breath. Something rare for him, even after a long run.

"Yes, I'm okay."

"Thank God." He squeezed her until she could hardly draw a breath.

"But what about you? You're wet?"

"Yeah. I'm fine. Tell you about it later." He looked at Daniel, who still had both hands on his weapon, gun half raised.

"Are you Daniel?"

He lowered his gun. "I am. Mr. Daniels, I presume?"

"Well it sure as heck ain't Dr. Livingstone. Daniel, your commander said they could use your help. But he said for you to approach from the south, near the jail cell, or you'll come under friendly fire. He said KC and I should take the motorcycle and skedaddle."

"Ski what?"

"Get out of here. We'll all rendezvous at the Ranger's motorhome in Sisters when this is over. He said you knew where that was."

"Yes. But what happened down there? We had them outnumbered."

"Evidently, that's what they wanted you to think. Somehow, a second detachment of Hannan's Special Forces moved in from the north. Maybe Hannan sent them because we killed four of their men."

Daniel looked confused. "Who's we?"

"Steve, Jeff, KC and I."

"That's very impressive for an improvised team. But, I need to go."

"Yeah. It looks like a stalemate down there, at the moment."

Daniel turned, facing the camp and the fighting. "Keep Mrs. Daniels safe."

"Will do, Daniel. We're praying for you." Brock relaxed his hold on her.

Daniel turned and ran silently down the hill.

"That sounded rather nice, Brock." Even if it was a slip of the tongue.

"What sounded nice?"

"Mrs. Daniels."

"Yeah, it did." Brock kissed her forehead. "But we gotta stay alive if we want to get there."

"Was that a proposal?"

"That we stay alive? I sure hope so."

KC shook her head.

"This is no time for proposals, silly girl. Got your motorcycle keys?"

She slapped a hand against her pocket. "Got them. Let's go, Brock. About fifty yards ahead and ... I'm not a girl." She stepped toward the motorcycle.

"Yeah. So, I've noticed."

Even with danger looming so close behind them, KC smiled, both her lips and her heart.

When they reached Southwest River Road, she scampered across the small dirt drive and circled the bush where she'd hidden her motorcycle.

"Brock, my bike's gone." *Not another disaster. Please, not another one.*

"Then let's go on foot."

"Wait a minute." She scanned the area around them. A larger bush grew a few feet further into the forest. She circled it and heaved a sigh when she saw her Honda, but her riding gear was gone.

"The Sayeret Matkal, or whatever this group calls themselves, must have moved it for me. Evidently, they didn't think I hid it well enough." She mounted the bike and hit the starter. "They didn't think my encryption scheme hid messages well enough either." KC eased off on the clutch, turned the bike around, and headed toward the road.

"What are you talking about, Kace?"

"Get on, Brock. They knew we were in trouble and came because they decrypted a message I sent when I stopped by Jeff and Allie's house."

Brock stood beside the motorcycle, silent, evidently thinking.

"So that's how we beat you here. I'm so thankful you stopped. We got to the camp first and then you brought the Israelis for us."

"It wasn't me that brought the Israelis. Climb on behind me and hang on, Brock. And I'd be thankful if you kept your big, body in line with me and the motorcycle. You know, balanced."

"Okay. But what do I hang on to?"

"If you can't figure that out, you're not the man I thought you were."

Brock's arms circled her waist and squeezed.

"Not so tight. I need to breathe." KC released the clutch and idled out onto the roadway.

"Hold it, Kace."

She stopped on the edge of the road. "Whatever it is, hurry. I feel like a sitting duck out here."

"Just a sec." Brock bumped her, pushing her forward. "Go, go, go! Let's get out of here."

She couldn't see whatever had alarmed Brock, but she shifted to second gear and goosed the engine. Out of sight of the camp now, she turned on the headlights.

"Faster, Kace."

"Why? What's happening?"

"The headlights of a vehicle came on, and it took off headed in our direction."

"Is it following us?" The glare of headlights hit her rearview mirror. "I guess it is."

KC's helmet bounced where she had hung it, still strapped onto the handlebars. Racing on a hilly road at night, wasn't safe. Without a helmet, dressed in shorts and a tank top, it was lunacy. But she wouldn't let them wreck, because KC had the best reason for staying alive she'd ever had sitting behind her, holding her like he'd never let go.

Brock leaned forward, placing his mouth by her ear. "It's following us and it's flying."

"Maybe it's not them."

"Maybe not, but it came from the area where their vehicles were parked."

"Then, like you said, we need to skedaddle."

When they hit the paved road, KC shifted to high gear and twisted hard on the throttle. She kept her speed slightly under insanity, but couldn't shake the headlights glaring in her mirror. "Hang on, Brock. There's a long straight stretch coming. I'm going to take us up to 110. Pray that a deer doesn't jump in front of us."

Brock didn't say anything. Maybe he couldn't hear her with an 80 mile-per-hour wind whistling in their ears.

When she hit 105, his arms tightened around her. At 110, she couldn't breathe.

KC slowed to seventy near the end of the straight stretch.

It was decision time. But their choices were down to two. "Which Way, Brock? Toward the main highway or to the ranch?"

"If we go toward the cities, the police will turn us over to the military. Go to the ranch. If anyone can hide there, it's you and I."

"I hope you've got a good hiding place in mind."

"Me too, Kace."

Chapter 41

KC kept the white line on the center of Chinook Drive under her left foot as she flew along the canyon rim. At 90 mph, she was over driving her motorcycle's headlights by 100 yards or more. If they hit any debris on the road, any dead animals, she and Brock would join the road kill.

In her mirror, headlights of her pursuer's SUV had shrunk to small, dim circles of light. She had opened up enough of a lead to lose them.

The fork in the road, where Rim Road and the road to the ranch split, lay only a short distance ahead.

KC backed off on the throttle. She tapped Brock's right arm, still coiled around her waist, then pointed to her right.

Brock would know her intent, but probably not all of it.

Time to become invisible. She cut the lights, shot a prayer heavenward, and shifted down, avoiding tell-tale brake lights.

The Honda responded, slowing.

Brock's arms around her waist tightened as the darkness claimed their vision.

She couldn't do this alone. The big turn at the top of the hill would test her small, but growing, faith. If they made it safely through the turn, they could easily reach the ranch without lights. If ...

Please, help me do this.

KC shifted down again. The engine wound tight, whining in complaint, then dropping half an octave in pitch as they slowed.

As her vision adjusted to the darkness, the white line reappeared, a gray blur, barely visible beneath her left foot. She needed to keep it there, her only means of navigation at the moment.

KC leaned right, veering off onto Ranch House Road, praying their pursuers didn't see her and that she could navigate the sharp turn ahead.

Brock leaned with her. He was trying to help her take the curve and lose the SUV, but the white line slipped steadily away to her left.

She wasn't holding the curve. Was it Brock or her? Regardless, she'd drifted too far to the right. The shoulder of the road, and its deadly gravel, lay somewhere in the blackness, a short distance to her right.

KC fought to get back to the centerline.

Brock leaned hard left, too far.

KC tightened her grip on the handlebars, refusing to let the bike drift further to her right, but trying to prevent the spin out Brock's leaning might cause.

Centrifugal force, luck, or something even more powerful, righted them and straightened the bike.

KC's stomach flip-flopped as they exited the turn and plunged downward, descending the steep hill to the ranch.

They had made it through the sharp turn.

Still afraid to touch the brake and let its red light advertise what she had done, KC shifted down to second gear. The engine whined its complaint, then wound down to a grumble and a sane speed.

The lights of Clubhouse Road lit an area 200 yards ahead on her right.

How many times had God intervened to save her life tonight? Regardless, she needed to trust Him to do it again, because this night was far from over.

"Kace, how close did we come to the shoulder?"

She lined up on the roadway using the light ahead as a reference point. "You don't want to know, Brock. I think we had some help getting through that curve. Hang on. I'm turning in here."

"Headed for the canyon, via the Old Hollywood Road?"

"Isn't that what you suggested?"

"I just said the ranch."

"But you meant Crooked River Canyon." She leaned into the right turn and idled through the buildings clustered around the club house.

"Yeah. The canyon. Great minds, Kace."

The motorcycle wobbled as Brock's weight shifted. "No lights on the hill. You lost them."

"Temporarily." She pulled the clutch and coasted at fifteen miles-per-hour past the church and through the motel. At the far end of the motel, she shifted to first and idled into the darkness. Beyond the motel was a locked gate. Beyond that lay the old road where a movie set and the entire cast had been hauled to the bottom of the canyon fifty years ago, leaving behind Brock's and KC's path of escape.

KC stopped the motorcycle near the fence, where the locked gate blocked their path.

Brock dismounted and studied the escarpment to the west, barely visible against the night sky.

KC pulled her motorcycle's keys out and slid them into her shorts pocket. She shivered as she looked around at the ground, hidden by the darkness, a darkness so deep it would hide nocturnal predators. *Like rattlesnakes.*

"Brock, if they don't find us, do we really need to go into the canyon?"

"Let me worry about the rattlesnakes." Like always, Brock knew her fears. He tapped her shoulder and pointed toward the cliff.

Headlights slowly descended the road cut into the escarpment to bring traffic down to the ranch.

"I see them. So we go into the canyon?"

"Yeah. Too bad there's no place to hide your bike. If they see it, it's a dead giveaway."

"Great choice of words."

He ignored her comment. "If they don't turn in at the golf course, we have a little time. I could hide your bike behind one of the yurts. They know I was staying there when all this started. It might throw them off, buy us a little time."

"But they're turning in."

"Let's go then." He pulled two barbed wires apart, leaving a two-foot gap between them. "Slip through here."

KC crouched, swung a leg between the two wires, and worked her body through.

Brock released the wires, grabbed a fence post, and vaulted over the four-foot-high fence. He took her hand. "Race you to the canyon, KC."

Their words from seven years ago, but the joy and exuberance had been replaced by the power of adrenaline and the necessity of staying alive.

She let Brock pull her along the road, but thoughts of rattlesnakes buzzing and striking sent shivers through her shoulders.

"It's okay, Kace." Brock knew, just like he always had. "We'll be flying by too fast for those little demons to get too defensive."

Unless I step on one.

Fifty yards ahead, the road turned sharply to the left. The turn would take them out of sight of any observers on the ranch, unless they stood at the cliff's edge and looked into the canyon.

KC glanced behind them. The vehicle came to a stop near Brock's room at the near edge of the motel. Maybe the men would search the room, giving her and Brock more time to escape and hide.

Car doors opened and people carrying lights jumped out, headed toward the Hollywood Road.

Now, the motivation to reach the sharp left turn eclipsed any possible danger from rattlesnakes. Desert vipers rarely killed a person, and they certainly couldn't do it as quickly as the deadly snakes behind them.

"Kace, I counted four. Run hard before they hit us with their lights."

Sprinting, they rounded the turn at the head of the Hollywood Road. Beyond the turn, the old road became little more than a trail, plunging downward into the blackness ahead of them, descending 600 feet in three-fourths of a mile.

KC glanced back one last time before rounding the turn. The last image emblazoned on her mind was a bright light hitting an object by the fence, her motorcycle.

"Hurry, KC, they've spotted—"

"I know, Brock. Now they'll know where we're headed," she managed between heavy breaths. "They can trap us in the canyon."

Brock kept running, pulling her. He didn't reply.

"What if they fly a plane or a chopper along the canyon?" She took a couple of deep breaths. "We can't climb the cliffs on either side."

"Don't worry, Kace. We'll hide."

"What if they split up and come down the canyon from both directions?"

Brock slowed.

She nearly ran into him.

He looked back up the road.

KC turned and followed Brock's line of vision.

Four hundred yards above them, four powerful lights bounced along, then stopped.

A single bright light hit the trail above KC and Brock. It swept down the trail, moving toward them.

Brock charged ahead, nearly yanking her off her feet.

The light hit them and adjusted its movement, following them.

"Sprint for the bottom, Kace." He shifted his grip, locking hands on wrists with KC.

She leaped in giant strides down the trail, pulled along by Brock's powerful legs and his hand. Running took no effort, so she concentrated on keeping her balance. A twisted ankle now would be a fatal injury.

No effort? After another minute of hard running, KC gasped for air. How long could she keep up this pace?

When the trail leveled off, Brock slowed.

KC struggled to catch her breath and prayed her rubbery legs held enough strength to keep up with Brock's furious pace.

Sounds of water rushing over rocks grew louder.

KC risked a glance back up the trail. Three lights bounced along.

When had four lights become three? Probably near the trailhead at the top of the canyon. "Brock, I haven't seen the fourth light since they reached the canyon rim."

"You're right. I wonder—oh, shoot!" Brock yanked her against a tall overhanging boulder. The now familiar tat, tat, tat of automatic weapon fire sent dust exploding into the air beside them, stinging KC's bare legs.

"Shoot's right. But how did he—"

"He must've driven their SUV down the canyon rim, following us."

"But there are fences, Brock."

"I don't think a barbed wire fence will stop these guys. He probably just plowed through them."

They were safe from bullets, for the moment, but they couldn't remain pinned down under the overhanging rock, while three men pursued them less than a half mile behind.

"Kace, we've got to find a way to get out of here before the others catch us."

KC looked up. The light on top was gone.

Gunfire sounded.

Brock yanked her in toward the rock.

No light on top, but the man was still shooting at them. "He's got a night vision scope. We're trapped and it's my fault. We should've stayed on my bike. I could've outrun them."

"Not your fault, Kace. But if he keeps moving down the rim above us, he'll eventually reach the—crud!"

"Crud is right. When he reaches the lookout tower, there'll be no places left for us to hide. It hangs out over the canyon."

Brock pulled her tightly against him under the sheltering rock. "I know a place he can never find us, provided he doesn't see us go in. And his night vision scope has one weakness."

"Weakness? Like it can't see rattlesnakes because they're cold-blooded?"

"Kace, think about it. If you and I are more than fifty yards apart, he can't see us both. The scope's field of vision is too small."

"Brock, I don't want to be fifty yards away from you. Never again."

"We don't have any more time. Just listen. The canyon wall steepens from here to the lookout. And on top, the footing along the edge is treacherous. He'll stay a few feet back. If we hug the wall, he can only see us part of the time."

"So what are you proposing?"

"First, I'll run to a safe spot. When I disappear from his view, he'll be looking through the scope for me to emerge further down. Then you sprint to me. When you reach me, I run to the next safe spot. In ten seconds, you follow. And we—"

"How long do we do this?" Brock was clever, maybe a genius.

"Until I tell you to jump into the river."

Brock was an idiot. "Are you crazy? The guys behind us can run a lot faster than we can swim."

"Kace, you'll have to trust me on this. When we get further down river than the shooter up on top, he'll run to a new position. While he's running, he won't be able to see us to shoot. Come on, if we keep moving like I said, the guys behind us won't catch us before we disappear."

"You mean drown, don't you? Forget it. Just go, Brock."

Brock tore out from under the rock. His feet pounded down the dim, gray line that lay between the dark shadows of the cliff on their left and the black depths of the canyon on their right.

Gunfire. Bullets ripped the ground somewhere ahead of KC. Other bullets ricocheted away, whining their complaint at being smashed on the rocks.

The shooting stopped.

KC waited a few more seconds, and then ran toward Brock's position somewhere in the dark canyon ahead, praying she wouldn't stumble over his body, praying that there were no rattlesnakes, and that she would simply run into his arms.

Darkness enveloped her. She grunted from the pain of the hard collision.

Brock's strong arms held her, a wonderful analgesic.

No more shooting. Either the man was on the move, or he'd looked for Brock and hadn't spotted him.

Brock pulled her head to his chest and kissed her forehead. "We're further downstream than I thought. He's probably running to the lookout now." He pointed up the trail. "The flashlights are gaining on us. We need to swim underwater for about forty or fifty yards. Can you do that?"

"I don't know." Brock was turning into an idiot again.

"There's a strong current here. It's only like swimming thirty yards in a pool. Thirty seconds underwater max, if I pull you."

"So what's forty yards downstream from us, a wardrobe leading to another world?"

"Kace, you don't want to go to Narnia. You hate cold weather. Besides, we've already got a witch, Hannan."

"So what *is* down there?"

"Our hiding place. I think."

"You think?" He was totally an idiot now.

"Nothing looks the same in the darkness. If it turns out to be farther, we poke our heads up, take a quick breath, and continue underwater. I don't think his scope will pick us up if we're under the water. We'll swim a couple of feet under, and I'll have your hand. Let's go."

Brock hadn't waited for her reply. Less than four hundred yards up the trail, three beams of light bounced along the trail toward them.

Brock held her hand and guided KC down a rock that sloped into swift water.

He waded in knee-deep, pulled her down into a crouch, then yanked her into the chilly water.

Chapter 42

The Crooked River meandered across the Eastern Oregon desert for a hundred and twenty miles, from east of Prineville to near Madras. Its desert origin made it warmer than the other rivers in the area, most of which began their journey to the sea from snow packs in the Cascade Mountains. Crooked River's sixty-something water temperature was near the ambient air temperature, maybe even warmer than the nighttime air.

She could do this. KC took a deep breath.

Brock pulled her under, and the current claimed her body.

As she kicked and paddled underwater with her free hand, KC realized Brock was angling toward the far side of the river.

KC followed him, clinging to his hand, frog kicking with her legs, and praying they didn't collide head-on with any boulders.

After what seemed like twenty or thirty seconds, the urge to breathe began its panic-inducing assault. She had to breathe. Now. KC jerked on Brock's hand.

He rolled her over onto her back and spun her around, feet pointing downstream to protect their heads.

Evidently, they were going to expose only their faces. She pushed the lower part of her body downward with an upward stroke of her free hand and floated feet first on her back. When her face broke the surface, KC drew several deep breaths.

Tat, tat, tat sounded from the canyon rim. Water splattered in small explosions around them.

Brock jerked her under, pulling her downward until her foot hit the rocks on the bottom of the river.

The strength in Brock's strokes that had whisked her through the water seemed to have diminished, considerably. His swimming motion seemed awkward.

Had Brock been hit? The thought jarred her. It wouldn't go away. KC prayed she was wrong, but knew she wasn't. Maybe it wasn't serious. But, even if it wasn't, it could force them to surface. A shooter on the lookout tower could finish them off as they floated by.

Brock jerked on KC's arm and swam hard along the bottom to the shallow water on the far side of the river. He swung his legs downstream, then angled upstream, dragging her with him. Finally, Brock surfaced.

KC came up beside him, gasping for air. "Brock … you were hit, weren't you?"

"It's okay." He pulled her three feet further upstream into a place so black she could see nothing. "Where are we?"

"After you left seven years ago, I came back down into the canyon to be alone. That's when I found this place. We're sheltered from the lookout by a large boulder, but if they keep moving downstream and shine their lights back upstream, they'll spot us in here." Brock dropped her hand and groaned softly.

"How bad is it, Brock?"

Brock leaned close to her ear. "He just nicked my upper arm. But we probably don't want to know how close some of those other bullets came. We need to move into the hiding place, now."

She didn't like the tone of Brock's voice, the emphatic tone he used to persuade her to do things she didn't want to do. "Where is this hiding place?"

"Only a few feet away, but you need to let me guide you under the rock to the cove. It's tucked away between the cliff on this side of the river and that big rock in front of us."

"We have to go *under* the rock?" Tight places gave her claustrophobia.

"Yeah. I'll take you down to the bottom. The river's only about five feet deep here. Then I'll push you through the tunnel. When you can't feel the rock above you anymore, surface. Then we're safe, completely hidden unless they explore this side of the river, on foot in the daylight. Even then, I don't think they could spot this tiny cove. It's covered by trees and sits against the thousand-foot cliff."

She was holding back and knew Brock sensed it.

"We need to go now, Kace, before they move into a position to spot us. Take a deep breath and kneel on the bottom."

She filled her lungs and dropped to the bottom. Her knees grated on the mixture of rocks and sand. The water had grown colder ... or she had.

Brock pulled her forward into the darkness under the rock.

When he shoved her inside the small tunnel, her battle with claustrophobia began. It came as a full frontal assault. The urge to turn around and swim back grew overpowering. She tried to spin around, but only conked her head on the side of the narrow passage.

Air. She needed it, now.

Brock put his hands on her rear and shoved.

KC shot through into a slightly brighter place and reached up. No more rock. She surfaced and took several breaths of the cool air. As her heart slowed and her panic subsided, her breathing relaxed.

Brock's head popped up beside her. "Come on, Kace," Brock whispered. "We need to get out of this water before it sucks out all our energy. Are you cold?"

"N–now that you m–mention it." Her teeth chattered as a shivering spasm shook her upper body. The adrenaline rush was over, leaving chills in its wake.

Brock stood and stepped out of the water. He took her hand and pulled her up to what felt like a long, flat rock about three feet above water level. "We need to get you warmed up."

What kind of place was this? It seemed to be a hole about eight feet in diameter. At its bottom lay three feet of river water and, on the sides, a lot of rocks, including the ten- or fifteen-foot-high boulder they'd swam under.

One long rock provided a bench to sit on. Above her, a canopy of trees appeared, silhouetted against the predawn sky. Above the trees, loomed the dark, thousand-foot escarpment on the east side of Crooked River Canyon, blocking her view of the entire eastern sky.

"H–how is y–your arm, Brock?"

"It throbs. Bleeding a little, but it's okay. Sit down beside me."

Brock leaned over, reclining on the rock bench. He pulled her against him and wrapped his body around hers.

"What are y–you doing? This is—"

"This is entirely necessary, Kace," he whispered into her ear. "I think the air temperature is in the upper fifties, and we're wet. We've already got four armed men chasing us. We don't need to fight hypothermia too."

"It *is* r–rather cozy." She pressed her cheek against his.

"Cozy? That's because I'm your mattress and your pillow. You ought to try the rock I'm lying on."

"I can move." She raised her head.

"No, just try to get warm. Let's listen and see if we can—"

She laid her head on his shoulder. "Brock?"

"Yeah."

"Can I ask you something? You don't have to answer if you don't want to."

"But, KC ... didn't we close out all of our issues before—"

"Issues, yes. Questions, no. You never told me what happened when they took you to the other tent. You were all wet when you met Daniel and me on the hill. Did they—"

"It's called waterboarding. I tried acting as if I was afraid of it. You know how long I can stay underwater. I thought it would be a piece of cake, and was just going to fake it bothering me. Get Abdul to waste a lot of time on me."

"Was it a piece of cake?"

"It surprised me. I had to concentrate on not panicking. Abdul stopped after about forty-five seconds. But when I wouldn't answer his questions, we went for another minute. That's when the Israelis showed up and shot him. Two times was enough for me. Don't know if I could've lasted through a third time."

"But you're okay ... nothing permanent ..." She stopped.

"I'm fine, Kace. No scars, mental or physical. Just a nicked arm when we surfaced in the river."

"That was my fault. I'm sorry I panicked and came up for air."

"It's okay. Maybe we should be quiet and listen to what the others are up to, unless you've got more questions."

Confession time. He needed to know that some things had changed over the past twenty-four hours. "Brock ... when the first Sayeret Matkal men came into the jail tent, I was flat on my face, praying for you. No ... I was groveling. I guess God heard me. He's saved us so many times in the last few days that I feel awful for not trusting Him more."

"Did you tell Him that?"

"Yes."

"Well, don't feel bad. 'These are the times that try men's souls'." He kissed her forehead.

"What?"

"Thomas Paine. The American Crisis."

"A history lesson? Brock, I would much rather have—"

"An appropriate history lesson. Paine said, 'Tyranny, like hell, is not easily conquered', and he couldn't believe that God would give us up to the care of devils. Devils like Hannan. Our founding fathers trusted God in 1776, and we can trust Him nearly a quarter of a millennium later. So, yeah, KC. We all learned a lot. But much of it is a repeat." He kissed her forehead again and wrapped her more completely with his body.

So, the history lesson was over. It had a very nice ending to it.

KC lay in Brock's arms listening to Crooked River rush through the canyon. The sounds of the water flowing over rocks and around boulders would damp out all but the loudest noises made by their pursuers. It would easily cover her and Brock's soft whispers.

"Who would have ever guessed? Seven years ago, as kids, we explored this canyon in the last days we had together before ..." Her voice broke.

"Yeah, before ..." He pulled her head against his chest.

"Then you came back by yourself and explored some more. What we did when our lives were being ripped apart is saving our lives tonight."

"Nicely put, but I didn't think you were a romantic."

"I'm not. But if I told that story to Allie, she would bawl her eyes out. I'm warmer now. Do you need to get in a more comfortable position, Brock?"

"I don't think that would be a good idea."

"What do you mean? That you don't want to?"

"I mean, look at us," he whispered.

"Look? It's so dark I can barely see anything."

"KC, we're ... uh, a bit closer than we've ever been. I'm comfortable enough."

"Brock, we're hiding in a hole, wet and freezing, while Hannan's Special Forces are trying to kill us, and all you can think about is—"

"Is you, Kace."

Brock's words from the jail cell had painted a picture of how long he had loved her, and how deeply. Their past was healed. No barriers between them. No reason to hold back feelings and every reason to think of their lives together as man and wife. "Have you noticed that it's getting rather warm in here?"

"Yeah. Maybe we should move."

"Okay." KC said the words, but made no attempt to move. "So, how long do we wait in here?"

"Craig will find us if we just sit tight."

"But what if it takes a day or two?"

"It won't. Besides, you said this was ... uh, rather cozy."

"And you said we should move. But someday, we won't have—" KC gasped.

Brock's arms tightened around her.

A large, yellow circle of light hit the cliff wall above them. The spot moved to the south and disappeared.

KC let out the breath she'd been holding.

But the light returned, and moved along the cliff, disappearing to the north. Clearly their hiding spot was under scrutiny.

"What if they cross over, Brock?"

Brock placed his mouth beside her ear. "We stay here and wait, no matter what."

"If they stood on that rock we swam under, they'd see us."

"They can't climb that rock. I tried. I tried to find this cove by walking down the shoreline. Even knowing that it's here, I couldn't find it in broad daylight."

"One curious, seventeen-year-old boy couldn't find it. That's so comforting."

"Kace, haven't you learned anything in the past twenty-four hours?"

"You mean like I can trust God more than I have been doing?"

"Yeah."

"I suppose I have."

"We need to trust Him now. He got us this far. And now it's out of our hands."

"Listen. Splashing sounds, Brock."

"Yeah. They're crossing the river. And look how much lighter the sky is."

"Just hold me close to you. Please?"

"Kace, I can't hold you any closer than I already am."

"If I start to yell or scream, clamp your hand over my mouth."

"That I can do. But we need to be quiet now. They won't find us, Kace."

The splashing grew louder. Light beams probed the cliff and the trees all around them.

Chapter 43

Brock pulled KC against him. Holding her tightly seemed to make her feel more secure, but his arms couldn't stop whoever had entered the water searching for them, nor could his body stop the armor-piercing rounds their weapons fired.

KC lifted her head from his neck, then froze.

Splashes sounded from the other side of the big boulder. Rocks on the shore crunched under a pair of boots. More splashing, then more crunching of rocks. Farther away this time.

Two men had just come ashore on the other side of the rock, one of them hardly more than ten feet from Brock and KC.

KC pulled her arm free and raised two fingers, clearly visible in the light of dawn.

Brock nodded.

"Was he shuh he saw them over here?" A man with a New York accent.

"No. But they were swimming near this side of the river, a few yards upstream from where he thinks he hit the guy." A man with a deep voice.

"Maybe he's at the bottom of the rivuh ... downstream."

"Maybe. But that would still leave the girl." Deep voice again.

"Did you get a good look at her?"

"The Banning girl?" The deep voice rose in pitch. "She's been all over the news."

"But did you see her in the flesh?"

"No." Deep voice continued. "But Abdul sure was obsessed with her."

"For good reason." The New York voice continued, now describing KC in crude, demeaning language.

KC stiffened in Brock's arms. She clenched her free hand into a fist. Her breathing became rapid, louder. KC was losing it. If she did, her temper could get them killed.

Brock clamped his hands over her ears.

She grabbed one of his hands, obviously intending to rip it away. Then her hand went limp. She exhaled slowly, kissed his cheek, and leaned her head against him.

New York City man finally ended his lewd description of KC. Someone tapped the big rock. "Hey, over here."

Boots crunched on the rocky shore line, growing louder.

Brock pulled his hands from her ears. She needed to hear this.

Though the thousand-foot cliff on the east bank of the river blocked the sunrise, it was now nearly daylight, and their probability of being spotted grew with the light.

Scraping sounds came from beyond the huge boulder. Boots pawing for traction on rocks.

"I could see every hiding place within 200 yards, if I could just get on top of this boulder." New Yorker's voice again. "Come here, Tom. Let me stand on yuh sholduz."

KC drew a sharp breath and clung more tightly to Brock as sounds of the men grunting and boots scraping on the rock continued for a couple of minutes.

Could the New York guy, even if he was determined, actually climb the vertical face of the boulder? Brock hadn't had any help when he tried and failed.

On the chance the man might make it on top of the boulder, Brock pushed up from the rock bench where he lay, forcing KC to sit beside him. He poked his index finger down into the rock bench and mouthed the word. "Stay."

The narrowing of KC's eyes was not reassuring, but this wasn't the place for an argument, even a mime argument.

Brock crept slowly up the wall of large rocks that lined the back of the small cove. On his way up, he fished out two baseball-size rocks caught in the crevices between larger rocks.

The New York City dude's grunts and heavy breathing sounded like he was nearly to the top of the boulder.

Brock tensed as a hand appeared over the rock. Its palm slapped down, fingers feeling for a handhold. They found one.

The other hand appeared, gripping an M4. The hand placed the rifle on top of the rock, then searched for a second hand hold.

With only limited places for his feet, Brock moved into an awkward, stretch throwing position. On level ground, this throw would be simple. At ninety miles-per-hour, the two-pound rock he held could dent the man's skull and rip him off the rock.

Movement behind him. KC had crept up the rock, nearly to his side.

He pointed down to the rock bench.

She shook her head.

When Brock looked back at the top of the boulder, a head popped up. The man's eyes scanned the top of the rock for more handholds. In another second he would see Brock and KC.

Brock let the rock fly.

The man looked up as the fierce throw caught him between the eyes with a sickening thud. His body flew backward off the rock and splashed into the river.

Before Brock could react, KC skirted him and scrambled to the top of the rock, grabbing the man's weapon.

Brock leaped forward to pull her back to safety.

A staccato burst of gunfire sounded from across the river.

Rock fragments exploded into the air.

Bullets whined off the rock. The noises echoed between the canyon walls, sounding like a long volley from an army of shooters.

KC's body dropped on top of the large boulder. She didn't move.

The rifle splashed into the river.

Panic pounded in his chest as he jumped to the top of the rock.

Please, God.

Blood ran down her face, nearly covering it.

It was a head wound. He nearly vomited from nausea as he scooped up KC's lifeless body.

Another burst of gunfire.

Bullets and rock particles sprayed the area around him.

With KC in his arms, Brock leaped from the ten-foot boulder into the shallow water of the cove, leaning backward as he fell.

KC's body slammed against his chest, smashing Brock's back on the river bottom.

Air exploded from his lungs.

Though he gasped for breath, he'd shielded KC's head when they landed. But the blood running down her face said that might have been an exercise in futility. That thought drove a knife into his gut. When he looked at her face again, someone jerked on the knife.

"Why, Kace? Why? You didn't have to get the gun."

Her blood soaked into his shirt as he carefully picked up her body and staggered to the rock bench. There he held her, rocking.

In what seemed like another dimension, splashing sounds faded away.

He laid KC's body on the rock bench and cradled her head in his lap. He had to stop this, try to do something. He couldn't give in to death.

Her neck. He needed to check for a heartbeat.

He laid his fingers on her soft skin. Pulsations against his fingertips. KC's heart was beating. But how long would it beat after being shot in the head?

Brock parted her hair, looking for the bullet wound. He couldn't see it.

For the first time, he noticed her chest, rising and falling. KC was breathing.

The question returned. For how long?

He parted her hair with his fingers near the bloodiest spot, two inches above her hairline.

A sound came from—was it from KC?

She groaned. Her arms moved. She held her head with both hands. "My head. It aches."

Her eyes popped open. A bloody face with eyes holding a dazed look stared up at him. "What happened, Brock?"

She was alive and she could talk. A bit of hope returned. "I need to check your head, Kace. Be still now." Brock parted her hair again at the source of all the blood and searched for the wound. This time he found it.

"Thank, God," he whispered.

"Maybe you can, but I'm not going to thank Him for this headache. What did you find?" KC wiped the blood dribbling into her left eye, and gasped as she looked at her hand.

"It's from a two-inch slice in your scalp, probably from a piece of rock." Tears spilled onto Brock's cheeks. "KC, I don't know whether to spank you or kiss you."

"How about neither. I'm a bloody mess."

Shots sounded from the other side of the river.

The other man? Had he swum back? He knew where Brock and KC were. How could Brock have just forgotten? Maybe he should try to fish the M4 out of the water.

KC struggled to sit up. "Brock, don't try to—"

More shooting.

Now, a cacophony of voices sounded from the other side of the river. Far more than three or four men. But now, they knew about Brock's hiding place.

He and KC were trapped.

Chapter 44

From the murmur of voices across the river, one voice rose above the rest.

Brock listened. It sounded familiar. Craig? Maybe their ordeal in the canyon was over. Maybe …

Brock gently pushed KC's head back to his lap and explored her scalp wound again.

"Ouch, Brock. Be careful. That stings."

"Do you hurt anywhere else?"

"Only my head. I must have hit it on something. Did I fall down?"

"You did. And I thought you were …"

"Don't say it. God wouldn't be that cruel. Not after all He's done to keep us together. I … I did something stupid and got a spanking for it."

"You got more than that. You're going to have a scar, Kace. Not gonna be perfect anymore."

"I never was. See the freckles." She gave him a weak smile, then pulled his hand away from her head and held it. "Brock, we all have scars from life. Some on our bodies, some deeper inside, in our hearts. Scars from things like someone telling us we're not good enough." She stared into his eyes. "We've got to live our lives and find happiness in spite of them." She looked down at the water below them. "But it's not fair."

"What's not fair?"

"That since you and I found each other again we've been constantly threatened with losing each other."

"But I think that's coming to an end." He cupped her cheek. "Can you stand?"

"Yes. If you hold me, I'll always be able to stand, Brock."

"Kace." He nodded toward a gap in the rocks that gave them a partial view of the far side of the river. "The Rangers *are* here."

"Then maybe you should help me up." KC stood and seemed steady on her feet.

He led her to the top of the boulder.

Across the river, Rangers had cuffed one of the four men who had chased them into the canyon.

To Brock's right, from the south, another group of armed men moved toward Craig's Rangers. They carried a body.

Captain Craig waved at the approaching group.

High on the canyon rim, more movement. Five armed men approached the outer edge of the lookout. They pushed a sixth man ahead of them, at gunpoint. The man's hands were bound behind him.

The strange uniforms looked familiar.

"Brock, it's the Israelis."

He blew out a breath. "Looks like it's all under control, finally." He focused on KC. "Kace, I need you to tell me the truth. Do you feel up to swimming back across the river?"

"I'm fine. I was just a little dazed from getting hit on the head."

"Next question. Are you up to jumping off this rock, out into the deep water?"

Fear flickered in her eyes.

"We could swim back under the rock, Kace."

"No. If you'll hold my hand, I'd rather jump."

"Yeah, I'll hold your hand. But we need to be careful not to hit your head again. You might have a concussion."

"Once I'm in the water I'll be fine. I'm not an invalid, you know." She smiled.

Even with a bloody face, it was so good to see her smiling again, when only minutes before he thought she was dead.

William Tecumseh Sherman had it right. War *was* hell and Brock felt like he'd been drug through its flames several times over the past week.

He squeezed KC's hand. "On three. We jump together."

KC started the count. "One, two, three."

They splashed into the water side-by-side.

When they surfaced, KC pulled her hand from his, rolled onto her back and kicked her feet, motoring across the river, while her hands washed the blood from her face and hair.

Brock reached the shore first. When he turned to pull her out of the water, blood trickled down KC's face again.

She wiped her face and looked at her bloody hand. "Crud! I can't even feel the blasted cut, but it just keeps bleeding."

Craig's medical sergeant, Cutter, trotted down to the water's edge to meet them. "What do we have here?"

"A scalp cut, about two inches long, from a piece of rock. She also fell and hit her head, so maybe a concussion, too," Brock said.

Cutter looked in a pack he carried and pulled out several items.

"You're not going to sew me up." She folded her arms and stared at Cutter.

"Wouldn't think of it. We'll just kill any bugs and glue it shut."

"Glue in my hair? I'll never get it out." She backed away from the medic.

"Don't worry. You won't lose any hair. But if I don't treat you, there could be an infection, and you'll just keep on bleeding. Come on, Ms. Banning. I'll have you repaired in three minutes flat or my name's not Cutter. But first, I want to have a look at those big green eyes." He raised KC's eyelid and peered into her eye.

"Cutter." KC half chuckled and half snorted.

"Be still, please. Now the other eye."

"A medic that's allowed to perform surgery on the battlefield—doesn't seem right to let anyone named Cutter do that."

"Just be glad I'm not cutting on you, Ms. Banning ... if you've got a concussion, it's mild. Be careful with your head for the next week. Now for the glue. There aren't any chairs out here, so kneel down and let me have a look at the cut."

As KC knelt, Captain Craig approached them. "I thought I told you two not to have too much fun while I was gone." He stood, hands on hips, looking from Brock to KC kneeling on the ground. "How's she doing, Cutter?"

"You're Irish, right, Banning?" Cutter grinned at her.

"That's none of your business, sergeant."

"So, you *are* Irish." Cutter glanced at Craig. "With a head this hard, she only got a scratch and possibly a very mild concussion. The wound's clean and I'm about to glue her up. Don't worry, your hair will hide the scar."

"My red badge of courage and I can't even show it off?"

Brock shook his head. "No, Kace. Your red badge of stup—"

"I don't want to hear your opinion regarding my wound, Mr. Daniels."

Craig stuck a thumb up toward the canyon rim. "They're giving us the friendly signal, and they have one of Hannan's men, but who *are* our new friends?"

With glue going into her hair, KC couldn't look up at Craig. "I take it you haven't talked to Steve yet."

"I was a little preoccupied trying to get here after the call I received by someone who fried my cell phone."

So she had Craig's phone all the time? Brock knelt down by KC and met her gaze. "KC, why didn't you call Craig to see—"

"Brock aren't you forgetting that we were going 110 on my motorcycle, followed by running through the canyon, then we swam the river, and that's when—" She looked up at Craig.

"Be still, Banning. I'm almost done." Cutter spread the fingers of his big hand and gripped KC's head like an NBA pro holding a basketball."

KC stopped moving. "Sorry. But how did you know I fried your cell phone?"

"I didn't. Just a guess. My cell's out of service and you two obviously swam the river. But I don't want to keep guessing about our friends on the rim. Who are they?"

"They're Israelis. From what they said, I think they're a team of select members of the Mossad, the Kidon, and the Sayeret Matkal, assembled specially for this mission."

Craig's eyebrows rose. "The Israelis came to *our* rescue? I guess it wouldn't be the first time."

Brock met the captain's gaze. "Craig, what do you mean?"

Craig hesitated. "Uh, the less said about that, the better."

Evidently, there was a lot Brock didn't know about the pre-Hannan, American-Israeli relationship. "They'd been reading my blog posts and knew I was working with KC. I don't think they knew for sure what to expect once they got here, so they sent their best."

"Including the Kidon." Craig looked up at the canyon rim, then lowered his gaze to them, rubbing his chin. "I hope they hadn't planned to assassinate Hannan."

"Sounds like a good idea to me," KC said.

Cutter patted her head. He was done with her.

She sprang to her feet. "If it bugs you that much, Craig, ask them."

"They came to rescue you and Brock. I think we'll just leave it at that. Come here, you two. I've got someone else to introduce you to, our latest recruits, a team of Navy SEALs."

KC lifted Brock's elbow, exposing his wound. "First, I think Cutter needs to glue up Brock's arm."

Sergeant Cutter's big hand clamped on Brock's shoulder and twisted him around until Cutter could see the wound. "You're a lucky man, Daniels. Another inch in and you might have lost an arm. I'll take care of it."

Forty-five minutes later, Brock and KC, along with the Ranger's, SEALs, and their captive, reached the top of the Hollywood Road. Brock took KC's hand and walked ahead of the group to meet the Israeli team, which waited between the head of the road and the gate.

"Mr. Daniels, Ms. Banning, I must apologize for not providing better protection for you. We are seldom surprised in the field. But we were not aware of the second team, hiding to the north of us."

"Nothing to apologize for, sir."

Brock looked at the man the Israeli's held in cuffs. This guy had nearly put a bullet through KC's head. Anger erupted, exploding from Brock's mouth. "You're a brave man, shooting an unarmed woman. I ought to break your scrawny little—"

KC's hand slapped over his mouth. "You can stop right there, Brock Daniels." She hooked her other arm around him. "You already broke one man's neck. While I agree with your assessment, you're in the company of a lady, and you will not use vile, profane language."

"But, Kace, this guy nearly killed you."

"He didn't. He couldn't, Brock. Not unless God allowed it."

"Where's all this coming from? Surely not from KC Banning."

"It sure didn't come from your mouth. I believe you were headed in another direction."

"Break it up you two." Captain Craig walked toward the Israeli leader. "I think it's time for some introductions."

The Israeli team commander stretched out a hand. "I'm Major Katz. It is good to meet you, Captain Craig. I've heard good things about you. But I suggest we leave this open area and find someplace private. There was a police car here a while ago."

Police were mostly dealing with problems around the cities. But one cruiser out here could cause them problems. "Major Katz, what did the police do?" Brock asked.

"They pulled in at the motel, like they were trying to get a good look at the trail leading into the canyon, but a woman came out of the motel office and talked to them."

"It was Debbie." Brock looked KC's way.

She smiled. "She's a sharp lady. Still covering for us, Brock. But, like the major said, we need to leave."

Major Katz turned toward Craig. "As I was about to say, I have some serious and urgent matters to discuss with you, Captain Craig."

Brock stuck out his thumb toward the west. "Then I suggest we all go to Steelhead Falls. It's private. We have two prisoners and it has a jail. I would love to lock this man in it."

"We will meet you there in thirty minutes." Major Katz turned to KC. "Ms. Banning, your motorcycle is parked by the gate. It hasn't been harmed or booby-trapped. My men checked it out."

"Thanks." KC looked up at Brock. "Will you ride with me to the falls?"

"Is that a good idea? You might have a concussion?" He held her by the shoulders and studied her face. "You'll wear your helmet and no more 110 miles-per-hour, right?"

She smirked. "I'll be sure to keep it under a hundred."

Chapter 45

Brock's arms tightened around KC's waist when she topped the hill overlooking the Steelhead Falls parking area, the scene of so much danger and drama for her and Brock over the past twenty-four hours. Now, in the bright morning sunshine, the beauty of the blue, swift flowing, waters of the Deschutes River seemed to erase all of that, setting KC's mind at ease. And Brock's body pressed snugly against her back, with his arms around her waist, set her heart at ease.

Brock loosened his hold on her.

KC slipped the bike into second gear and the engine rumbled as it backed off down the hill toward the camp.

Two vans, an SUV, and one motorhome sat in the parking area. Only one tent remained from the former encampment, the jail tent.

Where were the other tents, vehicles, and all the bodies? Major Katz had told her there were no survivors among the two Special Ops teams Hannan sent, except the two that were being led toward the jail tent by four Navy SEALs.

KC parked her motorcycle beside Craig's SUV and waited for Brock to slide off the back of the seat. She dismounted and took his hand. "What a difference a day makes."

"And a few Rangers, SEALs, and Israelis." He smiled and pointed ahead at the military men from two nations engaged in friendly conversation.

Captain Craig and Major Katz weren't among them. KC surveyed the parking area, then the Steelhead Falls trailhead. She tugged on Brock's hand. "Take a look at the trailhead."

Brock studied the two for a moment. "Craig and Katz all by themselves. It figures. Major Katz said he had some 'serious and urgent matters' to discuss with Craig."

KC hooked Brock's waist. "I'd sure like to be a little bird sitting in that Juniper by those two."

"Yeah. I got the feeling you and I are a topic on their agenda. Craig's on his cell. Wonder who he's calling."

She could guess. "Steve isn't here yet. And I have a feeling Jeff, Allie, and Julia will be on their agenda too. After all the trouble we've caused him, Hannan probably just wants all of us dead."

"Here they come, Kace. This is where we find out what our near-term future holds."

"I'm holding on to my future, and I'm not letting him go, no matter what *they* decide."

The two men walked across the gravel parking lot and approached Brock and her.

KC tightened her hold on Brock, trying to paint a clear picture that said any effort to pry them apart would fail.

Craig stopped a few steps from KC, cocked his head, then grinned. "Brock's a big man, but you keep squeezing him like that and you'll give him a hernia."

Brock cleared his throat. "Uh, Kace ... like he said."

She relaxed her arm. "When do we get to hear the master plan?"

"Soon. Steve, Ms. Weiss, and the Jacobs are on their way. We need to take care of business here and then all disappear. When Hannan's men fail to report, eventually

349

he'll send someone to look for them. We want to be gone by then."

But what if Hannan was already concerned about his men? "Captain Craig, do we have anyone watching out for—"

"Yes, Ms. Banning." He nodded toward Major Katz, talking to his men. "And, unlike Hannan's feckless espionage organizations, Israeli intelligence always keeps them a step ahead of their opponents."

In a few minutes, an SUV rolled into the parking area with Steve at the wheel and Julia riding shotgun. Jeff and Allie sat in the back seat.

Steve parked nearby and rushed to Julia's side of the vehicle. His intention was obvious, but he was a little late. Julia had opened her own door.

Jeff and Allie slid out on the passenger's side, concern written on their faces.

Julia surveyed the men crowded into three small clusters between the parking area and the jail tent. "Somehow this place just doesn't seem safe." She looked up at Steve, walking beside her. "Not after all that happened here."

"Don't worry," Steve said. "This is probably the safest spot in the USA for you right now." He hooked Julia's arm, "Come on. Let's see what Captain Craig has to say."

"That's an interesting development." KC looked up into Brock's eyes.

He was smiling. "Now I don't feel so bad."

"Feel bad?"

"For snubbing Julia," he whispered.

Steve and Julia stopped, a short distance away, having what appeared to be a serious conversation.

KC lowered her voice. "Snubbing her? That's what you were referring to when you talked about your mission trip to Guatemala?"

"Yeah. After all that's happened to her, maybe Julia will finally have something to celebrate out of all this."

KC wondered what was going through that male mind of his. "Brock, just leave them alone and let it develop. If it's supposed to happen, it will."

"Kace, you know me. I'm not the matchmaker type."

She grinned at him. "No, but *I* am. And Allie *definitely* is."

Craig seemed to be herding everyone out of the hot sun and into the shade of some large Juniper trees.

Julia turned their way and approached KC and Brock. Tears welled in her eyes, but she was smiling. She gave them both a quick hug. "Thank you—both of you—for what you did."

Brock grinned and nodded. "Maybe you shouldn't thank us until you've checked out all the bullet holes in your house."

"I was thanking you that there are no bullet holes in me." Julia turned, walked back to Steve, and sat on a big rock beside him.

KC and Brock walked hand-in-hand toward the group gathering for the meeting. As they passed Steve, Brock took Steve's arm and pulled him aside.

Julia gave them a curious glance, but remained seated on the rock.

KC followed Brock, listening. He stopped far enough away for the murmur of voices to keep Julia from hearing them. "Steve, how is Julia doing, really?"

"Well, the doctors say she got the vaccine in time, so they don't think she'll have any long-term effects from the Ebola. But only time will tell us that for sure."

"Us?" Brock studied Steve's face.

"Uh ... only time will tell us that too." Steve gave Brock a sheepish grin. "But Julia says God's in the business of turning bad into good. She's a sweet gir—I mean woman."

"Cute too," KC added.

Steve shook his head. "Beautiful."

Brock slapped Steve on the back. "That's all we wanted to know. Come on. The meeting is starting." He took KC's hand. "Let's see what these military masterminds have cooked up."

Captain Craig nodded to Major Katz, and the major turned to face the group, clustered in the shade of the trees.

"We have made some tentative plans to accomplish our two major objectives. The first objective is to keep the six civilians with us safe. The second is to wrest this nation from the hands of the usurper and murderer, Abe Hannan, eventually restoring the U.S. to its former state, a democratic republic under constitutional rule. But, as we do this, let us keep in mind the wise words of King Solomon. He said that a man's heart might plan his way, but it is the Lord who directs his steps. So, let us be prepared to change our steps, if He so directs."

Brock leaned close to her. "That's Proverbs sixteen nine. Bet you this guy is from the twenty percent of the Israelis who actually believe their religion. I'm liking this guy more all the time, Kace."

Major Katz waited for Brock's attention. "Mr. Daniels, Ms. Banning, Ms. Weiss, and Mr. and Mrs. Jacobs, there's only one way we can guarantee your safety. We have access to a Gulfstream 550 that will fly all of you, non-stop, from an *undisclosed* location in the Pacific Northwest to Israel, where you will remain until it is safe for us to fly you home."

Allie stared at the ground, frowning. Jeff and Julia both looked at Brock.

KC nudged him and whispered, "You need to say something, sweetheart."

Surprise on Brock's face turned to a warm smile as he looked into KC's eyes. "Yeah. But we all probably have questions." He rose from his seat on the ground. "Major Katz, we appreciate your offer of protection, especially after the danger we just came through, but what about my blog? Are you asking me to stop what I've been doing?"

The Major looked at Craig. "I'll let Captain Craig address that."

"No, Brock," Craig said. "We need you to keep blogging and KC to monitor the comments and help us coordinate the activities of military groups that join us. I hear the Sayeret Matkal commo guy has a great encryption scheme we can use to communicate."

"He's the guy who cracked mine," KC whispered to Brock.

Major Katz stepped beside the captain. "And Israel will provide you a secure server to host your blog. We'll also keep the hackers away, especially Hannan's hackers. That will free up more time for Ms. Banning to do strategic work. She won't have to find compromised blog servers and disguise her location."

He paused and made eye contact with KC and Brock. "I've heard a bit of your story. It reminds me of Queen Esther. Did it ever occur to you that you two extraordinary people were born for such a time as this? To save your nation and, perhaps, give America its own Purim for future generations to celebrate?"

"Major, I don't know about Brock and me," KC said. "But if you include yourself and Captain Craig, then maybe we were the people God chose and prepared."

"And protected," Brock added. "Then protected again by taking us to Israel."

Steve and Julia exchanged several glances. Their concern was obvious to KC. She wanted to say something, but the two might think she was intruding.

Captain Craig had also been watching Steve and Julia's reaction. Craig turned to the major. "Katz, considering you're taking on the burden of providing security for these U.S.

citizens, I will provide a Ranger to go with them so you don't have to babysit them 24-7."

Major Katz nodded to Craig. "That would be helpful. And, yes, we can easily accommodate six passengers on the flight."

Craig scanned his men. "Rangers, do I have any volunteers for ninety days TDY in Israel?"

Steve and Julia sat looking at each other as if unsure what to do.

KC jumped to her feet. "Steve will go."

"Kace, I told you to—"

She glared at Brock.

He closed his mouth.

Steve looked at Craig and nodded.

Julia blushed.

"Good." Craig grinned at them. "That's settled." He paused. "Now for the second objective. The longer Hannan stays in power, the more Americans we'll lose and the more difficult it will become to remove him. So, the major and I have come up with a plan. Let's call it the ninety-day plan, although, it might take a little longer than three months to carry out."

Craig paused, looking at KC and then Brock. "Our plan requires your help. I won't demand that you go to Israel, but I strongly recommend it. We don't have much time before we need to clear this area but, since this is a big decision we've blindsided you with, I'll give you five minutes to discuss it. Then you need to give the major and me your answers."

Brock placed a hand on her shoulder. "Kace, you and I still have some issues to discuss."

"No, we don't. Like what?"

"Like the only way I'm going to take you halfway around the world is on a honeymoon."

Once she got him off dead center, Brock moved fast. But, after all the waiting on him and wondering, KC wasn't going to make it too easy for him. "If that was a proposal, Brock Daniels, it was lame."

The smile spreading across his face faded.

She took his hand. "But I can't go running half-way around the world with a guy unless he's my husband."

"Are *you* asking *me* to marry you? That's supposed to be *my* job, KC."

"Then don't you think you should do your job?"

"Kace, it's not like we can just waltz into the courthouse and apply for a marriage license. We'd be arrested. Officially, we're still terrorists."

"And you're going to let a little thing like that stop you? Brock, we're going to another country where you're a hero ... well, sort of."

Brock stood, pulled KC to her feet, and escorted her to where Major Katz stood. "Sir ... about marriage in Israel."

"If the subject is marriage ..." the Major tapped the young man named Daniel on his shoulder. "Daniel, you're the expert on the nuances of marriage in our homeland, and there are many. Would you answer Mr. Daniels and Ms. Banning's questions?"

Daniel waved his hand between Brock and KC. "I assume this is for you two?"

Brock nodded.

"Then I need to know about your religious beliefs ... both of your religious beliefs."

Where was this going? Maybe it wasn't going to be easy to marry under their present circumstances. Were they jumping the gun? No. Everything within KC said, if anything, they had waited too long. They should have gotten together long before this.

Daniel looked at KC. "You're not Jewish, are you?"

"No."

"Mr. Daniels, please tell me you're not Jewish."

"I'm not Jewish."

"Okay. We're over hurdle number one."

"Hurdle number one? Are we in a race?" KC still wondered where this was going and why.

"Just bear with me a minute longer. Are either of you Catholic?"

"Neither of us is," KC said.

"How about any of the Orthodox ... uh, like Eastern Orthodox, Greek—"

"No we're not," Brock said. "We're just non-denominational Christians, Jesus followers."

Daniel rubbed his chin. "That must fall somewhere in the Protestant sector."

"I guess it does." KC took Brock's hand. "But we don't care what label you put on us, as long as it means that we're Christians."

"Maybe *you* don't care, but in Israel it presents a bit of a problem."

"You're not telling us that Christians can't get married in Israel, are you?"

"No, Mr. Daniels. But since you're both classified as Protestant, you have to apply and wait for approval on a case-by-case basis."

"What?" Brock shuffled his feet. He was getting antsy and irritated.

She needed to cut to the chase. "How long does the approval process take?"

"It will take two to four weeks to get the application approved. But Major Katz has connections. In your case, I'm guessing two weeks."

"Finally, an answer. Thanks for enlightening us, Daniel." Brock circled her waist with his arms.

KC sensed Captain Craig's tall form towering over her shoulder.

"If all this talk about marriage licenses is over, we have a tyrant to depose. I say this country has suffered under Abe

Hannan long enough. I need to know if you're willing to help us invoke the ninety-day plan. It's a calculated risk, one that could be dangerous if it backfires, but one that could bring a quick end to Hannan's power-play."

Brock released her.

KC turned and studied Craig's face. He gambled when necessary. They'd all seen that when the Apache helicopter bore down on them and he risked using the grenade launcher to save all his men.

Craig patted Brock's powerful right shoulder. "The plan requires a quarterback with a strong arm. And a corps of speedy wide receivers." Craig pointed to himself and gestured to his men. "It requires our quarterback to throw a long bomb."

Brock's eyes took on that intense, competitive look she had first seen thirteen years ago when Brock faced the bullies to protect her. "Long bomb as in what? A post pattern."

"Clever, Brock. Yes, a blog post pattern, a threatening, intimidating one." Craig studied Brock and waited.

"I don't feel very threatening right now. How can I intimidate Hannan?"

Craig poked a finger at Brock's chest. "That from a man who just caved in the skull of one of Hannan's special ops guys? From the man who drew fifteen million Americans to his blog, people who came looking for hope? A man who now has 100 million followers?"

Flattery would get you nowhere with Brock. KC could have predicted Brock's response.

"So, do you have something specific in mind?" Brock ignored Craig's finger in his chest.

"Somewhat specific," Craig said. "Katz and I discussed some interesting work the Mossad has done over the past seven years. They've put together a detailed psychological profile of Mr. Hannan. It's based upon the opinion of experts and years of Mossad intelligence."

"You said this was risky." Brock peered into Craig's eyes. "So, we're betting the farm on a psychological profile?"

"Daniels, Abe Hannan is what you called him in that rant a few days ago, a wuss. The Mossad think the man's a coward when he's personally threatened. And that is precisely what you are going to do, if you agree."

"After what he's done to KC and me, as well as a hundred thousand or more other Americans, I'd be glad to threaten Hannan. But, Craig ... what's the worst that could happen if this plan backfires?"

"If he goes into total paranoia mode, striking at everything like a cornered rattlesnake, he'll kill everyone who's a perceived threat. Some innocent people could die." Craig paused. "If Hannan's fortunate, and enough of the military sticks with him, he might hit us with a lucky strike. That would mean game over. The USA loses ... until the people have had enough of Hannan and they revolt at some point in the future. That would be a bloody revolt, and it would require the people to have the stomach for that sort of a revolution. But if our plan works, few lives would be lost." Craig studied Brock's face, waiting for his reaction.

Brock stared at the ground and kicked the dirt a few times. "So you're asking me to use the intelligence the Mossad have gathered to write something that will so terrorize Hannan that it paralyzes him?"

"Exactly." Craig folded his arms and waited.

"But if I fail, or Hannan gets lucky, people die and the USA becomes the Dystopian States of America?"

"That's about the size of it. So, Mr. Daniels, what will it be?"

KC closed her eyes and prayed Brock would say yes.

Chapter 46

An airfield somewhere in the Pacific Northwest

KC had already asked the pilot three times if they might be shot down by the U.S. military after they took off.

His reply had been the same each time. "Trust us. We've got it covered."

Now, the pilot was in the cabin, and the Gulfstream 550's twin jet engines started a low whine. The pilot agreed to wait while Brock finished blogging. After he posted it, they would take off for Ben Gurion Airport. From there, KC hadn't a clue where they would go.

Major Katz had said it was best if they didn't know, especially in advance.

KC didn't want to distract Brock as he sat in the ursa chair, performing final edits on his blog post. This post was crucial because it launched the ninety-day plan Major Katz and Captain Craig had explained to them at Steelhead Falls.

Brock had been working on the post since they started their drive to the airfield. Now, he was performing the final edits, and he'd asked KC to stand behind his chair reading while Brock edited.

To give her eyes a brief rest, KC scanned the cabin of the small jet.

Jeff and Allie sat on one of the couch seats lining the sides of the cabin. Steve and Julia sat on the couch seat across from them. Julia's hand lay on the seat between her and Steve, opened, palms-up, inviting.

Steve's eyes were focused on that hand.

Take it you idiot!

He did, finally.

Brock paged up to the beginning of his post, took his hands off the keyboard, and looked up at her, the warmth in his eyes so intense she could feel it. "I need a short break ... and I need to show you something." He shoved his right hand into his pants pocket. "Give me your hand."

She stretched out her hand, curious about what Brock had in his pocket.

He turned up her palm and placed a rock in it.

A smooth flat stone nearly three inches in diameter. "And the significance of this is?"

"You need to turn it over."

KC studied the rock for a moment. It was familiar looking. It was—no, it was too smooth. She cupped her hand and lowered it until the rock flipped over. Something was etched on it.

KB + BD

"Brock, you remembered and made another rock for me ... for us?"

"No, Kace. This is the rock you made me throw into Crooked River from the lookout tower."

She stared at their initials. Memories of wanting to be with Brock and the agony of their abrupt, forced parting played through her mind. The sweetness of young love fought against the pain of a separation she had partly blamed on him. When the love won, KC looked up into Brock's eyes. The love was there, just as it had always been. How could she ever have doubted Brock?

"Kace, I had to keep part of you with me. I couldn't have made it through those years without it."

He'd wanted that enough to ... "But how, Brock? You threw it 300 yards out and 600 feet down. Said you'd never thrown a rock so far." She sat down beside him.

He put his arms around her. "I watched where that splash came from. The day after you left, I went to the swimming pool and borrowed a guy's swimming goggles, then went down into the canyon and found what I thought was the spot. It was behind a large rock on the far side of the river. I spent a total of at least four hours underwater, swimming and searching. In the shadow of that big rock where we hid, I found it with our initials up, on the bottom of the river, right beside the opening to the hidden cove. It's been in my pocket every day since then."

"So, I make you throw a rock into the river, 600 feet below us, you go find it, and seven years later that saves our lives?"

"Yeah." Brock's eyes said a lot more than yeah.

KC held the rock to her heart. "Brock, why didn't you tell me this when we were in the cove?"

"Waxing romantic when four rattlesnakes were trying to kill us? The timing wasn't right."

"I've got to tell Allie." KC turned toward Jeff and Allie, but Brock pulled her closer to him.

"You can make Allie bawl her eyes out later. Right now, I need your help. This is important. Let's read this post one last time. In your mind, pretend you're Hannan as you read."

KC read along with him, looking over his shoulder.

A personal message for Abe Hannan, also known as president of the United States, until his term expires in January, unless he expires first.

When you took office you also took an oath, a very simple oath that only levied a single requirement on you, defend the

Constitution of the United States. You even chose to include so help you God.

I do not believe God helped you. He is neither a murderer nor a liar, nor does He help such. Satan, on the other hand, your mentor, is the father of lies, and it is he whom you have followed.

Mr. Hannan, you have not defended the Constitution, but have trampled it into the ground, violating it at will to suit your own selfish, twisted purposes.

Why do I make these accusations against you? I have personally witnessed the clinic in Guatemala where you infected children with your carefully engineered brand of Ebola, children dreaming of a better life. But you flew them to the United States border on a suicide mission, about which they were clueless. In so doing, you are personally responsible for the spread of the virus that has killed more than 100,000 Americans. You have used your vaccine, developed for this genetically altered Ebola, to control our population through fear. Families affected would do anything you asked in order to receive your vaccine. But the virus mutated, something viruses are designed to do. Thanks to you, another 50,000 Americans may die. At least your Secretary of Health and Human Resources, Patricia Weller, had the integrity to try controlling the new outbreak, integrity that you and your inner circle of cabinet members seem to lack.

You initiated the Wall Street crash and orchestrated the refinery explosions that led to further chaos and the eventual declaration of martial law, which was your plan all along. Foisting yourself on American citizens as a president who only sought to end the chaos, you intended to use your induced panic to seize control of the nation, and you had no intent to relinquish that control.

Besides your dereliction of duty, an impeachable offense, if not a capital offense due to the treason and murder *involved, I have something personal against you. My best friend, the most loyal American I have ever known, and the brave, beautiful woman soon to be my wife, Ms. KC Banning ...*

KC's breath caught in her throat as she read the words. Tears threatened to spill from her eyes. She wiped them with the back of her hand and continued reading. But, after Brock's words about her, it was impossible to read this from Hannan's perspective.

... you falsely branded a murderer and a terrorist to eliminate her testimony against you, after you discovered she could incriminate you. When she fled, you tried to murder her with an assault by a detachment of Special Forces and an Apache helicopter. That would seem easy enough to do, kill an unarmed, twenty-one-year-old woman using your hand-picked black ops team and enough firepower in the Apache to destroy a small city. But you failed, Mr. President. You failed, miserably. The helicopter was destroyed and, today, only two of your black ops team remain alive, and they are imprisoned by a man, an army captain, a commander of a detachment of Rangers who have not forgotten their oaths of enlistment or commissioning. This man wants me to deliver another personal message to you. Read it carefully and thoughtfully, as if your life hangs in the balance.

Mr. President,

Upon accepting my commission, I took an oath to defend this nation against all enemies, foreign and domestic. Now, I find I must defend this nation against you, sir, an enemy of the domestic variety. No single person has been responsible for as many deaths of Americans as you, since Adolf Hitler. So know this, Mr. President, we are coming for you. Not just my detachment of highly trained men, but Navy SEALs and other Rangers, all trained to move into any area on the planet, without being detected, and carry out our mission.

No one can stop us. Certainly not the gutless wonders you have placed in command. Some night you will awaken to fingers around your throat. They will be mine. But, I won't kill you. I want the satisfaction of seeing you tried, convicted of both treason and murder, and punished as prescribed by the Constitution.

Mr. President, as surely as the sun rises, we are coming for you, and no one except Almighty God has the ability to stop us.

See you soon ... when you least expect it.

Sleep well.

Captain C.

US Army Ranger

Brock had written more.

Mene Mene Tekel Upharsin.

That, Mr. President, was the handwriting on the wall. Let me interpret it for you.

The days of your presidency have been numbered. Your tyrannical reign is coming to an end. You have been weighed and found wanting. Your office will soon be given to another.

At that time, this nation will experience a new birth of freedom. Our allies will again trust us, especially Israel, whom you have betrayed.

Plans for governing our nation, until a new national election can be held, have already been made.

My final words today are for the American people. Take heart. Help is on the way. The filthy house will be swept clean, and we will start again as one nation, under God, indivisible, with liberty and justice for all.

May God bless the United States of America.

Your Voice in the Wilderness,

Brock Daniels

KC swallowed hard, trying to clear the lump in her throat. "Post it, Brock."

Brock clicked on the publish button.

The blog went live.

He looked up at KC. "Now we see who stays with Hannan and who deserts him."

Brock disconnected from the satellite connection set up by the Israeli commo guy, slipped his laptop into its case, turned and waved to the pilot, then sat and buckled into the ursa chair.

KC took the chair beside his and buckled her seatbelt as the twin engines of the Gulfstream 550 whined. "I am so proud of you, Brock."

"Let's not jump the gun, Kace. Remember Craig's warning. This could blow up in our faces. But we've rolled the dice. We'll see what comes up."

Chapter 47

6:00 a.m. the following morning

Randall Washington opened the door and entered the Oval Office, carrying papers in his hand, while his face carried a serious frown. He locked the door behind him.

What was this about? More bad news about the black ops mission? Hannan leaned back in his chair and propped his feet up on the Resolute desk. "What happy occasion brings my Attorney General here at 6:00 a.m.? You're not usually an early riser."

"I'm serving you papers, Mr. President."

"If that's a joke, it's in very poor taste, Randy."

"Brock Daniels doesn't think it's a joke."

Hannan swore, digging deep into his vocabulary to find words suitable for this thorn in his side. "He should be dead by now. Are you saying he isn't?"

"No. He says he isn't. And you can forget about Blanchard and his team." Randy tossed the stapled papers on Hannan's desk so they landed right side up in front of him.

He read the title. *A Personal Message to Abid Hannan: Mene Mene Tekel Upharsin*

"What sort of nonsense is this?"

"Many of your fine citizens think Brock Daniels is a modern-day prophet." Randy stood, studying Hannan's face. He didn't reply.

"For your sake, Mr. President, I hope he's not. Daniels is quoting from the book of Daniel. I suppose the name similarities are purely coincidental. But, evidently, the people don't think so. This post had at least fifty million hits in the last eight hours."

The heat rose under Hannan's collar, and he stifled the urge to shred the printed blog post with his hands. Fifty million hits? If this post had really gone that far beyond viral, he needed to read it.

"Oh ..." Randy pointed at the papers in front of Hannan. "You don't have to keep pinging Captain Blanchard. Read it. You'll understand."

Hannan took his eyes off the threatening papers on his desk, looking up at Randall Washington. "So, a little resistance was a little too much. Did Blanchard bail out on us?"

"The ultimate bail," Randy said. "Blanchard is dead. So are his men, all but the two who were captured." Randy walked across the Presidential Seal on the floor and sat on the end of the couch on Hannan's left. Not his usual seat.

Hannan tapped the papers several times with his finger, wishing he could make them disappear ... along with their author.

"You really need to read that." Randy's index finger pointed at the printed pages.

Though it angered Hannan to read it, Brock Daniels's accusations covered most of the actions Hannan had taken to force martial law. Daniels hadn't mentioned the preparatory actions, the hundreds of presidential memoranda, the 200 executive orders to support his actions, and numerous other end runs around the legislative branch, allowing him to seize control of the nation.

The Ebola accusation was damaging, but he could probably spin the success of Pat Weller so he could take credit for her actions. Banning was alive and probably going to be Daniels's wife?

Heat rose on his neck at the thought of Brock Daniels getting something he did not deserve and getting it at Hannan's expense. Blanchard and all his men were dead? Anger turned to rage. How could a country hick, hardly more than a kid, thwart the purposes of a man like Abe Hannan, the most powerful man who had ever lived.

He wadded the papers up and slammed them into the trashcan near his feet.

"Did you read it all?" Randy's cold stare was unnerving. Hannan had never seen Randy direct that expression at POTUS.

"I read enough."

"So, you read the note from the Ranger commander?"

"What Ranger commander?" Hannan reached for his trashcan and pulled out the wadded papers. If Blanchard was dead, it would have taken something like another team of Special Forces. How large was this insurgency?

He smoothed the crumpled papers out on his desk and turned to where he left off. So, this Ranger commander would try to hide behind his oath and the Constitution to justify his treachery. Hannan would ensure that did not work.

He read on. More than one ranger detachment? Navy SEALs? After today, maybe others. Anger, that had been molten lava, now froze, turning into an icy chill that ran down his back. Hannan's worst fears about his coup attempt became a horror movie playing in his mind.

Was this even a remote possibility? He had changed the culture of the military, silenced most of the people of faith, replaced the highest ranking officers with military politicians, yes-men who had helped him revamp the armed forces. But had the changes been enough? Yesterday, he would have said yes, but this wasn't yesterday.

He continued reading to the end of the post, dropped the papers on his desk, and stared across the room.

Randy watched him, studying him. "Mr. President, that wasn't simply a threat. If they're serious about coming after you, you are not safe in the Oval Office. You're not safe anywhere."

Hannan didn't reply. And he didn't like the look in Randall Washington's eyes.

Randy stood. "From the beginning, we knew this was a remote possibility. But it almost seems like someone stacked the deck against us."

"Stacked the deck? Certainly not God. I hope you aren't getting religious on me, Randy. Your references to the Almighty are usually reserved for yourself, not for—"

"I'm not religious," Randy said. "But you need to get the picture here. Your vice president kept his distance. Oh, he'll be implicated, but if he turns state's evidence, he'll never go to prison. It's the same with your cabinet, except the four of us, you, me, Dell, and Gerry Carter, whom you arrested, giving him good reason to testify against you." Randy paused. "I made plans for this contingency a long time ago. What do *you* intend to do?"

"So, the great Randall Washington is going to run like the coward he—"

"It won't work, Hannan. You and I have no shame. Honor is just too expensive to carry through life, especially for someone with political aspirations. Goodbye and good luck, Abid." Randy turned toward the door.

How dare Randy mock him with his unpublished birth name? "I'll have you arrested, Randall."

Randall Washington stopped and stared into Hannan's eyes. "You could shoot me right here, that would stop me. But you don't have the ... uh, intestinal fortitude. You could have me arrested, but I would cut a deal and testify against you. No, Abe, your only choice is to let me go. Once I walk out this door, Randall Washington will cease to exist."

When Randy walked out, Mitchell Dell stepped in, his eyes wide and anxious.

Hannan didn't have time for this. He needed to plot his next move. To get some intel on the military groups who were organizing an insurgency.

"Mr. President." Dell stopped at the edge of Hannan's desk.

"Make it quick, Dell."

"About thirty minutes ago, the White House networks came under attack. I can no longer guarantee they're not compromised. The only safe networks are the classified military networks in the DUCC."

"We've had attempted attacks before. Handle it, Dell."

"Never on this scale, sir. This appears to be a large-scale cyber-attack."

Who could be attacking? Banning? No. Before he died, Major Grieve, her supervisor, had said she was good, but no way could a twenty-one-year-old girl do this. Maybe she wasn't acting alone. "Where do the attacks appear to be coming from?"

"Uh ... from outside the U.S." Dell looked like he was holding something back. His feet shuffled on the floor and his gaze darted around the room, avoiding Hannan.

"What!" If it *was* another country, he could intimidate them with—

"Sir," Dell hesitated and swallowed, his Adam's apple bobbing. "If I was to guess, based upon what I've seen, I would say they're coming from Israel."

"Israel?" The picture of the opposition came into sharp focus. Hannan had antagonized Israel. Pushed them too far. For a country that fought daily for its survival— "Blast it! How did I ever decide to trust computing security to a ..."

Hannan cursed Mitchell Dell's abilities and everything else he could think of about the geek standing in front of him, the last person remaining of Hannan's inner circle.

He needed to keep his wits about him. He couldn't waste time ranting and couldn't afford to lose Mitchell Dell at this critical juncture. "I'm sorry, Mitchell. Too much bad news today. Just lost my temper. Can we keep the isolated military networks safe?"

"I'm not sure. Before I came up here something unauthorized came through the ... uh, through your—well, it went out on the classified networks and no alarms were tripped. We only saw it because I had instructed the network monitors to look for any traffic from your—"

"My study? But no one knew about that connection."

"That's not true, sir ..."

Hannan hurried out of the oval office. Mitchell Dell was still speaking, but Hannan only heard two words, "Katheryn Banning."

Banning knew about it. Hannan trotted down the hall to his study and unplugged the network cable, isolating the machine, then hurried back to the Oval Office.

Mitchell Dell was gone.

Hannan called a Secret Service agent, who strode into the Oval Office a few seconds later.

"Have you seen Mitchell Dell?"

"Yes, sir. He just left the White House. Seemed to be in a big hurry."

Hannan dismissed the agent, but couldn't dismiss his thoughts about Dell. The little twerp was running. If he was caught, he would plead out of any charges. And Dell had the most damning evidence against Hannan of anyone.

He had to stop all this spurious mental activity and think. He took a deep breath and released it, slowly. Israel hacks White House networks and gets access to a computer with a connection no one knew about except Dell and

Banning. Rangers, Navy SEALs, Banning, Daniels, Israel, the Mossad, Kidon. Kidon? Would they assassinate a sitting president? He wouldn't wait to find out.

Hannan locked himself in his private study. He needed a plan to protect himself. Maybe he could send another detachment of—no, that wouldn't work. There were some traitors left in the military. He needed to find them and eliminate them.

First and foremost, Hannan needed to stay alive, and he now had been threatened, personally. With Israel involved, he couldn't rule out the Kidon, especially if Israel became too desperate.

Hannan plugged his computer into the White House network, woke up the machine, and logged in. Was it safe to join the classified network and send orders to another group of Special Forces? Surely *they* could protect him.

Hannan reached for the network cable, then stopped when he saw a window open on the computer screen. It was a video window. A voice came through his computer speaker. "Turn on your webcam, Abe. This is Alexis."

It couldn't be good news. With Alexis, it seldom had been, lately. But these were the people who had bought him the White House. They would want to preserve their investment. Maybe the Organization would help him.

He clicked on the camera icon and saw Alexis smiling at him.

"Abe, we hear that your day got off to a bad start."

He sighed. "That's an understatement. But I need to tell you what we're up against."

"What *we're* up against? No, Abe. What *you* are up against."

"But I need some help here before all is lost."

"You don't understand. All is not lost."

"Look, if I were to be taken into custody by some military riffraff, they'll—"

"Exactly." Alexis's voice morphed to the singsong sound she reserved for mocking people. "That's why we're pulling the plug on you, Abe. You know, for the sake of the cause."

"But you've gotten eight years of hard work from—"

"No. You need to keep things in proper perspective. We bought you two terms in the White House. You were privileged to be the most powerful man in the world for nearly eight years, a dream life of luxury, with Air Force One at your disposal. The dream is over. Time to wake up."

"If you don't support me now, all *is* lost."

"That is also a matter of perspective. From ours, all isn't lost. Well, nothing but a few years. We'll continue to look for another left-leaning, charismatic politician and wait for the political pendulum in the country to swing our way."

"But I can implicate—"

"Don't even think about revenge, Abe. It will only make matters worse for you. And I'm truly sorry about Mitchell Dell. We needed to keep an eye on you and he was in a wonderful position to do that. Mitchell is not as klutzy as he seems. He has truly earned his new identity, the one he assumed a few minutes ago. Goodbye, Abe."

The window closed.

Alexis had disappeared from his life as quickly as she had entered it ten years ago, with the organization's deep pockets and a collection of personal groomers to prepare him for what? For this? For betrayal?

Hannan unlocked the door to his study. Secret Service Agent Belino stood against the wall, near the door to the Oval Office.

"Agent Belino, I have a question for you."

He walked over to the study door. "Yes, sir?"

"What would you do if someone tried to arrest POTUS?"

"I'm not sure, sir. But there's one thing you could count on. I would continue to keep the oath I took when I enlisted.

You know, sir, to support and defend the Constitution of the United States against all enemies, foreign and ... *domestic.*"

Was Agent Belino smirking? His crooked smile disappeared as quickly as it came.

Hannan wasn't safe, even in the White House. Couldn't trust the Secret Service. If one would betray him, all of them might. He needed people he could trust around him.

He locked himself in his study, and plugged in to the classified networks. According to Dell, these networks might possibly be compromised, but without some trusted military around him, Abe Hannan was compromised. The military networks provided the only direct access to the people he needed.

Hannan sent an encrypted message to Captain Deke, commander of another team he had used for black ops.

In a few minutes, Deke responded.

Cannot come to your aid, Mr. President. Some of my men have disappeared. Rumor has it they are seeking to join Brock Daniels and the insurgents. For the past eight hours, troops and munitions have been disappearing from locations on the East Coast, West Coast, Texas, and who knows where else. It's like somebody is coordinating everything, but we don't know who or how. Sir, for now, you will have to rely on resources at the White House.

Hannan powered off his computer, pulled his network cable from the jack, and strode out the door of the study, headed for the elevators that would take him down to the DUCC, the most secure spot in America. From there, he could regroup, issue commands, and see who obeyed them. That would tell him whom he could trust.

He could order the Joint Chiefs of Staff to join him. Surely they could force the military to defend him against any insurgency. But would they want to be confined to the Deep Underground Command Center with a man who had a bull's-eye painted on his back? And, what would they do if the insurgents appeared to be winning?

Hannan knew the answer. Every member of the JCS would posture themselves to jump to the winning side. They were what Brock Daniels had called them, politicians, yes men ... spineless. Ultimately, they would fail him.

If Hannan failed to hold on to power, it would be for the same reason that the Muslim Brotherhood lost power in Egypt, failure to control the military. His second term was coming to a close, and Hannan still hadn't been able to purge all of the religious zealots from the armed forces. In hindsight, it was a huge mistake, a mistake that Katheryn Banning and Brock Daniels, hardly more than kids, had taken advantage of to organize the dissidents in the military into an insurgency.

But there seemed to be more to this Banning-Daniels duo. Something that might enable them to stop the most powerful person on the planet and unravel a scheme years in the making, a scheme planned by the intellectually elite of the planet. What was it these two young people had?

Regardless, they hadn't won yet. For now, Abe Hannan was still the most powerful person on the planet, and he had only begun to fight.

EPILOGUE

A few hours later, 41,000 feet, over the mid-Pacific

Brock sat beside her, hand in hers, eyes closed, clearly dozing.

KC had so much she wanted to talk about with him, plans for their future, a future together. But he deserved a nap after all he'd gone through in the past week.

Brock's eyes popped open. More like half open. His head turned her way. "Hello, beautiful." He gave her a lazy smile.

"I'm glad you think so." She returned his smile but felt it fading. "When do you think we'll be able to go home?"

"Not until Hannan has surrendered and all of the military is under the command of the new president. And not until there are no Hannan supporters running loose to take potshots at us."

"But the people behind this attempt to steal our nation are still out there, somewhere. Brock, what do you think will happen to the group that brought Hannan to power? You know, the ideologues? They're the real enemy, but we don't know who they are, except for a few of the most wealthy. And there's probably no way to prove they broke the law."

"You're right. They've probably insulated themselves from Hannan. If we take Hannan down, they'll still be around, biding their time, spouting neo-Marxist platitudes, like economic justice and—"

"Economic justice? Marx and his modern-day proponents can make it sound so right."

Brock shook his head. "Kace, the Bible makes it sound right."

"You mean the Bible actually talks about economic justice?"

Brock grinned. "Yeah. If you won't work, you don't eat."

KC laughed. "That does sort of go against Marxist ideology."

'But his disciples will still be around, waiting for another shot at taking the USA down. Making it pay for its alleged economic crimes. That's why we have to teach our children well. We need to teach them history, about our Constitution, about the real origin of human rights, about the moral absolutes, God's laws and His truth."

"Teach our children ... that's something I think I want to do."

"Don't you want to keep doing computer security work?"

She shook her head. "Only for a short time. There are more important things."

Brock pulled his head back. "You're talking about *your* and *my* children, right?"

She nodded.

"You know, some things have to happen before we—"

"You got that right, Mr. Daniels. Like you have to propose. I have to accept. Then we have to navigate Israel's marriage application process, for starters."

"Here's something else to think about, Kace. When it's safe to go home, where do you want to live and raise our kids?"

"There's something about the ranch with its canyons, the rivers. I want to live somewhere near Crooked River Ranch.

And, if we have a daughter who's cursed with red hair and freckles—"

"You mean blessed with angel kisses, don't you?"

"I thought you said they were stars in the nighttime sky."

"And I thought you said that was cheesy."

"I lied." KC's enigmatic smile tweaked one corner of her mouth. "You're too good with words to let you—where were we? Our daughter. I want her to find a boy who will fight the bullies that call her carrot top, a boy to defend her honor, save her from all the rattlesnakes in the desert, and in life."

Brock put a hand on the back of her neck and pulled her face near his. "KC, you are so beautiful. What did I ever do to deserve someone like you? I'm not even—"

KC muted his lips with her fingers. "You saved me from rattlesnakes, rattlesnakes of all sorts. You helped me protect our nation. You showed me my father really did love me. And you helped me see that I can trust God, especially for the things that really matter. So, you see, you're more than just good enough for me, Brock Daniels. You're exactly what I need."

"Maybe I am." He kissed her softly.

She returned his kiss, trying to show Brock that he was exactly what she wanted and needed. When she finished, Allie's and Julia's clapping said she had succeeded.

And Brock's eyes confirmed it.

"See. No maybes about it, Brock."

"But, Kace, let's pray that our girl and the boy she finds never have to worry about saving the USA."

"Brock, we're living a piece of history that we *must* remember. If our nation survives this, we've got to talk about it, teach it to our kids, so its lessons are *never* forgotten. If all parents, grandparents, and schoolteachers would do that, our kids would know what it takes to keep a good nation alive and how to vote for good people, people who mean what they say."

He brushed a stray auburn curl from her face. "You mean like when they swear to support and defend the Constitution of the United States against all enemies?"

"Yes. That's exactly what I mean. And we want our kids to understand the lessons so well they won't need your voice in the wilderness to remind them."

The end ... of this book

AUTHOR'S NOTES

As an author and person of faith, I write stories like *Voice in the Wilderness* because I believe every reader who enjoys thrillers, stories dealing with high stakes and the grittier issues of life, ought to have the option of reading their favorite genre without being, as Oscar Wilde once put it, taken to the latrine and locked in. Violence can be shown without planting horrific images in people's minds, images they can never erase. Fiction, after all, is not reality. As author Dr. Donn Taylor often says, fiction is "... a construct that gives the illusion of reality ... we do not have to include every detail simply because it's there in real life."

I believe Donn is right. Characters' actions and words need include only what the author chooses to move the story forward. And, though my villains curse, I choose not to add to my readers' vocabularies of four-letter words. And though my villains kill, their killing is not overly graphic. If my characters close the bedroom door, the reader is not inside.

Before writing *Voice in the Wilderness*, I developed a detailed plan of what it would take to seize control of the USA. I read books by radicals who wished to accomplish that, as well as theoretical books on tyranny that warned people so history would not repeat itself. As I wrote my story, several incidents appeared in the headlines only weeks or days after I wrote about them. I didn't want to abandon my plot and, realizing mine was a character-driven story, I continued to write it, though the Associated Press seemed to be stealing part of my thunder with stories about Ebola, cultural changes in the military, federal pressure on lending institutions—the list goes on.

My conclusion from that experience, it's not as hard as one might think to take over this nation, if one has no moral restraint and can lull the citizens into political apathy until ... You'll have to read the series to fill in the rest.

The setting for most of the story, the Central Oregon Desert near Crooked River Ranch, is a place of incredible beauty. The confluence of desert-born rivers and other streams originating in the snow packs of the Cascades produces a diversity in geography, flora, and fauna that is spectacular. For the past six summers, my wife, Babe, and I have spent a week or more each summer near Crooked River Ranch. When the book releases, I'll post, for your enjoyment, some of the best of my 4 GB of digital photos from the book's setting.

Those familiar with Crooked River Ranch will note that I took a few liberties in describing it. First, I made the canyon a little deeper near the ranch, hyperbole for dramatic effect. Second, though there are rattlesnakes in the vicinity, they are not as populous as described in the story. The locals can tell you the few places where you shouldn't go wandering through the bushes or let your children play.

The Old Hollywood Road mentioned in the story was created for filming the 1967 western, *The Way West,* a story about one of the first wagon trains taking settlers to Oregon. Sally Field played her first movie role in this film. The old road has deteriorated over the past 50 years, but it still provides a great trail for hiking down into this miniature version of the Grand Canyon.

About the hero, Brock Daniels, and the heroine, KC Banning—I've known my wife since we were 3 or 4 years old. This gave me the idea of having a hero and heroine develop an unusually deep, childhood friendship that made it nearly impossible to pry them apart, as well as impossible for them to feel whole unless they were together. But KC's father, the senator and protective parent, manages to rip this relationship apart, deeply wounding the two kids, such that getting back together requires healing their wounds. But what if the two also had complementary abilities that, together, could save our nation, a nation now on the brink of tyranny? To work together, KC and Brock would first have to re-open their painful wounds. This idea created a lot of room for character growth, tension, conflict, and a first-class thriller plot with a strong romantic thread.

With these ideas for the characters, the Central Oregon setting, and my writing philosophy, *Voice in the Wilderness* was born. I hope you enjoyed it. If so, note that a sequel is planned, and there may be room for a third book in this series.

H L Wegley

JAMES L. RUBART

Rooms- "Two words. Blown away." Deborah Raney
Book of Days- "Couldn't put it down." Colleen Coble
The Chair- "James is one of my favorite authors." Terri Blackstock
Soul's Gate, Memory's Door, Spirit Bridge (The Wellspring series)- "Powerful ...
will leave you thinking long after you finish." Ted Dekker

"If you think fiction can't change
your life you need to read The Five
Times I Met Myself."
New York Times Bestselling
author Andy Andrews

james.rubart.com | @james.rubart | facebook.com/James.Rubart

SILENCE IN THE DARK
On Sale April 16, 2016

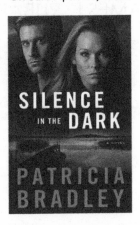

Two years ago, Bailey Adams broke off her engagement to Danny Maxwell and fled Logan Point for the mission field in Chihuahua, Mexico. Now she's about to return home to the States, but there's just one problem. After Bailey meets with the uncle of one of the mission children in the city, she barely escapes a sudden danger. Now she's on the run--she just doesn't know from whom. To make matters worse, people who help her along the way find themselves in danger too--including Danny. Who is after her? Will they ever let up? And in the midst of the chaos, can Bailey keep herself from falling in love with her rescuer all over again?

With lean, fast-paced prose that keeps readers turning the pages, Patricia Bradley pens a superb story of suspense and second chances.

Patricia Bradley

Patricia Bradley is the award-winning author of Shadows of the Past, A Promise to Protect, and Gone without a Trace. Winner of a Daphne du Maurier Award and a Touched by Love Award, Bradley is a member of American Christian Fiction Writers and Romance Writers of America, and makes her home in Mississippi.

Learn more at www.PTBradley.com

Made in the USA
Coppell, TX
26 October 2020

40188441R00229